Settling

Joan L. Cannon

PublishAmerica
Baltimore

© 2004 by Joan L. Cannon.
All rights reserved. No part of this book may be reproduced, stored in a retrieval system or transmitted in any form or by any means without the prior written permission of the publishers, except by a reviewer who may quote brief passages in a review to be printed in a newspaper, magazine or journal.

First printing

ISBN: 1-4137-4019-7
PUBLISHED BY PUBLISHAMERICA, LLLP
www.publishamerica.com
Baltimore

Printed in the United States of America

To Roger, who has put up with so much to support this project.

It has been said that it takes a village to raise a child, and I have found it takes more than an author to make a book. So I acknowledge with gratitude my teachers during my long preparation for writing fiction; my dear friends in our critique group during gestation: Joyce, Rosie, and Sole; and my serendipitous agent *cum* editor Adrian Streather for his faith in my efforts.

Joan L. Cannon
2004

CHAPTER ONE

Ruth March reached for the armrest to steady herself as the Buick slewed on a curve. She wondered why realtors felt such a pressing need to show how big and how new a car they could afford. Imagine driving everywhere in a '68 Riviera, and baby blue at that.

Her mind felt as unbalanced as her body, turning from one misgiving to another with the futility of a goldfish circling its bowl. She wound down her window to get some fresh air on her face. The view through the windshield showed her how far she was venturing from Greenwich Village, from everything she had known for more than twelve years. A moist wind blew across her face and pulled strands of her copper-colored hair free, dragging them into her eyes. She pulled down the visor and used the mirror to try to tuck them into place again. She was surprised at the face she saw there—not the features, which showed some distinction, with her short nose and wide mouth, high cheekbones and hazel eyes under level brows, but rather by the expression. She had been unaware of how mournful she looked.

Mrs. Chapin, the real estate broker, had a nasal voice, full of flat A's. "Don't you want to run the window up? The wind is spoiling your hair. You say you're moving out of the city?"

Slightly startled out of her reverie, Ruth nodded. "Yes." She pushed up the visor and made an attempt to arrange her face to look more cheerful.

"How's that?"

"Well, I've … It's time for a change." Ruth had known she would have to learn how to field questions like these, but certainly she wasn't ready now.

"Tch!" clucked Mrs. Chapin, twitching the wheel to avoid a pothole and making the car sway like something in an amusement park ride. "It's hard when things don't work out. You did say you were by yourself, didn't you?"

"Mm-hm." Ruth closed her eyes for an instant as if she could shut out even inward sights. She fingered the scarf at her neck, then pressed at the pins securing her chignon. Her long legs were cramped by a short driver's adjustment of the front seat. The scenery at least was soothing, but she longed for silence. She reminded herself that panic only thrust tranquility further out of reach, and did her best to resist it, but was unnerved by a sensation of sinking into a void.

Mrs. Chapin piped up again. "Just tell me if you want me to mind my own business. I suppose you're divorced. I'm sure you'll find some other young women to give you some sympathetic …" She rattled on, apparently oblivious of her passenger's discomfort. Ruth knew that Mrs. Chapin was only trying to do her job, which was to sell real estate, and maybe she even meant to be friendly, but she itched to tell the woman to be quiet.

Finally Mrs. Chapin said, "We turn here where the mailboxes are. It's the last house on the road, about a mile in from the highway. You wouldn't mind being alone? So few neighbors and all?"

Ruth said, "No, I was raised in the country." In the field on her side of the car, small dark junipers scattered among golden bunches of poverty grass showed that no one had mowed the pasture for some time. On its far side a small hill, wooded with oaks and beeches, rose against a sky roiling with massing clouds. Stone walls were partly hidden by young trees and brush, draped with hoary seed-heads of wild clematis, clumps of barberry, grape vines, and brambles. A clear brown stream, overhung by maples and ashes, angled off from a culvert they crossed. Early leaves were turning; Virginia creeper flamed against dark tree trunks and silvery fence posts. The catalogue of plants flowed comfortably through Ruth's mind like the names of old friends. She drew a deep breath, savoring the mossy smells, the scents of earth and dead leaves and coming rain. A flood of girlhood memories rushed into her mind.

She turned her gaze hungrily to the fading autumnal countryside. The scene was so unlike her childhood home on the coast of Maine. Here, horizons were close and cozy, formed by thick woods or the folds of hills. She recognized her rush to the rural as an atavistic move, but was already reassured. The country itself lifted her spirits. Maybe nature and solitude—a symbolic return to innocence—might help.

She leaned forward in the seat to see around her companion's plump bosom. A feathery hemlock partly hid the corner of a house, its weathered clapboard siding blending into the landscape like the plumage of a grouse in the woods. A small lawn separated it from the road and showed green through a drift of new-fallen, golden leaves.

When they stopped with a jerk, Ruth jumped out and hurried around the front of the car up to the paneled door of the house. Mrs. Chapin went on talking like a nervous hostess as she rummaged in her handbag.

"I'll just find the key, and then we can go inside." She raised her voice to cover the distance between them, as Ruth, standing on the porch, leaned sideways to look in a window. "There's a good, dependable water supply. You can see the spring house roof there back of that big rock ..."

Ruth didn't listen, waiting impatiently for Mrs. Chapin to bring the key. She looked up at a deserted phoebe's nest above one of the porch posts, saw a cracked pane in an eyebrow window, a row of neat dentils almost hidden by the gutter. The louvers of the shutters were lumpy with generations of repainting. Suddenly she felt like an exile returning, overcome with eagerness to see every detail, to compare this place with her unexpressed—indeed barely acknowledged—expectations. The woman's monologue ran on, praising meaningless details of renovation while she made her way across the lawn to Ruth on the porch.

Once inside, Ruth rebelled against the remorseless flow of information. "Mrs. Chapin, would you mind very much if I just spent a few minutes looking around by myself? I'll meet you at the car shortly."

Eyebrows raised, unmistakably miffed, her guide flounced back to the car, leaving Ruth alone in the quiet old house. The darkening day accentuated the sheltering character of low-ceilinged rooms and heavy beams, wide boards and paneling. Plaster, uneven over old lath, was scabrous; paint was smudged and faded on the woodwork. Mouse droppings littered corners, and when Ruth opened the cellar door, her nose told her the floor down there was earth. There were old-fashioned registers in the floor, but plumbing in kitchen and bathrooms looked less antiquated than what she had grown up with. She went up the steep boxed stairs, and looked at the three rooms on the second floor. When she stooped to one of the small-paned eyebrow windows, she could see over a granite outcrop to the mossy shingles on the spring house roof. Beyond thickets stretched the small meadow that went with the house, a clump of molting cattails showing where the ground was wet.

Something in this pastoral setting gave her a sense of second wind, like a tiring runner. In the few minutes since she had seen this house, her thoughts had taken an eager leap forward. It was the first time in long months that she began to feel less burdened by sadness, less hopeless. She pictured her great-grandmother's sampler hanging above a rocking chair, delphiniums and hollyhocks planted along a stone wall.

Downstairs again, she looked up at the beams that someone had exposed in what had well over a hundred years ago been a kitchen, but now would serve as living room. They ran out from the chimney wall, where she knew they were supported by the fieldstone structure in the middle of the house, which was divided into three rooms downstairs, each with its own fireplace. The kitchen, the center of the home, and the prop for the whole structure. Symbolic. Ruth bent to look up through the large opening and saw swifts' nests silhouetted on the sides of the chimney. A whiff of old smoke and ashes made her sneeze.

With a quick turn that was almost a pirouette, she scanned the room one more time, then went out the back door and headed for the spring house. A few large drops of rain fell heavily from the lowering sky. Where water overflowing from the spring drained away into the field, the small runnel was fringed with cattails, ferns, loosestrife, and wild flags. For an uplifted moment she stood, breathing the smells of wet earth and dry leaves. Like a tiny kingdom, this was complete. She held her palms up to the rain. Drops fell more rapidly as the air cooled abruptly, and a breeze sprang up.

Distracted with her impressions, she had no idea Mrs. Chapin was watching her from the driveway. "Mrs. Duchamp, don't you think we ought to be getting back?" The shrill voice slashed through the whisper of raindrops.

"Coming," Ruth called. Hugging herself as if she were protecting her joy, she hurried to head off this garrulous, anxious person she already viewed as an intruder.

As they drove away, Ruth kept silent, while Mrs. Chapin renewed her gush of superfluous data, punctuated by requests for agreement. Ruth tried to shut out the voice next to her; she wanted to review every detail of what she had seen before they reached the real estate office. She walked again in her mind through each room, recalling yet more delightful particulars: how the view through the small windows under the eaves provided a special slant on the world outside, the texture of worn chestnut planks, smoke stains on the mantels, even the corners where cobwebs hung fluttering gently in the air her passage stirred. She knew she could be at home there.

Ruth interrupted the monologue. "Would there be an option available, if I should be interested in buying later?"

Mrs. Chapin glanced away from the road. "I'll be happy to inquire for you, but I'm sure something could be arranged. It's part of an estate, and they're just beginning probate now, so I imagine they'd be happy to settle matters expeditiously."

"When could I move in?" Ruth blurted.

"Oh," Mrs. Chapin said, taking her eyes off the road and trying to see Ruth's expression. "Then you do like it? You didn't say—"

"My lease in the city is up in a very short time, and I want to spend the autumn here." Ruth couldn't hide a smile, but it was no longer important. At least now there was silence in the car. Mrs. Chapin was apparently satisfied. Clearly, nothing short of a deal could have stemmed her tide of maddening conversation.

Back in the office, Ruth signed necessary papers with a feeling of calm gratification mingled with anticipation.

CHAPTER TWO

On the day Ruth left New York to move to Connecticut, Nettie saw her off with a gruff goodbye and a hug that almost cracked a rib. Nettie: her mainstay through proverbial thick and thin. Ruth's eyes were blurry with tears as she sat twisted around in the taxi's back seat so she could watch the brownstone stoops, the trees with their yellowing leaves, the curving sidewalk and littered gutter—all the details of her street, so familiar after more than eleven years, reeling away from her through the rear window, passing out of sight like that part of her life.

Yet, as the distance grew, Ruth gained confidence, if only from a sense of inevitability—no going back now. The quiver of excitement reminded her of how she had felt when driving away from home in Devonport back in 1950, on her way from Maine to New York. She turned around and faced forward, lips tight, checked her watch, and settled back with her eye on the meter.

Once in the train, Ruth watched thinning suburbs sliding by the smeared window. They passed reservoirs with water calm under cobalt skies. She noticed several swans, floating like ornaments near tiny islets that dotted the tree-fringed lakes. How different were these inland waters, shaped and tended by the hand of man, from the fierce floods of the north Atlantic that bounded the landscape of her childhood. These lakes looked puny and domesticated, so unlike the wild, untrammeled view from the bluffs at home.

More than sixteen years ago, on the day she was to leave for the city, she and her brother Dan had walked out to look over the ocean. He had held the strands of barbed wire apart so she could duck between them. A veery chimed sweetly somewhere in the woods. Mosquitoes hummed around their heads.

"Damn things are like dive bombers." Dan smacked his cheek. "Let's go over to the edge. The breeze'll be stronger there." An opalescent afterglow had suffused the eastern sky; the water of the bay lay royal purple in the fading light, looking level and fixed as a table cloth. They crossed the pasture, knee-deep in June grass and yellow hawkweed, and sat down to take in the panorama of water and sky.

After a few minutes of silence, aware of Dan's downcast mood, Ruth had said, "You'll be fine, you know. Just hang in there. You have only a little while to go. Class of '52. Doesn't seem possible. It won't be long, and then you'll—"

"That's easy for you to say," Dan broke in. "You won't be here, sitting like a dummy in the parlor all evening, or cruising around with Pinky and Sam, or trying to keep from falling asleep in Miss Johnson's English classes. You'll be in New York, having a ball."

Ruth chuckled. "Some ball, on thirty-five or forty dollars a week. Secretaries don't live high on the hog. I just hope to goodness I can find a place to live on that kind of salary!"

Even though he was three years younger, Dan had been her anchor her whole life long, and that day she had found herself trying to calm his fears, when her own were about to drown her. She said, "And another thing, I'm scared stiff at the idea of going so far away all on my own. I don't know a soul, and it's the biggest city in the world."

They sat, gazing out over the dark sea and the glowing sky, two people brought up to hide emotion, keep troubles to themselves, and maintain pride and privacy as virtually interchangeable virtues. Two or three gulls wheeled below the edge of the cliff, white against the dark water, their cries leaking up through the shifting air. A bright star showed above the southern headland.

"It won't be the same around here," Dan said softly.

Ruth nodded. "I know." She stood up and reached for Dan's hand. He scrambled to his feet and took it. They walked back, swinging their joined hands between them. They had looked up at a group of twittering swifts wheeling over the roof. When they went into the house, the light in the kitchen was nearly blinding. Their mother stood at the sink, washing the supper dishes. For once, she hadn't called Ruth to help.

The next morning, Ruth's stomach was hollow as she sat next to Dan in the old Plymouth, on the way to the station, to the city, to the next step.

෩ ଔ

From where she sat now on the way to Connecticut, those scenes were a lifetime ago. Now she saw that ash trees along the tracks were nearly bare, and here and there bittersweet sparked the bronze of dying leaves. Autumn—preamble to short days, monochrome landscapes, the year closing in like sleep. Would winter days down here be anything like those at home had been—and perhaps still were?

There, when snow hung in the air so fine it was like floating mist veiling the edge of the woods and greying tree trunks against a skim-milk sky, Ruth used to sit with her books open on the drop-leaf table. She would look at the blank, blue-lined pages of her notebook and then gaze at the landscape as it grew fuzzier and dimmer and paler. Sometimes, in December, the light would fail so gradually she wasn't aware of it until her mother came into the room.

"Ruth," Elizabeth would say, "you must be trying to go blind before you're twenty. Why don't you turn on a light?"

One such dark afternoon, she and Dan and their mother had sat in the dining room. Glare from the three-armed lamp over the table whitened the cloth, shone on the silverware. They ate in silence. So much silence in that house. Elizabeth sat, as always, with her back to the kitchen door, Ruth on one side of her and Dan on the other.

Elizabeth's back was always straight, her collars always white. Ruth could not remember seeing lines in her mother's face, whose expression remained almost always serious and pleasant, and as smoothly unrevealing as her clothes.

When they heard Dad's pickup pulling into the driveway, Dan jumped up. Elizabeth said, "Just sit down and finish your supper."

"Can't I go say hello?"

"Your father will be in directly. Sit down." She reached for the pitcher and poured more milk into Dan's glass. He sank down in his chair. Ruth, showing off her greater self-control, had kept her eyes on her plate, eating steadily.

When they heard their father stamping the snow off his boots on the back porch, Elizabeth rose and went out. After the slam of the kitchen door, the children listened to the splash of water in the sink, then the rattle of the roller towel as he dried his hands. Soon he pushed through the dining room door and strode in from the kitchen, cold coming in with him like an invisible cocoon.

"Evenin', everybody." Nathan March's voice had a tendency to boom, perhaps from having to shout in the wind to his crew on the boat. His seamed face was ruddy from cold, his blue eyes glittered.

Dan bounced up and down in his chair, his eyes shining, face flushed. "Hello, Dad. You're late. We started without you. Was it a good trip? Is it still snowing?"

Ruth saw her mother coming from the kitchen with a laden plate to set at her husband's place. She shook her head at Dan, who subsided, though he continued to watch his father's every move. Nathan's jaws moved powerfully. He had a large head with grey hair, thick and wiry, and large hands with patches of hair over the knuckles. His shoulders were broad under his hand-knit sweater. He looked the part of a father to be idolized by a little boy.

Elizabeth sat opposite him, the harsh light from the three bulbs overhead casting shadows under her eyebrows and cheekbones. She wore her hair coiled low on the back of her neck. Ruth always thought of her mother like that: harshly lit, her hands folded in her lap, silently watching her husband. There were times when her mother seemed to be almost as still as a piece of the furniture.

Dan fidgeted.

"Pot roast is tender, Elizabeth."

"That's the last in the locker."

Nathan raised his eyes from the plate. "You'd best order another side, then." He looked at Dan while he buttered a slice of bread. "How'd your history test come out, young fella?"

"I got a B. Will you be home next weekend?"

Nathan lowered his eyes to his slice of bread, spreading carefully, slowly. "Not too bad, but A is better. Did you get your theme back, Ruth?"

"Yes, Dad. I got an A minus." Ruth felt chagrin for Dan when she saw him flush.

Nathan nodded, bit into the bread. "That's the ticket. You'll be right up there when you start high school next fall."

Elizabeth said, "More meat, Nathan?"

"No, my dear." He pushed peas on his fork with the piece of bread. "I have plenty."

"Can I please be excused?" Dan asked.

"May I," said Mother.

"May I?"

"Don't you want dessert?"

Dan hung his head. "Could I come back when you're ready?"

Nathan said, "Just sit tight, there, Daniel." He chewed. "Tell me what you did in school today."

Dan squirmed in his chair. "Nothin'."

Ruth offered, "We had a fire drill yesterday." She looked at her little brother, who was staring at his lap. He looked so small. "The bell got stuck, and they couldn't make it stop. It went on until it made your ears hurt."

Nathan chuckled without changing his facial expression. "Must have made Mr. Sandstrom about frantic."

Dan piped up. "He hopped up and down in the yard and yelled for Mr. Dugan to come and take out the fuse." Dan bobbed in his chair. "We almost froze out there, waiting for them to get it fixed. He wouldn't let us go back in till it stopped. He said we had to do everything as if there *was* a fire."

Nathan mopped gravy with the last piece of bread. "He would, the silly fool." Elizabeth raised her eyebrows, but kept silent. Nathan arranged his knife and fork on the plate and leaned back in his chair. He hooked his thumbs in his belt and sighed.

"'S good to be home. Boston harbor was a mess." He pronounced it "hahbah." "Between the ice and an apprentice pilot out there with a tanker, it's a wonder we didn't hit somethin'. That's the last time I go in there before daylight. It's too dangerous tryin' to maneuver a loaded barge when you can't see a hand afore your face."

"Ruth, you clear while I get the pie and coffee." Elizabeth took two plates and left for the kitchen.

Dan leaned forward, eyes fixed on his father. "Will you be home for the—"

"I'll be happy to get that contract for Savannah after this winter. Fog and ice and cold—they can drive you crazy."

Ruth carried dishes to the kitchen. Her mother stood at the white enamel table, putting slices of pie onto plates.

"Will he be leaving again before the Blue and Gold banquet?"

"He hasn't said, Ruth. We'll wait and see." Elizabeth handed her two plates, took two herself in one hand, picked up the coffee pot, and backed through the swinging door.

Nathan was talking. "They had to take those crates off the dock and get them into the hold 'fore the snow changed to rain."

He turned to look up at his wife as she set the plate before him. "Looks good, Elizabeth. We have any cheese to go on top?"

"Coming right away." She pushed through the swinging door again.

Ruth slid sideways into her chair. Dan was only nine. What could he understand about sea freight and details of lading?

Dan spoke up a little breathlessly, "Do you think you can stay home until the fifth, Daddy?" He held his fork poised above his pie, but his attention was fixed on his father.

"Pie always tastes best with a good slab of rat cheese. Don't start till your mother gets back." Dan put his fork down again. "In spite of all, it'll be a good season, though. Another year or so and we'll have the boat paid for."

Elizabeth brought the cheese, sat down in her place, and poured two cups of coffee. Ruth handed one to her father. "There was a time when I thought I'd never see the day."

They waited for Mother to pick up her fork and start on her pie. Father stirred his coffee. He continued, glancing at Dan, "You'll have a nice business when you grow up to it, fella." He sliced a chunk of cheese, placed it on his pie. "The sea's kept us for generations, but we've been mighty lucky in these times to keep our heads above water. Fine while every able body and seaworthy boat was needed for the war effort, but now, hard work hasn't been enough for a lot of people." He looked keenly at the boy. "Keep up in school and work hard, and you'll never have to worry where your next meal is coming from, like some we know." Nathan paused to savor his pie.

Ruth forgot her dessert and sat gazing from one face to the other. All as familiar as the furniture and wallpaper, and yet as strange as the formulas in the algebra book. Dan chewed slowly, as though he had a mouth full of cardboard. Nathan's voice paused when he took a bite, began again, paused.

When the meal was over, as was his custom, Nathan sat in the parlor, smoking his pipe, listening to Lowell Thomas and the evening news on the Philco. Dan curled in the corner of the couch, ignoring the book open in his lap, his eyes glued on his father. There was a lot of static on the radio; it was hard to understand what the announcer said.

Elizabeth and Ruth washed and dried the dishes. Ruth returned to the table and her homework. When the program was over, Dan got up, went to his father's chair, and sat down on the hassock. "Daddy?"

"Mm?"

"Will you be home for the Blue and ..."

"Ayuh."

"Oh, good! Then you'll get to see ..."

Nathan stretched out his legs and arched his back to get to his pocket watch. "'Bout time for you to go to bed, isn't it?" He snapped the lid closed.

"Yessir. But then when you come to the school on Friday night you can see my car ..."

"Best say good night. Sleep tight. See you in the morning."

"Yessir. Good night."

The boy directed a searching look at his father, who didn't seem to notice. Ruth followed Dan to the kitchen. Elizabeth was scouring the sink.

"Daddy says he'll be here on the weekend," Dan reported. Elizabeth wrung her dishcloth and hung it over the faucet. She leaned down, offering her cheek for Dan's kiss.

"That's fine, Daniel. Good night." She patted him gently on his behind as he turned away.

Ruth and her mother listened to Dan's footsteps fading as he climbed the bare back stairs. In the living room, the radio was silent.

Elizabeth entered and sat down on the couch with her mending basket beside her; she began to darn a sock. The newspaper rustled as Nathan turned a page and refolded it, tilting it to catch the light.

Ruth went to look out the window at the branches of the maple near the walk. In the dark glass she could see the room behind her, reflected like an illuminated stage set.

Nathan turned another page. "Says here they've had to delay starting that new road around Portland. May keep the tourist trade down. Too bad for the vacation charter people." Nathan turned another page.

"Daddy," Ruth faced the room again, "you *will* go to the banquet next week, won't you?"

Her father lowered the newspaper. "Reckoned all the fathers'll be there. I planned on it, yes." He addressed his wife. "They surely are concerned about that affair. Seems to me there isn't much connection 'tween that race and scouting." He raised the paper again.

Elizabeth continued to darn. After an interim, she said, "I'm told that the father-son banquet is an important part of the whole program. You'll enjoy it. The food will be good home cooking. All the mothers will bring covered dishes and desserts." Nathan grunted; Elizabeth darned. The wind gusted, rattling the shutters.

෩ ೦෪

Thinking about it now, Ruth recalled the glow of warm light along with the silent, pervasive cold that had filled her memory for so long. The evening would always represent, like a scene preserved in amber, life at home in Maine—details as sharp as steel engravings, overlaid by a golden veil of nostalgia.

After high school, Ruth had left for business school in Rhode Island. She regarded her homecomings in those days as times of recuperation. Among bricks and stone and paved streets, narrow views of sky, and constant man-made noise, she had felt like a foreigner. She had come back to her brother's undemanding affection and the familiar views and felt herself filling with a subtle joy the way a sponge fills slowly with liquid. Remembering her youthful love of the sights, scents, textures, and sounds of home, it occurred to her now (and she was surprised at the thought) that when dreams seem doomed, the cause might be fleshly as well as spiritual frailty. Perhaps pavement and smog had leached away something vital. She thought, *I need to touch the earth again.*

⁂

That last summer in Maine, the spell of good weather had held for several more days. Nathan had returned from a trip tanned, vigorous, taciturn as usual. This time he had brought a carved sandalwood box for Elizabeth. His last contract had taken him to Halifax, where he had bought it from a ship's master who had got it in Bangkok. The family passed it from hand to hand, examining the intricate carving, inhaling the musky but delicate fragrance.

Elizabeth had looked up at her husband and said, "Why thank you, Nathan." Ruth remembered searching her mother's face for a hint of how she liked her gift. She saw only a softening of the lips, too subtle to describe. Dan had run his fingers over the whorled arabesques and hollows, shaking his head slowly, wonderingly, smiling. "This is great work! How'd you think of that, Dad?"

Nathan shrugged. "Know your mother likes fine craftsmanship and beautiful things. This was special. Smell it." He lowered himself into his chair and took up his pipe. "Not the first foreign object to find its way into this house, after all."

Dan had held the box to his nose. Elizabeth remarked, "Seafaring's been work for the March men for four generations." Dan had seemed to examine his father's expression intently before he set the box on the table and left the room without speaking.

CHAPTER THREE

Alex Duchamp had always felt instinctively that his childhood was obvious proof of his difference from the rest of humanity. This was less a matter of conceit than simple alienation. Born in a rural Quebec village notable for the large size of its church and the small number of houses around it, he could not remember ever feeling as if he belonged there. Had he thought about it later on, he would have realized that this sense of displacement had never faded entirely.

His earliest memories were of what he thought of as "the chill of sanctity." He was one of many, cared for by nuns in a convent orphanage. He was, like the others, inured to sitting daily in a chapel that was always cold, squeezed next to the others in slippery pews, trying not to fall asleep during the unintelligible Latin liturgy.

In bits and pieces, over time, he had told Ruth what it was like, but only after they were married. "I remember how I hated the way we'd be herded across the gravel to the main building after Mass, marching in lines like bogus little soldiers." He had closed his eyes and gone on. "I'll never forget the smells. In the chapel it was hot candle wax and incense. Everywhere else, ammonia and soap they mopped the tiled floors with, and camphor and Lysol—and cabbage. Through most of the year, you could smell damp wool, and always, always children who hadn't had enough baths."

He had spoken of the sisters with combined disdain and fear. "They looked like a flock of giant black and white birds, predatory as vultures. I was grown up before I realized I'd been only another soul they felt responsible for. When I was little, I used to imagine I knew how a mouse feels within reach of an owl."

Ruth had not known a suitable response to this, though she hoped to hide her shock at his words.

"I think the worst was the glint in their eyes when one of us got caught out in a sin. Some of those holy women got their biggest yah-yahs from ferreting out what they called evil." He grimaced when he said that. "They either scared you into being good, or soured you on religion for the rest of your life. Now, of course, with the belated wisdom of hindsight, I see they were only trying to do the right thing by us, but at the time, every one of us felt like victims."

"Victims?"

Alex shrugged. "We always blamed the wrong ones for our predicament, of course."

"Who do you mean? Not the nuns?" She had not understood, though she could see how deeply his past rankled. Alex had pressed his lips together as if determined to say no more. She prompted, "Society? Or do you mean the mothers who abandoned their babies out of desperation?" He turned away from her then, but she persisted. "What about those orphaned by accident?" Finally, she had to accept his silence. She had known she would have to wait to return to the subject at some other time.

When Alex told stories of those days, he often tended to do it in a strange, abstracted voice, as if it were difficult to drag up the memories. "We ranged in age from infants up to about fifteen or sixteen. The uncertainty and misery affected our feelings about each other. We'd get into fights for no reason anybody could remember. I guess it was a way to let off steam. Rivalry was our one standard. The nuns lectured us till we were numb, but, of course, it didn't help."

"How awful," Ruth said. "You needed a brother or sister to look out for you."

Alex seemed not to hear. "When there was a rumor that someone was coming to look for a child to adopt, we'd crowd at the windows looking out over the courtyard and watch the visitors on their way to the wing where the nursery was. People were mostly interested in babies."

He didn't have to point out their growing despair as they got older. "Everybody had his own ways of surviving. Usually it was just plain toughness of body and mind that could save you, and plenty didn't have enough of either one. I took to mental escape."

When Alex talked about the village of St. Agathe, he nearly always described it in winter, with snow piled up along the roads in heaps, smoke rising from chimneys against skies as colorless as raw egg-white, surrounded by blotchy fields where clods of plowed earth showed through the snow. He never described the glitter of the landscape after a blizzard, or scarlet leaves in autumn. Only once did he mention spring.

"In spite of the cold, I ached to be out there, outside the walls that hemmed us in. Inside, all we knew was cold tile, waxed wood, sticky porridge, and the endless rustle of the nuns' habits and the click of their rosaries as they led us to chapel, to class, to meals." He looked at Ruth with a half smile. "I grew up thinking the natural way to walk was in straight lines; you only turned at right angles."

He said as if to himself, "One day in early spring, I looked out a window. There was a farm next to the convent, and they'd turned the plow horses loose in a field just beginning to show green. They whirled away from the gate like overweight race horses and galloped furiously in loops all around, avoiding the corners. They looked crazy, with those huge, shaggy feet. They kicked and bucked and tore up clods of earth that sailed over their heads. When I saw that—those enormous, plodding beasts—behaving as foolishly as colts, I imagined what it must feel like. After that, I dreamed night after night about never squaring a corner again."

Alex's descriptions of winter had made Ruth compare the fierce wind and sleet, the opaque fogs and driving snows of her own childhood winters. For her, they had meant sledding and skating, and the fragrant warmth of chocolate and popcorn and cookies fresh-baked when she and Dan dashed into the kitchen, their faces stiff with cold, and their noses red and running. Escape from home was the inverse of their wants; they had hurried to it in childhood.

"I met the Duchamps on a spring day," Alex had told her. "The window in the visitor's parlor was open, and we could hear a bird outside singing. They had four of us lined up for inspection. Sister Joseph-Madeleine glided back and forth behind us and introduced us one by one.

"I was scared to death of Sister Joseph-Madeleine. She used to catch me at the end of a line and give me a whack on the top of the head with her hand. Once when I was alone, she grabbed my hair at the back so she could tip my face up. Then she stared at me with her light-blue eyes that were cold as marbles. Her face looked like a mask with the white wimple around it. 'Bel ange,' she whispered, and then I found myself squeezed against her starched bib, smothered with her black serge sleeves, suffocating." He shuddered visibly. "I wriggled like an eel till I got free, and ran like hell to be with the other boys. It wasn't the first, or the last time it happened."

Sitting in the train, remembering, Ruth was still bewildered by this anecdote. Alex had gone on to describe that fateful day in the parlor. When he felt the sister's hand smoothing his hair in front of those people, he had trembled, trying not to bolt. "And then," he said, his voice changing timbre, "suddenly something told me this might be my chance. I thought—or maybe I just sensed—that maybe I could escape, if I could only do the right thing."

"And did you?"

He went on without answering. "The few visitors sat on a row of chairs like people watching a parade. Gabriel Duchamp was very tall and thin. He looked a little like Abe Lincoln without his beard. His wife was the picture of a comfortable matron, and had round cheeks shiny and red as a pair of apples. I don't know why, but I looked her in the eye and smiled. She reached a hand across the space between her and her husband and touched his wrist."

Mariette Duchamp had not taken her eyes off the beautiful child. The Duchamps took Alexander from the orphanage that day.

Alex told Ruth how even though he was dizzy with joy, he looked over his shoulder at the faces of the boys he'd vied with and whispered and endured punishments with, and his stomach hurt. "I felt like a traitor."

"But you knew everyone couldn't be lucky." She had always done her best to show the sympathy she felt.

Alex stared at her for a moment before he said, "No. Of course not. Until I left St. Agathe, I went to school with the nuns, but I lived in a house in the town, and had a room all to myself. I was lucky, all right."

He told Ruth, "I called the Duchamps by their first names, without those forbidding religious titles like *Soeur* or *Père* or *Frère*. Of course, eventually, I called them *Maman* and *Papa*. They adopted me formally as quickly as they could." He looked into space for a moment, then went on, "They were too poor to spoil me, but they hugged me a lot. Gabriel would help with my homework as much as he could. Mariette would try to read to me. The trouble was, I could read better than she could, and I'd squirm out of her arms so I could play with my toy trucks. I still saw plenty of the inside of the church. My parents saw to that. I went to catechism classes, to confession, made my first communion, even had to serve at the altar."

When he told her all this, Alex had sat down and looked into Ruth's eyes with an expression she could not read. It seemed somehow pleading. "It was hard, always under a shadow of sin and a threat of damnation, the duty of penance."

Gabriel Duchamp owned the gas station in town. As Alex got older, he went there daily after school to help out. By the time he got to high school, he was a better mechanic than Gabriel.

"I loved shop classes. I'd hear things in a motor and get a kind of gut feeling about what to do to make it right. I liked the logic. It made me think I had a kind of power."

After Ruth told him of her love of Maine summers, he confessed he too liked summers best because he could spend so many hours out of doors. "Mariette kept a house that was a nightmare for a kid, though it was no different from most of our neighbors'. It seemed that everything I did disarranged something or brought in dirt. And most of my activities involved grease and filth down at the garage." He chuckled. "It was the one thing I had in common with Gabriel—our endless masculine attempt to keep from getting anything dirty when we came home."

Except for shop, Alex had hated school. The nuns were forever shunting his fantasies and dreams aside. "The one class I could tolerate was geography. I loved maps, so I was forever at *The National Geographic*s from fifteen years before, which was all they had, and the atlases that were kept in the seventh grade room." Books had made his life bearable. There were not a lot of them, but they were a treasure trove.

Throughout their marriage, Ruth had found it hard to decide how to indicate her feelings when he launched into his rare reminiscences. He was prickly about his differences from his classmates. She understood he must have hoped not to appear overly studious.

"I played soccer and sneaked smokes with the other fellows, and read girlie magazines in the bathroom, but even then I knew the important part of my life was in my head, most of it put there by books. I spent so much time imagining other places and even other times, the nuns gave up on me. I was a typical adolescent daydreamer, and the nuns decided it was my problem and they couldn't solve it. They nicknamed me *le Voyageur*."

After this conversation, Ruth looked up the term in the dictionary, since she thought she remembered hearing it in her school days. She saw immediately the implications of risk and adventure conjured by the word.

When she asked, "How did you ever get to New York?" Alex looked up at the ceiling and said nothing for several moments, then turned his head to look at her. She realized that he would not tell her the whole story, at least not then.

For his part, even as he began to try, he was making up his mind whether to edit and how much. He even wished he could tell some things which had buried themselves out of sight like chiggers under the skin, causing no end of discomfort. He understood her wanting to know everything about him because he felt that way about her, but self-revelation had been dangerous or impossible for so long.

He cleared his throat like someone figuring out what the answer would be. "Well, when I was down at the garage I used to talk to anybody driving through when they stopped for gas. We learned English at school, and so I had no trouble with language if an American tourist or someone from Ontario happened along. One day, a guy came roaring in. His muffler was shot. He was a salesman from some place out at the edge of the prairie. He had a pile of sample cases full of business forms and stationery and office supplies stuffed in the trunk of the car. It was the end of the afternoon, so Gabriel told him he'd have to leave the car overnight, and we'd get to it in the morning. Once the fellow said where he was from, I kept thinking about it—a place with a wide horizon and no houses.

"I went home when we closed up, and sat down to eat. We always had supper at the oilcloth-covered table in the kitchen. I looked at my parents. Mariette still had those red cheeks, but they looked more chapped than healthy. She'd turned grey and was beginning to stoop, even though it was hard to notice it, because she'd gotten fat. Gabriel was still thin, but most of his hair was gone, and what was left was fading out like dye in the sun."

Alex had paused and swallowed. His eyes might have been focused on the scene he described. "I remember a row of African violets in pots on the window sill. There was a litho of Jesus next to the refrigerator. It showed him with long, brown curls and a cupid's-bow mouth, holding his robe open to expose his heart, glowing like a coal, with a gilded cross on top. The linoleum on the floor was worn through to the backing in places. Like every other room in the house, that one was painted a cream color, smeared with years of cooking grease.

"I ate a mouthful of *clafouti*, dropped my fork, excused myself, and ran upstairs to my room. I packed my canvas zipper bag that I took gym clothes to school in. Then I tiptoed down the stairs, and out the front door. On the way down the street to the garage, I looked at the buildings with asphalt shingle fronts on them, and said a mental goodbye. I didn't see Mariette and Gabriel after I left the table, so it was the best I could do."

He had taken a new muffler and some tools from the shop, stowed them in the trunk of the salesman's car, picked up a copy of every road map they had in the office, filled the car with gas, and driven away, popping and roaring like a Hell's Angel. "I knew at dinner time no one in town would leave a meal to find out what the noise was about. I found a bussing job in a Holiday Inn. I replaced the muffler, then left the car in a rest area out on Route 117. I thought maybe the repaired muffler might make up for the inconvenience I'd caused the poor salesman. I knew the police would return the car." He shook his head. "I don't know why I never thought Mariette and Gabriel might send the police after me. I don't even know if they did. Anyway, from then on, after I got enough tips, I'd move on, traveling by thumb. I was fifteen years old. Thank goodness they'd taught us English in school."

By the time Alex was twenty, he was in British Columbia, at a lumber camp. The wilderness had taken his breath away. It had also stripped away a veneer over his core that he had not been aware of until that time, despite his dreaming and longings when he was a boy.

He told Ruth, "It was terrible work, like being an apprentice devil. I used to dream that the trees screamed like tortured men, though I guess that was the sound of the saws. Still, I'd even think in broad daylight sometimes that the noises I heard weren't all from machinery."

He was afraid to show his horror in front of the other men, with whom he was pressed together as closely as he had been with the other boys in the orphanage. In the lumber camp, he discovered that in some ways he was not much of a social animal. He found the logger's life was even narrower than what he had escaped back in Quebec.

"Nobody could do that work and think at the same time, at least about anything but the work you were doing. A man could get killed if he didn't watch himself, and the foreman wasn't about to be held responsible, so he made sure we did watch ourselves. In our free time, we drank until the beer was gone; we wrestled and gambled and occasionally fought, and talked about women." Alex chuckled mirthlessly. "I'd have stolen again, if there'd been any books to steal anywhere. We weren't too far from a little village—just a tavern and different stores and services for the lumber business, like a gas station and machine repair shop, grocery store, and that sort of thing. Up there, though, it seemed like civilization. A half-breed called Old Wolf Bonaparte owned a saloon with a billiard table. Back east, it was books that kept me from going buggy, and there it got to be billiards. Old Wolf told me once that he got the money for his place by hustling games. He was a genius with a cue. He wouldn't tell where he'd learned how to play, but he was so proud if any white man asked his advice about anything, when I asked him to, he was happy to teach me. I found out I had a knack. I'd practice by the hour whenever I could get into town. Before the logging season was finished, I'd managed to hustle myself a stake that got me out of the woods."

At the time, Alex had been aware of the irony of his hurry to get away, but the forest loomed and sighed all the time they were attacking it. "It felt like scalping the world. Oh, I liked the yarning and roughness of the men, most of them okay guys, but I hated working like a killer from daylight to dark. The trees were so—majestic. As soon as I could, I headed back toward the plains."

Outside of Winnipeg, a ride left him off one night beside a carnival. "The steam-driven whistles on an old-fashioned calliope were cutting the air like music in a nightmare. I saw the ring of lights around the Ferris wheel turning slowly in the glow from floodlights on a dinky midway. The scene seemed like something out of one of my childhood fantasies. The whole collection of rides took up about the space of a city block. By then I'd worked in restaurants and on farms, in gas stations, and in the lumber camp. I looked at the carnies and thought, *This is it!* Of course, it wasn't. It was just another step along the twisty road I'd been traveling for more than five years already. The owner was a wizened little monkey of a man. He told me he'd been on the lookout for the right person to introduce his side shows. He looked at me and said he needed the right face to draw the ladies. 'You gotta snag 'em, or they won't bother with the freaks, or let their men folk spend money on them either.' It wasn't hard learning the spiel, and for a few weeks, I enjoyed it well enough. The best part about the job was the people I met. Once I was hired, I got to be one of the family. They made me feel I belonged to them. They asked no questions, just took me at face value."

Thinking back on all Alex had said, Ruth saw why his uneasy conscience, already lulled by time and distance, had fallen occasionally silent. It had taken years for Ruth to learn about Alex's youth on the road.

He told her one time how an aging girl called Arlene ran the little shooting gallery in the carnival. The customers could plink at wheels of ducks and pyramids of balls or balloons or bull's-eyes with rusting twenty-twos that were kept chained to the counter. She was a bottle blonde with an acrobat's body who had been with a circus until she broke her pelvis in a fall. She quit the circus when she had to give up the trapeze; she couldn't bear to watch the high acts. "I understood how she felt, and I admired her guts. Her dreams were shot down, but she wasn't about to throw in the towel. She got me to sit and talk to her about myself. She'd listen with her head cocked on one side like a poodle. She'd get a soft expression around her mouth and a dreamy look in her eyes, and I'd talk till I got hoarse." He did not mention to

Ruth that Arlene was the first woman he ever had that he hadn't paid for, or that she must have been at least ten years older than he.

"Every afternoon, I'd get dressed up in the outfit they gave me. With a top hat on, I'd stand on a little platform with a bullhorn. Arlene would be set up across the way from me, and she could see me from where she stood with the rifles in front of her. I'd feel her eyes on me, even when I was reeling off the line and taking money. She watched me all the time, even while she reloaded the rifles. She took to waiting every night on the step of the trailer I shared with the cook. In the mess tent, she wouldn't sit with anyone else. She did my laundry and nagged me when I needed a haircut. I began to feel like I was going in straight lines and squaring corners again."

ೞ ಆ

By the time they worked their way east to Kitchener, Alex had left the carnival. Near Stratford he was hired to do stable chores for a man who bred fine horses. Even though he grew up in a farming town, he knew not the first thing about animals. Long afterwards, when he was telling Ruth about that job, she saw he was embarrassed by how they had made him feel.

"I couldn't believe how beautiful those animals were. When I held a rope to lead one of them, I felt like a hero, just to have control over a creature that looked as noble as that. I'd stand, and breathe into their noses before I started to brush them. I got so I thought I could read the look in their eyes."

The owner had a son who rode most days, so Alex got to know him. One day he asked if Alex would like to play tennis after chores. They made it a habit.

"The kid taught me, I suppose because there weren't many near neighbors, and he was glad to have someone to play with." Alex looked hard at Ruth, seeming to decide whether to add the next words. "Knowing how to play tennis and billiards took me a long way from St. Agathe. Maybe one day I'll learn to ride too." They had both smiled at the foolishness of such a notion.

Alex had never stayed long in any job, and in time drifted into the US in some nameless prairie town near Minot, North Dakota. There he had been picked up by a man who ran a little aerial circus—almost the last of his breed. In the aftermath of the war, he told Alex, it beat crop dusting. He was looking for a fill-in for the stunt man who did the wing-walking act because his regular man had come down with mumps. For fifty dollars, Alex agreed. Between the need to prove himself fearless and his empty pockets, it was an offer he couldn't refuse.

Though he'd been roped on with safety harness, he was still pale and shaken afterwards when he got to the refreshment tent to down a restorative beer. A man came in and stood next to him at the plank bar. "You don't do that as a regular thing, do you?"

Alex shook his head and swallowed the rest of his beer. "And I won't again. Not for triple the pay!"

"What's your regular line of work?"

"I wish to hell I could find one!"

The man had held out his hand. "I'm Jerry Uhlik. I make documentary films." They had just finished shooting one on traveling performers like the carnival workers that roamed small towns in the heartland, the barnstormers and small circuses that used to crisscross the Midwest. One of his men had gone on his third drunk in a week and been fired. Jerry needed a strong back to take his place. Alex filled the bill.

By the time they got to Uhlik's New York base, Alex was grown. "It was the first time I had anything interesting to do that wasn't in some way destructive," he explained to Ruth. "The carnies were kind of diamonds in the rough, the best of them, but their way of life was too loose even for me. Besides, it was based on ... well, duping the rubes, as they used to say. The whole business was based on dishonesty, fakery. Even the horses I had so much pleasure out of were being bred for racing. After I saw a season of what that was like, the blush was off for me."

                                                      ಸ಼   ಞ

This ambiguous softness was one of the main traits that had captivated Ruth.

Alex had explained early in their acquaintance, "The movie

business is technically interesting, and it doesn't take anything from anybody—at least nothing they don't want to let go—or kill or injure anything or anyone. It begins with something—an idea, or a happening, or history—that already exists, and we make it into something new that can instruct and amuse people. I think that's why I liked it so much from the start."

"It's too bad you couldn't get an education so you could get into some kind of engineering," Ruth had remarked.

"Well, yeah, I was good with automotive machinery, but that was more like doing puzzles. When I learned how it worked or what was wrong with it and how to fix it, the fun was gone. Even if I'd had the chance, I doubt if I'd have had the sense to take it. I hated cutting trees, and anybody can see that carnival barker is a job for a horse's ass, not to mention all the laborer's jobs and bussing in fast food joints. After those experiments, what Jerry offered looked like a godsend."

୨୦ ୦୧

Sometimes Alex, once started on tales of his life before Ruth came into it, talked at length, as if he had been waiting for a chance to let some of his memories come into the open. "We made a movie once about how the Indians construct a canoe out of birch bark, and one on the life of itinerant tobacco pickers in the Connecticut River valley for a week at harvest time. I went with the crews on location, even once to Mexico. It was never dull, never has been."

There had been no limit to the sort of material Jerry could find to film. Those dry, hot prairie towns, skylines wavering in the heat, their dreary inhabitants rooted like the grass, could fade out of his life. Alex began to forget the down-at-heel villages and sway-backed barns in Quebec, the sky-blue upended bathtubs forming niches for the statues of the Virgin in those blank-faced churches, and eventually, even the flapping habits of the nuns.

CHAPTER FOUR

During her early weeks in the country, no longer surrounded by unavoidable reminders of Alex, Ruth discovered how therapeutic manual work could be. While she scrubbed, painted, waxed, reorganized from the chaos of the movers, thoughts that came while her hands were occupied were more soothing than upsetting. As her palms toughened and her muscles became accustomed to work, her mind gradually relaxed and opened.

Often she thought of times long gone, especially of Dan, who had been, when all was said and done, her closest and truest friend for most of her life. How she wished she could sit beside him and talk, not with the divisions of age between them as when they were children and the gap of a couple of years is so big, but freely as would work now that both were grownups.

She pictured her last summer at home, just before she left for Providence, when Dan had stood beside the lawn mower, frowning at her. She had seen that he was restless and dissatisfied, without an idea of how to direct his adolescent energy. "I like the sea to look at, Sis, but I can't see spending sixty percent of my time on it, away from land and family and ... and, I don't know ... I guess stillness. I can't stand the thought of being in motion twenty-four hours a day!"

"Well, you don't have to—"

"Are you kidding? Nathan March, Master, has his mind made up."

Ruth had watched him wrench the pull-cord, starting the mower instantly, then march away behind it in the enveloping roar as if he were setting out on a mission. The worst part had been that she couldn't offer him any kind of comfort or advice, not even a joke.

That same summer Nathan had told Ruth he regretted he would not be able to send her to a fancy school. "You'll need to support yourself, be independent till you marry, so a business college would be a good idea."

Ruth knew that kicking at the traces would profit her not at all, so she had gone to the business school, allowed herself to be molded into the daughter her parents wanted her to be. By nature a pacifist, she had learned by the age of ten to keep emotions and arguments to herself.

※ ※

Once away from home, Ruth had begun finally to imagine new horizons for herself, for she had never really dared to let fancy rule her thoughts. How fresh and fearless she and her friends had been! She was surprised that she enjoyed the companionship of dormitory life. It made her see how lonely she had often been without realizing it. She liked the lighthearted companionship, conversation, open doors, and even the noise of music and voices, after the comparative isolation of her girlhood. It was her first taste of being one of a group of peers, talking of matters she had never had a chance to discuss before.

One night after supper, her roommate, Eloise, was sitting on her unmade bed, painting her toenails. The radio was playing "Ragg Mop." With balls of cotton between her toes to keep from smearing the polish, her foot looked grotesque. Her straight brown hair fell in a curtain around her face as she reached with both arms past her knee to her toes. Ruth had been telling about Dan's problems with an admired girl.

Eloise, concentrating on what she was doing, spoke in an absent-minded way. "Pro'bly just wanted a guy with more to offer."

Ruth said sharply, "No one could offer more than Dan. He's good looking, intelligent—"

Eloise interrupted calmly, dipping her brush into the bottle, "You said yourself she got into a brand-new car with that other boy."

"I know." Ruth toyed with a pencil, turning it over and pushing it through her fingers, end over end. "But it isn't fair."

Eloise stretched her leg, examining her handiwork from a distance. "Well, nobody said life was fair, kiddo, did they?" She tossed her hair back over her shoulder with a jerk of her narrow head. "Anyway, what can you expect at sixteen? We all have to go through it."

Ruth was silent. The radio station had begun a medley of songs from *South Pacific*. She realized she had no idea how other girls had grown up. Through her childhood and Dan's, she had seen the two of them as lonely allies in a vaguely hostile camp, depending only on each other. Nathan and Elizabeth seemed somehow on a plane isolated from the two children. Ruth's college friends, Julie and Eloise, talked often of their parents and homes with ironic affection. Their uninhibited conversation only increased Ruth's sense that the Marches were different from other families; then she had stifled the thought as disloyal. To try to explain her brother's anguish over his first serious girlfriend seemed now impossible. She went back to her books.

In free time on dates, students from all over town met in the smoky amber gloom of Tony's Bar and Grill, where the rakish atmosphere made the girls feel daring. Patrons had to lean across the tables to hear one another above the din of the jukebox, clinking glasses, shouts, and gabble. Tony's was crowded, impersonal, but at the same time, comfortable and familiar. There was nothing like it back in Devonport. Ruth liked it because she thought the noisy surroundings forecast the unfettered life she could look forward to once she was on her own, with no one to answer to but her own conscience.

One night at Tony's, Ruth had sat across the table from Julie and her date, who were baiting each other on the subject of the recently finished World's Series, punctuating their friendly rivalry with casual obscenities. Ruth was amused because she knew Julie didn't care one way or the other about baseball. Eloise was there with Henderson, her fiancé, and Ruth had come with her perennial escort and comfortable pal, Norman, who was, as usual, trying to get her to have another drink before she finished the one in front of her. She knew he would vastly prefer to see her back to the dormitory if he thought she was sozzled, so he could hold it over her later.

Norman was a baby-faced lad who wore a crew cut that failed entirely to make him look as tough as he hoped. He told Ruth he wanted to get his degree before the Army got him and sent him to Korea. He reached for her hand, which lay curled loosely around her glass. She withdrew it gently, and wiped her fingers on a paper napkin before putting it in her lap. Norman never lost his good humor, however often she deflected his passes. She knew she could call the shots with him.

That night, she was tired. She looked around at the young crowd, at the harried waitress, twisting her way from the bar with a round tray balanced on one hand over her head, beer mugs inching slowly across to its lower side. She could see Henderson clasping Eloise's hand under the table, his thumb moving slowly back and forth above her knuckles. The sight caused a stab of envy of such a connection with another human being. The two were smiling at the rapid-fire banter between Julie and Frank, but Ruth was certain they were only half-hearing it. Whether it was fatigue or something else, she was suddenly overcome by a feeling of alienation. She peered through the jostling line-up at the bar, so dense it nearly hid the mirrored shelves in back. Everything glittered with glass and neon. She tried to see faces reflected in the etched panel behind the cash register, as if to anchor herself in reality, but images were fractured by the pearly patterns on the mirror.

She noticed a sailor's white cap, and next to him, two heads in profile, facing each other. One was a soft-featured man with grey hair, dressed in a business suit, who looked thoroughly out of place. The other, like most of the young men in the place, was wearing a crew-neck sweater over a shirt with the collar unbuttoned. His profile was arresting, clear-cut as a face on a coin, the features perfectly proportioned, masculine but refined. Oddly, as though his head were illuminated by a spotlight and the rest of the room were in darkness, Ruth now saw only his reflection and none of the others. She craned her neck, trying to glimpse the man himself rather than his mirrored image.

"See somebody you know?" Norman asked her.

She flushed, embarrassed as if she had been caught looking at something improper. "No. No, just watching the animals drinking."

Norman turned his head to seek the direction of her gaze. "Listen, Red, just don't forget who you came with." He winked, grinned, and waved at the waitress.

Ruth protested, "Norm, I haven't finished this one yet."

"It's flat now. You can make a fresh start."

"You just don't give up, do you?" Ruth smiled dutifully back at his impertinent expression. Her cheeks were beginning to feel stiff. It was already close to midnight. The noise seemed to be intensifying, as it often did near the end of the evening.

"Please, let's get out of here. I've got to get in before curfew."

"What about the beers?" Norman said in an aggrieved tone.

"Frank and Henderson can have them." She struggled out of her chair.

Eyebrows elevated, he followed. Near the door, where there was some floor space, he held her coat. As she reached for the sleeve, she saw the man at the bar again. Turned now in her direction, she saw his face head on. He was so handsome he took her breath away, literally.

He was young, not very tall; but like his face, his body was perfectly proportioned. He looked like a statue of a Greek athlete brought to life. She had trouble taking her eyes off him.

Norman took her arm, and they went out into the damp, fresh night, walking rapidly through patches of mist. He put an arm around her shoulder.

"How about sitting for a few minutes in the park?" He turned to cross the street in the middle of the block. "We have time before I have to get you back."

"Not tonight, Norm." Ruth pulled him back to the sidewalk. "I've got a couple of letters to write. Besides, it's cold for sitting outside."

He squeezed her against his side. "Be happy to warm you up."

She laughed and shook her head. "It was fun, and thank you for the nice evening."

After a few steps in silence, in a serious voice he asked, "Red, do you think you'll stay here when you graduate?"

"Not if I can go to New York. This may not be the worst of the sticks, but I want a chance to see the real world." She looked up at him, her eyes glittering as they passed street lights. "You know, there's too much going on that we never even get a chance to read about. I was in the library yesterday, looking for some information for that paper on corporate organization, and I was reading *The New York Times*. I know big cities have plenty of cultural opportunities, but until you look at the entertainment pages of a paper like that, you can't imagine what a variety there can be! Boston looks puny by comparison. It's not just museums and concerts and theater; it's universities and publishing, and all the literary and artistic community, politics and business, foreigners and—the UN is there, and another thing I only thought of recently—"

"Whoa, slow down. You'll wear me out!" Norman pulled her to a slower pace. "Your feet were going as fast as your tongue. Won't you feel kind of overwhelmed by that many choices? And what's a country girl like you going to find to do? You'll have to eat and pay the rent, you know."

"Sorry. I got carried away. Never mind about mundane things like a job. That's why I'm here now, and what I'll be prepared for by the time I leave. What I was going to say was that one of the best things of all will be anonymity!" She stopped and turned to him, her eyes flashing, her fatigue forgotten. "Can you imagine having nobody around who cares how you spend your time, or who with, or how late at night? Can you imagine what it will be like to have your spare time belong to you, all yours, to do anything with you want to?" She turned and almost skipped. "Norm, I could take a class in Swahili or join the Rosicrucians or engage in free love, and nobody would even notice!"

He looked down at her as they passed under a street lamp. Her hair, frosted with droplets, glistened, and he reached out to touch it. "You're right. I didn't know you were so het up about getting out of this neck of the woods." He squeezed her hand. "I wish you luck, Red. Maine's loss will be the Empire State's gain."

She smiled at his genuine good humor. They had come to the steps leading up to the dormitory entrance. "Thanks again for tonight. And thanks for being a buddy and letting me run off at the mouth."

He took hold of her shoulders and kissed her lightly. "Just something to remember me by. See you Saturday." He pulled her to him for another, slower kiss. Then he let her go, grinned in his boyish way, and watched her climb to the door.

Inside her room, she switched on the light, hung her coat up, and sat down in the chair at her desk. The text she had been studying lay open, a pencil in the gully between the pages. Terminology for the medical secretary—mostly Latin or multi-syllabic English words equally as strange. She pushed the book away and took a sheet of note paper from the drawer to write to Dan.

Eloise burst in. "Lord, I'll be glad when it's possible to come and go without being treated like a child!" She kicked off her heels and flopped on her bed. "To be answering to this sort of archaic regime at our age and in this day and time's enough to—"

"Weezie," Ruth cut in, "don't forget, the school's responsible for us while we're here."

Eloise sat up with a jerk. "Red, if you go all goody-goody on me right now, I may throw something. How old are you? How long has it been since you had to have your light out at a certain time at night? How long since you had to ask permission to go some place?"

"That's not the point—"

"The hell it isn't! That's precisely the point!" Eloise jumped up and flung her arms out. "It's just like what they did during the war—saying if a fellow was old enough to fight, he was old enough to buy a drink in a bar. Well, if we're old enough to go out into the world, earn our own livings and marry, we're old enough to decide when we want to go out and who with and when we want to go to bed—*and who with!*"

Julie appeared, her coat over her arm. Ruth was staring at Eloise, who stood for a moment, then dropped her arms. "Well, I'm sorry, but some days I get so fed up, I'm ready to chuck the whole thing." Eloise dropped back onto her bed. "I'm tired of Tony's too. All that idiot racket and the smoke so thick you can hardly breathe." She lay with her hands clasped under her head, eyes on the ceiling. There was a short silence.

Ruth said, "What's the trouble, Weezie?"

Julie came and sat down on the bed next to Eloise. "She's in love." She turned to Eloise. "I know just how you feel."

"Oh no, you don't, Julie. Thanks all the same." Again there was a pause. Then Julie got up, threw Ruth a look, and left the room.

Ruth took a deep breath, turned back to face the desk, but she did not begin her letter. Love—what was it? Would she ever find out, restrained and private and practical as she was? The profile seen in Tony's flashed before her mind's eye. *Idiot!* she said to herself.

Later, in the dark, thinking over the exchange between Julie and Eloise, Ruth tried to imagine how Eloise really was feeling, and discovered she had no idea. Was that the reason for her sense of a gap in her life?

☙ ❧

Graduation Day was a benchmark for Ruth that in her mind divided her childhood from long-awaited maturity. She thought how appropriate a name Commencement was for the ceremony. In the mirror she watched herself bend her head to one side to pull the brush through her long hair. Sunlight gave it a ruddy sheen like the wing of a wild bird. She gathered and twisted it, and inserted large tortoise-shell pins to secure it in a coil on the back of her head. Leaning forward, closer to the mirror, she applied lipstick.

Eloise had once called her *jolie laide*, and she had found a French dictionary to enlighten her. With her rather snub nose, high cheekbones, and full lips, she was not pretty, though now she had passed adolescence, she understood her looks were arresting, especially her polished copper hair and athletic body. She had a flashback to the days when she and her schoolmates had worried about growing up to be flat-chested. They had been jealous and she embarrassed when she was the first to need more than a cotton undershirt to support her developing figure. She stood erect, smoothing long-fingered hands over the front of her dress, and turned first to one side and then the other.

She looked around at the beds, each with a suitcase open on it, at the stacked cardboard cartons, brimming with books and framed pictures. The desks were cleared, patches in the dust showing where blotters and the bases of lamps had stood. A litter of bits of paper, lint, rubber bands, and paper clips was visible on the floor near the radiator. The room looked abandoned already.

Her family was waiting for her in the lobby of the hotel. When she pushed through the revolving door, Dan jumped up from his chair and hurried over, grinning widely. They hugged. Elizabeth and Nathan stood, waiting for her to approach them.

"Hi, Mom, Dad. Isn't it a wonderful day?"

Elizabeth smiled. "Lovely. Hadn't we better get over to the auditorium?"

Dan straightened his tie self-consciously. Had he grown just since Easter?

Nathan asked, "Are you going to wear that cap and gown, or just carry them for show?"

"Well, I was going to put them on when—Dad, you're pulling my leg!" Then she giggled, full of nervous pleasure. "I just don't want to be conspicuous on the street. Come on, everybody."

Walking beside her brother, she took his arm and looked up at him. "So, what's new at home? How's school going? You never write me anything about what you're up to."

"Everything's the same as always, Sis. Are you excited about getting finished? I can't wait to be out of school. Dad's been talking about college, but all I want to do is start working. What good is it to be sitting in classrooms for another four years?"

College? She examined her brother. He was taller than she by a good head, his cheekbones prominent like hers, his shoulders wide and angular. He walked with a free swing of his long arms, the breeze pressing his brown hair off his forehead, revealing a widow's peak. She couldn't read the expression of his eyes, squinted against city grit. She imagined him out on the boat, their father watching his every move. She knew he still got seasick. But college?

She spoke hesitantly. "I know how you feel, but if you think about it, you'll see he's right. No, let me finish. First off, if you get a good education, you'll find out about a lot of things you might not even know existed. In a little place like Devonport, all people think about is fishing, lobstering, and tourists in the summer. You'll be a lot better able to make intelligent choices about what you want to do. The other thing is that jobs aren't all that easy to get, not good ones. And promotions go to the best educated. A college degree would be a big plus."

The memory of that patronizing speech made her blush now. Maybe she should not have taken her role as big sister quite so seriously. Maybe she had wanted to dull the sting of envy for an opportunity she would have sacrificed mightily to have for herself.

Dan went on. "But Dad has his mind set on my taking over the boat when he retires. Why waste money on an engineering degree?" They walked a few paces while she digested his news.

Finally she said, "What do you want to do?" She thought she knew the answer.

"How do I know? I sure as hell don't want to work in the A & P or mow lawns for the rest of my life!"

She squeezed his arm. "That's the point! No matter what you're going to do next, it'll have a better chance of being something to satisfy you if you have that degree. Don't quit after high school, Danny. Don't. If Dad can help you go to college, don't miss it."

"Why didn't you go, if you think it's so great?"

Ruth glanced at his scowling face. She could not tell him she would give ten years off her life for that chance. Even the little taught here beyond shorthand, typing, and office procedures had enticed her with the hint of how much more there was. "I suppose because it's more important for a girl to earn a living until she gets married. And Dad can't afford to put us both through four expensive years." The last thing Nathan March would ever do would be to waste money knowingly. She wanted to look back at him, as though she might find a clue to this unexpected ambition for Dan.

Yet it was not as if there had not been other occasions when their father had surprised them. Once he arrived home from a trip to find Dan rolling and moaning in a welter of damp sheets, delirious with fever. Mother had kept calm and used cool wash cloths, but Dan got no better. Nathan had spent the night beside the boy's bed. In the morning, he and Mother had driven to the doctor with Dan wrapped in quilts. Ruth was hurried to the school bus, where she sat, pressing her face to the dirty window to watch their car following until the bus turned into the school driveway. She could see her father's scowl as he was forced to stop repeatedly for the bus to take on passengers. When she arrived home that afternoon, Dad was asleep on the living room sofa, the paper dropped across his middle. He had postponed his next trip for three days, waiting until Dan was better. For a brief time she puzzled over this odd behavior, but then forgot about it, until this day of promise for herself and surprise over his plans for Dan.

Now people were clustering on the sidewalk in front of the auditorium. Graduates in gowns were scattered among their parents and relatives like blackbirds in a field of flowers. A clock chimed overhead, sending a flock of pigeons into the air, and people began to go inside.

Ruth shrugged on her gown and put the flat cap on her head, opening a bobby pin with her teeth to fasten it. Mother adjusted the tassel, brushed her shoulders off, and patted her on the back. She turned in the doorway to wave to her family, then plunged into the dim interior to take her place in line. A solemn organ prelude reverberated over the crowded seats.

Through the long, boring ceremony, Ruth's attention had wandered. She opened her leatherette folder and read it and thought, *At last! Here's my passport.*

True enough, it had been, though now she saw that the journey had taken her to places for which she had no map, and whose language she seemed even now to be still learning.

CHAPTER FIVE

Ruth's first days in New York had raced by, crowded with new sights and the pressures of independence. Excitement staved off homesickness. Her eagerness to absorb as much as she could as fast as she could kept her from dwelling on her isolation.

On the day she found her job, gusts of hot, dusty wind swirled around, lifting grit under her skirt. She squinted to keep the grains of soot out of her eyes as she searched for the number written on her note from the employment agency. It was nearly noon, and her stomach growled. She wished she'd eaten more than a bowl of cornflakes for breakfast.

Then she saw an awning stretched across the sidewalk ahead, with the numbers on it. She pushed the revolving door with a damp palm, and found herself in a small lobby that looked discreet and dignified. On the directory next to the elevator she found, "Arthur Gentry, M. D., 8-B." Ruth took a deep breath and pressed the button.

She emerged into a silent, carpeted vestibule. The waiting room was furnished with understated taste in neutral tones, the creamy carpeting nearly hidden by a Chinese rug. A triple window overlooking Central Park admitted light through sheer casement curtains with tawny velvet drapes at the sides. Magazines on a low table were up-to-date issues of *The Smithsonian*, *Newsweek*, *Architectural Digest*, and *The New Yorker*. A long way from the uncushioned pine settle and linoleum floor of Dr. Brandon's office back in Devonport.

She stood in the center of the handsome rug, trying to smooth her hair. She felt suddenly chilled, whether by nerves or the air conditioning, she wasn't sure. She sat down and wiped her face with a clean handkerchief. It came away sooty.

When she heard the consulting room door open, she stood up hastily. A grey-haired man dressed in a light suit came into the room, hand outstretched.

"Good morning," he said. "I'm sorry to keep you waiting. I was on the telephone. You must be Miss March." He wore a neat Van Dyke beard and gold-rimmed spectacles. She thought he looked like a scholar from an earlier century.

"Yes, I am. Good morning."

"Please come in." He waved her ahead of him into the inner office, paneled and even more elegant than the waiting room. Indicating a chair in front of his large mahogany desk, he took his seat facing her.

"As I'm sure you have gathered, I'm Dr. Gentry." He picked up a folder from his desk. "I have the information forwarded to me by the agency, but suppose you tell me something about yourself." He folded his hands on the blotter, and gave Ruth a quiet smile.

She felt tongue-tied. "Well, you see I specialized in medical—"

"As you say, all that is here. I was thinking of learning more about you personally. Tell me about …" He opened the folder and glanced at the pages inside. "… about Devonport, Miss March."

It felt strange to be speaking of her home as if it were a place merely on a map. "It's a little town on the coast of Maine. There isn't much to say about it except that it's small, and pretty, at least to me."

"What is your work experience?" Dr. Gentry asked.

Of course, she should have known. "None, I'm afraid, apart from babysitting and cashiering at the SafeWay. There's not much to do in Devonport. My father owns an oceangoing tug. He moves freight up and down the coast."

"Why did you decide to go so far from home?" Dr. Gentry leaned back in his chair, resting his hands loosely on the arms.

Ruth was prepared for that question. "I wanted to see more. I've never traveled. I think New York, is the place to make—well, not my fortune, of course, but maybe I could say, the most of my life."

"Don't you like Maine?"

"I love it." Ruth felt her face flushing. "But there are a lot of things to see and learn in other places, and I want to be able to — to expand, I guess you might say."

Dr. Gentry smiled. "Any particular direction you want to expand in?"

"I don't know yet. I just know that the first thing I have to do is find a way to earn a living. I'll go on from there." Something about the doctor's expression made her feel free to smile.

Dr. Gentry got up from his chair. "Well, Miss March, let's see whether we can come to some arrangement. If you'll come out to the desk in the waiting room, I'll give you a little trial run. You can type a report on a patient, and let me see it when you're finished."

He showed Ruth the typewriter, gave her the pad with his longhand draft on it, and saw that she was comfortable. He left the door between them open, and returned to his office. As she typed, Ruth's brain buzzed with impressions, of the genial but correct and dapper man who was interviewing her, of the understated refinement she saw around her, even for an instant of how her mother and father would assess what she was seeing here. Was there some reason she should be cautious?

Nervousness caused her to make one or two mistakes she had to correct. When she finished, she took the pages in to the doctor. He had her sit down and take a couple of paragraphs of dictation. Later, after she'd transcribed these, she returned to her chair in his office. Like so much that she had attempted to picture beforehand, the interview was not at all what she expected. She found she was enjoying herself.

Dr. Gentry read through what she had done, aligned the pages carefully, got out a folder to put them in, and placed this precisely at one side of his blotter. Ruth began to be shaky with apprehension all over again.

Then he said, "When could you begin, Miss March?" He didn't smile.

Ruth tried to hide her delight, to be as professional and cool as he was. "As soon as you like, Doctor," she replied.

"Tell me where you're living now. Have you found something permanent?"

"Not yet. I'm staying in a women's residence, sort of like the Y."

"Well, if I may make a suggestion, allow me to give you some lunch and at the same time a little advice on where you might look around." He interrupted as Ruth began an embarrassed protest. "Don't be silly now. The least I can do is to try to make my new assistant comfortable enough in this strange place so that I can count on her to stay around for a long time." He treated her then to his gentle smile. She noticed how blue his eyes were, and the laugh lines partly concealed by his spectacles.

They had lunch in a small restaurant near the office, where they pored over the ads in a newspaper the doctor bought on the corner. His courtly manner inspired her trust. He talked about the city as if to coax her to like it. He persuaded Ruth to talk about her school days and her family. The experience was like meeting an uncle she had not known she had.

After lunch, with the newspaper containing the circled advertisements, Ruth had taken the subway down to Eighth Street. Where she emerged, the streets looked foreign. Indeed, much of the conversation she overheard was not in English. Even the traffic noises sounded hysterical after those near the office uptown. In the mid-fifties, Greenwich Village was as vibrant and crowded as it had been before the war. The narrow pavements were crowded with pedestrians who swirled like eddies in a river, their routes often eccentric and wavering. Jostled by passersby as she consulted her folded newspaper, Ruth searched for the first address, which was on a street with a name instead of a number. She wondered whether she would get lost and not be able to find her way back uptown.

The brick building was elderly, crumbling, less picturesque than decrepit. The surly superintendent who answered the bell took her up two flights of grubby, uncarpeted stairs, and threw open a door. A miasma of ancient cooking odors and fresh tomcat made her want to put her handkerchief to her nose. The room was dark, with a tiny hot plate and a sink in one corner. There was a fold-down bed against one wall, and a bathroom with a filthy tub, whose enamel was largely worn off. It was so depressing, she didn't bother to look at the closets. *Is this all I can hope for on my salary?* The filth made her shudder.

Three blocks away, after getting directions from a policeman, she had climbed the steps of an old brownstone that had obviously once been a private house. She stopped on the stoop and looked up and down the short, curving street. Young trees stood in squares of earth where the concrete had recently been broken away to make space for them. Someone must be interested in improving the neighborhood.

In the tiny vestibule, she scanned the row of tarnished brass mailboxes, looking for one belonging to the landlord or superintendent. Most of the half dozen cards were so grimy and faded they were all but illegible. While she was trying to decide what to do next, the outer door opened, and a plump woman entered, leading a child by the hand. She was very short, with a nimbus of orange hair surrounding her pudgy face. She was dressed in a sort of tent made out of apple green material. Ruth tried not to show her astonishment.

The woman asked in a friendly way, "You looking for somebody?"

"Yes. I've come about the apartment for rent, and I don't know—"

"Oh sure. Just go down under the stoop and ring the bell down there. Nettie's in for sure. She'll show it to you. Come on, Ziggy, you can meet the lady some other time." The little boy was staring fixedly at Ruth with his free hand almost entirely in his mouth.

"Good luck," his mother said. "Hope you like it. Maybe we'll meet again." She opened the inner door with a key and dragged the child along. He turned his head like a little owl to watch Ruth until he was tugged out of sight.

Ruth went down the steps again, and leaned over the wrought iron railing to look down into the areaway. She saw the door that must belong to the person called Nettie. In the top third was a window, the glass netted with wire, and so begrimed that there was no way to see through it, at least from the outside.

Ruth went down the steps. A small card attached to the door frame bore the ambiguous legend, "No Salesmen. Ring Bell." Ruth rang the bell. After a minute or two, just as she was reaching up to ring again, she heard footsteps approaching. There was a series of metallic clinks and rattles, and the door opened to reveal a woman so short that Ruth had to look down to speak to her. Her head was swathed in a kind of turban of printed material in electric blue and magenta and green. The face thus framed was doughy, its putty color accentuated by the brilliance surrounding it, and by the eyes, which were as dark as prunes.

"Yeah?" she said, with a rising inflection.

Trying to hide her surprise at the apparition in front of her, Ruth collected her wits. "Oh, hello. I came about your ad in the paper—"

The person interrupted brusquely. "It's eighty-five a month, you pay the electric and gas."

"Yes, well, I was wondering if I could—"

"Wait here. I'll get the key." The woman turned nimbly and disappeared into the gloom behind her. Ruth noted that her clothes draped a body built very much along the lines of a cube, its angles somewhat softened by layers of cloth. It seemed remarkable that she wasn't suffering from the heat.

Shortly she returned, jingling a ring full of keys. "This way." She led Ruth back up the steps of the front stoop, her skirts swaying from her broad bottom.

Inside the hall of the building, its ancestry as a town house became apparent. The floor, partly covered by a strip of dirty maroon carpet, was oak parquet. Plaster egg-and-dart molding decorated the cornices and followed the rise of the staircase. They went up to the back of the house, where Nettie opened a high, paneled door. With an abrupt swing of her short arm, she waved Ruth ahead of her.

They entered a minuscule foyer that opened into a high-ceilinged room about twenty feet square. Between a pair of tall French windows stood a blotchy pier glass, the gilding on its elaborate frame showing patches of soiled plaster in places, like a seedy dowager whose good bone structure indicates the beauty of her youth. In the center of the left-hand wall was a carved, white marble mantelpiece, under whose arch still nestled a little coal grate.

Ruth drew a quick breath of pure pleasure. She took several hesitant steps toward the center of the room, and turned slowly around. On the ceiling was an elaborate plaster cartouche of acanthus leaves that produced an esthetic shock, as if it might be a secret emblem. Its fanciful whorls set a seal of elegance on the whole airy space.

Opposite the fireplace were what appeared to be large closets. Bifold doors revealed a counter with a refrigerator underneath, a gas range, and cupboards and open shelves. To the right, a closed door hid a huge tub on ball-and-claw feet, along with the usual fixtures including a shower and another narrow cupboard fitted with shelves.

Trying again to look and sound cool and casual, Ruth returned to Nettie, who was planted in the doorway, arms akimbo, her feet planted far apart, as though preparing to do battle, if necessary.

Accustomed to looking at the fading grandeur of old New England mansions, Ruth felt pleasant recognition of what her mother might have called good structure and quality.

"It's very nice," Ruth said. "I take it that's a closet." She pointed to a door in the wall next to the entrance.

"Double size."

"When could I move in?"

"One month's rent in advance and you can suit yourself." Ruth mentally thanked Dr. Gentry for warning her about the security and offering a salary advance, should she need it.

"Well, I have to arrange to get some furniture, especially a bed. But as soon as I can, I'll come. How long will it take to have a phone put in?"

"Couple days, prob'ly. Come on down to my place and we'll get the paperwork out of the way." Nettie turned on her heel, and stumped out of the apartment without waiting to see if Ruth was following. "Just slam the door. It's locked," she called as she went.

Ruth hurried after her stocky landlady. She didn't know what she might have expected, with no experience of apartment houses, but something about this place made her feel less as if she had arrived in a foreign country, and apparently the exotic-looking inhabitants spoke a recognizable language.

It was surprisingly cool down below sidewalk level. At the end of the gloomy corridor that opened from the street door of Nettie's lair was a low-ceilinged room with a wide window next to a French door at the far end, looking out on a flag-stoned garden. A stamp-sized patch of emerald grass, recently mowed, surrounded a concrete birdbath. The walls on either side were wine-colored brick, hung with a heavy mat of English ivy. In one corner grew a pear tree, in the other, an evergreen. Privet and rhododendron brushed against the building, and pots of geraniums and petunias bloomed in clusters. Ruth realized that she would look down on this oasis from her room overhead.

Nettie's apartment inside was equally surprising. Nothing in it matched anything else. A thin, red oriental carpet lay in front of a brick fireplace. An ancient Morris chair, cushioned in a buzzing burnt orange stood on one side of it, and a broken-down Louis something armchair upholstered in powder-blue silk, soiled almost to the color of slate, was on the other. Under the window, a trestle table draped with a ragged paisley shawl, and flanked by a pair of Queen Anne chairs with rush seats enticed a person to sit and enjoy the limited vista. To Ruth's conventional eyes, the effect was rakish and enticing.

"Go ahead and sit. I'll get us a cup a coffee." Nettie disappeared back into the hallway. In a moment, Ruth heard running water along with the homelike rattle of crockery. She advanced into the room, looking around at the day bed along one wall, and at the posters and other objects hanging against the rough plaster. There was a print of a small, misty landscape in mossy greens and umber, framed in ornate gilt; a flat coiled basket, woven with a pattern of a stylized butterfly; a large Lautrec poster executed in vermilion and black and pumpkin yellow. On a copper tray sitting on folding legs next to the day bed was a large glass jar, filled with seashells and wired to make a lamp. The shade was tilted to throw light into the lap of someone who might sit on the bed. Heaps of colorful cushions were lined up against the wall. A vividly striped Mexican *serape* served as a bedspread. The whole place reminded Ruth of her mental pictures of artists' digs in Paris.

She sat down in one of the chairs at the table, looked out, and spotted an orange cat, sitting in a double-humped mound under the evergreen, his eyes shut and his front paws folded under his chest. Just looking at him pulled Ruth back to a sense of comfortable domesticity.

Nettie reappeared with a tray of coffee things. She handed Ruth a cup and seated herself in the other chair.

"Cream? Sugar?"

"No, thank you, just black. This is very nice of you."

"Might as well be comfortable. Don't have to be aloof just 'cause we're doin' business." Ruth sipped and looked out the window, and Nettie got a lease form from a desk in the corner.

"Who would have thought there would be such a pretty little green place right in the middle of the city? It's like finding a diamond in a Crackerjack box."

"Yep, but there's a whole lot of these. All these old buildings are like this. The blocks are hollow. Go on out and look; you'll see trees up over the walls all the way down. You can see even better from upstairs. What're you doing in New York?"

"I've come to get a job, see how life is in the big city."

"You're from up in New England, huh?"

"Yes, how—?"

"Listen to you talk. Maine?"

Ruth laughed and nodded. "Well, hope you like it. It's a damn sight diff'rent from the country. Where you gonna look for furniture?"

"I don't really know. Department stores? I can't afford much. I wish I could find some second-hand."

Nettie took a gulp of her coffee, and banged the cup down on its saucer. "I should hope so! Anybody can afford new stuff doesn't need to light in the Village in a place like this. I'll tell you how to find the Salvation Army store, and I know a guy has a truck'll help move stuff for you."

Startled, and even a bit suspicious of such open friendliness, Ruth hesitated before she managed to say, "Oh, that would be so kind! I don't know how to thank you, Miss, er—"

"No trouble. Call me Nettie. Everybody does." What could pass for a smile crinkled her face. "Can't call a mug like mine Antoinette."

On the subway, going back to the hotel, Ruth thought over her day. Whatever she might have expected, she could never have pictured what she had seen since her arrival. She thought the air around her would be the same everywhere. But here, there was something much more subtle and pervasive than smells that set the city canyons apart from the arching skies and fragrant airs of home.

Perhaps most surprising were the people she encountered. Surely the conventional wisdom was that in the "big city" a person was bound to be all on her own. Instead, she had already encountered kindness in two very dissimilar guises.

She went to bed and put a pad on her lap, intending to write home to tell all about it, but her eyes closed; she had not realized how tired she was. She had a dream in which she wandered with growing panic through a maze of streets with beetling, crooked houses overhanging them. She knew she must get to some destination she had forgotten and she was lost. She kept walking faster, until she was jogging and panting and she could feel her hair coming loose. She saw no other living thing anywhere. But the dream ended, and she slept soundly after it.

With Nettie by her side the next day to make sure no one tried to cheat her, Ruth got a studio couch, three Hitchcock-style chairs, and a gate-leg table from an antique shop on Third Avenue; from the Salvation Army store, a rump-sprung but welcoming wing chair, and a chest of drawers that had been painted a poisonous green. Nettie fairly danced on her abbreviated legs with impatience to get at stripping it, and infected Ruth with her eagerness. It took them a whole weekend when they finally did it, but they considered the result was well worth it when they uncovered solid cherry. Refinished and waxed, it was the beginning of Ruth's small collection of antiques.

Nettie's friend with a truck turned out to be a murderous looking Sicilian who peddled vegetables for a living all over the lower half of Manhattan. With white teeth flashing under his handlebar mustache, he heaved the furniture onto the flat bed of his truck. Then he humped everything into the house, while carrying on a running argument with Nettie on the virtues of communism. He never stopped smiling.

Ruth was so busy trying to understand what he was saying in his syncopated dialect that she forgot to consider the placement of her new treasures, and came to with a start to see that everything had been arranged, and the cheerful Francesco was gone. Using an old blanket for a skid, she managed to drag things around to suit herself after her helpers had departed.

Every weekend for a month she added to her possessions, beginning with some cookware from a nearby hotel supply company, another of Nettie's favorite places for a bargain. A carton of small items like the lamp from her desk at home arrived, and the room began to look like her own.

Between them, Ruth and Nettie decided that the onset of cold weather would be time enough to worry about floor covering. In the meantime, Ruth waxed and polished the beautiful parquet till it gleamed.

Her job had evolved rapidly. The first three months sped by, in part because after the work day was over, there were so many other things to be done, not just in her apartment, but by way of exploration and amusements.

The only drawback was a shortage of people her own age. But she loved to walk down one street or another, listening. She heard Chinese, Yiddish, Arabic, and all the European languages, along with accents from the Midwest and the South, the twangs of Long Island and Queens and Brooklyn.

Modes of dress, goods for sale, from peculiar and unheard-of fruits and vegetables, to imported clothing, crafts and art objects in store windows or push-carts, or even in unrolled peddlers' packs spread on the sidewalks gave the curving streets an exotic look.

Ruth felt sure that the eccentricities of Nettie's decor would never have flowered fully in the more staid, squared-off uptown parts of the city. In those days, Ruth tended to think of New York as The City, capitalized. But she was careful to keep the tone of letters home as subdued as she could, out of a sense that her parents might not have approved of how she was living if they had a true picture of it, though she could not have explained why. The only real cloud on her horizon was that she missed Dan.

Dr. Gentry had a busy general practice, consisting largely of well-to-do professional people. The duties of receptionist and bookkeeper took much of Ruth's time, but she preferred transcribing patient records, which gave her a sense of acquaintance with people, even though it was not the reality. In the first few weeks, in addition to office routine, Dr. Gentry taught her how to sterilize instruments, keep the inventory of medical supplies, and do the ordering. He explained that he intended her to be an assistant, not just a receptionist. His courtly manner of the day she applied for the position never varied, with the single exception that he began to call her by her first name.

A new era began the day Mrs. Gentry came into the office to meet her husband for lunch. She was a tiny woman with fine bones and aristocratic features that made her resemble engravings of an aged

Victorian heroine. She regarded Ruth with piercing blue eyes and an expression of undisguised appraisal that made Ruth blush.

Mrs. Gentry said in a melodious voice, "Arthur has said a good deal about you, my dear. I'm happy to meet you. My, your hair is a beautiful color. We have been wondering how you're liking life in the city. I understand that you come from Maine." She smiled. "We have a summer place there near Bar Harbor, where we have spent our happiest times." She seated herself on the waiting room couch. "I think it would be lovely to come from Maine." She cocked her head to one side like a quizzical little bird.

Ruth stammered, "Why, I never thought of it like that. I think perhaps it is. I'm liking New York very much."

"You're not lonely?"

"Not really. You're kind to ask. I love my work. I've made one or two acquaintances in the building where I live." Mrs. Gentry raised her eyebrows. "Oh, not friends exactly, but we exchange trivial conversation when we meet." Ruth smiled. "I even have a little friend called Ziggy to take care of when his parents go to an occasional movie. And my landlady is great. She's helped me very much in practical ways."

Dr. Gentry appeared, ushering a patient out. "Ah, Cornelia, my dear," he said, "I see you and Ruth have met."

"We have." Mrs. Gentry rose. "We were having a little talk about how Miss March is settling in here. I was about to suggest that she join us for dinner on Saturday next. I always think that the weekends are apt to be the loneliest," she added with a smile to Ruth.

"What a capital idea!" Dr. Gentry turned to Ruth. "We meet for a cocktail at six-thirty. I'll give you directions. We'll look forward to it. We must be off, or we shall be late." He took his diminutive wife by the arm, but turned at the door to say, "Mark your calendar, Ruth. And you may tell anyone who calls that I'll be back in the office by three o'clock."

Amid the myriad of new impressions, Ruth remembered her first evening with the Gentrys as an adventure. They lived in a townhouse that exemplified the parentage of her own abode in the Village. "My dear Ruth," Dr. Gentry said, holding out a hand as a maid ushered her into the living room. "How nice to have you here. May I present ..." and he introduced her to the other guests.

She had responded as best she could, but was distracted by the paintings on the walls, the textures and colors of fabrics, and numerous keepsakes and ornaments. She had difficulty attending to the conversation. Fresh flowers graced the dining table, the coffee table, and the vestibule. She thought, *If I could ever afford it, this is how I'd want my home to look.* She had to force herself to concentrate on the people instead of on the things around her.

There were three other guests. One was a young man with a sandy beard called Daryl Bates, who wrote dramatic criticism for an obscure magazine, and a middle-aged couple, both of whom were teachers at the New School. An animated discussion of modern music took place during the meal.

"I don't see what excuse there can be for making an artistic medium sound like a disaster in a pot factory," the professor stated, punctuating his comment by emptying his wine glass. Ruth felt the corners of her lips curling, and glanced hastily at her host to make sure a smile was an appropriate reaction.

Dr. Gentry's mustache twitched. "That's probably not a fair comment, Harold," he said mildly. "It's a question of what the ear is accustomed to."

"Rubbish!" came the rejoinder. The professor's full lips twisted into an ironic expression. "There's no possible excuse to listen to music unless it gives pleasure. If Cage can give you that, okay. But I'll bet a semi-quaver to a quid you'd be lying to make a claim like that."

"Now, Harold," his sleek wife interrupted, "don't reveal yourself as a complete Philistine." Her smile removed the sting from her words. Ruth tried to keep her expression impassive, while she determined to recall every word. Candlelight kept reflecting in the lenses of Daryl's spectacles as he gave his opinions, which brought tolerant smiles to the lips of the Gentrys. He defended the moderns hotly and cleverly. Ruth made a mental note to buy some records. She began to wonder whether she could hope to take in everything in that wondrous city.

Elvira, who served the meal, the silver candelabra, the consommé and pink lamb and lemon mousse, the wines, crystal, and Japanese prints, together with these people, all were as foreign to Ruth's experience as Hottentots. She felt a heady sense of adventure. The evening ended on the perfect note when Daryl saw her home and bade her good night with an ironic bow. He took down her phone number before he departed. Ruth undressed and went to bed in a daze, like someone exposed to too much sunlight after living in a cave for a month.

She accepted Daryl's invitation to dinner the following week. He introduced her to several of his friends, people on the fringes of the art world. The group often met for drinks or had an indifferent pseudo-Chinese meal at a dingy cafe below street level west of Greenwich Avenue, where the walls were decorated with pen-and-ink drawings of celebrities of the thirties. To Ruth the atmosphere was both intimate and daring. All the waiters were oriental, all wore their pants too long. She could not imagine how it had come to have a name like something out of Agatha Christy.

Among Daryl's friends were a couple of aspiring actors, a dancer, and a rangy girl who made welded sculptures. Over beers and whiskey sours, they would argue Marxist theory as it applied to anthropology and art, Oriental religion and Aristotelian structure, the merits of the two-party system, the virtues of free verse, and endlessly about the "police action" in Korea.

Since she was afraid to appear backward or reactionary, Ruth did a lot of listening. When she considered how her father would have viewed these people, though, she could see that some of their discussions appeared to be merely games—self-indulgent and removed from reality.

Daryl shared his midtown apartment with two other young men, both of whom worked for advertising agencies. They both wore grey flannels and white buck shoes, and affected Brooks Brothers Oxford-cloth shirts. They had the swarthy coloring of the Mediterranean, and though they did not share surnames, Ruth thought after she met them for the third time that it was a good thing that Ron parted his hair on the right, while Stan parted his on the left, or she might have mixed them up. She had to suppress mild shock when she understood their relationship, and was amused at their attitude toward Daryl. They seemed to feel that if they were patient, he would come to see the futility of his pursuit of the opposite sex. They were another first in the list of novelties in her new life.

That year for Ruth was like a child's first year in school: so crowded with material to be absorbed that there was simply no time for analysis or comparison. It was not until she was alone thirteen years later with time to go over those early days that she was able to make a sober comparison between her young self and the woman she had by then become.

CHAPTER SIX

One October Sunday, Ruth took her customary walk around Washington Square. She loved the park, dominated by the immense arch, lined with Georgian brick houses on the north, the undistinguished buildings of New York University on the east, and residential hotels on the west. The south side was a motley assortment of architecture, including the Judson Memorial's ugly yellow brick bulk and a couple of vacant lots.

The fountain, patronized on the hot days of the waning summer by droves of local urchins, floated the odd toy boat in comparative quiet now, since autumn was on the way. She liked the dusty-leaved plane trees and elms set in geometric plots of patchy grass, fenced with iron piping painted shiny black. Chess players sat on benches, there was the occasional street musician or juggler, baby carriages and dogs and strolling couples. Best of all, she enjoyed watching the tourists and not feeling like one of them.

An enterprising individual had installed a pair of asphalt-surfaced tennis courts in one of the vacant lots. From a tiny kiosk on the edge of the sidewalk, he sold tickets admitting players for specific hours. A slate attached to the wall by the window showed the schedule for each day. A drinking fountain was the only amenity available, but in spite of that, the courts were always full on fair weekends, and on summer evenings until dark. From a block away, one could hear the resonant pong of balls on taut strings, and the shouts and laughter of players. Ruth often stopped to watch.

Golden sunlight reflected from the wall of a five-story building looming on the left side of the courts. Behind them, dusty ailanthus trees waved over the walls of the gardens beyond the lot. An attractive blonde in a short, pleated skirt and a tanned young man with his back to the street were engaged in a singles match. On the other court, two middle-aged couples played sedate doubles.

The young couple played hard, running each other mercilessly from one side to the other. All at once, the young man hit a shot that bounced so high in front of his opponent that she tried a killing lob. She looked high, golden hair flowing, and smashed down on the ball. It made a false bounce against something on the ground, struck the brick wall next to it, and ricocheted over the man's head, over the fence, and into the street.

Without thinking, Ruth chased it and retrieved it from the opposite gutter. When she turned back toward the players with it in her hand, both were waiting, and the fat proprietor of the courts was holding the gate open. She trotted over, extending the ball toward the dark young man, who was holding his racquet out to take it.

Ruth's breath caught, and she stepped back when she saw his face. It was the one she had seen long ago in Tony's bar.

"Thanks very much."

"You're welcome," Ruth managed to get out. His eyes held hers. Though he reached his racquet out for her to drop the ball on the strings, she stood motionless, eyes wide. "Do I know you?"

"Oh—no!" She felt herself grow pale. "No, I don't think so. Oh, I'm sorry." She dropped the ball hastily onto the racquet, as if it were hot, and backed up, quivering.

The young man took the ball. "Do you play?"

Still mesmerized by his face, her voice sounding distant inside her head, she replied, "Yes, a little."

"Why don't you join us some Sunday? Do you live around here?"

"A few blocks away. But I'm not good enough to play with you. I could see that."

"I'll bet you are." He smiled. Ruth's eyes wavered, dazzled by the beauty of his face.

The blonde girl was calling from the other side of the net. He answered, "Coming, Sandy." With a wave to Ruth, he turned back to his game.

She turned away, numb. The remembered image in the smoky twilight of Tony's superimposed itself on the image she had just seen so closely, tanned and shiny with sweat, moist curls breaking the perfect hairline. She walked along the pavement, oblivious of other pedestrians, of the sunlight and shade, the yellowing leaves and the church bells, even of an organ-grinder with his audience of tots, of everything she had noticed with such pleasure just a few minutes before. She was disoriented, displaced from all objects and familiar impressions. A furious blast from an automobile horn and a shriek of tires brought her to her senses. She found herself with one foot on the curb and the other in the gutter. The driver was leaning out his window and making an obscene gesture as he rolled across the intersection. She had nearly walked in front of him.

Through the following week, she often reviewed the incident at the tennis court. Visual details of the meeting were crystalline. She pictured how the light flickered across the tops of the ailanthus trees, the pattern of shadows like a fish net cast across the macadam from the hurricane fence, red lacquer stripes around the frame and down the handle of the racquet in the young man's hand. She could still see the texture of his browned skin under its film of moisture, the glistening hairs on his arm, the rounded corners of the base of his thumbnail with its perfect half-moon, pressed on the handle of the extended racquet. Especially she remembered his lips, with a nearly imperceptible rim of paler skin outlining their margins.

The scene replayed itself over and over behind her closed eyes at night, every sensory detail etched on the surface of her mind.

By the next Sunday, she was too nervous to prepare the leisurely brunch she had promised herself. Instead of blueberry pancakes, she ate half of a slice of toast and drank a cup of coffee. In an effort at self-control, she sat at her desk and tried to write a letter home, but threw away two crumpled sheets and gave up. She got a sweater and went out.

On the north side of the park, she sat down on one of the benches facing the white stoops and fanlights of the brick row-houses. The neighborhood organ-grinder was cranking out his wheezy, tinkling music, the instrument rocking on its single prop in time with his movements. She concentrated on the metallic, not-quite-rhythmic song, trying to tune out the sounds of a tennis game behind her. The little monkey in its pillbox hat and tiny bolero held a tin cup and hopped nervously from one of his master's shoulders to the organ, with its garish landscape painted on the side, to his master's other shoulder, and back again.

From behind, the man reminded her of the scarecrows her father used to make for the vegetable garden at home. Every mud-colored rag he wore seemed to flap loosely on him. His scrawny neck looked too frail to support his head with its filthy fedora perched at a jaunty angle on top of a brush of grizzled, overgrown curls. She concentrated on details, planning to describe them to Dan.

As one of the tunes was ending, a woman emerged from one of the Georgian house's white door. She was neatly dressed in a blazer and tartan skirt. She ran down the steps, dropped a bill into the monkey's cup, lifted a hand in greeting, and ran up again to disappear behind the paneled door with its shiny knocker. When she first appeared, the organ-grinder had cranked faster and nodded his head rapidly, turning himself toward his hoped-for patron, and for a few moments Ruth saw his face, furrowed, dark, eyes nearly hidden by shaggy brows. He was smiling with an expression of exaggerated glee—a rictus of anticipation that he maintained until his donor's form had disappeared from view.

The sun, which had been shining in a clear sky, was suddenly dimmed by a cloud. In an instant, the scene had lost its gloss. Ruth rose, chilled, and walked over to stand under the majestic Washington arch. She gazed up Fifth Avenue until perspective cut off the invisible horizon with converging verticals of trees, lamp posts, and soaring towers. She kept her back to the tennis courts.

Finally, she turned and went in the opposite direction until she could see the hurricane fence and the white figures darting about behind it, and hear the voices of the players. This time he was playing facing the street.

Ruth pivoted, and cutting diagonally through the park, hurried home.

Daryl called, and Ruth suggested they try to rent a court for some tennis before the weather got too cold. The moment he agreed, she wished her words back. What was happening to her? She was not the sort to pursue a man!

Two weekends in a row, they played on the south side of the

square, but the other court was occupied by people she had never seen before.

Gradually, as winter arrived, most of the time she was able to push the image of the handsome stranger's face to the back of her mind. One evening, Daryl and Ruth walked home through the busy night life of Greenwich Village. They had stopped for drinks after the theater. She welcomed his companionship, and enjoyed his raffish conversation. Besides, he was the only young man she knew in town. He had an arm around her waist, and they strolled, talking about the production they had seen. She had a moment's recollection of the damp street in drab Providence, where she had walked beside Norman and voiced her ambitions for the future.

Under a street light, Daryl stopped suddenly, pulling her around to face him. He had a strange expression on his usually relaxed features. The yellowish glare accentuated his unruly hair and beard. She noticed a line between his sandy eyebrows, and the sheen of the whites of his eyes.

He demanded, "Who the hell are we trying to fool, Red?" Ruth was startled. She tried to imagine what he could mean, but before she could ask him, he continued in a hoarse voice. "You know I don't give a shit about Mielziner or whether the damn show ever makes a nickel. Ask me in tonight."

She stammered, "Daryl, I ... What are you talking about?" Yet she knew she should not have been surprised. She'd felt tension between them the last three or four times they had been together. He tightened his arm around her. She pulled her head back as she saw his lips approaching. But he kissed her hard, pressing her head to his with one hand. She went cold with anger and apprehension combined.

"Don't act, Red. I can't stand coyness. Come on, let's get to your place." He grasped her hand and began to walk rapidly, dragging her along the sidewalk toward the steps leading up to the door of her building, while she pulled back instinctively.

"Daryl, wait!" She tried to slow his headlong pace.

"We'll talk when we get inside," he growled. "Where's your key?"

"Daryl, please! No, I can't let you in."

"You must be joking!" he barked. "This is the twentieth century. Give me the key!" His eyes glittered; he held his hand out.

Ruth pulled away from him, her back against the railing. She made her voice calm with an effort. "Maybe some other time, Daryl. Thank you for the evening. It was a lot of fun."

"Give me the fucking key, Red!"

"You'll wake everybody up. Not tonight. But thanks for everything." Never had her inexperience been more obvious to her. She was becoming frightened.

He lowered his voice. "If you don't want to wake everybody up, then let's get inside." He reached for her handbag, tugged at it while she hung on. They pulled back and forth for a moment like a couple of children with a disputed toy.

Daryl's breath was heavy with whiskey. As they struggled, Ruth began to seethe with anger and embarrassment. She wanted to sink out of sight, but she was powerless to control this new person, panting in front of her like an excited dog. What had become of her humorous, witty, intellectual escort with his irreverent commentary and ironic attitudes?

As suddenly as he had begun his aggressive behavior, Daryl ceased. His hand dropped from the purse, so that Ruth staggered back against the railing. They stared at each other for a moment in a silence broken by the sounds of their rapid breathing.

"Sorry. I'm sorry. You just don't understand what … I'm sorry. I better get going. I'll call you." He turned and hurried unsteadily down the steps. She heard a muffled "Good night."

Ruth, breathing hard, dropped back to lean against the stone banister, and closed her eyes. After a moment, she found her key. Once in her apartment, she sat staring at the blank windows and wondering how to learn about men. For the first time in a year, she truly longed for someone to talk to.

She dreaded hearing from Daryl again, yet there was no one else available to take her out. Days passed, and she told herself he had just had one drink too many. After a week, he did call, sounding as though nothing had happened. She decided she should behave the same way. They arranged to meet for Sunday brunch.

Sitting at the bar at the Hotel Brevoort, Ruth and Daryl quibbled amiably about a film revival they had just seen. "You have to admit the whole thing was exaggerated to make the point," Ruth insisted. "There wasn't anything real about it! And the title doesn't help—'It

Happened One Night!' Can you imagine anybody having a night like that?" She was sitting on the bar stool, half turned to Daryl.

He drank from his glass and wiped foam from his lip with the back of one hand. "Come on, Red. It was a comedy—for fun. It made you laugh. God, the way that woman can keep a straight face and her charm while being so outrageous, so sexy—"

"Dammit, Daryl, would you stop and pick up some strange female with gorgeous legs just because she lifted her skirt above her knee at the roadside?"

"Well, if I wouldn't," he said with a wicked grin, "it would be because of my insurance." He allowed his gaze to fall to Ruth's legs, where her skirt exposed her knees.

She couldn't suppress a laugh. "You're a pain, you know that? A regular reactionary. But you're right. Claudette Colbert could probably do just about anything she pleased, no matter how outrageous, and still look like a lady."

"Since you want to be so serious, how about going to the Fifth Avenue Playhouse with me on Thursday? I'll take you to that Jean Gabin revival. I have to review it, and maybe your somewhat benighted, not to mention archaic, point of view will suggest something different for me to say about it."

She was relieved that they seemed to have regained their old, casual footing. She turned to pick up her glass from the bar. "Thank you very much," she said. "I'd like to."

Daryl held his beer up, grinning. "Here's to beautiful girls ... "

"And to handsome men to admire them," she put in, lifting her own glass. It occurred to her that maybe she was getting the hang of it.

Just as their glasses were about to touch, someone fell against her back, shoving her forward against Daryl, and spilling both their drinks into her lap.

A man's voice cried, "Holy—I'm sorry! Are you all right? God, I'm sorry!" Ruth and Daryl scrambled for handfuls of cocktail napkins from the bar to brush the worst of the liquid out of her lap, trying to dry her off.

She looked down at her drenched skirt, "It's okay—just a bit damp." She turned to see who was apologizing and had to reach out to hold onto the edge of the bar. She was looking straight into the sable brown eyes of the tennis player, the Greek god from Tony's. She was breathing too fast and her hands had begun to shake. She saw the man's tanned profile, his glossy hair feathered above a shapely ear as he bent over her lap, patting at it with his handkerchief. Disconnected details of the scene imposed themselves on her confusion. Oddly, she was sharply aware of the bright sidewalk outside, pedestrians passing in the sunlight, green and yellow double-decker buses rolling up the avenue like a frieze in motion on the other side of the glass. It was as if her connections to reality were purely visual.

"I'm so embarrassed!" he was saying. He held out his hand. "My name is Alexander Duchamp. Call me Alex. Would you let me take care of the cleaning?"

Something seemed to have happened to ordinary social rhythms; Ruth struggled to answer through a dizzy pause she was powerless to shorten.

Finally, she managed, "Of course not. It's nothing. Besides, this skirt is washable." She met his eyes and her heart seemed to fill her throat.

"But I was so stupid, so clumsy. I really do beg your pardon, Miss?"

"M-March. Ruth March." Was there a subtle foreign sound to his speech? She realized she was staring at him. Making a major effort to appear composed, she gestured, but without shifting her gaze. "And this is Daryl Bates." Daryl nodded, and she caught an expression of prim disapproval on his face. Alex Duchamp extended a hand, and Daryl shook it once.

"Why don't we move over to a table? The least I can do is offer to buy you both a drink, if only to replace the ones I spilled." He had taken Ruth's arm, helped her down from the bar stool, and began to lead her to one of the banquettes. His touch shocked like electricity. "I've got to do something to prove to you that I'm not in the habit of staggering around in bars and lurching into innocent patrons."

Dazzled, enticed by the hint of accent she detected in his pleasant voice, Ruth was shy of the frankly appraising expression in his eyes; they lingered on her hair, ran down her figure and back up, stiffening her with embarrassment, while he continued to chat easily as he seated her. "Somehow I'll have to convince you I'm a civilized type, in spite of recent events." He slid onto the seat next to her, and waved to the bartender.

For a quarter of an hour, while Alex made genial small talk, Daryl maintained silence, eyeing the newcomer suspiciously, and replying to questions in monosyllables. Ruth gradually regained her composure, while Alex thawed Daryl with appeals to his judgment and invitations to express his opinions, ploys as irresistible to Daryl as to anyone.

Ruth remembered later that Daryl had scarcely spoken on the way home. She could hardly have answered in any case.

CHAPTER SEVEN

Alex invited Ruth to play tennis. Had she given him her telephone number? Since he knew her name and that she lived near the park, perhaps he'd found her in the book. Now, thinking back on those first minutes of their first date still made her cringe. She remembered how she had walked out on the court in her short white skirt, rigid with nerves. At first she couldn't concentrate. She was even afraid to run, sure she would stumble.

The blonde girl called Sandy and a prematurely balding young broker made up the party. When her turn came to serve, the game finally forced her to pay attention, and after an hour, she was playing as well as the others and enjoying herself. Some of her hypersensitivity to Alex was buffered by the presence of others. Once she overcame her obvious shyness, she was athletic and graceful, and her height gave her a distinct advantage over Sandy. Ruth and Alex had no trouble winning almost every set.

After that tennis game, Ruth knew she was lost. When she was not with Alex, she longed for him like someone without food longing for a meal. If this was what Dan had felt, if this is what Eloise meant—she thought, *How do people manage to live ordinary lives in this condition?* She had wit enough to reprimand herself for such foolishness, but not strength enough to escape feeling as if she were under a spell.

Desperate to talk to someone, twice she sat down to write a confession to Dan. If she could just discuss how she was feeling, maybe she could gain perspective from a listener. But she crumpled the paper and threw it away. Her habits of self-restraint were ingrained. It took all her willpower not to allow her work to suffer.

She was unaware that Alex had been almost as tense as she, but was better at hiding his feelings. He made up his mind that he must get to know this long-legged, dignified redhead. Her reserve made her unlike any other young woman he had yet seen. In that first game, he had played well, but carefully, so as not to intimidate her. Wavering between a growing desire to capture this intriguing girl and his sense that they had almost nothing in common, Alex hurried home daily to call her, forgetting about the other young women of his acquaintance. Current events went into his head from the newspapers, and as quickly as he read the articles, they evaporated from his mind. He allowed this preoccupation to sweep him along, enjoying the chase, he told himself. Perhaps because he saw he could reach Ruth only with care and delicacy because of her innocence and inexperience, this novelty added to her allure. He had no conscious desire to deceive her, but he certainly saw her as a challenge. She would need careful handling.

In the long, sunny days of that autumn, they played tennis regularly, until it got too cold, and shared coffee-shop post mortems full of puns, hilarity, and friendly rivalry with other couples. Ruth's singles game improved. Alex was even amenable to losing to her once in a while, which surprised them both, though neither mentioned it.

One evening Alex took her to a small restaurant below sidewalk level on Eleventh Street. The scene would forever glow in Ruth's memory like a stage set—exotic, framed in darkness, and evocative. At the back of the dim dining room was a tiny flagged patio, roofed over by a trellis festooned with creeper and grape vines, among which hung Japanese paper lanterns. There, sounds of traffic were so muted, it was almost like a country setting. Every table had a candle; there was a mandolin player, and the food was spicy and full of garlic.

"I never thought a meal could taste so strange and be so good!" Ruth sipped wine. "There were Italian restaurants in Providence, but nothing like this." She looked into Alex's eyes and saw that their expression was affectionate, quizzical, and almost as soft as the curious eyes of deer, seemingly at variance with his forthright charm and easy conversation. In the haze of her fascination with him, she, nevertheless, wondered why the very mildness of his expression should increase her own unrest so much. Could he be in some way hypnotizing her? She felt a delicate shiver of apprehension. She scarcely dared dream that such a plain person as she would appeal to the likes of Alexander Duchamp.

Ruth realized he was probably aware of her uncertainty, though she hoped not of its source. Alex talked of ordinary things. "What kind of food do you have at home?"

"Well, I suppose you'd say, plain food. Mother's an excellent cook, but I don't think she'd have garlic in the house, and I doubt if she's ever made a sauce except to cream onions or potatoes." Ruth leaned back in her chair, her long fingers rolling a spoon over and over. Feeling Alex's glance like a subtle command to go on, she looked up. "But you've never had a better meal than her pot roast with vegetables, or her fish chowder and biscuits, or roast turkey with cranberry sauce and stuffed squash, or chicken with dumplings, or apple—" She stopped. Alex was shaking with laughter. "What's so funny?"

"The way you can think of all that food when you've just finished a whole dinner."

Ruth, to her own surprise, answered his laugh without embarrassment. "Terrible, isn't it? I guess I'm just greedy, but I can cook too. I'll show you some time." As soon as the words were out of her mouth, she wondered how she could be so forward. She said, "Tell me about your work."

Over coffee and liqueur he did. "It's a funny kind of job, I suppose, but that's why it suits me." He searched her face for a clue to how much he dared reveal. "I work for a man who makes special short films, documentaries, mostly. I do a bit of everything, from lugging equipment to building blinds for filming wild life. I make repairs on the van, on lighting equipment, or even sometimes on the cameras. We make films about anything you can imagine: animals and birds, politics, poverty, avant-garde art. Once we did one on a flood in Louisiana. Anything out of the ordinary. Life is full of things people don't know anything about, or if they do, all they have is misinformation."

"How fascinating."

"Really I'm a sort of glorified *gofer*." His tone changed, hardened. "But some day I'm going to make my own films. I'll choose the subjects, produce and direct them. I might even try writing the continuity for the voice-over, but with a different slant—mine!" His enthusiasm made his dark eyes glitter. He gestured often and expressively and words poured out. It seemed to Ruth he was hungry for an audience to share his ambitions. "When I get a chance, I'm going to make my own statement, create my own films with my own commentary. Mine will be a name everyone in the business will know!"

"I'm sure it will," Ruth murmured, awed. It crossed her mind that he looked as commanding in his own way as her father did in his, though this man was as outlandish as a panther to her New England eyes.

Abruptly, Alex ceased his energetic monologue. He captured her eyes with his. "I want to know about you. Where were you born? Tell me about home."

A longing to show him everything dear to her made Ruth suddenly shy again, since such an emotion was so unfamiliar. "Oh, it's just a small place on the coast. You wouldn't have heard of it." She saw his eyes focused on hers and looked down, but let the words come. "It's picturesque. It smells of the ocean a lot of the time. The weather is like a cranky person whose temper you can't be sure about. Seasons are distinct." She hesitated, then added, "And it's so ... provincial."

Alex nodded. "Do you get homesick?"

Ruth shook her head. "I simply haven't had time to, I guess. I came to New York on purpose, and I'm so glad I did."

"You like your job, then?"

"Love it."

His next word seemed to telegraph to Ruth an astonishing intensity and curiosity beyond small talk. It produced a pleasant little shock. "Dreams?"

While it struck her as demanding, importunate, she longed to tell him everything, to open herself to him. His probing made her uncomfortable at the same that it thrilled her. She paused, trying to quell her feelings and collect her thoughts, to find a way to keep herself safe. "Well, of course—I guess so, like anyone." She felt humble, tongue-tied and naive. Sophistication, fame, learning, romance, children … . What exactly were her dreams?

Alex seemed about to press her, but after a long look, to her relief, he smiled and rose to pull her chair back for her. She was grateful that once again, on the verge of embarrassing or testing her, he seemed to sense her unease.

They strolled back to her apartment, chatting. Alex made her feel about sixteen, instead of twenty-two. His self-assurance and charm, his magnetism, his amazing looks, but above all, his apparent sensitivity awed her. Until that evening, she had been sure, with a feeling near despair, that she was too colorless really to interest him.

At the door, Alex took Ruth's keys from her hand and ushered her into the entry as though it belonged to him. She stopped just inside and held out her hand for the keys. Alex raised his eyebrows. "Thank you for a lovely evening." Why did conventional words always fail to convey anything important, hiding as they seemed to, so much?

Alex made no response, his eyes fixed on hers.

She tried again. "For the great food, and good talk, and …" His expression made her swallow her words. His mouth wore the slightest hint of a smile, and his eyelids were lowered just enough to give him an expression of extreme irony. A momentary picture of herself struggling childishly with Daryl flashed into Ruth's mind.

Still holding her gaze, Alex stepped close to her and folded his arms tightly around her. He brought his mouth down on her lips, very deliberately, very slowly. He pressed her shoulders to his chest with one hand, with the other, he pulled her pelvis tightly against his body as he increased the pressure of his mouth on hers.

The instant Ruth felt his touch and the inescapable evidence of his feelings, she was shaken between panic and delight; she had trouble breathing. She tried to loosen his hold by pressing her hands against his upper arms, but he increased the tightness of his grip. A languorous current washed through her, weakening her knees. She tried to draw her head back, away from his insistent mouth, but he followed hers. In spite of her pleasure, she was instinctively fearful. She felt danger and delight equally in a whirlpool of emotion and sexual excitement.

At last Alex allowed her to move, though he still clasped her in his arms. The springy muscles of his torso and the hard columns of his thighs asserted themselves against her body and legs. She gasped.

"What's wrong?" His voice was low, vibrant.

"Let me get a breath." He relaxed his arms a little, but did not release her. She attempted a light touch. "That was quite a kiss for a first—"

"Believe me, it won't be the last." He pulled her slowly and firmly to him again.

Breathless, she turned her face away. "Alex, enough for now. Please!" There was a tremor in her voice.

He studied her intently for the space of a breath, before he said, "Do you mean it?"

The weakness that had threatened her a few moments before began to give way to annoyance at herself. "Yes," she said, striving for firmness. "I certainly do."

Alex continued to study her face in the yellowish light of the drab hallway. Ruth forced herself to look steadily back at him. Very gradually he relaxed his hold. She was careful not to break away from him, but lowered her hands from his chest as he removed his arms; then she stepped slowly free of him. His eyes never left hers, nor could she look away. They moved formally, as in a *pas de deux*.

She stretched out her hand again for the keys and saw a shadow pass across his face. Disappointment, puzzlement, or perhaps anger? She said softly, "Good night."

Alex reacted as if she'd punched him. He dropped the keys with a jangle into her outstretched palm, breaking the inertia that seemed to grip them. Before she turned to the inner door, he summoned a smile, gave a mock salute, and went out.

That night Ruth had lain awake a long time. She replayed in her mind all the times she had seen Alex, making leaps in chronology; she could not think about him in logical sequence. She saw the glowing flush of his moist skin in the brilliant autumn sun with the tennis court behind him; the modeling of the base of his throat, and his tanned, muscular arms. She saw him again, his head wreathed in cigarette smoke, reflected by the mirror behind the bar in Tony's; recalled his charm as he apologized for the spilled drinks. The warmth and texture of his lips and hands filled her with apprehension and exhilaration in equal measure. The degree of her infatuation frightened her.

It was not only his looks. Alex was enigmatic. He seldom answered personal questions. His smooth exterior suggested depths she could not plumb. What went on behind those brown eyes, whose gaze seemed to see into her very brain? And why did she so much want him to? She tossed herself onto her other side. But she was afraid. What if this came to nothing?

As weeks passed, Alex multiplied his requests for Ruth's time. He wanted to see her every day, and revealed a shortened temper if she had to refuse. Ruth found herself less and less willing to disappoint him, or indeed, herself.

He took her to a concert. In Carnegie Hall, surrounded by gilded plaster and red plush, she heard for the first time the incomparable sound of a live symphony orchestra. It was a feeling like drowning in the living pulse of the music. All the way to the subway afterwards, she was speechless. It took the inescapable din of the train to obliterate the echoes of Beethoven, so that she was finally able to talk haltingly of her impressions.

"I knew you'd like it," he said.

"How? We never talked about—"

"Not about music, no, but I've watched you, and I've listened to you talk. You could say I recognized your sense of—" He hesitated, looked away from her at the advertising cards fixed above the windows in the subway car.

"Sense of what?" she prompted.

He looked back at her intently, then said gently, "I don't want to sound presumptuous, but I was going to say, your sense of beauty. I thought it would extend to your ears."

A thin, hot thrill made Ruth falter when she murmured, "What a very nice thing to say." She was profoundly stirred by his perception of her. He was aware of a side of her that she'd never considered herself, and that no one else ever noted, not even Dan. Or was she being changed by association with Alex?

At Ruth's door, he made a point of holding out his hand for her keys, as before. He unlocked it for her, accepted her thanks for the evening, and left her with no more than a warm clasp of her hand between his.

Every time they said good night like that, she watched from the open doorway as he walked away from her, the street light casting a momentary halo over his glossy dark head when he passed beneath it. She began to ache for him to renew his embraces.

As they spent more time together, she met more of Alex's friends. His clear eagerness to share her with others gave her a new sense of her own worth. She began to forget to be afraid that he would lose interest and to allow herself to look forward to their next meeting.

With groups, Alex was not as talkative as he ordinarily was with her. She noticed how he seemed to watch everybody, almost like someone making mental notes. Sometimes his observations of those around him made Ruth uncomfortable, as if their being together implicated her in his scrutiny.

"You know Daryl sees himself as a bit of a radical," Alex said.

"How do you know? You only met him that once."

"Just take a look at his hair and beard," he replied coolly.

At a party, he said, "Sandy and Hank have had a fight."

Ruth looked across the room at Sandy, who was talking to someone. Hank, standing next to her, was raising his glass to his lips. "Did she say something? Did he?"

"He hasn't spoken to her since they came in, and she got her own drink. Besides, she usually drinks highballs, and that's on the rocks."

Ruth looked at Alex with new respect, but quickly forgot her resolution to learn to be as perceptive as he. She was frustrated by how difficult it was to make him talk about himself. His adeptness at fending off questions and directing the conversation away from himself meant she picked up little but hints.

On one occasion he asked her, "Did you have what they call a happy childhood?"

"I think you'd say so. I'm not sure what that means really." An instantaneous flash of the coastline under stormy skies crossed her mind. "My parents aren't at all demonstrative, but I think they love us. They always took care that we were taught—"

"You said, 'us.' You have brothers and sisters?"

"Just my younger brother."

"Are you close?"

"Very, but we don't correspond a great deal. He's in college in Maine now."

"Do you miss him?"

"Well, yes, I do. We always talked to each other so easily. He's always been my best friend, I guess. I don't know, there were times when it seemed like the two of us against the world." She laughed.

"Does he look like you?"

"He doesn't have red hair, if that's what you mean. What about you, do you have any brothers or sisters?"

Alex shook his head. "What did you do in the summers? Sail?"

Ruth laughed at the idea that they could have afforded a boat for fun. She told him about their house and tried to explain their life.

She asked, "What does your father do?"

He hesitated, as though deciding whether or not to give in to her curiosity, shifted in his chair, and began to twist the stem of his wineglass. Without looking at her, he said, "To tell the truth, I don't know. I was raised in an orphanage, at least until I was almost seven." He glanced up at her and smiled at the expression on her face. "It wasn't like Dickens. In Quebec they know how to cook, and most of the nuns weren't trying to make us into little saints. By and large, I think they had a pretty down-to-earth attitude toward us. Of course, I didn't appreciate them at the time. They taught us by rote, cracked us with a ruler when we misbehaved, dinned a sense of sin into those they could, and fed and clothed us as well as they could afford to." He shrugged. "It probably wasn't so different from growing up in a big family, except there were a lot of brothers and no sisters."

"And too many mothers, one father who didn't sleep at home, and church every day, isn't that right?"

Alex grinned at her. "Okay, I see your point. But we did survive without bedtime stories. And we did have to do chores like putting out the garbage."

"Do you know anything about your parents?" She needed a frame into which to fit him.

Alex looked down at a roll he was crumbling. "Only the name on my birth certificate, and that's not the one I have now. The nuns weren't interested in the past. They wanted to save our souls if they could, I guess, and get us out of a place that had too many of us and into families who would take over." There was a silence. Then he went on, "I do remember once hearing Gabriel and Mariette talking to someone in the parlor one day. I heard the word *abandonné*. It stuck in my head for a while, but I decided not to think about it." He looked then at Ruth. "I haven't let it come back till now."

For a long breath Ruth knew no response to this. It would be years later before she understood the full importance of that revelation. She said, "I'd hate not knowing. I'd think it was so hard not to ... I guess you could call it, *belong*."

"How do you mean?"

"Well," she had said slowly, "there was never a question about what was expected of us because there were so many precedents, I guess. There wasn't a stick of furniture in our house that didn't have some sort of anecdote attached to it. You could say the Marches almost live by tradition."

Alex had succeeded again in deflecting inquiries about himself.

Yet, as time passed and Alex continued his practice of treating her with utmost restraint, failing to touch her except casually. She was at first dismayed and later shocked by the effect he had on her if he took her hand, or if they danced. She would find herself gritting her teeth, as if that might stiffen her knees, along with her resolve not to reveal how she was stirred by contact with his flesh.

Early in the winter, Alex took her to a party in a partially renovated building. It was an old factory whose vast floor space had not yet been partitioned. No one knew how the host had managed to rent the premises at all, even though facilities for cooking and sanitation had already been installed.

When Ruth and Alex arrived, a billiard game was already in progress, accompanied by much laughter and jeers as shots went awry. Eventually they got Alex to the table. The game was a sort of round-robin pool, though no one was taking it seriously.

When his turn came, Alex cleared the table. The conversation and jokes died down as people watched him pot ball after ball with a smooth, unemphatic stroke, as though he had a hinge where his shoulder should be and a pin in his elbow that allowed his forearm to swing like a pendulum.

"How the hell did you learn to do that?" someone said.

Alex straightened up and chalked his cue with a bland expression. He shrugged. "It wasn't very hard. You should try billiards."

"No, no kidding. Can you do that again?"

"I think so."

They racked up the balls, Alex broke them, and then for fun, he played balls people chose for him into the pockets they specified. His ability to use the cushions to direct a ball to a destination behind several intervening ones had everyone spellbound. Finally they got him to tell how he had acquired his skill. It was almost the first hint of his past away from his home that Ruth had.

"Well, I spent almost a year up in BC in a lumber camp. About the only entertainment was a billiard table in the one gin mill in the town we were nearest to. So I practiced when the snow wasn't too deep to get into town. The owner of the bar had bought it with money he made hustling games during the Depression. He taught me." Alex laid his cue across the table.

Later, when Ruth tried to get him to tell more about that part of his life, he said, "Oh, it's a long story. Some other time." Eventually, he had told her.

Another time Ruth asked him whether he had ever been to Providence. "Did you ever go to a bar there called Tony's?"

"God, I don't know. Yes, we did stop off there on our way back from shooting a film about Newfoundland dogs. I don't remember the name of the place. Why?"

"I've never told you this, but I've seen you before. I mean, before we met at the tennis court. I saw you in that bar with a short man with grey hair." She felt herself flush, but added, "I thought he looked like a gangster."

Alex laughed. "That was Jerry, all right. Why would you remember me, though? I didn't see you."

"I was with a group of students." Ruth lowered her eyes. "I almost died when I saw who you were that day I returned your tennis ball."

Alex studied her face for a minute without speaking. Finally he said, "Well, what do you know?"

※ ※

It had been some time before Ruth dared to acknowledge to herself that she was being courted. On their first evening out, she had been insulted by Alex's tacit assumption that he could make love to her. Later, she wished desperately that he would. She felt like a silly adolescent. Alex had demonstrated his acceptance of her attitude by changing his behavior immediately to an easy informality that had restored her confidence. Then she had tried to deny to herself how much she wished he might renew his ardor. But the intense awareness of his masculinity, the force of his physical presence, along with her growing awareness of his increasing desire had become pressures she realized she wouldn't be able to deflect indefinitely. She lived in a delicious state of suspended animation, only hoping that the impulse, when it came, would not destroy her semblance of control. She had given up negative thoughts by then, certain that in the end, Alex would offer to make love to her again.

Alex, for his part, was surprised at his own capacity for restraint. All the while he kept up small talk, Alex realized he was prey to a turmoil of emotion for which he was completely unprepared. His adventures with girls and women had always had only the most obvious purpose. Ruth March, however, was not only interesting, even handsome—with her striking hair, lithe and sumptuous body—she was also mysterious. She kept her self to herself. He realized he could not take her lightly.

After that first concert, he took her to more, and to the ballet and the theater. They went to gallery openings uptown and to two Armory art shows. As if he were trying to give her as much of what she wanted from New York as he could, he was endlessly inventive in the activities he planned for them. He knew a lot of people in the arts and in the entertainment business, because of his work. Frequently he took her to parties, or they met other couples for dinner or the theater.

Being surrounded by people in numbers helped Alex remember his determination to hold impulses in check in order to lure Ruth so carefully that she could not escape when he decided the time was right to spring his trap. He thought of catching her in terms like that: like a hunter with elusive and intelligent prey. Or he did until he was with her, when he found himself full of determination to protect her, though he wouldn't have been able to explain from what.

They ate in Armenian and French cafés, and Chinese and German and Italian restaurants. They rented bicycles on Sunday, and rode down to the Battery. Before Christmas, they even went skating in Rockefeller Center.

Ruth's vitality increased; she discovered energy she never suspected. She was incredibly happy. For a time after she began to go out with Alex, she'd seen Daryl occasionally. But before long, the Gentrys became almost the only other people with whom she maintained social contact. They included her in some family entertainment almost monthly, treating her like a young niece. They and her job were all that kept her from total preoccupation with Alex.

Maine had come to seem like a place she had known in some other life. Ruth wrote nothing specific about Alex to her parents, though she mentioned him in all her letters to Dan, who seldom answered. She wanted to keep Alex a secret, not out of shame or embarrassment, but from a superstitious notion that she risked losing him if anyone were to know how vital a part of her life he had become.

By New Year's Eve, Ruth sensed that soon some climax was bound to come. The sexual tension was becoming intolerable. She perceived how much it cost Alex to restrain himself when they touched, and her assurance grew. She wondered briefly if he thought her cold, and chided herself for being so ambivalent about revealing her feelings.

The sense of something perhaps vital held back in him continued to trouble her. It was not so much that he kept the facts of his life secret (though they were for the most part hidden), as it was that she sensed an inner layer that he concealed from everyone. She longed to uncover it.

ಬ ಣ

On the night of the big New Year's Eve party, sleet struck the windows in short rattling bursts. Ruth stood in front of the pier glass. She had spent half a week's salary on the taffeta to make her gown, and now that she had it on, she wondered whether she had chosen the right shade after all. On the whole, olive green suited her coloring, making her eyes look like dark amber. She had applied makeup to give her skin a glow as if she had been in the sun. She arranged her hair in a knot of falling curls that accentuated the length of her neck and the curve of her shoulders. As always, its color was glorious. Brought up to deplore vanity, she yearned now to be a match for her comely Alex, but gazing into the glass gave her the sense of looking at a stranger.

SETTLING

When she answered his ring, he came along the corridor to where she stood holding the door open for him, her skirt sweeping the floor. He carried a corsage box. "My God, Red, you are something to behold!" She realized he had never before commented on her appearance. She felt her face get hot.

"I think that's a compliment, isn't it?"

He whispered, "In spades!" The melting expression in his eyes at that moment took her breath away. He seemed to have trouble taking his eyes from her face, then looked down at the corsage box in his hand. "Here, I think these will go fine with that dress, though when you said green, I was thinking of something brighter." He leaned forward to kiss her cheek softly.

"It'll take just a minute to pin—" She opened the box. "Oh Alex! They're gorgeous!" She lifted a pair of lemon yellow lady slipper orchids, shiny as wax, to the low neck of her dress. She looked in the mirror to pin them on. The thought flashed across her mind that she would never be as beautiful again. They stood together in front of the pier glass in their formal clothes like a couple painted by Sargent or Whistler. In the lamp-light burnishing hair and fabric, each felt a soft shock like the touch of destiny. Neither knew how or whether to mention it.

Alex said soberly, "You look beautiful."

Like all large parties, that one had been noisy, crowded, hot. Sandy Archer was a good hostess, and she had a commodious apartment in Chelsea, so there was room for dancing. When they went in, they heard more laughter than talk, with music underlying all. Mingling with the noisy crowd, Ruth enjoyed the feeling of isolation with her man among all those festive strangers. Ruth loved Alex's arm around her waist, his hand pressing her to his chest so she could rest her cheek against his as they danced. She looked at all the other men, and felt a childish pride that hers was by far the handsomest one there.

"What is that secret smile about?" Alex held a glass out to her, smiling himself, searching her eyes.

She sipped. "Nothing at all." Once again, he surprised her with his perception when he kept silence, while gazing into her eyes.

At midnight, the guests had stood in a huge circle in the dining room, hushing each other so they could hear the announcer on the radio, champagne glasses poised, waiting for the ball to drop in

Times Square. Ruth looked around at the bright colors of the dresses, and the black and white of the men's evening clothes. She had a momentary vision of the living room at home in Main—small, cozy but drab, and almost silent. Elizabeth and Nathan would be sitting on opposite sides of the fireplace, listening to the radio too, counting down to bid the old year farewell, waiting for Guy Lombardo to play "Auld Lang Syne."

A cheer rang out, glasses clinked and splashed, everyone shouted, "Happy New Year!" to one another as though they were all deaf. And then the scene was blotted out from Ruth's view as Alex's mouth descended on hers, his face hiding everything. Her initial stiffness melted and she sank into his kiss as into a warm bath, her legs and arms seeming to bend like dampened clay. As he drew away from her, he looked into her eyes with an expression that made him appear almost to be angry.

"Happy New Year," he said softly. The gentle tone of his voice belied his expression. Breathless and shaken, Ruth watched him turn and walk away. Within a few minutes, he'd found their coats, thanked Sandy, and led her outside.

They had to walk a long way on slushy pavement before they could get a cab. Ruth's feet were wet and icy in her sandals. When they finally found a taxi, she sank gratefully against Alex's shoulder. When they arrived at her building, Alex told the driver to wait.

He took Ruth to the door, and again embraced her. She clung for a moment, wanting the night to last forever.

With his lips against her hair, Alex said, "Red, I think it's time some changes were made. Let me come for brunch tomorrow."

Her answer had sounded muffled in her own ears. "All right. About noon." He continued to hold one of her hands for a long moment, looking deeply into her eyes.

At last, as if it cost him an effort to take his gaze from hers, he said, "Good night," and turned away, letting her limp hand slide from his.

Suddenly Ruth realized her feet were like blocks of ice.

CHAPTER EIGHT

When Ruth woke, stripes of sunlight shone between the slats of the blinds onto the parquet. As a child, she had loved to choose an object, and close first one eye and then the other so she could watch it jump from side to side. She did that with a golden ribbon of sunlight. She concentrated on this with a superstitious fear that if she allowed herself to think of what she so much wanted, she might anger the gods and prevent it. She rolled over, and followed with her eyes the river pattern of a crack in the ceiling, until it disappeared in the acanthus leaves of the plaster cartouche. Lulled by suggestions of symbolism in the random line, she lay with a half smile on her lips, her thoughts drifting and misty.

Alex had asked her if she had dreams, and she had not known how to answer. Her dream was his image, however soft the focus. Behind every other thought hovered his face. She had always prided herself on an ability to look at facts, to demolish castles in Spain before they could take over her horizons, but now she had completely lost that objectivity, and she didn't care.

She got up, opened the blinds, and smiled at the day. She sang in the shower. By half past eleven, she had the table set in front of the window, and was pacing the length of the room as if caged. She changed her sweater and paced some more. She kept glancing at herself in the pier glass, smoothing her hair, allowing herself to be pleased with her figure, then mentally chastising herself for vanity. In spite of knowing Alex was interested in her, she seemed to hear a voice cautioning her not to be a fool. The words sounded in her head in her mother's voice. She bit her lip.

When at last she heard the bell, she ran to the door. Alex paused on the threshold as he had the night before, now facing a sunlit room, his eyes moving from Ruth to the scene behind her and back again. She saw his nostrils flare, perhaps at the fragrances of coffee and food.

"Good afternoon, Red." She heard the smile in his voice, though there was none on his face; saw his eyes soften into dark velvet. She felt light and empty, and couldn't support his gaze. She looked down and waved her arm to usher him in.

"You have a great place here. It looks sensational in the daylight." He leaned over to kiss her lightly. "You look sensational in the daylight too." He unbuttoned his coat and shrugged it off. Ruth took it to the closet, wearing an involuntary smile, like a child with a secret. "Sit down, please," she said. She was as shy as a little girl entertaining her first guest. "Will scrambled eggs doctored up a bit be all right?"

"Sounds great." He followed her to the alcove that housed the kitchen, and leaned against the wall.

"I'm starving," he said. "Can I do anything to help?"

"Not a thing, thanks; it's almost ready."

Always she would remember details of that meal: the basket lined with a napkin and filled with muffins hot from the oven, the yellow orchids as a center piece in a glass bowl, reflected sunlight dancing on the ceiling from the moving surface of coffee when she filled their cups. Like a light-drenched Impressionist painting, every visual detail seemed a sparkling emblem of the anticipation she felt. In retrospect, she recognized an irony in the fact that it was her education at Daryl's and the Gentrys' hands that made it possible for her to have such a notion.

She had made simple food, but it was perfect. The bacon was crisp, eggs creamy and spicy with onion and Parmesan, muffins light and nutty. Hangover of a New England country upbringing, she felt more self-confident with food she had prepared, in her own home, than anywhere else. When they sat down, the sun warmed them through the windows. The view of leafless branches, sooty bricks, and limp washing on a line, a gaunt cat on top of the fence, and a ribbon of contrail against the sky—all, like the grain of the wood she had looked at from her bed, were beautiful.

Ruth glanced at Alex's face, at the modeling of his hands, at his neck above his unbuttoned shirt collar. In the depths of her, she knew the picture of this morning and of this man would be indelible for as long as she could remember anything at all.

She could not understand how it was that they talked about the party, the weather, their mutual acquaintances, yet she was able to hold up her end of the small talk. She knew Alex was watching her, studying her face with his characteristic intensity. Some of the airy joy she had felt on awakening began to slip away, as her feeling of suspense intensified.

At last, Alex had sighed and leaned back in his chair, his eyes still on her. She endured this examination bravely, without looking away. Neither spoke. They heard a distant siren, the gurgle of melt water running down the bricks outside.

Finally Alex put his napkin on the table, leaned toward her slightly, and said, "I wanted to ask you something today, something serious." She noticed that his voice was more low-pitched, his words slower than his usual rhythm. "I wouldn't blame you if you said something like, 'This is so sudden,' because maybe it is." He compressed one side of his mouth, pulling his regular features out of symmetry. His eyes flickered for an instant, then resumed their steady focus on her. "Now I don't know what I want to say." He reached across the table with one hand, his eyes again on Ruth's. "That's not the truth either. I want to ask you …" He paused, as though considering the precise wording he wanted to use.

Ruth glanced down at his hand, extended palm up on the table. It had seemed that she ought to say something, but her mind was empty, her body vibrating with tension as she clasped her own hands in her lap so as not to grasp his, which his gesture seemed to suggest. Remembering, she recognized her hesitation as a sort of odd cowardice.

When he broke the silence, his voice was so quiet, it was almost as though he feared being overheard. "Will you marry me, Red?"

She heard him with a lack of immediate emotion, as one might listen to the radio. One layer of her mind registered the meaning, while another reacted like a slug to the touch of a sharp stick—with an involuntary shrinking. At some level of her mind, this ambivalent reaction astonished her.

She withdrew her gaze from his with an effort and stared out the window for a moment. Then she looked back at Alex, whose expression had softened so that his eyes held a dreamy look, and his mouth seemed ready to smile, though it did not. He looked wistful and boyish, and Ruth had a fleeting impression of what he might have looked like in childhood, of the appeal that had gained him a home and left other boys behind. Her thoughts felt damped down like a clock under a pillow.

"Why?" She could not imagine why she said that. Older and wiser, she would recognize fear as the reason—of the unknown, of failure even. At the time, she knew she should try to explain herself, but could not manage to do it. She had never felt such confusion before in her life. At the same time she wanted to abandon herself to his arms, where she could drown in his warmth and strength and maleness. Then she forgot what she had just said, wondering what was holding him back from further speech. She gazed at him, wide-eyed and frowning with alarm.

Alex stood up, thrust his hands in his pockets, and turned to the window, with his profile to her. His body cast a shadow across the table. "You're the most desirable woman I've ever met." Once again, she heard emotion resonate in his voice and was unnerved. "I can't stop wanting you. I have from that first day when you gave me the tennis ball. You're different from … I've tried to be the way you wanted me to be. I *have* been patient, haven't I?" He turned and faced her. "I want you for good, for me, always. You feel it, don't you? That we ought to be together?"

Slowly she nodded. Her mind was reeling. She was astonished at the romantic tone of his last question. She hesitated over the vast areas of his past and mind about which she had a sudden sense of her ignorance, but desire shocked and weakened her. She felt joy swelling.

"Then why… Why haven't you—" She stammered, groping for a way to ask what she wanted to know. "Only once, a long time ago, you really—really tried …"

Reaching out his arms, Alex had moved to Ruth's side of the table to raise her from her chair, drawing her into his chest, enfolding her. With his lips against her temple, he murmured, "Make love to you?" She nodded silently. He raised her chin, looking into her eyes. "I had to show you that you could trust me. And I had to prove something for myself too. Have I? *Will* you marry me, Ruth?"

He had never called her that. The sound of her name pierced her with vivid understanding of his seriousness. She could see herself reflected in the dark pools of his eyes, two tiny, pale ovals crowned with auburn. She felt suddenly as she thought a butterfly newly emerged from the chrysalis must feel—as though she was blooming into some new and beautiful form.

He lowered his lips on hers, pressing, moving, questing. Ruth tightened her arms around his neck, leaning against his body, melting against him. When his tongue opened her lips, she tasted it first with trepidation, then with eagerness. Finally she pulled back, panting, shaken. "Yes," she said breathlessly. "Yes, of course I will!"

Aware of his growing desire, she had felt compelled to try to restore her own self control, thinking, *One of us has to stay sane.* She broke out of his arms, took him by the hand, and led him to the couch.

"Let's sit down so we can talk sensibly." She tried to take a deep breath and smiled. "I mean, there are a few things to talk about, don't you think?" She asked herself, *What had he meant when he said that about proving something to himself? What would he be like to live with? As a lover?* She flushed at the thought.

He was still standing where she had led him, looking down on her, his hand in hers. "Yes, sure, but do you mean it? You will?" His tone was incredulous; he resisted her gesture to make him sit.

"Yes," she said fervently, consciously throwing caution to the winds. "I mean it!" She laughed with pure joy. And with the words, at his brilliant smile, she sensed a release, like the abandonment in air of a diver once his feet have left the springboard. No way back.

They decided to live in her apartment, to have a small civil ceremony, to combine their favorite possessions. They discussed whom to notify and whom to invite to the wedding. By the time they went out to dinner in the early dark, they were both exhausted.

Before he left, Alex embraced her again, leaning his cheek against her hair, his eyes closed as he murmured good night. She felt him tremble before he released her and went away. She understood now that this control had indeed been his proof of sincerity, and trembled herself.

Alone, she had stood in front of the pier glass. Still no beauty, but her coppery hair, her narrow waist, her shapely breasts, her long legs were, after all, enough. To be desired, perhaps that was the most pressing dream of all—the one she had not even been aware of when Alex had asked about her dreams those months ago.

Then she sat wearily at the desk to call home, surprised at the fatigue emotion engendered. As she listened to the ringing, she thought about the last time she had seen her mother. Her father had been away when she left for New York; Dan had driven her to the station. Was it only seven months ago? She'd hugged Mother and kissed her cheek. They were standing on the top step outside the kitchen door. Ruth had noticed that the paint on the doorjamb was scaly and cracked, like the shell of a hard-boiled egg that has been dropped. The once dark green was weathered to a bluish hue that seemed like the color of the world on that sweltering day, with its lowering sky full of the threat of thunder. She remembered thinking how the storm, when it did break, would be a relief. When she had looked backward as Dan drove her away, her mother had already gone back inside the house.

A police siren whooped in the distance, shaking her back to her mission—to notify her parents of the impending marriage. She heard her mother saying, "Hello?"

"Hello, Mother. It's Ruth. How are you?"

"Fine, thank you. Is anything wrong?"

Ruth laughed, delighted again, her fatigue forgotten. "Not at all—quite the contrary. Is Dad at home?"

"No, he left yesterday for a ten-day trip. He'll be sorry to have missed your call."

"Well, I'm calling to give you both some news." Ruth took a deep breath. "I'm engaged to be married."

There was no answer, just the faint hum of the line. Ruth gripped the receiver, staring at the ornamentation on the frame surrounding the pier glass: fruit and leaves in tarnished gilt, and a fat cherub holding plaster ribbons. She should not have failed for so long to mention Alex, she realized.

At last she heard her mother say, "I see."

When Ruth realized that she wasn't going to add anything, she said, "I met him here in New York more than six months ago. His name is Alexander Duchamp."

"Is he French Canadian?"

"Why, yes."

"What does he do?"

"He's an assistant to a film producer. They make documentaries."

"I see."

Was that the only comment her mother was going to make? Ruth shifted the phone to her other ear, and wiped her hand on her slacks. "We'd like to be married quite soon. While we don't plan anything elaborate, we want you both here, of course."

"What sort of family is he from?"

Why didn't her mother ask any of the questions she wanted so much to answer? Wasn't she happy at the news? "His foster father owned and operated an automo—"

Her mother interrupted. "He's adopted?"

"Yes; he was an orphan. He lived in an institution until he was six. He grew up in Quebec, in the country."

"Does he have an education?"

"Not college, no."

"Is he Catholic?"

Ruth hesitated. Except for references to the orphanage and his feelings about the nuns, Alex had never discussed religion. She said, "Well, I doubt it, though I think he was in a convent orphanage, but I don't think he's religious, Mother."

"I see."

"Mother, we want you and Dad to come."

"You're not planning to come home to be married?"

Ruth shifted in the chair. This was turning out to be almost as though she were trying to explain something she knew nothing about. Once again, she felt suddenly overwhelmed with weariness. She said a little desperately, "Well, it seemed most sensible to be married here, since neither of us is in a position to take much time off just now."

"Just now? You're getting married right away?"

All at once Ruth felt a rush of guilt, as she used to when she helped herself from the cookie jar. If only she had laid a little groundwork for this discussion. "Well, pretty soon. We thought before the end of next month."

"Ruth, is there something you're not telling me?"

"No, of course not!" Hot with humiliation, she decided to ignore the implication. Then her mother's voice changed timbre, now sounding subdued and lower pitched.

"Ruth, for goodness sake, I hope you are thinking clearly." She began to speak with deliberation, enunciating carefully, as though she were reading aloud. "What is your hurry? I do not have to remind you that marriage is a serious step, but I must tell you that I fear for your future when I think how little experience you have. You are not ready to—to assess a character. You haven't known enough men to make comparisons—" Elizabeth broke off to take an audible breath, and began again with a rising inflection, as if she were introducing a new subject in a lecture. "Choosing a man with whom you will spend the rest of your life is probably the most important choice you will ever make. You cannot change your mind about it later. You must be sure that you have seen enough—that you know enough—to be able to select, not settle."

Ruth had expected some coolness, perhaps even disapproval, but not this troubled concern. Why was her mother so fearful? Was it only because she hadn't met Alex? Ruth began to dread her father's reaction, if this was her mother's.

"Mother, it'll be fine. We met right after I got to the city, so I've known him for months. You'll like him. I'm sure you will." She tried to think of something reassuring to say. "He has an excellent job, good prospects, interesting friends." She wanted to add, *He melts my bones; he's as beautiful as a god; he loves me!*

Elizabeth said, "You are too far away ..."

Ruth interrupted. "Mother, this life, here in New York, suits me. It's so stimulating. I've tried to tell you in my letters ..." She faltered to a stop. She had not told them in her letters that it was the feeling of freedom and possibilities and surprise that made her happy in the city, knowing that all they hoped to hear was that she was working hard at a creditable job and making a success of it. She could never describe the emotions Alex stirred in her, at least not to her parents. Again there was that humming silence of an unsatisfactory phone call.

Her mother's voice, sounding a little far away, as if she had moved the receiver away from her mouth, said, "I'm sorry you won't come home to be married, Ruth." The tone was resigned. "Let us know the date when you decide, and we will answer you then. I don't have your father's schedule for February."

"All right then." Ruth closed her eyes momentarily. "Give Dad my love when he gets home, won't you? I'll call again as soon as we set the date, probably next week." She added, "Don't worry, Mother." She waited for a response. When none came, she added, "Wish me luck?"

"Yes, of course. Thank you for calling. Good night, Ruth."

Setting the phone down slowly, Ruth had been on the verge of tears. She had pushed the feeling away, remembering the dutiful care that was so important to her parents. It was wrong to blame them for worrying over her. Why couldn't Mother understand what it was like to be in love? She didn't think that perhaps her daughter's wedding might have special significance to her mother.

ೞ ೞ

The end of February produced the worst weather of the entire winter. As she sat writing invitations to their few friends by hand, Ruth had prayed for one of the brilliant blue days she had seen in January. But snowstorms closed roads from New London to Bangor. Ruth saw with a sinking heart that her parents would never be able to make the trip. But Dan traveled for twenty-four hours to get to New York. When he called her from the bus station, Ruth burst into tears of relief.

The wedding day dawned with a light so dull that the whole city took on the aspect of an etching. A pewter sky dropped heavy, wet snowflakes onto slushy streets. Only the bright yellow of taxis relieved the monochrome effect. Ruth and Dan rode down to the financial district, where they met the little group of well-wishers she and Alex had invited.

The ceremony, such as it was, had taken place in a chilly room in City Hall that smelled of dust and wet rubber. Dan gave Ruth away, and Nettie stood up with her. There had been no question of Eloise or Julie being able to come on such short notice, and in midwinter. Alex's best friend, Pete, from the film company held the ring for him. The Gentrys both came, wreathed in smiles and bearing a set of

Georgian silver dessert spoons as a wedding gift. Jerry Uhlik appeared with a case of scotch. The little gathering left ugly wet marks on the floor where they stood with snow melting off their shoes.

Instead of a wedding dress, Ruth wore a sensible, heathery lavender wool suit with a frilly blouse. Alex gave her a corsage of yellow orchids like those he had brought on New Year's Eve. As they left the looming, neoclassic building, Ruth walked between her two men and held Dan's arm as tightly as Alex's.

"Danny, thank you so much for all you went through to get here! It wouldn't have felt right without you, especially since neither of us has parents here." She glanced at Alex, wondering suddenly if she had said something to injure his feelings.

"I'd have gone through a lot more not to miss your big day, Sis. I can catch up on sleep any time." Dan smiled down at her, his eyes shadowed by fatigue. He had leaned around Ruth to say to Alex, "Just remember, old buddy, you'd better treat this sister of mine like a princess."

Alex replied with a thumbs-up gesture, and then raised Ruth's hand to his unsmiling lips, looking her in the eyes.

The Gentrys gave a buffet and reception for them at a hotel on Gramercy Park. There, as Ruth looked at the smiles around them, she began at last to feel some of the gaiety she had hoped for. Here was a group of new friends, who represented so much of her new life, enjoying the party and the occasion for it. She pushed the thought of the night to come from the front of her mind, reminding herself of the countless brides who had gone before her.

When they stopped by the apartment to pick up their bags, they had found a telegram from Maine. "Best wishes for a happy life together, love— "

Their honeymoon was two days at the Plaza.

In those early weeks, Ruth felt as if she were being made over, becoming a person that she had never suspected she could be. She continued to be awed by Alex's physical beauty. His body affected her like some delicious drug. She kept having the feeling that no real person could look like that.

Because he told her over and over how beautiful she was, she began to lose her inbred modesty. As she learned to accept his lovemaking, gentle yet intense, all other pleasures seemed heightened, enhanced now by a new dimension she was learning through the voice and face and body of her husband. Everything she touched, from the petal of a flower to the texture of a scrub brush, she took note of. She was like someone who had been anesthetized, and was coming awake gradually.

Alex, deeply and now humbly proud of having won her, found himself examining his reactions not only to Ruth, but to every person with whom he came in contact. His powers of observation, already well developed through necessity, took on a new subtlety. He thought it was because of intimacy with her. He began to realize that the woman he had taken as his wife had much more to uncover even than he had thought. He was glad of his forbearance both before and after the ceremony. He recognized with some surprise that she was truly virginal, and felt subtly guilty that he was surprised. He was profoundly grateful not only that she had given herself to him, but that somehow he had perceived her value.

They nourished each other in every sense, and told each other that they had never felt so complete and so happy before. Alex seemed to have learned a new language that he used to tell her repeatedly how he adored her. He could hardly believe himself that he was willing to give voice so freely to his feelings.

Ruth had felt herself opening like a blossom. Alex's passion caught her up and carried her on its current to shores she had never imagined. When she was timid, he was slow and undemanding, but he drew her with him, deeper into the realm of delight with which he seemed so familiar. No modern cynicism could erase her conviction that she would never be the same again.

※

In Connecticut, when she set about arranging her belongings in the new house, Ruth found the album with their wedding pictures. She opened it and turned the pages slowly, gritting her teeth against the pangs the images brought. The photographs showed her and Alex side by side with golden oak paneling behind them. The flash accentuated Alex's chiseled features, his dark brows and hair, and washed out Ruth's fair coloring, but under the soft white cloud of her angora hat, her hair glowed. In one photograph her eyes were on Alex's face, while he looked directly at the camera. Ruth recalled the rough feel of tweed under her hand. The wide band of her wedding ring was shiny and prominent. There were several candid shots taken at the reception: Dan handing Ruth a glass, their friends laughing as bride and groom shared a slice of cake—the usual fleeting images of every wedding party. The photographer had caught Ruth in the act of toasting Alex, her profile turned to the camera, chin up and mouth laughing as champagne slanted up to the rim of the glass, its sparkle frozen by the flash, forever untasted and unspilled.

CHAPTER NINE

Recalling those green days of their lives together, Ruth thought now that perhaps the calm had been less a matter of good luck than dissembling—each of them hiding, or perhaps unaware of incipient stresses and imperfections. She had not wanted to waken from her dream of delight, perhaps she had been merely oblivious to anything that might threaten her security as a wife, and so had failed to notice signs that must, she now thought, have been present. Maybe Alex felt insecure as well. What might he have kept to himself that they would both have been better off airing? Oh, not at once and not all the time, of course. Bitterly, she understood what harm had perhaps been done by pride.

She recalled her sadness when she received intimations of matrimonial disillusion from Eloise. She had sat with the letter in her hand, looking out the window. At almost six o'clock in the evening, the branches of the pear tree caught a rosy afterglow, looking like pale, crinkled ribbons against the murky brick behind them. In their living room, a lamp spilled a pool of light across the desk top and into Ruth's lap, leaving the rest of the room obscured by encroaching darkness.

Ruth and Eloise both had been married for more than three years by then. Having read her friend's letter, Ruth remembered a pang of guilt that she seemed to be by far the more contented.

Henderson and I are trying to work out all these problems, but I tell you in all honesty, I wonder how we can. This move has been such a mistake, and now with all our bridges burned, there are too few options.

Sorry to be so gloomy, but I feel better now that you know. Silly, but it helps. Write your news. It's good to hear about your success—your satisfaction with your job and all.

Best to Alex, of course, and love to you.

Eloise had made it clear she disliked the Midwest, was bored and unhappy in her suburban house with a toddler. She didn't enjoy the morning coffee and gossip with her friendly, but pedestrian neighbors. She was frustrated and homesick.

Ruth recalled their late night discussions on deep and serious questions that are so enticing at age twenty. Eloise had always been the one to drag them all back to earth, unwilling to waste energy on flights of abstraction and fancy, few as these were in the practical world of business education. Now, it seemed, Eloise was finding she wished for a little romance. Ruth, feeling worldly wise, had decided to suggest as gently as she could that there were bound to be changes as years went by. When she heard Alex's key grate in the lock, she got up to turn on another light.

"Greetings." He hung his coat in the closet and went to the kitchen. She heard him cracking ice from the tray. "The usual?" he asked.

"Yes, please. What did you have for lunch today?"

"Lousy tempura. As it happens, I had lunch with Daryl. He turned up at the studio looking for something to do an article on. He'd heard about the film Jerry's planning. You know, on that artists' cooperative up near Hartford, where they have glass blowers and weavers—all those craft types. He took me to lunch at a new Japanese place over near the river to discuss the possibility of doing an illustrated article. Color photos, the whole thing. It was a mistake." Alex poured scotch over ice, brought Ruth's glass. "The lunch, not the article idea."

"That's too bad. Will warmed-over lasagna and some French bread and salad be okay? I've got plenty. I stopped to get some fresh strawberries on the way home." Ruth sat down at her end of the couch. "I had a letter from Eloise today. Kind of upsetting. She's miserable in Eau Claire. Henderson thinks he's getting a raw deal on his job, and I guess they both wish they'd never left Providence."

Alex was unfolding the newspaper, his drink on the end table beside his chair. "That's tough."

Ruth finished preparing the meal; the paper rustled as Alex turned pages. Now and again melting ice cracked softly in one of the glasses. Ruth said, "We have about half an hour till it's ready. Mind if I turn on the news?"

"Sure, go ahead," Alex said from behind the paper.

Thinking back on those evenings, Ruth now saw the ironic similarity of New York days' ends to those in the house in Maine.

At night things were wonderfully different, however. Until one particular one. Alex had drawn Ruth close to him, sliding his hand under her gown. She arched eagerly toward him, but all at once she stiffened at something unfamiliar in his touch. With a sudden insistent tug, Alex pulled her gown up above her waist, pushing her to a half-sitting position so he could get it over her head. She helped him, then lowered herself over his chest, but he took her ribcage in his hands, twisting her around with rough force.

Ruth was surprised and becoming apprehensive. "What do you want?" she whispered.

"Turn—turn over. We'll try something new tonight." His voice sounded strained and husky. Wanting to please him, Ruth tried to comply with his wishes, but he handled her more and more roughly, and she became less and less pliant. His breathing was heavy and rapid, but she could not match his eagerness. He was prodding her into awkward positions that were peculiar, uncomfortable, even embarrassing. She felt suddenly chilled, not by cold, but by dread. She made an effort to comply with his wishes, but there was an iron quality in his hands, in the tension of his body.

Finally, breathless, she said, "No! I'm sorry, I can't!" She wrenched free, crouching on the edge of the mattress, huddled.

"Sure you can," he had coaxed. "Come on, sweet. Just let me show you." Ruth shook her head dumbly. She sat in the splash of streetlight from the window. He reached for her; she flinched away. "Ruth, don't be foolish."

"Please, Alex. Let's not ..."

His voice roughening again, he said, "Where's your sense of adventure?" He took her by the upper arms, pulling her back. Again, he twisted against her resistance. With a little despairing cry, she rolled strongly away and off the bed. She stood panting and shivering. She could hear his exhalations as well.

"I'm sorry," she whispered. Unaccountably, she had felt at fault. She stood wrapped in her own arms.

Alex fell back on his pillow, his eyes closed. After a silence he rasped, "*Moi aussi.*"

Finally Ruth lay down again. Rigidly she waited for sleep, remembering her early incredulous joy in lovemaking. She determined not to think about what had just happened, to deny a peculiar, stony space that had opened between them. When she heard Alex's breathing become even and slow, she willed herself to relax, and filled her mind with details of matters she wanted to attend to the next day.

In the limbo just before sinking into sleep, time had seemed to turn into something palpable, a sort of slippery rope that was sliding inexorably through her grasp. The notion, not quite a thought, had come to her that she should make an effort to slow it, keep it from running out so quickly. Phrases from Eloise's letter drifted through her mind. She hovered on the edge of sleep. *I wish we had a child.*

℘ ℘

Ruth had always enjoyed the occasions when she sat with Ziggy. She had become more and more convinced that parenthood would change the tone of her marriage. At the time, it had seemed wise not to mention it to Alex. Why had she been so cowardly?

Alex traveled often in those days. Uhlik had at least three projects in hand at a time, and they were scattered over the whole country. Sometimes Alex was involved with one, sometimes another. He began to be restless if he had to stay home for more than a week at a time, and was often grouchy and sarcastic. Once a new project was under way, he would regain his usual good temper, and arrive home full of pent-up sexual energy and affection.

During his absences, Ruth had become accustomed to free time to read and to listen to music and meet friends, and she learned not to feel abandoned when Alex wasn't there. Their lives, while not exactly separate, often ran on parallel tracks. When he was home, they indulged in theater and concerts and restaurant dining, as their income permitted. She had considered her life to be busy and even luxurious.

She knew she should consult Alex about her desire for a child, but something about his almost incessant restless activity had made her hold back. She had not become pregnant, and they never discussed it, though on several occasions she was aware that Alex was about to initiate a discussion she was afraid to begin. She felt as if her desire for a baby was somehow disloyal, a sign of feeling insecure in some way. In time, when nothing happened, she nearly stopped thinking about it altogether, until the strange attempt at lovemaking that had so upset them both. That was when she first wondered specifically whether fatherhood might tame Alex's fierce drive and restlessness.

It had taken a long time for her to stop reliving the day she had come home from a fateful doctor's appointment. She had stood at the window, looking out at the neat geometry of Nettie's little walled garden and beyond, to scraggly patches of sour dirt and contorted bare branches in the partitioned plots down the block. Much of the sky was cut off by the buildings. Dingy walls were marked with zigzag patterns of fire escapes, and spotted here and there with a white milk carton, or a flower pot on a window sill. After staring at this view for ten minutes, she was overwhelmed with a wave of homesickness. She pictured the field at the back of the March house, how the grass would be dun colored under November skies, crackling under her feet. She would just be able to make out smoke from a ship, hull down, if she happened to look at exactly the right spot on the horizon. Like giant blimps, clouds would be crowding the edge of the sea in the northwest, seething and changing shape in the winds aloft. The gulls would be roosting with the cormorants on the cliffs south of the cove. The wind would be light, smelling of seaweed and salt and fish, instead of soot and gasoline fumes. The flat planes of masonry and the constricted view of the heavens afforded by her window made her feel suddenly trapped.

By the time Alex came home, she had stirred herself to begin to prepare a meal. She decided to wait until after dinner to give him her news. But he studied her face and asked, "Something on your mind?" She nodded, grateful that he could still notice her. She kept her eyes on the carrot she was scraping. "Tell me."

"After dinner." Alex reached for her hands, and she dropped the knife and carrot in the sink. She scrabbled to pick them up again.

"Come on, Red. Now is better." His voice was soft as in those courtship days. He took hold of her shoulders and turned her toward him. "Get it over, whatever it is."

She took a quivering breath. "You remember I went to see Dr. Abrams today?" Alex nodded. "Well, he gave me—gave us bad news." She stopped and swallowed, pulled away, and turned her back.

"Okay—it'll be okay," Alex said gently. "Let's have it."

"I'm never going to make you a father." She tried to square her shoulders, still with her back turned. "And no, there isn't a treatment. Something about—something to do with my tubes. I don't know. I think I didn't really listen. I'm so sorry!" Her voice broke and she turned then to face him, her eyes blurred with tears. He had wrapped her in his arms.

As Ruth remembered, she realized now that Alex had seemed rocked, as if thrust off balance. Had she been aware of it at the time? He had seemed to pull himself together, to deliberately control his voice. "Listen, it's not your fault. It's too bad, and I'm sorry too, but it's not your fault." She had been rigid in his embrace. He went on, "I guess I always thought we'd have a kid some day, but I guess I was also thinking, *Not yet*. Didn't you too?"

She had nodded, tears beginning to wet his shoulder. "We're busy people. Maybe it's for the best." But she had heard the sorrowful note in his voice.

He had stroked her back for several moments. Then he took a deep breath and took her by the arms, holding her gently away from him to look into her face. "Think of it this way." His tone lightened. "We'll have more freedom, more carefree rolls between the sheets, no worries about braces or college educations." He lifted her chin. "We'll still have each other. We're a pair, no matter what. We'll make out. It'll be okay." He kissed her on the forehead. "My poor love," he murmured.

That night he had made love to her patiently, much as in their first nights together, until she relaxed at last, accepted his solace, and afterwards lay limp as a drowning victim next to him, cheeks wet, until she sank into welcome sleep.

☙ ❧

During that year even more than before, Ruth had become absorbed in her work. President Kennedy's assassination was the salient recollection of that time. The repetitive tempo of her working days came close to insulating her from outside events. As she came to know Dr. Gentry better, she began to admire him more. His interest in his patients was genuine and sensitive; he kept abreast of new theory and the latest experimentation. Ruth was proud of his confidence in her and gained ever more self-confidence as he increased her responsibilities. He trained her to act as his medical assistant—work she found even more interesting than the clerical duties.

Sometimes Mrs. Gentry enlisted Ruth's aid in getting the doctor to take time off. Together, over the years, they indulged in various little deceptions over such matters as Christmas presents and surprise birthday parties. Alex was included in these affairs when he was home. As she made out checks for the Gentrys' charitable donations, and arranged for tickets to theaters and concerts, and ordered family gifts, Ruth reflected that it was like having a new set of relatives.

As the doctor relied on her more, she had become more intimately acquainted with his private life, and came to understand that she was in the employ of an exceptional man— humorous, compassionate, intellectual. The pressures of his profession meant that someone in the sort of position she occupied could do a great deal to make his schedule run smoothly, and to shield him from unnecessary distractions. She had found a career.

☙ ❧

Eloise had written that she and Henderson had moved to St. Louis when a better job was offered. As Ruth imagined the daily irritations of dealing with small children in a strange city, mortgage and car payments, and all the usual stresses of young families, she confessed to herself that the picture had become only marginally attractive to her. She realized how much she valued her relatively unruffled life.

Her guilt and sadness faded gradually, overcome with the quotidian. She had assumed that Alex had adjusted to the fact that they would never become parents. Ruth wrote about this to Eloise, trying not to sound self-pitying, and received one of those wisely cynical responses that echoed their days in school. At the end of her letter Eloise had put in a PS:

You mustn't get the wrong impression. What I really mean is that it's all a balancing act. Balance the money worries against the warm body next to you at four in the morning, balance the wet beds and nightmares against the first word and the night-light shining on curly heads—that kind of thing. I found out the real trouble comes when you forget how to keep the see-saw level. It'll all work out, Red, you'll see.

Ruth had kept that letter folded in the pages of her medical dictionary, as if she expected to refer to it again some day.

In those days, if she happened to reflect on her own satisfactions, she was still worried about Dan. He wrote so seldom, and told so little of what was in his mind that she feared they were becoming estranged. He had gone to work for a contractor in Bar Harbor.

She wrote, "What about your future? How long are you going to pound ten-penny nails into two-by-fours? Please, drop me a line and tell me what you're really doing."

But for the most part, she forgot the small chills in the general comfort of her days.

Until, on a cold January afternoon, when Ruth was unlocking the apartment door, she had heard the phone ringing. She dropped the paper bag she was carrying, and ran to answer it. As always, her mother's voice sounded like that of a young woman. But this time it was faint. At first Ruth had thought it was a bad connection.

"Ruth, I have some bad news."

"Mother, are you all right? I can hardly hear you."

"Yes, I'm all right. It's your father."

Ruth waited, hearing the faint sighing of the open line. "Dad? Has something happened to Dad?"

"Yes." Again silence. A trickle of fear seeped through Ruth like ice water. Again she waited, afraid to ask what the trouble was.

"Ruth?"

"I'm here, Mother."

"It was very sudden, very quick. I'm still at the hospital, but there was absolutely nothing they could do." Again, that silence. Ruth swallowed two or three times. She understood the words, few as they were, but knew she had yet to feel them.

"Mother, I'll get the first train. Mother?" No answer. Ruth rubbed her hand across her eyes. "Does Dan know?"

"No."

"I'll call him. I'll catch the first train I can. I'll see you in the morning. Mother—is anyone with you?"

"Eileen brought me to the hospital. She'll stay until ..." Ruth thought she heard a muffled sob.

"Ask her to stay, Mother. I'll be there in the morning. Mother, I'm so—so sorry! Take care of yourself. I'll see you tomorrow. Thanks for calling. Good night."

She stood up still clutching the phone. It had grown dark; the only light came through the door she'd left open when she ran to answer the phone. When she noticed the receiver still in her hand, she slowly replaced it in the cradle. She moved as if in a trance to turn on a light, close the door, take the bag of groceries to the kitchen. Then she sat down to call Dan. One of his housemates answered, took her message. Dan would call when he got in.

Numb, she got out a suitcase, began to take clothes from her drawers. She stopped in the middle of folding a blouse and went to telephone Dr. Gentry.

When Alex got home, she realized she'd done nothing about supper, nor put away the groceries. He heard her news, then made them an omelet.

When Dan finally returned her call, Alex held her hand while she talked to him.

"It's Dad. Mother called a little while ago."

"What's happened?" Alarm altered Dan's familiar voice.

"I don't know, Dan, I don't know. But Dad is—he's gone."

"What do you mean, you don't know?"

"Oh, Dan, Mother could hardly talk. What difference does it make? We'll find out when we get there. I'll take the next train out of Grand Central. Will you meet me?"

Under the immensity of the heavens in the station dome and the resounding echoes, Alex had put his arms around her. His voice, next to her ear was warm, intimate, on the human scale she felt she was losing, though whether from the immensity of the place, or from fear or the unknown, she couldn't tell.

"Try to take it easy, Red. I'm sorry I can't come with you." He hugged her. "I know it's tough." He kissed her. "I'll be thinking of you."

She had not seen the worry on his face, nor that he stood watching until the train pulled out.

※ ※

She had sat rigid on the rough plush, her head rocking with the train's motion, eyes closed, remembering. She relived the day Dad had come home at two in the afternoon, his weathered face creased with a huge smile. He had an envelope in his hand that he tossed onto the kitchen table with a gesture as graceful and free as a Little League pitcher's. Mother was putting a pie in the oven and she turned, surprised to see him home in the middle of the day like that. Dan and Ruth had been playing Monopoly in the living room. When they heard Nathan's steps on the back porch, they ran into the kitchen. If it had not been Easter vacation, they would not have been there to see.

"There it is." Nathan took off the dark woolen cap he always wore, and ran his hand over his springy hair. The children had been so astonished at his uncharacteristic grin that neither spoke. They stood together in the doorway to the dining room and watched.

Elizabeth closed the oven door carefully before turning to stand with her back to the stove, the pot holder still in her hands. Her eyes were on the envelope where it had fallen, almost among the scraps of piecrust and flour still on the table. Without speaking, she walked to the table, rubbing one hand down the front of her apron, and laid the pot holder down. She took the envelope and raised the flap, took out the sheets of stiff paper, and held the folds apart to read and reread.

Suspense froze Ruth and Dan in the doorway. When Elizabeth finished, she went to her husband, who stood, still smiling, near the back door. With the papers in her hand, she raised her chin and kissed him on the mouth. Ruth remembered the extraordinary look of his bowed head in profile as he met his wife's lips. The intimacy of their posture made them look momentarily like strangers.

Dan had broken the silence, at last. "Dad, what are you doing home?"

He looked up. "It's a special day for the Marches. I just collected the title to the boat from the bank. As of this day, in the year of our lord, 1949, the *Marbeth* is all ours." He went to the door where Dan was standing next to Ruth and tousled his hair roughly. *"Now* your dad's a real master!" The four of them had gone down to Denholme's and had lobsters for dinner that night.

The train rocked on and Ruth fell into a restless doze.

A fine, chilling rain was liquefying piles of snow when Ruth got off the train. Dan, tall and solemn, had stood under the station shed, waiting for her. They hugged, hurried to his car, and made for the house.

"I'm so glad you were close by," Ruth told him. She pulled her collar up, against the damp cold. "Lord, it's penetrating. I'm frozen."

Dan was driving with both hands on the top of the wheel, his shoulders hunched. "I'm worried about Mother," he said without taking his eyes from the road. He was frowning, his lips compressed.

"It must have been an awful shock for her."

"That's just it." Dan tossed her a glance. "She's shocked all right, but not so she doesn't know what to do. She isn't acting lost, if you know what I mean. She had most of the arrangements made by the time I got here. Eileen said she spent over an hour making phone calls when they got back from the hospital, and the only thing left to do is pick out the Bible passages to read at the funeral."

"Really?" Ruth was chagrined. "I thought making the arrangements would be my job. What seems to be the trouble then?"

"She doesn't talk. I haven't seen her eat. She doesn't make any effort to ... to do anything to ..." He floundered.

"Don't you think she just feels numb? I do."

"Yeah, well, I do too. But it's different. It's as if she's ... I don't know. As if she didn't want to be in the same room as everybody else.

As if she felt like she belongs somewhere else. You'll see what I mean."

When they got out of the car into the wet wind, Eileen came to the door to let them in. She was their mother's oldest friend, known from the children's school days. A heavyset woman with the complexion of a girl, she moved like a burglar—silently and lightly. Her smile warmed everyone it touched. In Devonport everyone counted on her whenever emergencies arose. Her quiet efficiency always soothed the families she entered. Colicky babies and querulous old people, even the household pets, quieted in her presence. She kissed Ruth and patted Dan on the cheek. Then she turned to the table, where she had a tray with cups and a pot of coffee.

"Come into the living room. Your mother's in there." Ruth glanced at Dan, who nodded slightly, and they went in. The room was dim. They had to strain to see Elizabeth, who sat in her usual chair. There was a faint tapping sound as the drizzle began to change to sleet outside, striking the windows with a hardening touch.

Ruth said, "Hello, Mother." She went to her. "May I turn on a light? I can't see you in the dark." She bent to kiss her. Her mother's face felt soft and cool and as unresponsive as a doll's.

"As you like," Elizabeth's voice was expressionless, ordinary. The room brightened as Ruth turned on a lamp, and she saw her mother cradled Nathan's gift of the sandalwood box in her lap, absently stroking the carving without looking down at it.

"Here's coffee for everybody," Eileen said, setting the tray down. "Would you like some, Elizabeth?" She handed a filled cup to her friend. They passed cups and cream and sugar. Elizabeth accepted a cup without removing the box from her lap, stirred her coffee and sipped. Added to the whisper of sleet was the tinkle of the spoons against china. Dan and Ruth might not have come; their mother seemed not to notice them.

Dan drained his cup thirstily and went to pour another. As he turned from the tray, he had looked at Ruth meaningfully. She lowered her eyes, wondering what to say, how to help. Her mind was teeming with images of the thousands of times she had sat in this room. Over the years of her marriage, she had been back only once, when she and Alex had come for the first Christmas after their wedding. That had been a stiff, unhappy week, punctuated with strained, elaborate meals Ruth had tried to help Elizabeth prepare, only to be rebuffed. Alex and Nathan had found no common ground, but had addressed each other like strangers in church, formally and in monosyllables.

Involuntarily, Ruth had looked at her father's chair, and for the first time, knew with a visceral shock that he would not sit in it again. Her hand trembled so that she had to set her cup down.

Eileen sat quietly, eyes on her friend. Dan got up and paced to the window. Thrusting his hands into his pockets, he rattled his change. Ruth's ears began to ring with tension. She couldn't trust herself to speak without breaking down. Elizabeth set her cup and saucer on the table next to her chair, folded her hands over the box in her lap, and continued to sit motionless, her eyes on the brass bed-warmer hanging next to the mantel.

Finally Eileen's soft voice insinuated itself into the unnatural quiet of the room. "Elizabeth, would you like to tell Ruth what plans you've made?" And Elizabeth, like a well-brought-up child, obediently explained how she had arranged things for the church service and the burial at sea, from the deck of the *Marbeth*, on the following day, weather permitting.

In the three days she was at home, Ruth never found out details of what had happened except for the barest medical jargon. "Myocardial infarction." She was back in New York at the local library before she found out what that meant.

She and Dan had spent two hours, whispering guiltily in Ruth's old room after the visiting hours at the funeral home, trying to piece together the information gleaned from Eileen and the minister.

When asked, their mother had wordlessly handed them a piece of paper on which she had written the Bible verses she had chosen to be read at the service. Except for the demands of courtesy or necessity, she uttered not a word to anyone.

The day of the funeral, was overcast, cold, with a dense bank of fog visible out to sea, but the air was still and the water calm. By nine o'clock the coffin was aboard the boat, and they were motoring out of the bay.

Ruth had stood holding the railing outside the pilot house. She'd wrapped a woolen scarf around her head against the wet wind on the water. Her feet buzzed with the engine's vibrations. She looked back at the shore, at the rocky water's edge and the cliff looming above, revealing a few silhouettes of trees and a church spire. To the right, along the curving shore, spots of white and color showed the marina and the town, bounded by the point and breakwater on the sea side. Nothing looked familiar. She had seldom been out on the water, and when she had, it had been in sparkling weather under sunny skies.

Dan had stayed with Elizabeth and the minister in the tiny galley. Crenshaw, the mate, stood at the wheel, chewing slowly and ceaselessly, his eyes first on the obscured horizon, then on the compass. After what seemed a very long time, Dr. Raymond put on his stole, took Elizabeth by the arm to help her outside the pilot house, and the four of them joined the two crew members on the rear deck, where they stood on either side of the coffin draped with an American flag, while the minister read the committal. As he raised his hand in benediction, the two sailors had lifted one end of the plank on which the coffin rested, and it slid sedately into the heaving, glassy green of the Atlantic, leaving no mark. The half dozen people on the little boat bobbed silently on the waves like flotsam.

ℰ ⸱ ℛ

When she got back to New York, Ruth had tried to describe those days at home to Alex. She was by then overcome equally by her sense of loss and by puzzlement. "Mother was like a stranger. I couldn't see her, not the way I always knew her. She seemed to be ... just to be completely out of reach."

Alex murmured something consoling that Ruth did not hear. "She didn't cry, she didn't reminisce, she didn't even talk to us. Something ... crucial was missing for the whole time I was home. And I don't really know what it was. Mother was like someone looking on at all the rest of us. Dan always adored Dad, and his death hit him hard. He had tears running down his cheeks in church, though he was better on the boat. But Mother looked the way she looks every day, except she was wearing black. She said, 'Thank you' when friends offered sympathy, but she never looked anyone in the eye. Not even Dan and me. He said she seemed to want to be somewhere else. I thought she acted as if she were somewhere else."

Alex put an arm around Ruth's shoulders. "She's still in shock, honey. How long were they married?"

"Thirty-three years." Ruth looked up at Alex. "But it wasn't like that. It was ... You know, she acts like someone that's only around in the flesh, as if the spirit had gone out of her." Ruth pulled her feet up, and snuggled into Alex's side. She was quiet for a while. Alex stroked the back of her hand.

"All my life, I almost never saw her touch him, except to give him a kiss when he left on a trip." As she mused aloud, Ruth's mind seemed to clear a little. "But she seems now like someone waiting—waiting for him to return, for something to happen, for some change. It's as if she were worrying about him on a trip and waiting bravely for news. She's so controlled I wonder if she won't ... I don't know—fly apart. And yet, that isn't quite right either. It's more as if, with him gone, she isn't there anymore either."

"That sounds a mite farfetched," Alex had commented gently.

Ruth sat up suddenly, facing him. "I know, but it just hit me, just this minute. I never thought of it before. She must have been in love with him." Ruth saw the expression on Alex's face change. For a beat he said nothing. His eyes searched hers.

Finally he asked, "Well, she married him, didn't she?"

"You wouldn't understand. You almost never saw them together. But in spite of how little they showed, at least in front of us, I guess they must have ... I guess it was a happy marriage!" She heard the surprise in her own voice. "And Dad always seemed so—cold almost, and Mother so unemotional. Isn't it remarkable?"

Alex had pulled Ruth into his arms and kissed her. "It's not too easy to tell how happy people are," he said thoughtfully, "or aren't. We could go up and see her some time in the spring if you're worried about her."

"Thanks. Maybe we should." Ruth sighed, memories nagging at her like unfinished business. "It was a pretty strange few days."

Alex took her hand again and turned the wedding ring on her finger as they sat in silence, close together. Then he said, "Honey, death is the one loss you absolutely know is permanent. It's going to take time for her to adjust to that."

Later on in the year of her father's death, Ruth had thought a lot about a remark Alex had made to her while she was still trying to sort out her feelings after the funeral. He had been restless, impatient, showing frustration she didn't understand at the time. He told her, "You're all wrapped up like a snail in a shell."

Indeed, there seemed to be a sort of membrane growing between them in those days, tough as fiberglass. Looking back, she saw that neither of them had seemed to know how to break it. They never talked again about marriage or loss.

One day the following summer, a letter arrived from Dan. His long silences between communications were customary, and no longer worried Ruth. He was doing reasonably well as a contractor who specialized in alterations and additions. The boat had been sold, which had added to their mother's security. Dan was sometimes hired to build private homes, many of them vacation places for people from many faraway states. As Ruth unfolded the sheets of the letter, a wallet-sized photo fell out. "Dear Sis," the letter said. "First, here is a picture of your new sister-in-law. At least she will be when we're married the end of the summer."

Ruth took up the small picture. It showed a young woman with a squarish face, turned to look back over her shoulder at the camera. She had a wide mouth whose corners turned upward a little, and level dark brows over large eyes. A short, straight nose gave her features a symmetrical strength emphasized by a slight cleft in her chin. Her dark hair waved across her forehead and onto her shoulders and the blue of her eyes was as pale as a summer sky. She was lovely.

> That's Lacey. I wish I had the time to take her down to meet you, but when you come up to visit, we'll take care of that. She wants us to be married quickly and quietly since she's alone. 'No fuss,' she says. He had told her the date and time, and continued, I could use a lot of paper and try to tell you all about her, but I'd rather wait until we can talk, and you two can spend some time together. The main thing is that I wanted you to know that your little brother has got it all

together at last. It's just like they say it is, isn't it? Love, I mean.

Ruth smiled. She answered him immediately. Now you'll find out how it feels to have someone always there, just for you, she wrote. I'm so happy for you!

Had she understood when she wrote them, how important those words were? Was there someone always there for her? Perhaps once, but not now.

When they had gone to Maine for the wedding, Ruth and Alex found Elizabeth subdued, but more approachable. She was thinner. She seemed to be fading, as though she were dissolving quietly into the foggy air that so often cloaks the Maine coast. Dan, now preoccupied with his own life, understandably no longer seemed worried about her.

Ruth had noticed that Elizabeth treated Lacey with a gentle tolerance that somehow lacked any real enthusiasm, but Dan seemed not to be unaware of that. Ruth had loved Lacey at once.

When the festivities were over, Ruth had watched her mother looking at Lacey and Dan standing together next to their car, waving goodbye. Alex was at the bottom of the steps, waiting for Ruth and looking across the field toward the horizon. Cicadas shrilled in the woods, and a warm breeze brought a scent of seaweed up from the bottom of the cliff.

"It's been lovely to be here, and we'll see you next year, Mother." Ruth kissed Elizabeth on the cheek. "You must be glad to see him getting settled at last."

Elizabeth studied Ruth's face, a tremulous smile beginning at the corners of her mouth. "Indeed I am. It's just what he needs." She looked searchingly at Ruth for a moment, then glanced at the back of Alex's shapely head before returning her gaze. "I hope you have what you need, Ruth."

"Oh, Mother, of course I do," Ruth had said quickly. She had hugged her mother, then gone down the steps and taken Alex by the hand.

CHAPTER TEN

Ruth sat at a table in the window of the old Connecticut house, looking out across the small meadow while she ate her evening meal. The earlier darkness as October ended gave her an excuse to light candles. She and Alex had burned candles every evening at supper time. She compared this view with the one from the apartment window. The exercise was painful. She kept seeing a transparent Alex reflected in the glass, his face turned to hers, his eyes meeting hers.

Alex. Surely there was a lesson in it all. Her pain must not be completely wasted. She let her eyes blur the outline of the hillside that formed her horizon. The soothing curves lulled her tired mind; her thoughts drifted, back to the times when he *had* talked. She wondered now whether by trying to answer her he had hoped to clarify his own thoughts.

She took comfort in recalling the days when she first was drowned with love. True, he had changed her from the person she had known herself to be: in control, sensible, to one obsessed—unable, and soon unwilling, to break away from his magnetism. It had seemed to her unquestioning mind, that she need never try. Was she wrong to think she had come to know him—that he was not a stranger? *My love,* she thought, *but my torment now!*

Alex had, eventually, told about himself, little by little, over the years. Gradually as the emerging skeletons of the trees in autumn winds, the framework of his personality had been revealed.

He mentioned once that he had looked up the word "home" in the dictionary when he was still a schoolboy. She had not known how to respond. Who would not know the meaning of such a common noun? Now, so far from their initial closeness, she wondered whether he blamed her for her incomprehension. Surely by then, after years of marriage, he should have understood! How could she have been expected to share automatically in a perspective so foreign to her?

She had been surprised whenever he spoke of himself over the whole span of their married life because his words were often so vivid. He said about getting his job with Uhlik in the city, "You don't know how good it felt, knowing I'd never again have to hole up in somebody's barn for the night, or stand on a highway shoulder with rain running down inside my collar and my thumb out. I was actually through with minimum wages or hazardous jobs just to keep myself alive! My God! I was saved!" Ruth was still trying to absorb the impact of what he had just told her when he added, "I admit I missed Mariette's cooking. Her red face, sweaty from the heat of the stove, still came back to me now and then, but once I met Jerry and landed in New York, I knew I was on my way. I could let the past go."

Alex, in response to Ruth's urging, had told her he thought that he might write home some day, though as far as she knew, he never had. She could see that he was restless, rootless, even irresponsible, she realized, but above all, what had mattered to her was that he had, somehow miraculously, loved her. Haunted by memories, she clung to the best of them.

"You made me feel I had a place in the world," Alex had said once. "When I met you, I'd known my friends for more than two years, a long time for me. I had a real apartment, money in my pocket, and a library card. I'd applied for citizenship papers. But it was you who gave me a home place—a place to live my life in."

The words had brought tears to her eyes and melted her heart. He had made no secret of the fact that there had never been a shortage of women around him. What had happened to change his mind? She had been unable to resist asking him once, "Why me?"

He had thought for a minute. "Well, you *looked* so different from the girls I'd known. Not just your long hair and the way you wore it, but the expression in your eyes. It reminded me of those horses I'd worked with—shy, skittish, wary, but soft—and strong." He shook his head, smiling a little. "And you didn't come after *me*. After a while, though, when I was with you, I began to feel like I was sinking." He searched her eyes. "Being with you was like walking on river ice in March. There was no way of telling when it would crack, and either leave me afloat on a melting raft on the way to the next rapids, or dump me into the current. Either way, I'd drown for sure if the cold didn't get me first."

She couldn't forget the intensity of his gaze. "Our relationship was just like that to me, slippery—and vital."

His words had astonished her. Now, thinking of them, she quaked inwardly. What if she were never to see again the look in Alex's eyes as he let his guard down? Now, on her own, her future undecided, she knew how he must have felt—now that *she* was grasping desperately for anchorage, while spinning like a nutshell in a flood.

After five or six years of marriage, which Ruth thought of as the middle years, an increasing amount of her time had been devoted to the Gentrys' private needs. Mrs. Gentry's health had become frail. Ruth had taken charge of their Christmas card list and made all arrangements for their holidays, when they were able to get away. The Gentry house became almost as familiar as her own apartment, and she was often a dinner guest there when Alex was on a trip.

Their kindness had not diminished with familiarity. On her thirtieth birthday, they gave a small party for her. Alex was in East Africa filming wildlife, native villages, and dramatic scenery, destined to become stock footage for cutting into Hollywood's epics.

The younger Gentrys, whom she and Alex had met a few of times, were present. Alex had commented after their first meeting, "That Darla Gentry is going to make trouble for Malcolm. I'll bet money on it."

"How can you be so sure?" Ruth had inquired.

Alex had shrugged and smiled. "Maybe I don't trust tall blondes."

After that, Ruth found herself studying the couple carefully. From her perspective in her new solitude, remembering, she thought ruefully that she should have spotted undercurrents that could have helped her own marriage, despite different circumstances. Yet that party had given another indication of just how astute, or intuitive Alex was.

Malcolm Gentry was a civil engineer. He and his family lived in suburban New Jersey, from which he commuted to a large construction company office in the city. At the time, the two Gentry granddaughters were eleven and fourteen.

The four were a group whose picture might have graced the pages of *Town and Country*. Darla Gentry sat on her father-in-law's right, her ash blonde hair falling to her bare shoulders. Though not a conventionally pretty woman, her narrow face and sharp features gave her a look of aristocratic severity. Her daughters both had her coloring, though only the younger one, Hazel, displayed her mother's coolness of manner, which made Ruth wonder on first meeting whether the child was arrogant or shy.

Malcolm was taller than his father, but looked very much like him, though he was clean-shaven. His eyes, however, were his mother's: a translucent blue under dark lashes, and endowed with her same inquisitive expression. The ruddy tone of his skin and sun streaks in his hair suggested he must spend considerable time outdoors.

"I couldn't believe she was serious," Darla was saying in her cool voice. "There's nothing she could have bought that would have been uglier than that cast cement statue, unless it might be plastic flamingos." She took a sip from her soup spoon. "So I had to bite my tongue when she informed me that she was going to enter the Garden Club competition for handsomest landscaping this year." The sarcasm was unmistakable.

Malcolm had broken a roll in half and begun to butter it. He said in a musing tone, "And besides, she's lowering the standards in the neighborhood by hiring those refugees to work around the place." Ruth had glanced at him, surprised at his words.

"Exactly," Darla said. "The bitter end is, she's given them the top of the garage to live in!"

"And you know what that means, with the way they breed—like rabbits," Malcolm murmured. "They'll be all over the school before we know it."

Darla was opening her mouth to speak, but Cornelia Gentry, with a meaning look at her son's lowered eyes, had interrupted. "Tell us about school this year, girls. How do you like it now that you've moved out of elementary school, Alice?"

The elder daughter began a recital of her grievances against her algebra teacher. Like her father, she had a flair for irony. She took a sip of water while the adults were laughing at her confession (made with a certain pride) that it was she who had coined the class nickname for an unfortunate teacher: the Walrus. "It's not just his mustache. He talks in bursts, like belches."

Ruth, a little shocked, suppressed a smile.

"That isn't the worst, though. What's really awful is that he won't ever try to explain anything another way." Alice glared at her nearly empty plate, as if to transmit her frustration to it. "He keeps repeating what he's just said, as if saying it fifty times will make you understand what you didn't get the third time he said it. He drives us crazy."

Hazel looked at her sister with an expression of exaggerated scorn. "You're just mad because you have to stay late every Wednesday."

"Well, you would be too. It's not fair if he can't get it across. They ought to get somebody— "

Her father interrupted, his tone softened now. "Well, don't get too shook, honey. I didn't know this was such a problem. I'll give you a hand with it from now on, and we'll get you straightened out." Malcolm had given Darla a narrow-eyed look across the table. Clearly this was the first time he had heard Alice's complaint and was wondering why.

Alice beamed. "Oh great, Daddy!" Then her expression sobered. "But do you think it'll help really? I'm such a dope about math."

"Don't be negative, pussy cat," Malcolm said. "We'll work it out." He smiled at the child across the table. "I can probably remember enough from those ancient days when I took algebra to be some help."

"Just don't forget, Alice," Darla put in, "no one can do your work for you. When you get to college, you won't have your father for a tutor."

Ruth had caught Malcolm's grim expression. For an instant she thought he was going to answer his wife. A muscle jumped in his jaw. Alice glared at her mother. Her retort was forestalled when Malcolm caught her eye and shook his head.

After dinner and the birthday cake, Darla had hurried the girls upstairs to bed as if she wanted them out of the way, while Malcolm scowled and headed for the decanter of port.

The evening left Ruth puzzling over undercurrents among the younger Gentrys. When she got home, she found a cable from Alex, wishing her a happy birthday. He said he would be back in less than two weeks.

※ ※

Ruth had adjusted to his absences, though she slept restlessly without his warmth beside her, and missed having him to cook for. She lay awake a long time, planning his homecoming meal, and what to wear.

A month or two later, when Alex was away again for a night, Ruth had met Nettie at the corner on her way home from the office, and they walked back to the apartment together. "Would you like to take potluck with me tonight?" Ruth asked. While not a habit, the two often shared a meal in Alex's absence. "We could watch a movie on TV or something." She hesitated at the foot of the stoop. "I haven't had a chance to talk to you for ages."

Nettie peered over her paper bag, her eyes quizzical. Then she said, "Why not? I'll bring a bottle of Guinea red."

She had arrived with the straw-wrapped bottle in one hand and her cigarettes in the other, still turbaned in her customary garish colors. Ruth had wondered once fleetingly if Nettie might be bald.

They each had a glass of wine, and exchanged notes on the comings and goings of the other tenants in the house, while supper cooked. Nettie, however, kept peering around the room as if she were looking for something she thought should be there. Finally she said, "Alex is gone a lot, isn't he?"

"Sometimes it seems so."

"Man that handsome, you might want to keep an eye on him." Nettie poured herself a second glass of wine.

Ruth chuckled. "I know what you mean, but there's no sense borrowing trouble, is there?"

Nettie had followed her to the kitchen alcove. She stood leaning against the wall and watched while Ruth made salad. She said in an offhand manner, "Truth is, I thought by now you'd be looking for another place."

"Why?" Ruth straightened up from peeking into the oven. "You know how much we like it here."

With a hitch of her shoulders, Nettie cleared her throat. "Thought by now it'd be too small for you." Ruth stopped meal preparations to look straight at her friend. The old pain rushed back. Was this any of Nettie's business?

After a distinct pause, she said, "Well, maybe we will want more space one day, but for now, this is fine." She got the casserole out of the oven and carried it to the table.

All at once, Ruth wished for Eloise or Julie, or especially Dan. This odd, friendly, prying woman was really a stranger.

Nettie said, "Sorry, Red. Didn't mean to …"

Ruth had forced a smile. "Don't be silly. Come and sit down; let's eat it while it's hot."

"No point in pretending," Nettie said while Ruth served plates. "I'm interested in you two. Always have been. If I'm too nosy, just tell me to butt out and I will. No hard feelings. But you're pretty much on your own here, seems to me, and maybe you'd be glad to have someone to …"

Ruth broke in, "Of course I would." She saw suddenly that it was true. Her feelings from a minute earlier forgotten, she added, ""Oh, would I ever!" Smiling, she held out her hand to Nettie. "May I have a match, please?" She lit the candles. "So don't think about being nosy. It's nice to have someone interested."

"You figure on working forever?" Nettie inquired with her mouth full. "This is good."

Ruth looked up from her plate. "I hadn't thought … what I mean is, we … I don't know. Maybe." She had not been able to voice the truth just then.

Nettie was eating steadily, her eyes shifting from the plate to Ruth's face, and back to her food. Ruth felt her scrutiny with some discomfort. At the same time, she was grateful for what she took for sympathy.

Nettie had changed the subject, and they chatted amiably about work and the neighborhood. Nettie finished her meal and poured herself another glass of wine. Then she leaned back with a sigh, and held her glass to the light, then took a swallow. Her head tilted, she studied Ruth again.

"You ever wonder what life is like for people you meet? I mean, just casually. People you know well are different. But take the guy runs the newsstand on the corner of Greenwich. You ever wonder what his life is like?"

Ruth had pictured the kiosk, fringed on three sides by fluttering magazine covers, framing the gnome-like vendor in his greasy cap. She thought of the times she had dropped coins on the stack of papers, slid a copy out, and gone on without even a word. Like everyone else in the neighborhood, she knew he was blind.

"I can't imagine," she confessed. "I can't even figure out how he gets to and from work, or even where he could live." Nettie's fixed stare made her uneasy.

"Didn't think so." Nettie leaned back in her chair and picked up the book of matches. With the dexterity of a sailor, she struck one with the thumb of the hand that held it, and lit a cigarette. She inhaled so deeply that she was nearly finished with the next sentence before the smoke began to emerge. "You ever even think about what goes on with people you can't see right now? What's Alex doing this minute? Your mother, say? Or your best friend?"

Nettie's questions had made Ruth feel the way she had as a little girl, when her father would quiz her as he sometimes did, when she didn't know what sin she might have committed. She was apprehensive and defensive, without knowing why. She remembered that vague feeling of guilt and that she did realize she was being accused of lack of imagination, though she had not understood the point in her friend's inquisition. If she had been more perceptive, might matters have turned out differently?

She had asked, "Are you suggesting I'm unimaginative, or unsympathetic?" and trying to suppress her resentment, had attempted a laugh. "Or both?"

Nettie took another long drag on her cigarette, her focus now on the picture hanging on the wall behind Ruth. Her expression was serious. "I don't know," she had answered thoughtfully. "I think maybe you could be missing a lot." She shifted her gaze to Ruth. "And you're the kind could take advantage of it all, seems to me. Isn't everybody that can." She stood up, stubbing her cigarette out with impatient stabs at the ash tray. "Let's get the dishes done."

Lying in bed that night, Ruth had thought over their conversation. With an insidious, acid feeling running through her bones, she had begun to wonder what Alex was doing that very minute. Nettie, as she doubtless intended, had planted a seed.

CHAPTER ELEVEN

While Ruth's routine was her job and helping the Gentrys, Alex was becoming steadily more restless and irritable. The change in his attitude had come about gradually, in fits of sudden hostility or depression that would pass off, but which became more frequent.

Ruth wondered now whether the night after only a few months of marriage when he had become a stranger in bed had been a symptom of some latent and fundamental dissatisfaction. Still hoping not to have to shoulder too much blame, she wondered if he had shown his feelings more consistently she might have taken note of them sooner.

One evening not too long after her conversation with Nettie, Alex had come in and slammed the door behind him. She saw his scowl as he tossed his jacket at a chair and failed to pick it up when it landed on the floor. Wary of his moods by then, Ruth said nothing. She accepted the drink he handed her and went on getting their meal ready.

At the table, he pushed his food around on the plate, eating little, making monosyllabic comments on what she offered in the way of conversation about her day. She saw marks on either side of his lips like fine pencil lines that she had never noticed before.

As if talking to himself, Alex said, "I've begun to think that every day comes without any mystery, with no promise, with nothing that makes the life of a human being different from an animal's."

"Oh, Alex," she had murmured, "aren't you exaggerating?"

He growled, "Either Jerry turns me loose on a project of my own, or I'm going to snap my tether and gallop across lots, so to speak."

Ruth had a vivid mental picture of the workhorses Alex had told her about on the farm near the orphanage. "Sometimes, when we were shuffling in those dark hallways, crowded so our shoulders brushed the walls, I'd think about running in zigzags, the way we saw the farm horses do when they were turned out after a day of plowing. Their tracks went every which way. We were never allowed to move except in line, while even working animals got some time to run wild. And now I'm beginning to feel like that again."

She had not known what to say, but had watched him gulp from his wine glass, his gaze clearly bent on the past. "Eventually we got old enough to play volleyball outside in the playground, but even then you could only play inside the lines." He shifted his eyes to hers. "When I think of my childhood, I still think of straight lines. I thought I'd left all that behind years ago."

"But things aren't really like that for you now. For us, they're not that bad, are they?" Her brow furrowed, she searched his face for a glimmer of his usual enthusiasm.

As if he hadn't heard, he went on, "I stood in front of a pet store window today and watched a little hamster. I got a sensation of whizzing around and around in the exercise wheel, as if I were in there too. I watched that poor little bastard bounding along, going nowhere, and I was right behind him. I could feel the crosswires. We spun the wheel till it looked solid but transparent, as if it were made of glass. Then he stopped. We rocked back and forth, enough to get seasick, both of us panting and quivering. I saw how everything through the cage blurred. The end never came. Nothing changed at all after he stopped." Alex ran a hand through his hair, turned away from Ruth, and got up to make another drink. She had no words.

It always frightened her when Alex spoke that way. He did it only occasionally, but when he fell into a mood like that, she felt separated from him—almost in touch, but not quite. Alex's disquiet infected her with a sense of sinister imminence.

He had turned to her. "I don't want to go back to the days when I was a green kid, bumming around back and forth across the Canadian border, a driver's license for identification, half the time not knowing if I'd have the price of a meal the next day. In five years,

I had a dozen jobs, and the only repeats were the ones I did in diners and roadhouses. Now I feel so—mired, trapped, in routine and geography …."

"Maybe we should go on a trip," Ruth cut in, and saw Alex flush with exasperation.

He gazed with eyes unfocussed again across the room. "Listen. I keep having this dream: I'm in a huge cave with spikes of stone hanging off the roof and sticking up out of the floor. It's dark, but I can see, at least for a few feet in front of me. I'm calling, and my voice reverberates. I don't get an answer, and I get scared as I walk farther and farther into the earth, trying to find someone. I don't even know who. It's black in there, but you know how dreams are. I can almost see, until suddenly I step off a precipice and begin to fall. I spin slowly around like a leaf coming off a tree, sailing along in utter silence past the wall of the cliff, that somehow I can dimly see. I don't know why, but I'm not afraid of hitting the bottom. I wake up drenched with sweat because I know I'm going to go on turning in space, in slow motion, past that wall—forever."

She had stared at him then as he turned and searched her face with an expression of pleading. She moved to give him a hug. Only now she wondered, *What was the source of that dream?*

Alex had got up, moved restlessly away from her, and turned on the television set as if to use its images to substitute for the ones in his mind.

෨ ෬

Ruth had continued through those times to do her best to behave as though she were content. But without realizing it, she became more precise, more orderly, more subdued. Having gained self-confidence from her job, and having established a settled life, she maintained a routine and took sanctuary in it. She pushed disquieting thoughts away. In retrospect, she saw how foolish she'd been. She'd not been completely blind. If only she had had the courage … . But now it was too late.

Alex had begun to pester Jerry about his future. In the past couple of years he had stopped being so much of a jack-of-all-trades. Jerry allowed him to do a lot of pre-production legwork and made him responsible for many of the details of actual shooting, though he kept the director's authority for himself. Finally Alex had extracted a promise that if he could choose a subject Jerry thought was worth spending money on, he would let Alex direct it.

For a time, that promise sustained him. He began to concentrate on finding just the right vehicle to set himself on his way. He read all the small back-page stories in the papers, hoping to turn up an idea. Ruth watched him calmly, assuming that he was again reconciled to his work and his hopes for the future.

Alex was aware of Ruth's worry over him. He felt guilty about leaving her so often and would tell her stories to amuse her, since she couldn't accompany him. After a trip for a documentary on labor troubles in Appalachia, he said, "I wish you could have seen it, then you'd know what I mean. There's so much more in the universe than Manhattan, as well as the coast of Maine." He had not disguised the derisive tone on the last word. Ruth had felt a stab of annoyance that she suppressed.

When Ruth sensed that Alex was disappointed in her, she would temporize. "I'm sorry, honey, I guess I don't have much imagination."

Sometimes he had tried to make her laugh. "You should have seen Pete after the strike leader poured a bucket of paint over his head. It was dripping all over the floor. He looked like an escapee from one of those places where they try to 'raise your consciousness,' or whatever the jargon is." He made no effort to hide his disdain, when Ruth looked her question. "Well, you know who I mean. They make you fall over with your eyes shut, so you can't see if anyone will catch you, or they make you feel somebody else all over and then you have to let them do it to you?"

And Ruth, though she was trying to join his mood, had said in spite of herself, "I don't see how you made that connection just because he was covered with blue paint."

"That's what they do to people in those screwy groups out in California. I figure the people who fall for that must look as stupid and at a loss as Pete—"

"But I thought the idea was to teach people to trust each ..." Ruth was still groping to get a hold on the connection.

"I'm talking about humiliation!" Alex shouted. "Any dumb-head that gets himself in a situation like that doesn't need to be taught how to trust! He needs to be paper trained like a puppy! It's all he's good for!"

She had kept quiet then, trying to figure out what had become of the funny story. Pete was Alex's closest friend.

Doggedly, Alex had picked up the thread. "My God, there we were, everyone in hysterics, falling all over, laughing like damned idiots. Anyway, the end of the story was that the miners decided to letter their protest sign in blue because they didn't want to waste the paint."

Ruth spoke hesitantly, "How did you happen to have the crew there at the right time? Had someone tipped you off?"

Alex had barked, "We don't need tipoffs! It's our job to know where to be when!"

At times like that she had always been confused and hurt by Alex's irritability. It was clear that her comments didn't seem to be what he was looking for by way of response.

On another occasion, Alex was trying to be funny about one of the girls in the crew whose room had been invaded by the motel owner when an anonymous caller had reported that the occupants were harboring a pet snake. It was a prank one of the camera men thought up because he was annoyed at her for turning down his request for a date that night.

Alex had told his story brandishing a can of beer. "And there the poor bastard was with this gorgeous chick, bare-assed and shrieking like a banshee, not because they'd been caught together, but because, as soon as he opened the door with his master key, old Logan yells, 'All right, you get them snakes out of there!' and scared her to death—she hated snakes. She lit out for the next county!"

After a tiny pause, Ruth had asked, "Sort of a mean prank, though, wasn't it?"

"Well, I thought it was pretty funny. We have to blow off some steam sometimes. In this business, you're either up all night and working twenty hours at a stretch, or you're standing around for eight hours a day, waiting for something to happen. Feast or famine."

"Still, you seem to have time for fun."

"Listen, Red, I'm always going to have time for fun." Had he taken her remark as a criticism?

⚜

The time came when Jerry Uhlik, enamored of the money to be made in TV commercials, had accepted an offer for his small business that would enable him to make the necessary equipment and personnel changes to open a more elaborate studio, so he could film in-house and meet the demands of that specialty. Alex could hardly believe it.

"The son of a—! He had the balls to tell me after the fact! He didn't even think to ask me! I only found out when the new people came to do an inventory! And then, as if he hadn't had enough fun shafting me already, he told me I might be able to work for the new people if I could learn to—get this—keep my temper!"

Half afraid to say anything, Ruth had ventured, "Well, maybe you could …" But Alex would hear no encouragement. He never forgave Jerry for doubting his ability to raise money, or to manage the production of the films he dreamed of making. "It makes me sick to think of all the work we've put in to get a rep for good documentaries, and then to throw it away on that whoring business of TV commercials! Well, maybe he'll see the light and change his mind before it's too late."

When Alex came home that day, after the final row with Jerry, he got out the scotch immediately. By the time Ruth came in, he could not have cared less about dinner.

"But what will the new owners do with the company?" She asked. "Couldn't you ask them—"

He had burst out, "They specialize in stag films, and the kind of dramatized sermons they show to kids to teach them bike safety and how to avoid venereal disease and kidnapping. What the fuck could I contribute to that kind of asinine propaganda? It's worse than making sales pitches for detergents and beer." He sneered and took a swig from his glass. "Now, if they were making grade-A blue movies, that might have something to recommend it."

"I'm sorry, honey. Are you thinking he should have offered you a chance at buying him out yourself?"

He gave a bitter laugh. "Not anymore. Not after he told me how much he was asking. Shit, he knew there was no way I could raise that kind of money." He took another swallow of his drink. "Bastard!" He'd paced for a few minutes, while Ruth racked her brain for the right thing to say to soothe him.

He burst out, "I s'pose you're thinking I ought to be glad you've got a good job, so we can eat until I find something else."

She said quickly, "No, of course I wasn't. Besides, you won't be out of work for long. With your experience, you'll find something very soon."

"Yeah," he growled, dropping onto the couch. "A job. But how'm I going to find anything that I can stand for more than six months?"

Ruth sat down next to him. "There must be hundreds of interesting jobs in this city. Don't worry, darling. It'll be fine. We'll be fine." She leaned over to kiss him on the cheek.

Something in that gesture stung him. She should have seen that he was in no mood to be patronized. He jumped up and walked unsteadily to the window, glass in hand, where he stood staring out at the buildings silhouetted against the dull, rosy glow of a cloudy city sky.

"If I had any guts, I'd move to California," he muttered. "If you want to make any kind of movies, that's where the action is."

Had he been testing her? If so, she ought to have passed. She hadn't said a word, though her stomach had tightened and she had felt her palms go damp. Fear that he might be serious about moving had chilled her like a drench of cold water. In the silence, the ice rattled as Alex tipped his glass.

He stood motionless at the window. "But hell," he said without turning around, "I can't gamble with your life as well as mine." His words were coming more slowly, and his voice was beginning to sound muffled. "If it didn't work out, you'd have lost your job too. Can't make a move to do something new or something different; can't take chances. We don't have enough saved to live on for more than three months."

Watching, Ruth had seen that his thoughts were beginning to blur like his speech. "If I couldn't find anybody to back me, I'd never even get a chance to find out if I could — could show — tell the world — make something great like de — de Rochemont ..." He was having trouble with the French name, his native tongue. "Takes money to prove ... if I could make something that'd stop the bastards in their tracks." He looked at Ruth muzzily.

The tone of his voice had become plaintive. "Anybody gets an original idea, there's no way to get it on film unless — same as it's always been. You gotta have money to make money." He raised his voice. "Can't be any damn good in this lousy world without deep pockets and plenty to line 'em!"

Ruth had tried with a note of entreaty in her voice, "You said once that we're a team. We'll have each other ..."

He had turned on her, mouth distorted, eyes wide. "That's what I call cold fucking comfort, Red! It's a long time to retirement. I don't want to be a sick — stick-in-the-mud, old fart with a bay window when I'm fifty!"

Alex was not usually given to bad language, and Ruth had watched with growing alarm as he brandished his nearly empty glass and took a couple of wobbly steps back toward her. "Still, you'd think the son of a bitch'd at least ask me ..." He broke off, began on a new tack. "Maybe *you're* satisfied stuck in one place doing the same damn thing every damn day, seeing the same faces, never having anything rock your precious little boat!" He waved his arm, and the glass flew from his hand, crashing onto the bare floor. Ruth had jumped up and gone to pick up the larger shards and the ice cubes.

"Christ!" Alex shouted, suddenly out of control, frustration pouring out of him like water over a dike. "I mustn't mess up your nice little ... little f-fucking floor! Don't spoil the dandy décor or break ... break glasses. Or appointments, or habits ..." He began weaving in the direction of the bed. "Don't get rough!" he ranted. "Don't fucking act like a red-blooded male, don't screw your woman. Hell, you got to *make love* to your dear little wife!" Acid dripping from every word, he went on, and on.

Ruth was crouching motionless, her hand still extended to pick up the pieces of glass, her eyes glued to her husband, while he continued to shout and rave. He was near the bed by then. His voice was hoarser, words slower. She had a queer sensation, as if the scene must be happening to two other people. Transfixed, she had wondered who this inebriated and foul-mouthed stranger was.

"'S a good thing you never see anything but what's in front of your turned-up nose. 'S a good thing you like your clean, quiet, goody little unreal world." He had turned around, sat down abruptly on the bed, and stared in Ruth's direction. She wasn't sure he could see her. His unfocused eyes told her his mind had gone blank. He licked his lips; his eyelids drooped; then slowly he leaned sideways until he was lying down, his legs over the side of the bed and his feet touching the floor. Ruth had remained crouched, frozen, like a rabbit with the hounds coming near.

※ ※

In the half light of dawn, Alex had wakened and found Ruth curled in her corner of the couch, enveloped in the afghan so that her face was nearly hidden. She had feigned sleep, afraid of what would happen next, but between slitted lids, she saw him sit up to take off his shoes, wincing as he bent over to untie them. Very carefully he walked into the bathroom. She heard him open the medicine cabinet, run water, flush the toilet. Then he came back and turned down the bed. Tiptoeing, he went to the couch, stooped, and kissed the top of her head. When she dared to look up at him, he gathered her up and carried her to the bed.

Gently he took off her shoes and her skirt, then his trousers, and crawled in next to her. He cradled her head on his shoulder, his body curled against hers, saying nothing. She had slept at last against his familiar warmth until the alarm went off.

※ ※

It had taken almost two months for Alex to find work with a large advertising agency. Naturally, it was filming commercials. He had swallowed the irony, and taken the job. Sometimes they still made some tacky little trailers for car dealerships and catering palaces that

SETTLING

specialized in wedding receptions—the sort of thing still occasionally shown in those days in small-town movie theaters. Alex was permitted to direct those.

He did try to make the best of it. He told Ruth, "With any luck, I'll end up an account executive, and the money's good. At least it's not just paperwork."

But she was unable to forget the day Jerry announced the sale of his company. She feared another scene like it, even though she tried to hide her anxiety. She and Alex had always routinely avoided subjects she considered were better left unmentioned, and he had never insisted on pursuing them.

Changes of season and holidays, varying degrees of job pressure, occasional parties were the only ripples on the surface of their lives, once Alex was working again. Ruth had tried to relax and have faith that all would be well.

One night Alex had come home in an almost manic mood. He had dreamed up a commercial featuring a hot-air balloon as a sort of emblem of the high-flying, adventurous spirit the client wanted to project as the most prominent characteristic of his product—a line of men's cosmetics. Half thinking that his idea would be rejected, Alex had suggested the balloon as a selling tool for the toiletries. The staff and client alike thought he was inspired. That day, as they started filming the first of a series, they'd taken Alex up for a ride.

Pacing around the room, words tumbled out of his mouth as from an excited child. "Red, it took me back. I tell you, it took ten years off my life! Not a sound except the roar of the burner and the wind in the rigging and the basket creaking! It was great! Made those rackety little stunt planes out in the Dakotas seem like outboard motors compared to twelve-meter yachts. That's what ballooning is like! It's flying the high-class way—quiet, leisurely, and the best way there is to see things. You've gotta try it! We've got to save up and get one."

Ruth stared at him. "A balloon?"

"Damn right!"

"Don't they cost a lot?" she had finally asked meekly.

"Hell, I don't know what they cost, but I'm going to learn to fly one first, naturally, and then we'll go on from there. We've got a date with Hank on Saturday morning up near Stormville. He'll take us up and ..."

"Us?"

"Of course."

"I couldn't. I'm sorry, darling, I can't. I'm terrified at the whole idea. No, if you're serious, you'll have to go without me. It's bad enough just to think of you ..."

"Don't be such a spoil sport!" Alex had cried.

"I'm not," Ruth answered, stung. "I'm not trying to interfere with what you want to do, even if I do think you're crazy, but I can't do it with you."

"Won't, you mean," he'd rejoined, scowling. "God, haven't you any ... any gumption?" he finished lamely. "You don't want to try anything new."

She saw he was trying to control himself, but he was seething. He snatched up the newspaper and dropped into his chair, making a show of unfolding and shaking out the pages. Ruth bit her lip.

Ballooning! She had seen in her mind's eye one of Alex's word pictures, painted years before. One night in bed, after making love, he'd begun to talk. Even as she heard him, she'd thought, *He wouldn't speak like this with the light on.*

"On winter nights when I was kid, I could hear a sort of musical buzz I thought was other worlds spinning in space. I don't know where I got the idea there'd be a sound, but there's something about the silence of sub-zero winter nights and the brilliance of the stars, that touched off my imagination. It was like weird music, like humming tops." He turned on his side. "It seemed to be calling, and I'd feel myself sail out the window into the sky, like a puff of milkweed floss. I never felt cold. It was like floating wrapped in down."

He described how he would look down on the convent and the town of St. Agathe, the fields and barns and woods, and see the gleaming aluminum roof on the church. "It shone just in starlight, without any moon. Inanimate and cold as a silver ingot."

In the end, of course, though he did take Ruth with him to watch him take off in a balloon, nothing more had come of his flight of fancy. Alex had remained tied to earth.

CHAPTER TWELVE

Dr. Gentry had telephoned Ruth at home the evening before he was to leave for a conference. She had been in his employ for ten years by then, and was accustomed to acting as much more than a mere office assistant. "My dear, I must ask you to look after Cornelia. Now that she's confined to the house, she'll need to see a friendly face, and perhaps you can run an errand for her from time to time."

"Don't worry, Dr. Gentry. I'll stop in every day." She had turned from the phone to explain to Alex.

He interrupted her without looking around the pages of his paper. "Yeah, you're elected to play maid, I suppose."

As usual, she had tried to fend off trouble. "Well, I won't have to be in the office all day, just check the answering service. Besides, the Gentrys have always treated me more like a daughter than an employee. I'm beholden and I'm glad to help."

Alex had merely grunted and turned a page. He knew his attitude was unreasonable, but his wife was being treated like a family retainer. She was his *wife*, after all, not a servant.

When Ruth thought back on these exchanges, she saw the irony of a maverick like Alex taking such an old-fashioned view. At the same time, she now realized she had not reckoned with his pride.

It was almost six o'clock the next evening when she had arrived at the Gentry house with library books. She rang the bell and waited, looking along the block of restored brownstones. Window boxes filled with ivy and flowers, and young plane trees planted at intervals along the curb gave the street a festive air. Ruth wondered how much it must cost to live in this style in this neighborhood. The door was opened not, as she had expected, by Elvira, but by Malcolm Gentry.

"Oh—how do you do?" she stammered.

"Hello, Ruth. Come on in. Mother's expecting you." He led her upstairs.

"Is she worse?" Ruth asked. "I mean, since you're here ..."

"No, she's the same, but too lame to get around." He said nothing further to explain his presence, and left her at his mother's door.

He was waiting in the hall when she came down. "Can I offer you a drink?"

She had examined his face, looking for a clue to the tension she sensed. She heard coins rattle in his pocket, where he'd put one hand.

Then he said, "Perhaps I should explain. I suppose you're wondering what I'm doing here." He turned toward the living room door, as if to escape her scrutiny. "Scotch?"

"Thank you." Curiosity made her follow slowly. His expression was grim. He occupied himself with the drinks, his back to her. She sat on the edge of one of the settees that flanked the fireplace, her feet together, her back primly straight.

"I don't want to embarrass you," he was saying, "but you'll be hearing about it, I'm sure." He carried a glass to her, and seated himself facing her across the coffee table. Looking down at the ice in his glass, he stirred it around with one finger. "I'm staying here temporarily for personal reasons." He looked up, and Ruth realized he was as nervous as she was. "Darla and I are having—problems. We've decided on a temporary separation."

"Oh, I am sorry!" There was an awkward silence. Then they both began to speak at the same time.

Malcolm said, "I beg your pardon. What were you going to say?"

"Well, I just was thinking how—how it would—I was thinking about your girls." She took a sip from her glass. Malcolm said nothing. "I mean, I was thinking how difficult it must be for you all to get through a time like this. It must be hard for Alice and Hazel not to have you there." She stopped, unsure of how much to reveal of her impressions from the last time she had seen the family together at her birthday party. Embarrassment made her want to babble.

He nodded. "You're right, of course." He stood up and began to walk about the room. "But I felt the only thing that made any sense after our last ... argument ... would be to let things cool down for a while." He smiled wryly. "I never can learn to hold my tongue, at least not consistently enough." He drank deeply. "Forgive me for discussing my problems."

Ruth interrupted, "Please don't apologize!" She wanted somehow to remove the awkwardness that was making them both so stiff. "I'd hardly say we were discussing anything ..."

"Well, I should be asking about you and your husband," he broke in. "How does he like his new work?"

"It's fine," she had said automatically. "He had hopes of doing more directing. Just of the sort of short subjects and specialty productions he did with Uhlik. This advertising thing is just enough of a challenge to keep him interested, I guess, but it isn't what he'd do if he had a choice. It really isn't creative enough, I think. I'm afraid he's really bored."

"It's too bad he doesn't have some connection with one of the little theaters. You live in the Village, don't you? Did he ever think of finding one of those off-Broadway groups, for instance? They'd be mighty glad to find someone with his experience, even if it isn't on the stage. He knows about lighting, and that sort of thing, doesn't he?"

"What a wonderful idea!" Ruth exclaimed.

"Well, it's just a thought."

"But it's inspired! Why didn't one of us think of that?" She took a swallow of her whiskey. "I can hardly wait to get home to suggest it." She set her glass on the coffee table and got up hastily. "Thank you for the drink. I'll see you tomorrow then, unless I get here too early."

"I usually get back around five-fifteen, now that I don't have the long commute."

He accompanied her to the door. As he held it for her, he said, "I'll be anxious to hear what Alex thinks of the idea."

Alex was home before Ruth. She mentioned Malcolm's idea while she was getting dinner.

"I never thought of that!" Ruth had heard the excitement in his voice. "But I don't know if I could deal with a play. Still, I'm used to thinking in scenes, and trying to figure out transitions and angles. But you know," he said, his words coming more and more rapidly, "when I was with Jerry, I always wished we could do more original stuff and less pure reporting. It used to drive me nuts to see how strong you could make something if only you could control it as it was being shot. If I could handle actors on a stage, I could really make an audience feel ..." He stood and went to the middle of the room, gesturing as he talked, smiling and animated. "It'd be a great way to learn! God, do you think I could do it? Maybe some amateur outfit would let me try. They meet in the evening and on weekends, don't they? Most everyone has to work ..." He broke off again as another thought came to him. "But how in blazes can I find one of these groups?"

"I'll bet Nettie will know, or if not, she'll know how to find out. She knows everything that goes on around here."

Nettie had proved to be quick and efficient. "Let me just look at the *Voice* and see if I can find that piece ... Here it is. They call themselves The Castoffs." She put a derisive emphasis on the title. "But what d' you know! I know the guy that owns the place where they rehearse, and the fairy that does the lighting for them is an old buddy from high school days. And it says here they've got a call out to cast—would you believe—*The Great God Brown*?"

Ruth asked, "That's the name of a play?" Nettie took a drag on her cigarette, flicked ashes in the general direction of an ash tray, and folded up the tabloid she'd been reading. She dropped the paper on the table and gave it a decisive smack as she stood up.

"O'Neill. First off, you better start educating yourself. At least enough to know something about whatever he ends up working on." She was rummaging among her disorganized collection of books. "Here. Here's a copy for you to read. At least you'll know the kind of stuff that's going on even if you're not around to see it." She handed Ruth a worn anthology.

"Do you think they'll let him ..."

"Listen, any warm body would make them happy, believe me. And if they get a chance at somebody with half a brain, they'll kidnap him if they have to, especially a man." Nettie stubbed out her cigarette. "Just one thing, though. Don't be surprised if they try to draft him to act for them."

"Oh, I don't think he's interested in ..."

"One look at that profile, friend, and you'll be lucky if you get him home in the same condition he goes out in, if you get my drift." Nettie pursed her lips and shook her head. "That's the only part that worries me about this. Are you sure you want him to get mixed up with all those 'artistes'?" Quotation marks were clearly audible.

Ruth had considered being honest with Nettie. She had yearned to confide the sort of misgivings she had, but felt shy of baring what she already thought of as problems. She said, "He needs some creative outlet, and this theatrical group seems like something made to order for his interests."

Nettie shrugged. "Well, it's your funeral," she said in what had turned into a lugubrious tone. She handed Ruth the paper, and brushed aside her thanks. Alex called the number in the ad. A fruity voice told him that the group would be delighted to make use of his services, and they would welcome him at their next meeting, which was the last of the casting sessions for the proposed play.

Alex had been on pins and needles with anticipation. He took Nettie's book and hastily read through the play. Ruth watched happily as his enthusiasm increased. Though she had taken the trouble to read the introduction to the book, and at least now understood O'Neill's standing as a playwright, she had found the play ponderous and over-symbolic, and wondered why anyone would want to produce it. She was wise enough to keep her opinion to herself, however.

After his first visit to the empty store that served The Castoffs as a meeting and rehearsal hall, Alex had come back to the apartment ebullient. He walked up and down in his usual way when he was excited, telling about his introduction to the group. "They're a dedicated bunch, you have to hand them that. And some of them are really pros who just can't find work and want to keep their hand in. And you'll never guess who's a member. Someone you know."

"Who?"

"Remember Ron, one of that pair that roomed with Daryl?"

"Yes. I kept getting him mixed up with his—friend. What was his name? Stan."

"Well, he was there in all his glory, with a new boyfriend, and he remembered me. So that was great, because then it was as if they all knew me. Anyway, they have a director, of course. Big, ugly bastard who thinks he's God's gift to the ladies, but he seems to know what he's doing. At least he talks a hell of line about *expressionism* and Freudian psychology. I thought he asked the people who were reading for the parts the right questions. But they don't have a stage manager. Well, they didn't, but they asked me if I could do it."

"That's terrific!" As an afterthought, Ruth had asked, "Are you pleased?"

Alex dropped into a chair and stretched out his legs. He put his hands behind his head and looked up at the acanthus leaves on the ceiling. "Yeah. It sure will take the curse off all that commercial jive I have to slog through all the time. I mean, to be thinking of the—I hate to use the term, but I can't think of a better one right now—artistic side of putting ideas into stage pictures. At least I can watch how it's done. It'll be a change." He leaned forward, elbows on his knees. He was smiling; the frown that Ruth had been seeing for so long seemed to have melted away, and he looked younger.

"You know, a proscenium isn't the same thing as a motion picture screen, but there are elements that aren't too different. You have to make sure that all the gestures and expressions are bigger and clearer on a stage than for the camera. You don't have a close-up lens, but you still have to make pictures. And you won't have the element of chance we always had to cope with on the documentaries. Everyone on the stage will be in the same place when they say the same thing, performance after performance. But the best of all is, there isn't a God-damned storyboard you have to follow like it was engraved on stone tablets!"

Ruth began to see how she had underestimated his restiveness and frustration in recent months. She decided not to suggest that the playwright's words might be sacrosanct.

"Harry Offenbach may be a pain, but I'll learn from him. Maybe I could even end up in the business myself—get shut of this advertising crap." He had talked until after midnight, when he finally noticed Ruth's yawns, and went happily, if reluctantly to bed.

☙ ❧

After his trip, Dr. Gentry had told Ruth that he was worried about his wife. She seemed not to have recovered from the fall she had had a month before his departure, though nothing was broken. He hinted that he felt Malcolm's problems were weighing on her mind. Ruth wished she could offer comforting words.

On her visits to Mrs. Gentry, she had found her less formal, more sad, though she didn't mention what was worrying her. Ruth concluded that the problem must be her son's situation. Malcolm, for his part, was friendly and had renewed his invitation to stay for a drink on the one other occasion when he was present. Ruth had refused, and hurried home. She noticed that he was depressed, but she was reluctant to encourage any confidences from him. Intuition warned of danger, though he was unfailingly correct when they were alone.

Everything about Ruth and Alex's lives had seemed to pick up speed as reluctant spring sidled into the city. Dr. Gentry had reduced office hours, in order to increase the amount of time he devoted to his wife. There were more requests for Ruth's time to help with shopping and personal correspondence, so that her days continued as full as always. The Castoffs cast their play and went into rehearsal by the end of March. Alex continued to come home full of tales of humorous disasters, and what he considered to be phony temperament. Though he often complained of the foolishness of individuals, Ruth knew he was enjoying himself hugely.

※ ※

In May, Ruth had brought up their annual visit to Maine with some trepidation.

"Why don't you go ahead as usual?" Alex urged. "I can't leave now, with the play schedule. You'll have a better time with Dan and your mother if I'm not around anyway."

"I hate to leave you alone to live on pizza and Chinese take-out," she said. "But I know you only go to please me. Maybe I should just take the train and stay for a few days." She paused. "But I wonder if I ought to go at all. I can't get it out of my head that something is going to go wrong with the Gentrys. The doctor isn't himself at all lately, and I can't get him to talk about it. When Malcolm moved back to the city, it upset the two old people, you know. That was when I was going to the house every day to look in on Mrs. Gentry. But I don't really know …"

Alex broke in, "You worry about them too much. They have their son home now, so they ought to be able to manage without you for a while, especially since it's the same vacation time you've taken for years."

"I suppose you're right, but still …"

"You've got two weeks. Why not stay up there and get some sun and enjoy the beach and all?" Alex was collecting his script and clip board. "Don't worry about me. I was a bachelor a long time before you caught me." He hugged her and dropped a light kiss on her forehead, then went off, whistling.

Outside, Ruth had watched the flush of sunset on the brick walls and dusty windows of the buildings beyond the garden. A starling was trilling its musical mating song, and a wisp of contrail glowed across the darkening sky. Even there in the city, full spring was making itself felt. The ground under the pear tree was still sprinkled with fallen petals.

When she sat down to write to Dan, she leaned back in her chair, dreaming, remembering spring in Maine. The apple trees would still be clouds of blossom, the geese still crying at night as they flew northward, or settled on Hungerford's pond over the hill from the house. She drew a long breath, as if she might smell the fragrance of the grass after its first mowing. At last, she bent to the paper, and began to write.

She pictured her little nephew, who would be running now, perhaps talking in sentences—Josh, the picture of his mother, but with something of Dan's shyness. She began to look for ideas of what to take for his gift. As she read her letter over, she had experienced a stab of homesickness. She missed the scent of low tide, the breadth of sky to the earth's distant curve, the sound of waves and the faint taps made by a gull breaking a crab or mussel on a rock.

She went out to mail her letter, walking on the quiet street. Cars were parked bumper to bumper along the pavement; no one was visible. Walking to the corner, she was astonished at the number of odors drifting to her nose: a hint of salt water, a faint leafy smell suggesting green things, a whiff of hot oil coming from an open kitchen window, diesel fumes diluted by the evanescent scent from a window box filled with blooming daffodils.

She dawdled on her way back, amusing herself by looking into windows at vignettes of other lives in strange, lighted rooms. She caught a glimpse of a brawny young man in a light-blue T-shirt with his back to the window, just as he made an angry gesture. She felt a sudden desire to see the person in the room with him, to peek at the scene so she might catch the significance of his motions. She actually paused on the sidewalk, but his muscular back was too broad for her to see around it, or the other person was too far to one side for her to catch sight of him, or was it her? Though she could not understand what he was saying, through the open window she could hear that his voice was high-pitched and excited. The approach of another pedestrian made her start walking again hastily.

When she reached their building, impulsively she had turned down to Nettie's apartment instead of climbing the steps to the first floor. She pressed the bell, and waited for the series of clinks that signified the unlocking of the street door.

"Oh, it's you." Nettie stopped as if she intended to say no more.

"Have I come at a bad time?"

"Ah, well... oh hell, come on in." Nettie opened the door all the way.

"No, no. I just thought I'd stop in for a few minutes since Alex is off at rehearsal. If you're busy, I don't want to intrude. I'll come another ..."

"Oh come on in, Red. I wasn't really doing anything." Nettie was walking away. Her broad figure almost blotted out the light filtering into the corridor from the living room beyond. Ruth realized that she would either have to follow, or close the door and leave without further conversation.

"Just snap the Yale lock," Nettie called. A floor lamp stood close to the table in the window. Several piles of manila folders and a litter of sheets of typescript covered the surface of the table, along with three or four spiral notebooks, a jar filled with pencils and pens, one ash tray full of paper clips, and another full of cigarette butts. A space in front of one of the two chairs had been cleared to accommodate a yellow legal pad and still another ash tray, where a cigarette smoldered unattended.

"Nettie, what on earth are you working on? Honestly, I'll come back another time."

"Now you're in, why don't you just sit down?" Nettie was running water into her kettle in the kitchen. "Time for a cup of tea anyway."

Ruth took off her coat and laid it across a chair back. She hesitated to walk over to the table, for fear it might look as though she were prying. Not knowing what else to do, she sat down on the day bed, with its piles of garish pillows. Nettie came back for her abandoned cigarette. Dressed in her usual headgear and an ankle-length skirt of Indian cotton, she stood with her back to the table, the cigarette hanging from her mouth, arms folded, and looked steadily at Ruth through the banner of smoke rising in front of her eyes. "Guess you caught me," she said enigmatically.

Ruth had looked her question. Nettie pushed off from the table edge, and went back to the kitchen, where she rattled crockery. "How long you been here now?" she called.

"It must be close to eleven—no, twelve years now. Lord, it doesn't seem possible."

"Yeah, well, I guess I ought to be willing to let you in on my little secret after all this time." Nettie emerged with a tray and the tea things. Setting them down, she handed Ruth a cup, and plumped down beside her.

"I was just working this evening. But I was kinda stuck, so I really don't mind you coming in now."

"Working?"

"Yeah. Writing." She paused, then added, "Poetry."

Ruth failed to hide her astonishment. "Poetry!"

Nettie narrowed her eyes in anger. "That's just what I figured you, or anybody else, would say. Who's she think she is, pretending to write, let alone write poetry? Well, you can all go ..."

"But, Nettie, I think it's marvelous! I just don't understand how you've—*why* you've kept quiet about it all these years. Tell me."

"Well, Antoinette, Lady Tennyson I ain't," Nettie said with a grimace. She squinted her eyes at Ruth. "But didn't you ever wonder what I did with my time every day?"

Ruth had laughed. "Did I!" She drank from her cup. "Alex and I used to have a theory that you must be into the stock market or reviewing daytime television shows. We thought you had to have some home industry that took plenty of time and energy to keep you happy. After all, even in this old place, the number of complaints and vacancies can't take all your attention."

"That's the point. Being the super here is perfect. Leaves me plenty of time for my work." She looked up sideways, appearing for the first time to be embarrassed. "Keeps a roof over my head, and pays for groceries too." Then she became abruptly matter-of-fact again. "Well," she said, taking a slurp from her cup, "what'd you come for?"

"Nothing. I just went out to mail a letter and thought I'd see if you were free. I told you, Alex is out. Nettie, I don't know anything about literature."

"For my stuff, I reckon that'd be an advantage." Again Nettie changed the subject. "Alex likes the theater bit, eh?"

"He does, Nettie. He's got all his old enthusiasm back. Thanks for your help in finding this."

"Hmph," Nettie had said. Then with another abrupt change of mental direction, she got up and went to the littered table. She pushed the papers around busily for a minute or two and came back with a handful of sheets. Thrusting them out to Ruth, she smiled, transforming her bulldog look to that of a friendly Persian cat. "Take these, and some time you can tell me what you think."

Ruth took the proffered sheets, carefully, as though she feared soiling them. She thought how seldom she had seen such a sweet expression on Nettie's usually dour features. It was a little as if the mask of her public personality had been momentarily moved aside, like the lace curtain at a genteel window in a prying neighborhood. Ruth felt privileged, as if she had had an instant's glimpse into an unsuspected and private interior.

"Don't try to read them now," Nettie was saying. "You got to concentrate on poetry, you know. You can't just up and read it straight through like a book or a newspaper, not and understand it. Takes time and takes effort."

Ruth nodded. "How did you happen to get into this?"

Nettie dropped down onto the couch. She seemed to be thinking about what her answer would be. She leaned back and rubbed her eyes with the fingers of both hands. "Basically, I guess it's just misery." She gave one of her characteristic grunting chuckles. "You step in shit often enough, you start looking for ways to forget about the smell, I guess." She looked sidelong at Ruth again, her black eyes gleaming with malevolence. "Nothing I want to talk about now. But you get my meaning, don't you?"

"I suppose so. You read about the artist having to suffer …"

"Bullshit. All it takes is a certain amount of being unhappy and a certain scarcity of ordinary sympathy and *voilà*: an instant potential writer or painter or composer or what have you. And most of them turn back into ordinary chumps again, once the mood has worn off." She paused and Ruth waited. "I guess I'm just one of those cases that hung on," Nettie finished, her voice dropping. "Anyway, *suffering* is much too fancy a word for whatever got me going."

"Is your work published?"

"Whenever possible. You can count the times and places on your fingers." She gave one of her huge shrugs. "You know, pal, would-be poets are thick as fallen leaves in this neighborhood, and a lot of them are better than I am. You can picture my chances."

"Isn't it discouraging if you don't get readers?"

"Sure. But if you have the real urge, you don't let that stop you. I could put together a book, if I could just find somebody to sell it for me."

"An agent?"

"Whatever, but they don't usually handle poetry, especially when it's by a nobody. No, I'll just have to peddle it over the transom."

Ruth had been fascinated. What kind of verse might Nettie produce? She seemed so taciturn. Never a reader of poetry except when assigned in school, she knew she would not be a good judge of it, but she wanted the opportunity to see behind the façade of someone she had known so little, though for so long. It occurred to her that the poems could be revealing.

"You don't mind my reading these?" she asked.

"Why not, if you want to?" Nettie answered. "I tried to pick some I like best. Enjoy." The tone of the last word had made Ruth feel the time had come to leave. She thanked her friend, said good night, and went home with her sheaf of Nettie's secrets, impatient to look into them, and perhaps into Nettie through them.

CHAPTER THIRTEEN

In spite of Alex's enthusiasm for the theater group and the load of her own work, Ruth had not been able to forget the awful evening when she had come home to find him so drunk. The memory returned to haunt her at odd moments. Then, something in the often bitter notes of Nettie's poems spoke to the shades of Ruth's feelings at that time—compounded of astonishment, fear, and finally anger. She read a poem called "The Eremite":

... however sweet the honey on the tongue
No balm will soothe the sting nor scent make fresh
The rising stench of rotting pledges.
Clench the jaw and keep my want at bay—
Learn the discipline of saints to save my soul today.

Where had blunt-tongued Nettie ever drawn that formal diction from? The hints of past unhappiness of a kind that Ruth couldn't associate with her toad-like neighbor made an intriguing mystery. The suspicion dawned on her that ignorance is not always a matter of lack of education; she was humbled by the thought.

Nettie's poems had stimulated Ruth to a new curiosity. After reading them, she took to sitting with a book open in her lap, looking across the room at Alex, at the face that had captured her when she was still really but a girl. Maturity had done nothing to lessen its beauty. In bright light, a sprinkling of white hairs barely showed at his temples, and the structure of his skull began to be revealed with greater definition and strength as his cheeks had become leaner, and shallow grooves began to show on either side of his lips. The fresh color of his skin, which tanned without appearing weathered, gave him a virile glow of youth and health. Except when he was tense, his gestures and ordinary movements were unconsciously graceful and energetic. His physical appeal was undeniable. She had always taken pleasure in walking beside him into a room, and derived pride from the envy in the eyes of women when they glanced at her with her arm linked in his, though she would not have admitted it.

When he had shown her how to express love by making love to her, by returning in kind her offers of intimacy, she had felt like the heroine of a fairy tale that ends with "and they lived happily ever after." She expected normal moods and fluctuations of temper, for after all, she wasn't a child, and yet, she had for some time been unable to escape a sensation that all was not as it should be, though searching her husband's features for a clue yielded none.

A combination of unresolved conflict and the notions stirred by Nettie's poems had begun to change Ruth. Those verses pricked her mind like the touch of spurs on the flanks of a sluggish horse, urging her forward into territory she wanted to avoid. In words of often unlovely precision, Nettie frequently depicted the arid emotional landscape of the ugly, the bereaved, and especially the betrayed. All the poems were not about loneliness in one way or another. There were several lyrical fantasies on the possibilities of joy. Ruth liked their transparent symbolism. Surprisingly, when she would stop and reread, she was sometimes half frightened by the ideas Nettie's words stirred in her own mind. But part of her pleasure was in the frequent surprises.

A poem called "Harvest" was an example of the sort of imagery she found herself unable to associate with the stocky, gruff person with whom she was familiar.

> When the sting of hardening cider tingles on my tongue
> I'll see your eyes' soft signals sent to lure me on
> To glean the sheaves of ripening promises that sun

And storm and gentle twilights slowly swell to spring's reward.
And in the fullness of your fields and orchards will I run
And laugh and leap and lie and dream and come at length to
harvest home.

However, themes of treachery and commitment reappeared often. Ruth wondered for the first time what Nettie's life had been before the years since they had become acquainted. The more Ruth read, the more she gradually began to perceive what Nettie had been hinting at when she had taken Ruth to task over her lack of insight. She began to think seriously and at length about the hidden rivers in a personality's landscape.

Ruth had begun to look at Alex with new eyes too, seeking different details from those that had satisfied her in the past. She had begun to have a sense of exclusion that was new to her, and she began to be afraid, of what she could neither describe nor understand. She began to think of Alex as having a dark side—not evil, but dark like the far side of the moon: unseen and unknown. For so long, she'd put the knowledge aside, pretending it made no difference to their compatibility. It was not that she was afraid of him; she realized he had allowed her from time to time to glimpse a hidden scene whose dimensions and significance she was unable to assess. She wanted to get behind the screen of the obvious.

ಸಾ ಣ

One evening, she had asked Alex to take her with him to a Castoffs rehearsal.

"What for?" he demanded. "We're still in a very rough state, lots of technical details to be worked out, and the actors are just beginning to get ready …"

"I'd like to see a production before it's ready for an audience. It would make it so much more interesting to see the finished product if I had some idea of what it had to go through to get to that point."

"Well, I don't know if the actors would want to be seen by an outsider at this stage. Besides, I'd have to clear it with Harry."

"Harry?"

"Harry Offenbach, the director. He doesn't like to have people kibitzing."

Despite his resistance, Ruth pressed him. "I'll sit in the back row and never utter a word. Please, darling, it means a lot to me to see how you spend so much of your time. Besides, it's lonesome here night after night."

With a sulky note in his voice, Alex agreed to ask Offenbach. It was clear he didn't want her to go to the theater, and she wondered why, since he had always been eager to show her whatever he worked on when he was with Jerry.

In the end, she got her wish. When they arrived, Alex didn't introduce her to anyone, and she sat in the back of the musty smelling, shadowy old hall, unnoticed.

On the bright stage, unadorned with any sort of scenery, but equipped with necessary furniture, the actors looked like mannequins in a store window—afloat, a little like fish in a lighted aquarium. The often-stilted and sonorous dialogue enhanced this impression.

Offenbach sat, leaning forward over a card table, in the front row of seats, gesturing elaborately when he gave instructions. He was a huge, hunched man with an untidy beard and horn-rimmed spectacles. Alex was not visible.

Ruth felt that special electricity that permeates the surroundings when a group of eager Thespians is running full throttle. Here and there in the auditorium, an occasional pair of people who were not required on stage would sit together, watching raptly as each scene was rehearsed.

Ruth couldn't take her eyes from the actress playing the part of the prostitute. A tall, voluptuous woman, her sensuality pervaded the stage and overflowed. She had a voice whose middle pitch was made noteworthy by breathy overtones that lent it a woodwind quality. She radiated allure. At first, Ruth assumed she was a consummate actress. But when her short scene was over, and she descended to watch the later scenes with two of the others, her posture and gestures offstage reinforced the impression she had created when she was on it. That overwhelming sexuality was entirely natural to her. In the dim light, Ruth could not see well enough to guess at her age.

After the rehearsal, Alex took her to the seedy little green room, and introduced her to the cast and staff. The girl's name was Honor Ringwold. Ruth immediately forgot almost all the other cast members.

"Well, how did you like it?" Honor asked, lifting a can of Coke to her mouth.

Ruth hesitated, afraid of seeming rude. "I thought it was—very unusual—all the masks." She accepted a cold can from Alex and sipped. "But I'm not sure what an audience will make of it. You're all very good. I mean, you make the most of the parts you have, but, well, I'm not familiar with anything of this kind. I'm the wrong person to ask."

Honor smiled at Ruth. "Why not? You represent the average audience."

"Average be damned," boomed Harry. "Don't be an intellectual snob, Honor baby. This is an allegory, and if we don't make it clear, it's our fault." He turned a beaming grin on Ruth. "You come whenever you can for the next couple of weeks while we put the finishing touches on it, and if there's anything you think is fuzzy, let me know. We'll work on fixing it."

"Well, I wouldn't want to be in the way ..."

"Crap. We can use a fresh eye. O'Neill isn't your average cup of tea, and we may need to do some extra work to keep audiences in their seats. You get Alex to bring you along." He lumbered off after his lighting man, who was leaving, without waiting for an answer from either Alex or Ruth. Alex avoided her look.

On the way home, she had ventured, "They were very nice. They didn't seem to mind my being there, did they?"

Alex responded with an unintelligible grunt. She looked at him as they passed under a streetlight. His mouth looked tight. She had the distinct impression that he did not intend to discuss their evening at the theater.

Alex went to the next rehearsal without Ruth. He came home and announced gruffly that Harry had requested her presence again. After that, she sat quietly in the auditorium every night and watched the final weeks of readying the play for production.

Honor dominated Ruth's perceptions about the play. Once, when she went back toward the dressing rooms, Ruth saw her standing so close to Alex that he was holding his clipboard out to one side. She was bending her sinuous neck to bring her mouth to his ear. The intimacy of their pose shocked Ruth. The image of their bodies, nearly touching in the darkness of backstage clutter, burned itself on her retina.

She had begun to watch them with special attention. From this, she gained no reassurance. Honor nodded to her in the green room, but made no further attempts at conversation. She would take Alex's arm, and lead him to the proscenium steps to sit down so he could take notes on his clipboard as she talked. He never told Ruth what special attentions Honor required on those occasions.

In the two weeks of rehearsals remaining at the time, they were often invisible behind the scenes, along with the rest of the cast and crew, and Ruth's new talent at imagining flourished. Twice Alex sent her home by herself because he said certain short sections were going to have special rehearsal, and there was no need for her to stay. She did not want to reveal her fears, and so went without comment. She was tempted to spend the waiting time rereading Nettie's disquieting verse. She had made it a point to be in bed with a book when Alex returned.

֍ ֍

The Castoffs became Alex's true life at that time. Like so many of the people he had seen around him all his life, he managed to get through his working days with the greater part of his mind elsewhere. He was caught up in the excitement of bringing imaginary people and circumstances to life. Since stage managing was so detailed and so vital to the production, it made him feel important and useful. When he took his clip board and script in hand, he might never have sat at a desk and dealt with what he called "the myopia of an advertising client with only money in view." It was true recreation, in the literal sense.

֍ ֍

SETTLING

Honor Ringwold had proved to be the catalyst that changed everything for Ruth and Alex. After they were finished with a dress rehearsal one night, he invited Honor to have a drink. She tilted her head, looking out of the corners of her eyes, and said, "I was beginning to think you'd never ask."

They sat in a booth at a bar, and he watched Honor drink Ricard, sipping the milky mixture through a straw, looking at him through her lashes, her lips moist and puckered. She had a fluid, languid way of moving, not unlike a cat, and equally as deliberate. Her calculating eyes and open sensuousness were hypnotic.

They talked about the play, and about the people in it. Alex listened enthralled. Every sentence Honor spoke seemed to be hiding a meaning much more intriguing than what she actually said. She was vicious about the one other woman in the cast, who played the small part of the mother, remarking on her figure (which was stocky) and her face (which was ordinary) in scathing terms. Alex recognized the woman's aspirations as entirely pragmatic; she was interested only in character parts. It occurred to him to wonder why Honor troubled to be so nasty about her.

He was to discover that Honor was like a force of nature. "Take me home," she coaxed, when they left the bar.

"All right. I'll see if I can find a cab."

"Don't bother. We can walk. I just live over on Christopher." She had linked one arm through his and reached around to hold it with her other hand so that her body was half turned to his, his hip and thigh moving against her stomach. "You know, I'd love to have you come up with me—for a nightcap."

"Thanks, but I better not." He had wanted to pull away from such close proximity to her body, but could not decide how to do it.

"Scared of your wife?"

He looked at her, startled. "Why do you say that?"

"Why don't you want to accept my invitation?"

"Honor, it's late. We're both a bit wound up, but I'm tired, and tomorrow's another day."

She removed her hand from his arm and faced front, striding out rapidly. "In that case, the sooner we get home the better."

Alex stretched his legs to keep up with her, wondering what her peculiar emphasis could mean.

"Good evening, Andy," Honor said brightly to the doorman. She led Alex rapidly to the elevator and pressed the door-closing button as soon as they were inside. Then she sank to her knees, reached for the zipper on his trousers and pulled.

He had stepped back and looked down at the top of her head. She tilted her face sideways and smiled at him while her fingers reached through his flies. Then he saw only the shiny top of her dark head. As she made contact, he gasped and closed his eyes.

Still dizzy when they arrived at her floor, he had followed her in a half daze. Once inside, he was sufficiently back in command of himself to be astonished at Honor's apartment. It seemed to belong to another order of existence. The windows were darkened by heavy drapes—daylight would be banished. All the furniture was cushioned and soft. Her bed, like a prop in an old movie, was draped in folds of some filmy, transparent fabric in pleated loops from the four tall posts, heaped with small, silk cushions trimmed with lace. He was sure the sheets would be satin.

Honor would remain forever in Ruth's memory as she appeared in that play. Her long hair loose on her shoulders, she wore a dress on stage that was made of some kind of clinging stuff in an electric blue shade that revealed even the contours of her nipples. When she walked, she swayed, and her arms looked more flexible than ordinary arms, in the way that a dancer's do. She never looked at anyone—on stage or off—directly. Always she tilted her head, and kept it turned a little away, so that her glance was sidelong, enticing, suggestive. Ruth had been unable to still her anxiety and her growing sense of helplessness.

CHAPTER FOURTEEN

In the midst of Ruth's worries over Alex and Honor, Dr. Gentry had emerged from his office one morning, smiling and holding out an envelope. "I have something for you, my dear. Cornelia isn't feeling up to it, and it would be a pity to waste it, especially since Alex is out so much lately."

"Thank you. What is it?"

"Cornelia's ticket to the theater for Friday night. Malcolm and I will meet you there. You will come, won't you?"

Ruth hesitated only briefly. She was tired of evenings alone when she wasn't wanted at the theater and very tired of the insidious jealousy that plagued her. "Thank you so much. I'd love to go. I'm sorry Mrs. Gentry isn't feeling well enough."

Dr. Gentry said, "She's no worse. but late evenings are really too much for her these days. As you know, we have season tickets, and we included Malcolm when he moved. So the two of us shall look forward to seeing you." Inside the envelope was a ticket for a revival of *The Glass Menagerie*.

It had been a memorable evening, not solely because of the performance. After the play, pressed together in the crowded doorway, Malcolm placed an arm across Ruth's back to help her through the crush.

"Did you enjoy it?"

"Very much! But it wasn't a happy sort of play. I feel a little foolish with my eyes all teary still."

Out on the sidewalk, Malcolm looked down at her with a serious expression. "Your eyes look as beautiful as ever," he said, and turned abruptly away to seek a taxi.

Ruth felt a shock that wasn't unpleasant. She was grateful for the street lighting that might disguise the flush she felt on her cheeks. She looked after Malcolm, but he was moving away from her, saving her from the necessity of a response.

Having broken free of the crowd, the doctor came up beside her. "Perhaps the greatest tragedy in everyday life is the hopelessness of unrealistic expectations," he said. "Williams is almost too good at depicting that." Ruth was still watching Malcolm, whose words remained in her ears, and for an instant was unable to grasp what his father was talking about. Then the old gentleman's genial smile helped her to pull herself together.

"Yes, but their hopes weren't extravagant or unreasonable. Those people were trapped in …" She groped for a way to explain her thought. "…a sort of cage—a genteel trap. They didn't choose it, and they had no way out. And they all were so brave, in a way."

Dr. Gentry nodded. "In a way that so many others are in so many other kinds of places." Someone rushing through the crowd emerging from the theater knocked into him. Dr. Gentry turned his head to look after the man, then shrugged and smiled at Ruth. "The past, either as heritage or as history, grasps nearly everyone with tentacles. Very few can break loose, and the women in that play never thought of trying," he said.

A taxi was approaching the curb. "Why don't you let Malcolm see you home without me? I'll walk over to the avenue and get a cab there. If you'll forgive me, that will get me home a bit earlier." He looked at his watch.

"Of course. And thank you again, so much, for this wonderful evening."

He kissed her on the cheek. "Nonsense. I'm glad you enjoyed it. Here's your cab. Good night."

"Your father wanted to go straight home," Ruth explained, climbing in.

"I was going to suggest that myself," Malcolm said. "He likes to get back to Mother as quickly as he can. How about a nightcap?"

"Well, I don't …"

"Where to?" the cab driver asked, without turning his head.

"The Carlyle," Malcolm directed. To Ruth, "All right?"

She had nodded uncomfortably, suddenly unnaturally aware of their isolation together. She was glad of the noisy motor, the sound of horns tooting, and the raucous music on the radio up front with the driver, all of which seemed to make conversation unnecessary.

She tried to get a look at Malcolm's profile in the shifting light and dark in the interior of the rattling cab. He was sitting rigidly, his torso tilting jerkily as the taxi jolted and swerved. With his chin lifted and his erect posture, he looked as if he were preparing for an ordeal. Ruth shifted on the sticky seat, trying to relax. She could think of nothing to say. They endured their lurching transport in silence, like prisoners. Though he hadn't moved, Malcolm suddenly seemed to be taking up all the space and too much of the air inside the squalid enclosure. Ruth took a deep breath, and tried to let it out silently.

At the hotel, the maitre d' showed them to a table in a corner, out of sight of the spotlighted piano. In the welcome dimness, Malcolm leaned toward Ruth, and then reached across the table. Without thinking, she placed her hand in his, as instinctively as she might have given her hand to a relative or her best friend. The warmth of his grasp, and its pliable strength seemed like comfort, like water to a thirsty plant. She looked at his eyes, and saw his expressions was serious, even mournful. She wondered if it was the light, or rather the lack of it, that gave his face such a shadowed look, that made his eyes look sunken. A waiter approached, and Malcolm released Ruth's hand, looking away to give their order. Ruth asked for coffee. Malcolm ordered Irish Mist for her as well. As they waited, she glanced around the room as if trying to memorize the faces at each table, as tongue-tied as a fourteen-year-old on her first date. Malcolm, whose eyes she could not meet, was as silent as she. They sat like a couple who had quarreled.

When the liqueurs and coffee were brought, and the waiter had retired, Malcolm picked up his glass.

"Thank you for coming," he said gravely. "Here's to—to friendship."

Ruth touched her glass to his, and met his look. His lips smiled slightly. His poignant expression touched her as if she had caught him in tears. They each took a sip from their glasses.

"I hope you like French songs from between the wars," Malcolm said, after a long pause, nodding in the direction of the piano.

"Of course." She sipped again. The smoky sweetness lay on her tongue with a savor unequaled by anything she had tasted before.

The small dance floor was crowded, and Malcolm turned to look at the people. When he faced Ruth again, his smile was happier. "Will you dance?"

He was taller than Alex, his body more angular. The pressure of his arm was delicate, its springy touch holding her carefully slightly away from him, as if to deny the intimacy of their positions.

Once they surrendered to the movements of dancing, their tension faded, and they began to talk. She remembered nothing they said, yet she knew they shared memories and theories, politics and humor, everything except the Vietnam conflict and the future. Neither mentioned aspirations or plans. Ruth finished her coffee and liqueur. Malcolm offered another drink, then waved the waiter away when she refused, and they continued their conversation. Words flowed from them as freely as if they shared a past.

When they had looked up at the hovering waiter much later on, they noticed for the first time that the piano was silent, and they were the only patrons left. They hurried away, arm in arm, smothering embarrassed laughter. Out on the street, Ruth tried to see her watch under a streetlight.

"Do you realize what time it is?"

"It has to be pretty late for them to be closing the place down, but why worry? It's Friday, and neither of us has to go to work tomorrow." He looked into Ruth's face. "I'm sorry. Are you tired?"

She shook her head. It had surprised her to find that she was not. When they left the theater, she had thought she wanted to get to bed as soon as possible. Now she had energy as in her college days, when she had been able to stay awake till daylight.

She wanted more time to speak of more things, to discover more of her companion and his thoughts, to reveal more of her own. Her mouth was full of words, and she wanted to go on releasing them—that was how it seemed to her—releasing them, like captive birds. She had a vision of their words like a cloud of starlings, whirling and darting out of sight over rooftops.

Out on the street, Malcolm said, "Excuse me for talking too much and keeping you out so long. Let's go on over to Madison. Maybe we can flag a cab." Malcolm offered his arm with a smile, and she took it.

At her building, she had held out her hand. "Thank you, thank you for a lovely evening." She smiled, to banish the gravity of her tone. "I enjoyed the theater, and the dancing. Please, don't get out. I'll see you soon." She opened the door of the taxi, jumped out, and ran up the steps. As she fumbled in her bag for the key, she heard him call good night before the taxi drove away.

She opened the apartment door as silently as she was able. In the light from the one lamp she had left on when she went out, she could see that Alex wasn't home. For a moment she stood looking all around the room, as if he might be hiding in some shadowy corner. She looked at her watch. Well after two. She hung up her coat and sat down on the couch to wait, determined not to dwell on where he might be.

Deliberately she had reviewed her evening, and realized that Malcolm had not said a word about Darla, or even about his daughters. The talk had been the sort one has with an appealing stranger without thought of secrets—full of revelations of attitudes and tastes, devoid of any intimations about the near past. Yet he had spoken of his childhood, of trips with his parents, of some of the more colorful Irish maids that had served in his parents' house, of how he had become fond of sailing, music, and mountains. It was as if she had just met a man who had no commitments, and only a happy history.

And that was the way she had responded. Much of the time she had described Devonport, the favorite pieces of furniture in her home, the times she remembered best with Dan. And Nathan's funeral. They had talked about the problem of knowing one's parents, and trying to understand them correctly. They had laughed over their embarrassments as adolescents, and their pet peeves.

Finally Ruth had undressed and gotten into bed. She had fallen into a restless sleep, hearing every traffic sound, and once she waked fully to hear cats howling in the garden. Later, somewhere a siren wailed, and she had opened her eyes to weak light filtering into the room from the window. Dawn was breaking, and Alex had not come home.

⁌ ⁍

The next morning Nettie came in to see Ruth. She said without preamble, "What are you going to do about it?" She was standing with her legs apart, her back to the window, arms akimbo, tilting her head to keep the smoke from a lighted cigarette sticking out of one corner of her mouth from drifting into her eyes. Her fierce squint, the pose, her black slacks, and the turban made her look like a Disney pirate.

Ruth sat in the wing chair, chin resting on her clasped hands. She looked at the floor, as though she might find some answer in the pattern of the carpet. She was afraid to try to speak.

After a silence, Nettie moved from the window to knock ashes off her cigarette. She sat on the edge of the couch. "I know, Red. It's really none of my damn business, is it?"

Ruth said, "No. I don't feel like that. I don't know, is the answer. I couldn't believe it the first time, I told you. He sent me home by myself, saying he had to 'go over' some things with Honor. Now I don't …"

"Do you believe that name?" Nettie broke in.

Ruth smiled. "I guess so. She's English, though she grew up in Short Hills. Anyway, what can I do? Heaven knows, a scene wouldn't have helped the—at least not there. And he isn't around enough for me to find a chance to have one here, even if I could face it." She shivered.

"You want me to ask around? See if I can get a line on this broad?"

Ruth had straightened up, and looked at Nettie's earnest face. "I don't know. I don't know even what I feel really, let alone what I want to do." She got up and went to the window, looked down on the little garden, where she could see the bright red of geraniums in pots. Without turning, she nodded. "Yes," she said with sudden firmness. "Yes, I think I would like to know about her." She was consumed with curiosity and fear in about equal parts. She went back to her chair. Nettie watched. "Yes, I want to know everything about her." She began to rub her hands together, as if they were cold. "If I have enough—information—maybe I'll find her weaknesses, or worse, maybe even that she doesn't have any. I won't go and watch them anymore. I've already seen three performances." She pressed both hands to her face, then pulled them back and up, stretching the skin on her cheeks and around her eyes. "I don't know what I'm going to do, but maybe if I find out enough—if I can see inside her a little, maybe it'll help me decide."

"Well, kiddo, I'll be here if you need me." Nettie was stubbing out her cigarette. "In the meantime, I'll put out some feelers and see what I can come up with." She started for the door.

"Thanks," Ruth said, in a voice that betrayed how weary she was. "Oh, Nettie, here." She went to the desk and picked up the folder of poems. "Thank you for letting me read them. They're terrific."

"Glad you like them." Nettie saluted with the folder, and let herself out.

∞ ☙

Even later, when the same thing happened again, Ruth had been unable to explain to herself what kept her silent. She had said not a word to Alex, but behaved as though it were perfectly normal for him to spend an occasional night away from home.

The first time, she sensed his apprehension when he came home for dinner the following evening, and she decided coldly to let him squirm. It gave her some pleasure to see him struggling with conscience, or perhaps only curiosity about how she was going to react. After that, with a queer twist to his lips, he, too, behaved as if nothing unusual had happened and kept as silent as she.

Thinking back on that time, she wondered what excuse he might have given, or whether he would have told the truth, if she had asked. In retrospect, she realized with considerable chagrin that she had been cowardly, as if by pretending all was well, she might avoid facing facts. If only she could go back and try another tack, the outcome might have been forestalled. She said to herself that she shouldn't be a fool! *You can't go back, ever—there's only one direction in life.*

∞ ☙

As weeks went by, and the play finally closed, still Ruth had said nothing. A sort of ritual seemed to develop in mutual avoidance of the issue. They were both behaving as though committed to a pattern of tacit acceptance. Alex stayed away several times, always without any attempt at an excuse. The worst thing about it for Ruth after the first shock was that she saw that each time it became less uncomfortable for him. How much time would it take for him to get used to it, as if silence gave consent? What if *she* became accustomed? What then?

After her conversation with Nettie, Ruth began to frame a resolve. It might take a long time, but she thought she knew what to do. She would wait. The suspicion did come to her that this might be a form of weakness, but she rationalized by thinking that a person gains strength gradually, through exercise and determination. She would need practice to gain equilibrium. She would give herself time. If she were strong enough, she could somehow vanquish Honor.

In her mind's eye she had seen the clouds that raced above the harbor at home, gulls riding the gusts, and tossing about almost as if they were afloat on water. Up on the cliff, one could see them at eye level sometimes, their yellow eyes looking into the human ones until they turned their serpentine necks away, and tilted their wings to bank and slide downward in the air. Tossed and buffeted though they were, they were never wholly out of control. The strength and balance of their skill enabled them to use the invisible currents so that only the most violent storms could threaten them. In her apartment in New York, Ruth had yearned for some earthbound equivalent of wings.

One afternoon, shortly after she came in, the telephone had rung. She had been brooding, and she reacted slowly, as though she had just awakened. She fumbled with the receiver.

"Hello, Ruth. Is this a bad time?"

"Oh, Malcolm. No, of course not."

"I wonder if you ... please don't think I'm being, well, presumptuous, but I wondered if we could arrange to meet again, maybe for lunch, or for a drink, or ..."

"Is anything wrong?" Ruth asked.

Malcolm cleared his throat. "Well, not exactly. I'd like to have a talk with you, if you can spare the time."

"Yes, well, I have the time certainly." How should she deal with this complication? "When would you like?"

"The sooner the better."

The empty apartment seemed suddenly oppressive. Impulsively she asked, "Would you like us to meet for dinner tonight?"

"Tonight? That would be great!" He didn't ask where Alex was. After they made arrangements, Ruth wondered if she could carry off a social evening in her present state of mind. But if Alex were to find her missing, perhaps he would stop and consider his own behavior.

She went to wash her hair. Standing under the hot water calmed her. Even the pace of her thoughts slowed as the bathroom filled with steam. For the first time in several weeks, she thought with pleasure of the hours ahead. Only a moment's concern about Alex's reaction if he returned to find her out interfered with her anticipation. She firmed her lips. Fleeting shame at her desire for a small revenge failed to spoil her mood.

It was not until after the meal that Malcolm had spoken of the reason he wanted to see her so urgently. "I wanted you to know that Darla and I are not going to be reconciled. We're going to get a divorce." He spoke without visible emotion.

Ruth said, "I'm very sorry. It must be terribly difficult to go through that." Thoughts of the New York state divorce laws raced through her mind. She wondered what they could claim for grounds and who would bring the action. She felt dizzy from the strain of keeping silence about her own situation.

He went on, "Thank you for letting me talk to you about it. I don't mean to burden you, but I'm grateful for your ear. The greatest difficulty right now is the girls. They don't get it, naturally. I wish I thought Darla would be fair about me with them, but I guess that's unrealistic."

"Oh, surely she wouldn't …" Ruth hesitated, wondering what Darla wouldn't.

He gave her a wry grin. "Oh, but she would! It doesn't occur to her, you see, that there could be any harm in embroidering, or bending the facts." He shook his head. "She doesn't really have an imagination. If it feels good, she does it. The only consequences that trouble her enough to think ahead about are social ones."

"I'm sorry," Ruth said again. How unsatisfactory that was! "But surely the girls are close to you?"

Malcolm made an impatient gesture, his brow furrowed. "It's true enough, but it won't cut any ice in court. The reason I wanted you to know is that—I thought, I wanted to explain to you how it's been. Mother and Dad are great, but they will always feel that I'm at fault for not forcing Darla to stay, for not insisting on keeping our household intact, at least until the girls are grown. There just isn't any place in their philosophies for my hope that there might be time for me to make a new start. They really just want me to patch it up, repair the damage, and get on with my marriage." He shook his head again, then raised his eyes to Ruth's. "Do you understand how I feel?"

She had noticed the subtle emphasis he placed on the first pronoun. She nodded slowly. "I think I do." She felt her face getting hot, but went on. "I can imagine how it would be to find yourself with a wife who's no longer a friend." She hesitated, then added, "But perhaps that's something she never was." She would not have said that, if not for her memory of the dinner party.

Malcolm gave her a searching look and said, "Exactly so." There was an awkward pause as they then avoided each other's eyes. Ruth saw Malcolm's hand on the stem of his glass, turning it slowly around.

She murmured, "I wish you all the best. I hope you'll be—that it will work out for you the way you hope."

His lips moved in the faint beginning of a smile. "Ruth, forgive me for asking, but how is it that you're free tonight? Is Alex away?"

She had felt jolted as though she hadn't been waiting all evening for the question. She tried to make up her mind what to say. *How remarkable,* she thought, *the things one can carry in one's mind, and push out of sight as if they didn't exist.* Suddenly she had seen how risky a position she was in with Malcolm, but the aftermath of their previous evening together had been a feeling of safety after the initial chilly tension. She had felt warmth, the security of friendship. Only then did she begin to acknowledge to herself the possibility of a broader emotion. Looking at him, she saw the same melancholy expression she remembered from before and decided to tell him the truth.

"I don't know where Alex is tonight. The truth is that he's been behaving oddly for quite a while. That night I went to the theater with you and your father, he never came home."

Malcolm murmured something, and she continued, wanting to tell it. "I know who he's with, or I'm pretty sure. I don't know where. For some time he's been—taken—with an actress." She looked up, but Malcolm said nothing. "She's very striking." Flatly, she said, "I'm positive he's involved with her."

Malcolm's expression was shocked. "Lord, Ruth! How could he? What are you going to do about it? You don't have to stand for that sort of ..."

"No, I suppose I don't. But I haven't made up my mind really about what to do." She felt enormously relieved to be speaking. "Right now I'm not prepared to do anything. Maybe it will—maybe he'll get over ..."

"You can't be serious! What good is any change after this?" Malcolm was frowning, drumming on the table with his fingers. "I can't believe he'd treat you this way."

"You know," she said musingly, "I don't believe he's thinking of me at all. It's as if this woman had taken over his whole attention. I'm just beginning to come to terms with the whole situation." She shook her head. "Would you believe we haven't even discussed it?"

"Let's get out of here." Malcolm got up abruptly, and pulled Ruth's chair out for her.

She had risen obediently and followed him out. They found a taxi, and Malcolm gave his father's address. Ruth became nervous again. "I should really get home. If Alex ..."

"Let him stew, if he does. We'll have a nightcap and then I'll get you home." He took her hand, and held it tightly. They rode in silence. Ruth had felt as if she were afloat in some element unfamiliar to her. None of her usual responses seemed available or appropriate in her state of exhausted, passive suspense. She rested her head on the back of the seat, and closed her eyes.

In the Gentry living room, Malcolm carried a snifter to her, and sat beside her on the settee with his own in his hand. A scent of polish, rose petals, and leather spiced the air. The room had an atmosphere of fastness, as if it were impervious to ugliness in any form. Malcolm, his shapely hands curled around the brandy glass, dressed in tweed, might have been painted into the scene, Ruth thought, like a model in an advertisement.

"I have to make a selfish confession to you," he said, looking down into the amber liquid in his glass. "We've known each other for how many years now? More than ten, anyway. I've admired you through all that time. Now that I'm getting to know you …"

Ruth had interrupted in a soft voice, "Please, don't say anything more now." She set her glass on the coffee table, and looked at Malcolm's profile. He turned his head to catch her eye.

He spoke urgently, though quietly. "I'm going to say it now, because there's no need to wait. Now that I'm getting to know you, I see even more clearly how much there is to admire in you. Please don't look away. We're grown people, Ruth, with some life behind us, it's true, but there's a lot ahead of us. I want to say that …" He paused, his gaze penetrating and insistent, holding hers. "I want to say that this may be the perfect time to see if we could take advantage of our mutual—disarray, and look for a new future. I don't know how, what form it might take. But please, I implore you, gentle Ruth, think about making a new start. Something pushes me toward you …" He stopped, reached for her hand and stood up. "And perhaps you toward me. Don't try to give an answer now. Just think about it." He walked away several steps and looked down at the rug, rubbing his chin with one hand.

She sat motionless and speechless, watching him. Her bruised ego was soothed by his words, but she feared a new involvement. While she craved his sympathy and the affection visible in his attitude, she doubted her own mind. He stood in the center of the hearth rug with head bent. The affinity she had felt the night of the play had remained with her, but she sensed the threat to her personal stability, as if she were in danger of stumbling over a precipice. She took up her glass, and swallowed some of the fragrant brandy.

"Forgive me for surprising you." Malcolm spoke in the voice one might use to a child, frightened by something strange. "It's just that it seemed like providence, that we find ourselves as we do at this moment." He walked over to her, and placed a hand along her cheek, looking down on her intently. Then he straightened. "I'll take you home now."

CHAPTER FIFTEEN

After her dinner with Malcolm, Ruth had felt as if she were in a current tugging at her, carrying her toward shoals she could not see, but knew were hazardous. From time to time, Alex seemed to regain some of his energetic enthusiasm; he even talked to her again sometimes as if nothing were wrong between them, and her sense of danger would be lulled. She tried to take a spurious refuge from the facts of their relationship by pretending nothing had changed. Still, the weight of all that hadn't been said imposed an artificiality on every exchange.

Though he still kissed her good night, Alex no longer cradled her in his arms. If he did begin to caress her, she felt her joints turn as stiff as if she were carved out of a single piece of wood. Her thoughts would boil to the surface when he tried to make love to her. Jealousy and anger turned her stony. When she rolled away from him and turned her back, he took his hands from her, and they lay rigidly separate, like strangers.

Ironically, their continuing life together became bearable for Ruth because of Alex's frequent absences on business or without a stated reason. When he was gone, she did her best to concentrate on the mechanics of daily life. She went through the motions without being aware of what she was doing unless her full attention was necessary, as it was in the office. Even there, she often found herself morbidly trying to picture just what particular blandishments Honor might be using to tether Alex to her. Sometimes, usually in the night, she would be amazed at the fertility of her imagination and she would struggle to banish mental images that shocked her, though not another soul would ever know what they were.

Nettie came in occasionally and brought grapevine reports on Honor. She tended to adopt a matter-of-fact tone when passing on information. "Honor and Harry Offenbach founded the Castoffs. They were an item for two or three years. Randy as goats. You know, anybody who knows Honor knows she's a pro when it comes to erotic frills. She's notorious, Red. They tell stories about how she likes to set the stage, as you might say. Don't think about her."

Ruth flushed. "I try not to."

"Why should a lady like you give one tinker's damn about a trollop her friends made up a rhyme about?"

"Rhyme?"

"Sure. The people who know her best. Listen to this:

There was a young lady theatrical,
Could send a man's brains on sabbatical.
Mid incense and veils, Salome pales
When compared with this vamp fanatical."

Nettie finished with an evil wink and leer. Ruth tried to smile. Nettie had added grimly, "You can't do much, you know. When a man takes that kind of bait, you just have to wait for him to feel the hook. And he will, in the end." She gave one of her elaborate shrugs. "Right now, it's up to you. You want to hang in there, or cut loose?"

Ruth couldn't look Nettie in the eye. She had not made up her mind to do anything decisive, nor could she summon the courage to admit even to her friend that she was still in love with her husband.

She didn't tell Nettie about Malcolm. Some instinct stopped her, as if even such an acknowledgment might make a still doubtful outcome inevitable. In the depths of her mind, she clung with a stubborn determination to the notion that if she were sufficiently brave, persevering, loyal, Alex would come around. She loved him; he knew how completely she belonged to him. He would have to respect that bond, if she refused to allow it to break!

It had not occurred to her that he might be humiliated if his affair were to end, and thus unable to face her, even if he wanted to. She continued to flounder. Between Malcolm's phone calls, she tried to comprehend her own motives. Her marriage was her lifeblood. She would not let it go!

At the same time, she lacked strength to refuse Malcolm's sympathy, which she found comforting in a way Nettie's would never be. She had come to depend on his obvious admiration to bolster her faltering self confidence. She even sometimes ached for the touch of his hand or his gentle farewell embraces. Twice she put him off when he asked her to meet him because she needed to prove to herself that she could resist what she was beginning to want so badly.

She had begun to feel that all the threads of her life were fraying. Dr. Gentry said nothing to her about Malcolm's marital problems, but in the office, he seemed weary and preoccupied. Ruth was concerned about the fact that she had to remind him of appointments—a new thing in her experience. She knew he fretted over his wife's health and seemed often to have his mind on things other than his day-to-day commitments. When she was not too preoccupied with her own concerns, she worried about him.

One evening when she opened the mailbox, she found a note from Malcolm.

> Dear Ruth, I have moved into my own apartment. Forgive my putting it this way, but I need to see you.

He added his address and phone number and signed it only with his initials. She hid the note in her wallet, her wrist weak with emotion.

When Alex came home that night, she could see he was agitated, distracted. He could not sit still, but paced to the window where he looked blindly at the darkness beyond the mirroring glass, then went to the bookshelf where he stood, hands in his pockets, as if examining titles. He paced back to the window again.

Ruth continued getting their meal, trying to remain calm, but she was aware of his every move with growing nervousness. He was more restless than she had ever seen him before, even at the time he left Jerry.

"What's wrong?" she had asked at last.

He had been standing at the window, his back to the room. He didn't answer, but his shoulders tensed visibly. After what seemed to be an interminable wait, he turned to face her. All his usual grace seemed to have disappeared; his movements were abrupt and jerky.

"We can't keep this up." His voice, normally strong and resonant, was thin and nasal.

Ruth came out of the kitchen, wiping her hands on her apron. She was trembling. "I know."

Alex followed her to the couch, where she sat and looked up at him. He stood over her, bent slightly at the waist. "I'll move out."

"No!" Her sharp word, spoken out of reflex and instinct, had caused a change in his face. She saw a shadow that looked like fear; his eyes shifted so rapidly that she couldn't catch his glance. She tried to add something. "I think we should ..."

He burst out, "Red, you're off in a world of your own! You can't expect me to believe..." He broke off and began to walk back and forth in front of her, gesturing as he talked, his voice guttural now, and low, as if he were afraid of shouting. "Don't you know what's happening? Don't you want to know where I am when I'm not here? I'm having an affair!" He stopped and turned burning eyes on her. His expression was truculent. "I've been cheating on you!" He glared at her fiercely, spacing his words deliberately, harshly. "I've been sleeping with somebody else!"

He paused, but Ruth said nothing, felt nothing except a hollow sensation in her stomach. Now that the fact was verbalized, she waited for emotion to shake her. Instead, she discovered she was numb.

Alex raised his voice. "Do you expect me to go on living here? What do you think? That if I have a bed here, I'll be ready to come back home like a naughty child, ready to take my punishment, or something?" He put his hands on his hips and glared at her, his handsome face distorted by emotion. "Well, don't hold your breath!" His tone turned venomous. "You must be crazy! I'm sorry—sorry, but we're through! You and I are ... " He had made a slicing gesture "... finished!" He turned away, resuming his nervous, aimless motion. "No excuses. I've made a wreck of our marriage. I admit it, but it's ruined now—beyond repair." He had kept rubbing the back of his neck, as if it were stiff. He turned toward Ruth again and halted.

"We're going to have to face it. All these weeks without a word—Christ, I can't believe it!" He resumed his pacing. "God, no one but you would have kept quiet when ..." He spun on his heel to face her again. "How can you be such a damned icicle? I guess it was knowing—knowing how Goddamned *orderly* you'd be that kept me quiet too, made me go along with it. I didn't have the guts to face ... Well it's an impossible way to live! Christ, even *you* must see that!" For an instant she thought he was finished, but then he added, almost inaudibly, "You can have a divorce."

The word had seemed to pierce Ruth physically, the first real reaction she was aware of. She sat still on the couch, her back straight, hands folded in her lap. She watched Alex's movements with a sort of concentrated attention, as if she could derive some crucial hidden signals from them. There was a long silence, broken by the sounds of his steps passing from wood to the carpet and back to bare floor.

At last, she spoke, formally, as if she had been handed a gift. Her voice had seemed to belong to someone else, as it had when she accepted his marriage proposal. "Thank you, but I think I'll refuse your offer." Alex opened his mouth, but she continued, cutting him off, her voice strengthening as the words came. "We're fortunate not to have to make any decisions in haste. We have no children. We both have jobs. We're free." She looked up at him as he passed in front of her without looking at her. "I'm free," she said with wonder in her voice. "Maybe I was a fool. I thought marriage was a permanent state. Well, I'm not ready to enter some other situation even more permanent right now. Not now." When he tried again to interrupt her, she continued with measured emphasis, discovering what she wanted to say as she was saying it. "I'm not sure what's in our future, yours and mine, but I'm not ready to close off any options, at least not yet."

Alex halted, legs apart, staring at her. "My God! You want me to stay here? You must be out of your mind! Well, I won't. I'm leaving." He strode to the closet and pulled out a suitcase. He opened it and threw it on the bed.

"Alex," Ruth said, "she's very—alluring, I guess is the word." She continued as he went back and forth from the dresser to the bed with clothes in his hands. "I understand that. But she's not—she doesn't have any—she's ruthless. She won't stick with you. She'll hurt you, Alex."

Fury transfigured his face. "What the fuck do you know about her?"

Ruth quailed inwardly. "I know enough to be afraid for your sake."

Alex stopped thrusting shirts and underwear into the case. He stood for a minute, trembling slightly. Then he growled, "You sanctimonious bitch!" He finished packing in silence, though he was breathing heavily as if he had been exercising hard. Ruth was still sitting silently, adamant, numb, hopeless, eyes riveted to him, when he turned in the doorway with several suits tossed over his arm, still on their hangers, and set down his suitcase so as to reach into his pocket for keys, which he tossed onto the bed. Then without another word, he turned and slammed the door behind him.

Silence had pressed on her like something physical, in the form of a sound in her ears as if shells were cupped over them. She unclenched her fingers with an effort. All sense of time passing was gone. After a long while, she rose and went back into the kitchen. Moving slowly and precisely, she scraped the food she had been preparing into the garbage, washed the pans, wiped the counters, hung up the towel and her apron. The church clock struck in the next block. Eight.

She had found herself moving in air that felt thick, like swimming in cream, slowing every gesture and step. Her vision was narrowed like a driver's at night when constricted by the headlights' beams. She noticed how dark it seemed. She turned on the rest of the lamps.

Maybe if I put down on paper some of this, I might be able to order my thoughts better, she thought. She sat down, laid a pad in front of her, held her pen. She found she could not write a word. She meticulously put away the stationery, arranged the pen and blotter on the desk, settled a picture frame precisely in relation to the edge, and stared at it. Every move seemed to require great effort. After many more minutes, she got up from her chair, took her coat and purse from the closet and went out.

On the street, she began to walk rapidly, as if she knew where she was going. She went down into the subway, boarded a train and sat blindly in the din, unaware of passing stations, grateful that at that hour she needn't swing from one of the overhead handholds like a boat moored in a storm. While her eyes failed to register what passed in front of them, her mind seemed to have turned itself off, leaving a kind of distorted after-image of the scene with Alex, so that she kept seeing his face and gestures, hearing again some of his words, but was unable to remember others.

Without noticing the station, impulsively she stood up at a stop and left the train. She climbed the ironclad steps, and was surprised to see, when she emerged, that she had traveled down to the Battery. She looked around at the railings of the park, the looming towers of the financial district, and the lights across the water in Brooklyn, Staten Island, New Jersey. As if she had intended to go there all along, she went to the ferry slip and bought a ticket. She breathed in the familiar smell of salt water, acrid diesel fumes, smoke from someone's pipe. She stood at the rail, blindly facing the bay. The wind off the water brought tears to her eyes as she watched the curving ranks of lights on an approaching ferry. When hers docked, she went through the iron gates and walked the length of the boat to the other end, to stand again in the full blast of the wind.

She remembered that ride as if it had happened to someone else, someone who stood in a bell jar, able to feel the vibrations under her feet, to hear the grumble of the huge engines, the sounds of whistle and bell, the voices of other passengers speaking to one another. In that shell, the crossing of the bay had stretched into a limbo time, the distance from shore to shore expanding as if she were still, and the wake raced away behind her.

She saw the black, oily water heaving and breaking into foam dotted with flotsam, the distant moving glitter of shore lights, but she was so detached from these things that she nearly fell when the boat abruptly thundered into the slip, thumping the pilings off-center and rebounding like some behemoth, groping for its lair.

When the motion stopped, she came to, came back to some realization of where she was. She looked around, smiled sheepishly at the ticket-taker, showed her return stub, and walked hastily to the other end of the boat, where she stood, staring back at the Manhattan skyline.

All at once she was cold, freezing. On the return trip, she sat shivering, huddled in a corner of the almost deserted cabin, squinting against the glare of unshaded bulbs and struggling to sit erect on the slippery curve of the wooden bench. She concentrated on a pair of teenage lovers outside, nuzzling each other and sliding their hands up and down each other's backs as they leaned over the rail. It had seemed important to remember the exact color of the girl's cerise scarf, the way the wind whipped locks of the boy's hair around his ears, the shape of his nose in profile. Her grasp of such details seemed as if they might signify her sanity.

She took a cab back home. She didn't remember going to bed, but the next morning she was as groggy and disoriented as if she'd been drugged.

CHAPTER SIXTEEN

Ruth had come to dread Nettie's righteous indignation, though she knew it was entirely in her favor. She was afraid Nettie might sway her, trick her somehow into making some irrevocable move she would regret. The sense of disorientation, of alienation was like being adrift in a tempest at night. She could be fatally shipwrecked at any moment.

When she was capable of thought, it was of Dan. Dan would receive her with open arms, wounded and utterly dismayed as she was. He would show sympathy and anger, but wouldn't try to influence her. But Dan was far away. How she craved the unquestioning support he would offer!

Looking in her handbag one day to find her pen in order to write to him, she saw Malcolm's note. As she read it again, the sight of his handwriting gave her a sudden lift, as if she had discovered a treasure she had forgotten. Carefully she set the note on the desk, leaning against the lamp. Then she sat down and wrote to Dan—a conversational, ordinary letter, like so many she had penned over the years. In a PS she told him without embellishments or explanation that Alex had left her.

℘ ☙

It was several weeks later when, with determined strides, Ruth had walked uptown. She felt safer in the open than underground. The air seemed fresher, and the night sky more luminous than she had seen them for a long time. The exercise refreshed her; she had begun to feel as if she were recovering from an illness.

Drawing a deep breath, like someone about to make a dive, she went into the lobby of Malcolm's building. A small self-service elevator stood waiting, its doors open to reveal scratched imitation mahogany paneling and a smudgy mirror.

When he answered her ring, Malcolm's tentative smile seemed anticlimactic. Ruth's nerves were strung so taut, she had been unconsciously braced. His apparent composure threatened to deflate her attempt at bravado.

"I'm glad you came," he said. He took both her hands and drew her close to him. Very gently he embraced her, almost as though he feared she might be fragile. His touch soothed her, and she began to relax.

"I've wanted to see you so much," he murmured against her hair. "Thank you for coming." He seated her on the couch. "I've made coffee, but maybe you'd like a drink."

"I'd love coffee, thank you." She stood up to follow him to the kitchen. "Let me help you."

"No, let me see if I can manage to be a proper host. I'll be right out."

She looked around the room, wondering how the conventions seemed so necessary regardless of the situation. She saw from the bland tidiness that this must be a furnished apartment. The pictures on the walls were trite prints of landscapes and one still life, framed in narrow gilded moldings. A student lamp stood on a writing table, but there was no desk. A Parson's table with a wire basket containing a pair of desiccated oranges defined the dining area. There were no books except for two in library covers on a table next to the easy chair. She noticed a Lucite-covered stack of stereo components next to the doorway into the kitchen, with a pile of records on the floor next to it.

When Malcolm had poured the coffee, they went through a period of being tongue-tied that reminded Ruth of the first evening they had spent together. While they seemed to have nothing to say, the atmosphere fairly bulged with unexpressed emotion like a storm cloud with rain.

Malcolm had seen her looking at the room. "No, it's not a home, but it will have to serve as one for the time being."

"I know." She looked directly at him for the first time since she had arrived. His face, lean to begin with, looked hollowed at the temples. There were shadows under his brows and cheekbones. His nose seemed larger and his lips wider than she remembered. These subtle changes in his face accentuated his thick, sun-streaked hair, and his fading tan. He looked almost the same as he had when she first met him, yet she realized that he had the aspect of someone who had been ill, or who had undergone an ordeal.

He said, "It's funny. When you make a big enough alteration in your life, you run into a hundred smaller ones that are part of it, that you didn't think about ahead of time. When Darla and I split, it wasn't so bad at first because I just moved to my old home again and because I was the one to make the decision. But I'm too old to share my parents' house, even as easy and undemanding as they are. I didn't think about the fact that most of our friends live in New Jersey, where we'd been all our married lives. I had no idea how much I'd miss the girls. Darla has moved and taken them to California. I thought the privacy you can find in a big city was just what I wanted, but I didn't reckon with the loneliness."

"I know," Ruth said again.

"What has made it even harder has been—it's been you." Looking hard at her, he added, "I don't mean just the contrast between a busy social life and none at all. I mean you as yourself. If we had seen more of each other sooner, I would have been talking to you like this much sooner."

"Oh, I can't imagine ..."

"No, I don't suppose you could. Forgive me. I can't keep it in my mind now that you were happily married. I saw so little of you with Alex over the years."

She feared he might question whether indeed she had been happy and was relieved when he didn't. She struggled to respond. "Well, he always traveled a good deal, worked long hours."

Malcolm broke in. "I didn't mean to bring him up. Dad told me about—your situation now. I just want you to know how much I've wished I could sit with you, talk to you." He stopped, looked away from her, then reached for the coffee pot.

She shook her head when he offered more. "I have a friend. She lives in our building. In fact, she's the super, and she's taken me under her wing. Way back when I was new in the city, she showed me the ropes and helped me out with everything. Now that this has happened, she's so incensed for my sake that I can't get her to look at my situation in perspective. But it means she provides all the sympathy I need." Ruth tried a brave smile, but her chin was stiff.

"It's hard to assess your own problems," he agreed. "But that's where another person's view ought to be a help, isn't it?"

"View, yes, but I'm afraid of being ... steered, right now. However kind the pilot's motives might be, it's not what I need. It's beginning to sink in pretty fast that I'm alone ..."

"No," he broke in, "you aren't that! Not unless you choose to be."

"That's just what I do choose. I've got to make my own decisions and stand on my own feet." The question flashed into her mind, *Then what am I doing here?*

"I'm sure you've always done that."

"Well, maybe I knew how once, but I think in recent years I've forgotten a lot of what goes into that kind of living." She looked away from Malcolm's eyes. The tension of her earlier mood was waning, and she found her mind beginning to work with the special clarity that comes occasionally when one expects it least.

All at once, she felt filled with insight and optimism. At the same time, she was aware that this was a temporary condition, and all her matter-of-fact caution hovered over the experience even as she was having it. Yet, here she was, however delayed, in response to Malcolm's note. Despite the fact that she was at sea among doubts, she felt calm and determined, at least for now.

She wanted to offer him an explanation. "Gradually I've begun to live by rote, sort of going through motions without thinking about them at all. Habits have taken over, even in how I react. I'd learned to make do. I understand that perfection isn't possible. But a jolt like this makes you wake up. Everything familiar takes on a new look, people included. It's a little like being very young again, with a lot to learn. I have to find out how not to be too scared to take advantage of that."

She smoothed the hair from her temples with both hands, stretched her legs, and leaned back against the cushions. "I've earned my living and enjoyed it. When I was a girl, I looked out for my brother and tried to be a proper daughter to my parents. But you know," she turned to Malcolm, "I don't think I ever learned ...what do I want to say? I never learned what the possibilities are. No, that's not it. I see how little I've accomplished. There's so much I should have been doing all this time! Oh, Malcolm, I'm sorry. I sound like a hazy adolescent." She felt a blush rising. "I think I'm beginning finally to have an idea of what sort of a person I might be able to be, if I set my mind on it. Do I sound mad?"

"You sound a little bit inspired." Malcolm reached for her hand, clasping it strongly. "You sound like a woman with so much to offer ..."

"Not now," she interrupted. "But the way I feel today, I hope that some day, maybe."

"Sooner than you may think," he said decisively. He let her hand go and rose. She could see by his uncertain steps away from her that he was anxious to speak and unsure of whether to do so. He put his hands in his pockets and paced slowly around the room. With an effort, Ruth studied him, pushing her own resolutions into the background. Patiently, she waited for him to say what was in his mind.

At last he spoke without looking at her. "Do you have any idea what it's like to have no available ear to understand anything you say? To live like an outsider in your own house?" He shook his head roughly. "Forget I said that. It's not fair to cut Darla up behind her back. You know," he turned to Ruth, "you're everything she isn't. And what makes me ashamed is that I didn't see it—not until it was too late. Oh, I don't mean I didn't understand Darla until now. I've known for years, but I ran out of patience to live like that any more. You mention possibilities. I know what you mean. Life's too short to ignore them." He ran his hand over his hair, shook his head like someone denying something.

She began to speak in agreement, but Malcolm continued. "Now Alice and Hazel have to pay part of the price of my blindness. I feel like a traitor." He stood with head bowed and his back to her. "If there's one thing I've learned in these last weeks," he said, "it's the futility of self-pity." He turned around, his face again suffused with sadness. "Failure's bad enough when it's your own, but God! When you drag others along with you, and you love them ..."

"Malcolm," Ruth broke in, "you mustn't let yourself suffer for what you can't help. You're not to blame! The girls are bright. Of course they'll have a hard time with this, but nothing they won't be able to handle, I'm sure. Think of how many children have divorced parents and live through it."

"But it's Darla too," he said miserably. "The years I took were, for her, the best ones. Someone like Darla cares so much for youth and elegance."

"But she isn't old yet, for goodness sake! She'll find someone else, and so will you."

"That's my problem."

"What do you mean?"

"I already have."

He was standing near the middle of the room. In the sudden silence traffic noises were magnified. The refrigerator came on with a muffled rattle. They looked at each other. Then Malcolm took the steps which separated them, reached for Ruth's hand and raised her to her feet. She stiffened automatically, but in a few seconds she rested her head against his chest and put her arms around his waist. She felt the long, hard muscles of his back through the cloth of his jacket. His breath was warm on her neck. She felt hairpins loosening as he embraced her. She raised her face and he met her mouth with his. They pressed together more tightly, in contact to their knees. She drew away from the kiss slowly, reluctantly, but continued to hold her lower body against Malcolm's lean frame. Pulling her head back so as to see him clearly, she studied his face, looking for a reassurance that she dared to surrender to his comfort, his warmth, his maleness.

"Should I apologize?" he asked softly.

Slowly she shook her head. The coil of her hair loosened, and she freed one arm to reach for it. Malcolm slid a hand up her back, felt for the remaining pins and slipped them out so that her hair fell down. She sighed, and he bent once again to her lips. Then he lifted her in his arms and carried her toward the bedroom. She lay against his chest with her head on his shoulder until he set her on the bed.

"Malcolm, what are we doing?" she murmured, but she could not summon resistance. He knelt beside her, and laid his head in her lap, his arms circling her hips. He spoke slowly and sedately, as if explaining something important. "If you're willing, we're going to practice the oldest natural healing in the world."

Ruth had found her mouth was dry. "I'm not sure ..."

"I'm sure for both of us." He bent and took off her shoes. Then he stood and began to take off his clothes. She watched him until he had removed his trousers. Then she, too, arose, and they finished undressing together.

The blinds were drawn so that the only light came from the open door into the living room. In twilight they had stood on opposite sides of the bed to turn back the spread, and looked at each other. Ruth thought how graceful the lines of his body were, elongated and angular, like those of a thoroughbred. With her hair falling over her shoulders, she felt like a young girl, but oddly without embarrassment. It had been as if she could sense what he was thinking about her lithe, slim body with its breasts more like those of a girl than the thirty-four-year-old she already was. She smiled.

It had been like slipping into feathers, rocking as if on waves of calm, deep water. Under her hands was silk and sinew—warm as embers—of shoulder and nape and groin, firm and moving, curling and molding and melting her own flesh, until the sense of time present was drained. Body and mind blurred, and she was tossed somewhere on the edge of dream until she fell into the abyss of release.

CHAPTER SEVENTEEN

When she got back to her apartment the next day, Ruth had found a letter from Dan. In it he urged her to divorce Alex, get a settlement out of him and forget him. Grateful though she was for his evident concern, her instinctive and instantaneous reaction was against his advice. He begged her to come for a visit and to stay with his family. She had considered it for an hour or so. In the end, she wrote back to thank him and to promise that she would be in Maine again in the summer, as was her custom.

There were to be other changes in her life. Dr. Gentry, increasingly distracted by his wife's failing health, was making plans to close his practice. Ruth's duties at the office began to comprise more and more details of sorting and packing attendant on his retirement. At another time, she would have been distressed at the imminent termination of her employment, especially given the close relationship she enjoyed with the Gentry family, but just then, the event seemed to fit remarkably well into her changed prospects. It pleased her to see that the doctor was eager to get on with his new plans. The result was that the last weeks in the office were scarcely tinged with regret.

Dr. Gentry did not talk about Malcolm, and Ruth hadn't mentioned him in her letters to Dan. To her mother, she wrote no details at all, only stating her intention of making a change. Without saying it, she had been depending on Dan to transmit the news of Alex's departure. She could not bring herself to discuss her own problems, but wrote about Dr. Gentry instead. She implied deliberately that she was going to take advantage of the end of her job because she craved a change. Yet the sense of Malcolm's presence clung to her, providing a comforting backdrop for the nebulous plans she was trying to crystallize for herself. She knew that if necessary, he would be there for her to fall back on, but the knowledge was an invisible prop. Often in her mind's eye was his face, his mouth smiling over the coffee cups, his long hand covering hers on the table. A stab of sensual memory would grip her like a cramp. She had not dared to picture Alex nor make comparisons. She couldn't get over her amazement that she could have such feelings for anyone—anyone except her husband.

> She wrote to Dan, I don't know just what the timing will be, but I hope to find a new job by midsummer. When I do and I know where I'll be, I'll let you know and then I'll come for our visit the way we—she crossed out 'we,' I always do.

She had been tortured by the question of whether she ever would go home with her husband again. The thought of never seeing his hair blown by the onshore wind had banished Malcolm's image immediately.

> I can't wait to see you and Lacey and the boys. You have no idea what a comfort it is to know that you're settled, busy, happy, and there for me to run to. And I promise I will, if need be. But I think, in time, there will be some obvious choice for me, if I have the patience to wait until I see what it is. Don't you think it's lucky that my changes seem to be coming all together? I feel as if I can look forward to a kind of complete new start.

She had raised her eyes to the window, gazing at the tracery of branches moving gently against the dirty brick walls. Her mind drifted, still liberated by lovemaking and the relief of sharing. She recognized the feeling as kin to what she had experienced almost thirty years ago, on the afternoon before she left for New York, when she had walked with Dan on the cliff, and they had listened to the twitter of the swallows dipping and swooping over the house—a sense of freedom and limitless horizons. How strange to have it now, at such a distance from where she had felt it first, and with disaster so close.

The remedy for her psychic discomfort had been the job. She was pleased and relieved see the optimism with which the doctor made his referrals, attended farewell luncheons given by old friends and colleagues. He arranged the long cruise he planned to take with his wife.

Ruth would arrive back at her apartment, wearied and satisfied, ready for Malcolm's call. The sound of his voice on the phone was enough to refresh her. They would often go out to eat, to talk, and at last, to return to his bed and the solace of each other's arms.

With a conscious effort, Ruth had pushed thoughts of Alex out of her mind. She took the photograph of the two of them off the table and put it in a drawer. It was like consigning her love to storage, ready to be returned to the light of day at her bidding. As if forcing herself to recover from an aberration, she refused to allow herself to brood anymore. She concentrated on each day with a sort of avarice, as though she might not be treated to another of equal value. She compared her emotional state to that of someone making every effort to recover from a serious illness. She quashed the murmurs of a conservative conscience. She allowed Malcolm to revive the conscious sensuality awakened by Alex, which had flagged in recent years. The taste of food or wine, the textures of skin and fabrics and fog, the resonance of a voice, or the timbre of a bell, all became noteworthy, memorable, evocative. She had pretended to forget how she had experienced those same sensations when she was first in love and newly married.

Nevertheless, she had been prey to doubts. Malcolm tried to reassure her. "We don't need to look ahead. Not now, not yet," he said once, as if reading her mind. "If what we have can help us both, we'd be foolish to throw it away. The future will show us what we should do as it unfolds." He had smiled, though his eyes were serious. "We need to have faith." And so Ruth tried to and found it not too hard.

Nettie's attitude was different. The forthrightness of her curiosity, her insistence on details, despite her friendliness, made Ruth begin to avoid her if she could. There was something about her uncompromising practicality that was too harsh for Ruth's state of mind at that time. Nettie expected her to move forward, full of purpose, with a clear goal in view. And there she was, trying to sail toward an unknown shore that was shrouded in mists of confusion, injured ego, and turbulent emotions.

"Have you been to a lawyer yet?" Nettie asked, brows arched, eyes narrowed.

"Not yet."

"What are you waiting for? You want him to make the first move?" Nettie never minded how impertinent she was.

"He said he wanted a divorce, Nettie, but I told you. I don't want to make any final decisions now." Ruth quailed under Nettie's piercing gaze. "There's no hurry."

"If you ask me, you're scared to take the bull by the horns, you should excuse the expression," Nettie had said. "It's not as if you didn't have somebody else."

"Nettie! That's none of your ... how did you know?" Ruth felt herself flush with embarrassment and anger.

Nettie looked at her over the flame of her cigarette lighter as she inhaled a huge cloud of smoke. "I've got eyes, kid. Sorry. I don't mean to be a nosy Parker, but I worry about you."

"Well, thank you, Nettie, but please, let me work myself out of this my way. I'll be fine."

"Okay, but I don't think you've figured out the first step. You don't have a clue how!" Nettie snapped.

Ruth felt guilty as she watched Nettie go out, the angle of her head telegraphing injured feelings. Yet she had clung to her privacy and even to her uncertainty. She told herself she was setting clear emotional challenges, the way an athlete in training would. She was choosing deliberately, to build mental muscle and psychic endurance.

Never a gambler, in those days, she seemed to crave risks, as if she could prove her intestinal fortitude. Practical decisions and concrete actions were not what she was ready for. Ruth was hoping for great change—in her work, perhaps in her abode, even in her way of living. She had to flex and train new emotional muscles. But how? Malcolm was her backboard, her bench, and her coach. A tiny nugget of apprehension lay under the cushion of her relationship with him, but she ignored it as resolutely as she could, while learning to turn her back on her recent misery.

One day, with the pages of the Sunday *Times* spread out on Malcolm's dining table, Ruth held a coffee cup in one hand as she read the classified real estate ads. She enjoyed trying to picture what was described.

"Doesn't this sound nice? 'Five acre plot, remodeled farmhouse on town road, three bedrooms, one and a half baths. Southern views over lake. Twenty-five thousand.' Or this: 'Hilltop contemporary, eat-in kitchen with fireplace and custom cabinets, privacy and convenience, only forty-nine five.' What do you think they mean by 'gentleman's retreat'?"

Malcolm looked around the section of the paper he was reading. He smiled at Ruth's studious pose. "Planning to move to the country?"

She turned in her chair to face him. There was a perceptible pause. Finally she said, "How I wish I could!"

Malcolm lowered the paper to his lap. "Do you mean it?"

"Yes!" She discovered it was true. "I've loved the city, but I've missed the country and all the nice things about it."

She got up and went to the window. The sunny street below was lined with cars at the curb, but had the deserted look of Sunday morning, without pedestrians or traffic. Trees were spaced evenly along the pavement, their leaves twisting in a light breeze. Open windows across the street showed curtains fluttering under raised sashes; sparrows were chirping and quarreling with the pigeons beside a cluster of garbage cans.

"Sometimes I want so badly to walk on dirt or grass. The park isn't the same. I guess most of all, I miss the sky at night."

"Maybe you're a bit homesick."

"Maybe, but I don't think I'd ever want to go back to Maine for good. I've been spoiled for the sort of isolation we had up there, much as I loved it years ago—still love it, for that matter. But I do wish ... Oh well, it's silly, I know."

"Ruth," Malcolm said quietly, "what do you plan to do? About the apartment, I mean. Do you intend to keep it?"

She turned from the window. "No. The lease is up in another five weeks. I don't want to stay there anymore. I've been trying to work up the courage to tell Nettie. I know I have to do it this week." She sat down at the table again. "I can't seem to decide to look for something else, though."

Malcolm crossed the room to her. He bent over and kissed the back of her neck. "Sometimes you seem almost dim," he said chuckling. "Now's the perfect time to move in here with me. You know I want you with me all the time." He closed his arms around her, and nuzzled her hair. "You know I love you."

"Oh, Malcolm, thank you." She struggled to turn from the embrace, pressing against the edge of the table with both hands. She was amazed at her sudden feeling of panic at what he was saying. Malcolm released her and stepped back.

She turned to face him. "You are so dear, but I don't want to." She stood up, rubbing her forehead with one hand. "I don't know how to explain it," she said as gently as she could, "but I think I need to get my feet under me somehow." She had looked at his troubled expression. "Oh, please forgive me. It's just that I can't let myself take an easy path only because it's the only one in sight. Do you know what I mean?" She walked back to put her arms around him. "You're so good for me. I just hope I am for you."

"Oh, my dear, you know you are! Better than anyone I've ever known."

At the back of her mind when she was with Malcolm had lingered the notion that if she were forced to put enough into words, she might eventually be able to figure out what she thought. His unquestioning sympathy enabled her to speak more freely than she ever had with another person, except to Dan. Malcolm had suggested that they might heal each other, and probably to a large extent, they had.

But she had to answer him. Her head was turned to the side, resting against his shoulder. He lifted her chin up with his right hand so that he could look into her eyes. "It won't be so long now. My divorce will be final before fall. Things go quicker in California. Then we can ..."

She was shaking her head slowly. "I can't. I can't yet. Please don't ask me. I have too much unresolved, too many problems we haven't talked about, and I don't want to talk about them yet." She pushed away from Malcolm's arms gently. "I don't have my mind clear." She tried a smile. "Maybe I never will, but I'm not ready to make any final moves now. Forgive me if I hurt you by saying this. I know you deserve better of me." She faltered. They had reached a turning point, she knew, and she saw as well that she had avoided the inevitable from the beginning.

"I understand," he had said, but she could tell by the tone of his voice that he did not. Indeed, how should he? She had felt swamped by guilt.

ಸಾ ಣ

Later, in her own apartment, she stood in the center of the large room, hugging her elbows. It was evening. Ruth could see her reflection in the dark glass of the tall windows as well as in the pier glass. A flood of recollections washed into her mind: the wicked laughing face of Francesco as he carefully adjusted the angle of the desk the day she moved in; Alex, reflected in the pier glass as he reached to pull her into his embrace when she came home from work; the sunlight falling across the table in the window while they ate Sunday brunch; the sounds of cats howling in the garden at night; the pear tree foaming with bloom in spring; Alex's low laughter in bed. She shivered suddenly.

Then, a bit grimly, she had gone down to see Nettie. "I've come to give notice that I'll not be renewing the lease." She cleared her throat. "I know you won't have trouble renting, but I want to give you plenty of notice."

Nettie had shown no surprise. "I'm sorry to see you go, Red." They were standing in Nettie's narrow entry, the light from the living room glowing in the background.

"Oh shit," Nettie growled, turning her back and walking away down the hall. "Come on in and sit down. I'll make us some coffee." Ruth followed slowly. Nettie spoke from her little kitchen. "You know, you don't have to be embarrassed about this. I don't blame you for wanting to get out of here. In your shoes, anyone'd want to do the same." She poked her turbaned head around the doorjamb. "Where are you planning to move to?"

"I haven't decided," Ruth admitted miserably. She felt foolish, childish, vexed. Nettie's matter-of-fact attitude emphasized her own lack of direction. She sat down on the couch among the vivid cushions to wait for the coffee.

"Are you going to be in trouble for money?" Nettie was as forthright as ever.

"No, I've saved a fair amount over the years. Since we have no children, we haven't needed to spend everything we made. Dr. Gentry is giving me a very generous severance settlement."

Nettie came and sat down next to her. She picked up her cigarettes and lighted one before she spoke again. "How much of a change are you looking to make?"

"What do you mean?"

"Well, are you thinking of just finding another job and another apartment and maybe another man—or are you thinking of going away to a completely new place and changing everything?" She cocked her head as she eyed Ruth with a critical expression. "You're lucky, you know, to be able to jump right out of the old life if you feel like it." Ruth looked down without answering. "I know you don't feel lucky, but think about it. Most women would be stuck if they were in your shoes. They'd have been entirely dependent on their husbands. They might have children to think about. They wouldn't have alternatives." Coffee aroma filled the air. Nettie rose and went into the kitchen. Ruth leaned forward, elbows on knees, chin in her hands. Her eyes wandered along the pattern in the rug. Little curlicues of royal blue and maroon twined around each other on a brownish background, leading into geometric tracings in black and dull gold. Medallions of a sort of bitter green, and leafy shapes in lighter blue and black and red were scattered across the center field. The lines and masses of the eastern design swam in her vision, dimmed and brightened.

She started slightly when Nettie set the tray down with a tinkle of spoons and china. Nettie held out a cup. Ruth sat up as if she were waking from sleep, and took it. She scalded her throat with the first swallow.

"Have you heard from Alex?" Nettie spoke as flatly as if she had asked if Ruth had seen the paper.

"Not since he came for the rest of his clothes." Ruth was proud of her calm. Where was the familiar rush of anxiety and misery she so feared? The thought that she might be adjusting already was, in a surprising way, as chilling as her previous despair.

"You better tell him you're giving up the apartment. He might think it's here to come back to some time."

"Nettie, I've got an idea." For the first time in weeks, Ruth turned to her friend, looking eagerly into her face. "Tell me if I'm crazy. You just said how lucky I was to have alternatives. I've just thought of a new one. I have enough saved to consider it, and I can work anywhere." She paused to sip cautiously at the hot coffee, and to give a second quick thought to what she was going to say. "What if I moved to the country? Say Connecticut or New Jersey or Long Island? Right out in the country?"

Nettie demanded, "What's in the country you don't have here?"

Ruth thought of saying, Memories, but instead, "Air and light and quiet," she blurted, "animals and birds and good smells!" She laughed. "Power failures and storms and mud in the spring!" She jumped up from her place on the couch. "I haven't seen dew since the last time Alex and I went up to see my mother—or fireflies!" She felt like dancing with excitement.

"Okay, okay, I get the message." Nettie's voice was as nasal and uninflected as always. "Just a country girl at heart. Thought I'd taught you how the other half lives, and you liked it well enough."

"Oh, Nettie, you did, and I did. I do! But I want to ... I don't know what I want to do, but something tells me I should try to get away from *here*. Things look very different when you see them in relation to the sky and the ocean and ..."

"So go. Maybe you'll let me come and visit." Nettie was smiling with one side of her mouth. Ruth recognized warmth in those odd eyes, despite the cynical expression on her friend's face. "You'll have to buy a car, you know. No subways in the Hamptons," said practical Nettie.

Ruth sat down again and drank more of her coffee. "Mm, I know. Used will be cheaper. Should I look for a rent, or will I have to buy something, do you think?"

"Maybe rent would be better, so you're not stuck if you decide it's not for you."

Ruth took a hasty gulp and set down her cup. "Thanks for the coffee, Nettie. I've got to get back and take a look at the paper, make some plans for next week. Thanks for the coffee, and the talk."

Nettie went to the door with her. "Good luck," she called as Ruth ran up the stairs.

CHAPTER EIGHTEEN

The following week, Ruth and Alex had met at a diner. Ruth had insisted on neutral territory. She and Alex faced each other across a sticky table set with the usual sugar jar, squeeze bottles, salt and pepper in a wire basket, and a flyspecked chrome napkin dispenser. A fug of cigarette smoke and frying oil made the air between them visible.

Alex fidgeted, tapping a spoon handle on the edge of a saucer. Ruth had to raise her voice over the clashing crockery, taped rock music, and shouted orders. It wasn't the best place to talk seriously, but had the advantage of complete privacy because of the ambient din. Having asked Alex to meet her, she knew it was up to her to speak first, but now she quailed inwardly. She kept asking herself how she could ever relinquish what they had? "Thanks for meeting me," she said at last. Alex cocked his head, craning toward her without lifting his eyes, indicating he couldn't hear. His lips were tense and he wore a faint frown. Ruth noticed that he looked thinner. She raised her voice. "It's just that ... I don't want to give you any surprises."

Alex examined the spoon in his hand and said nothing. Ruth didn't know how to go on. At last he looked up at her with brows arched. His eyes were hard; their only expression was one of inquiry. He remained resolutely silent.

She struggled on. "About leaving the apartment ..."

"You told me that on the phone," Alex said, looking down at the spoon again.

He was clearly going to do nothing to help her. "I know, but there's more. Dr. Gentry's retiring, and by the end of the month I won't have a job, so …"

His eyes jumped to hers. "Gee, Red, I never guessed. That's tough." He sounded genuinely concerned. "But you can get work without any trouble. You're a hell of a good secretary." His words broke through her attempt at self-possession, recalling how he had always been concerned for her, had offered support and warmth to which she had become so accustomed she had never before doubted him.

She collected herself as best she could, her hand trembling on the handle of her coffee cup. What had become of that Alex? "Well, that's the thing. I'm thinking of going away. I'm looking for a place outside the city."

She watched his face for a reaction. Once again, he was avoiding her eyes. Had he understood that she was giving him notice that the apartment would no longer be available unless he stepped in to pick up the lease? He looked puzzled and surprised, but then she saw he wasn't concentrating fully on what she was saying. He kept shifting his glance, looking around the coffee shop, then to the window and the people passing outside. Ruth's mouth felt chalky.

"Where are you going?" he asked finally.

She'd been expecting him to ask why she was leaving. "I'm not sure, but maybe Connecticut."

He straightened his back against the leatherette bench. With a movement of his chin like that of someone bracing for an ordeal, he cleared his throat and stared intently into Ruth's eyes. "Red, look, I've done what you wanted. I've been patient. It's time we got this thing settled. I want a divorce. If you won't give me one, I'll …"

That stinging word! Feeling her resolve harden again, Ruth struggled to speak calmly. "You'll what?" Before, when she had tried to defend herself, her words had sounded weak and ineffectual. Now she heard a note of challenge, though she had not intended it. "You need grounds, Alex." As she spoke, she wondered if he might know about Malcolm. No, it would never occur to Alex that she would become involved with another man.

She saw the muscles in his jaw moving under the skin as he strove to control his mounting anger. "Why, Red? Why not make a clean break?"

Why indeed? She shook her head slowly, looking into her lap, where she'd clenched both hands into fists. "Honestly, I can't answer that, except to tell you that I don't think it's the right thing to do." She stared at the remains of her hamburger on the plate in front of her: pebbly crumbs surrounded by congealing fat. "Not for either of us." Interrupting as Alex began to argue with her, she added, "I have only my instincts to go by." She raised her eyes as she lowered her voice. "And they're telling me not to make any hasty decisions."

He burst out, his eyes narrowed now and steely, "Hasty! For God's sake, it's been four months! What the—? What are you waiting for?"

For this to be over; for you to give me back my life! For you to love me again!

After a pause which neither seemed willing to break, Ruth managed, "How are things with—with Honor?" She tried to hide how she was searching Alex's face, aware of the risk she took with his temper.

His eyes turned opaque with emotion. When he spoke, his tone was sneering, and his voice trembled. "What do you mean, 'How are things?' Things are just fine." His cheeks, suffused with a deep flush, paled suddenly. A line showed at each side of his mouth, freezing his expression and giving his face a mask-like look.

"I'm glad for you," Ruth murmured.

Half rising, Alex suddenly leaned belligerently across the table and spat out, "Oh, come off it, Red!" He dropped back onto the bench, lowering his voice to a near-hiss, chin thrust toward her. "Don't give me that plaster saint crap! You know, you're beginning to get to me." His hand vibrated as he moved a cup out of his way. "I'm not proud of all this, but everything has two sides to it."

"You're absolutely right," Ruth interrupted. "That's why I'm insisting on taking time enough to figure both of them out, if I can. It's too soon. We're both too tense to talk sensibly." Seeing Alex about to interrupt again, she hurried on. "So I'm asking you to let me take my share out of our joint account. I'm going to use my savings and see about finding a place to live out of town. As soon as I'm settled, I'll let you know where I am."

"What the hell are you trying to do?" Alex's voice had risen again. "You want it all your way, don't you? Well take the damn money! I don't want your money! All I want from you is to get *loose*! Untie the fucking cord and go my own way!"

Ruth could scarcely believe how ugly that handsome face had become. She felt as if she were sinking in quicksand. It was hard to breathe, and her vision narrowed as if she were looking through a tube. She yearned to reach out to Alex, to grasp his hand, so he could pull her out of this morass, even while she knew she could do nothing of the kind. He would not save her. Yet she could not stem the tide in her very blood. Alex was the only one who could.

She shut her eyes, forcing herself to speak. "I know," she murmured. "Yes, I do understand. I promise to make up my mind as soon as I can." Her breathing was shallow, and she felt faint. She blinked, trying to clear her head. "But not yet!" She felt across the seat for her purse and then began to try to slide off the bench. She had to escape.

Alex closed his eyes. "I'm sorry. I swore I wouldn't lose my temper. Wait! Let's not leave it like this. I'm sorry!"

Ruth was shaking her head blindly, still maneuvering to get out into the aisle. "It's no good. I can't talk to you. I'll send you a note." Her words tumbled over each other. "We've been together for almost twelve years. You can stand a month or two more."

She stumbled out without another word, into the bright street, not noticing that she'd turned the wrong way to go back to the office until she looked up and noticed a street sign.

❧ ☙

Since that frustrating day in the luncheonette, time had slowed. The only ripples in it were her meetings with Malcolm. Then, with regret and rising spirits both, she had come away, to this venerable, sheltering little house, that had seemed from first viewing to open its arms and welcome her to the backwater where she might catch her breath, look back, and attempt to assess the rapids ahead. Surely, in time she would comprehend the lessons taught by those she'd already run, and even find a way to navigate serenely again.

CHAPTER NINETEEN

When Ruth first moved to Connecticut, Malcolm had called several times a week. Each time, Ruth heard his voice with a mixture of gratitude and chagrin. They talked as if she were away for a visit. He kept her up-to-date on the progress of his divorce, and she heard the note of fear and loneliness when he spoke of his girls. She missed him more than she'd thought possible, but was convinced they had no future together, mostly because she was unable to banish Alex from her inmost mind and heart. She also understood what Malcolm hadn't yet realized—that his relationship with his daughters would have to determine how he was to go on with his life.

Eventually, she gathered nerve enough to invite him for a weekend. The happiness in his tone as he accepted wasn't lost on her. She resolved not to weaken. When he arrived, they both tried to behave casually, yet there was a subtle and unmistakable awkwardness.

"You've done a wonderful job with this place, Ruth."

She smiled as she set a platter on the table. "I'm glad you like it. I've enjoyed every minute I've worked on it. It's been fun furnishing the bedrooms and finding how to fit in my pets from the city. Come and eat." She pulled out his chair. "Thank goodness I had Nettie's instructions on thrift shopping. There's still so much I want to do, but my budget is used up for now, so I'll have to wait." She began to serve their plates. "I've found a part-time job now, so I can begin to make plans." She hoped he'd understand that the word implied that she had taken hold once more, that she was beginning to look forward. She wanted him to see that in the weeks she had devoted to the house while completely alone, she had done her looking backward and was resolved to move away from the past.

Malcolm accepted the plate she held out to him. "What are you doing? You didn't say when we talked on the phone the other night."

"I'm working in Lewisville, secretary to a doctor. It's perfect because it's only thirty hours a week, and it's what I know how to do." Malcolm glanced away from her. She saw he was trying to hide his face. "Is there something wrong with that?"

"No, of course not." He put his fork down and leaned toward her. "You really mean to stay here, don't you?" She nodded. She heard discouragement in his voice when he said, "Getting a job sort of clinches it, I guess."

"Well," she said, perhaps a little too lightly, "I do have to make a living."

"Yes, I know." Malcolm began to eat again.

"Malcolm, what's the matter?"

"This is great. You're a wonderful cook." He looked up. "I don't want to spoil dinner. We'll talk later, okay?"

"All right." She ground some pepper over her salad. "Tell me how things are going with you. How are the girls?"

"They're fine, as far as I know. Darla isn't much of a correspondent, and the girls are—well, you know—kids. Their mother insists on tennis lessons and piano lessons and ballet lessons. On top of school, it's no surprise they don't write." He shook his head. "I can't stop worrying. But I said I wasn't going to spoil supper. Let me tell you about Dad and Mother."

Ashamed she hadn't already asked about them, Ruth urged, "Oh, please do!"

So Malcolm related their plans to build a house on Sanibel Island and how much improved his mother seemed since the cruise. "I don't know if they're planning to sell the house in New York, but it wouldn't surprise me. They could get a hefty price for it and they'd be happy to stay in Florida all the time. I think it's what they should do."

"How fast things seem to change, as you get older," Ruth said. "It's a complete surprise to me, since I thought it was the young who had to adjust to new things all the time. I thought when I first visited your parents' house that it was like a small museum or something. To me is was a real institution. It was so perfect. I can't imagine any change taking place there."

Malcolm smiled. "I never thought of it that way. It was always just home to me. I see what you mean, though. Still, it's just a house."

"With some of the most beautiful things in it I ever hope to see."

"Why, thank you for all of us," he said with a smile.

When Ruth rose to clear the table, Malcolm began to get up too. She touched his shoulder. "No, you sit still. I'll only be a minute. Do you want ice cream on your pie?"

After the meal, they sat in front of the fire with their coffee. Ruth could see the tension in his face and posture. She wondered if he would have been eased if she had let him help her in the kitchen. They sipped in silence.

Ruth was trying to decide how to approach the subject they both had in mind. Once again, she doubted her courage. Subtle night noises, insects and rustling leaves and readjustments of old timbers, whisperings of the fire, little percussions of china and silver, emphasized her house's cozy exclusiveness. It made her feel cocooned, as one does when escaping from a storm into the haven of home. Outside was a chilly, clear night with, Ruth knew, a sky full of stars.

She looked at Malcolm's profile, highlighted by the firelight and thought he looked weary, his mouth sad. "More coffee?"

He shook his head. "No, thanks. Ruth, thank you for letting me come and see you. I've missed you, but you know that." He smiled slowly. "I've told you each time I called. I have a problem, I think."

When he seemed to be waiting for her to speak, she said, "What is it?"

"I think it may be this place. Seeing you in this house is like seeing you for the first time. I've never known you to be the way you seem to be here."

"What do you mean?"

"I don't know how to explain it, but you seem more at ease, more at home, I guess, here than any other time we've met."

"Oh," she said with a little chuckle, "after all, you never saw me at home before. It was always at your parents' or at your apartment."

But she knew he had seen something that was true. Not since her childhood had she felt so integrated with a place, nor so dependent on it. Though she'd loved the apartment, valued the city, cherished the home she'd made there, nothing had fitted her in the way this house did. There was an organic connection that she had sensed when she first looked at it with the distracting, foolish real estate agent.

Malcolm took her hand and stroked it with his thumb as he talked, but he looked away from her face, into the fire. "I had to see you, Ruth, because I want to ask you, seriously, honestly, hopefully, to marry me."

"Oh, Malcolm, I hoped you wouldn't ask me that now."

"I know it, but I must ask you now. It's because of Hazel and Alice. If I don't want to lose my children, I've got to face facts. I know how it will be if I don't see them often. Darla loves San Diego and she's doing everything she can to make sure the girls do too. If I'm going to keep any part of my daughters, I'm going to have to make a major change." Misery showed in his eyes.

"You're going west too." It was not a question.

He nodded. "Please, my darling Ruth—please come with me!"

She squeezed his hand, then freed hers and stood up. She went to the mantel, stood with hands folded in front of her, her head bowed as she looked down into the fire. She said in a low voice, "I owe you so much. Please try not to be hurt by what I say, if I can say it. You're too good for me ..."

He interrupted, "What nonsense! We're good for each other. We always have been, from the first time we admitted it. You knew it then too."

Ruth turned her back to the fire and looked at him. "Yes, I did, but I told you at the beginning that I couldn't say what was going to happen, to me—with me—and you agreed. Now I have to repeat that."

She returned to sit beside him, her body turned so she could face him. "In the time I've been here, something has changed, or at least is changing, now—in me. I've got a lot of space for thinking, and there's something about looking at country things and listening to earth sounds, that makes it easier to be quiet inside my head. It sounds farfetched, fanciful you might say, but lately I've been learning—

about me, and about Alex too. And oh, my goodness, have I got a lot still to figure out!" Her lips softened in a small smile.

The firelight warmed their faces. She could see in Malcolm's expression that he was in awe of her, of her new determination. And she sensed his desire. She was glad of it. She accepted the feeling without the pang of guilt she'd felt even a few months ago, but she was cautious too, knowing now that her own insecurities were still too strong and that she could not add to someone else's. "I know enough to know that I can't go anywhere just now, or do anything other than what I'm doing." She touched his arm. "Please don't look so unhappy. You know what they say about gaining perspective. I haven't discovered enough of me yet to be able to give you, or perhaps anyone, what you deserve." She was distressed for his sake by her oblique reference to Alex, but it was imperative to be clear. "You've given me the gift of—of appreciation. I sound like an adolescent again, don't I? Well, I am in a way. I can't say yes to you, dear Malcolm. You deserve a mature ..."

Malcolm shook his head hard. "I love you as you are! I'll help you in your self-discovery!" He took her hands. "If you'll come with me, we'll have a whole life of discovery ahead of us!"

Ruth suffered a real pang of sorrow, even as her resolve crystallized. As if she had needed this confrontation to harden her, she felt a growing certainty.

Softly she said, "No. Your children are the center of your life, as they should be. You have your career to reestablish in a new place. It wouldn't be right for you."

"*You're* right for me!"

"And it wouldn't be right for me," she finished quietly. "I'm absolutely sure. I cannot make up my mind to give up my marriage yet. I have to say no." She offered a sad little smile. "I'm so sorry, but I'm so sure."

Malcolm's grip on her hands tightened. They looked silently at each other, and she wanted to lean into his arms and rest her head on his chest. She felt the current of attraction drawing her. With a tiny mewing sound, she pulled her hands away from Malcolm's strong grasp and jumped up. She went to the far end of the room to lean her forehead against a chill pane in the window, squeezing her eyelids against tears. *What if I'm wrong?*

After a minute or two, she heard Malcolm pouring more coffee. She took a shuddering breath and turned slowly around. His posture was drooping; he was leaning forward, his elbows on his knees, a cup cradled between his hands, staring at the fire. The silence lengthened.

When he spoke, his voice was hoarse. "Do you want me to leave?"

Ruth went quickly to stand close to him. "Oh no, please ..."

He raised his eyes. Softly he said, "A sort of farewell?"

She nodded. "For both of us," she whispered.

☙ ❧

From the beginning of her flight to the country, Ruth kept in touch with Nettie. Often they spoke on the telephone, exchanged notes, and sometimes letters. It was February by the time Nettie agreed finally to desert the city for a country weekend.

Ruth went to the station to pick her up. Snowflakes spun like the contents of one of those globes that, when shaken, creates a miniature storm. Flakes reflected her headlights so that it was like driving into a shifting wall. Leaning forward as though that could help her see, she concentrated on keeping a loose grip on the steering wheel. "Thank heaven for the yellow lines!" she said.

Nettie sat beside her, smoking. "You better have a bottle of something good and strong waiting," she growled. "The train was like the Trans-Siberian Express, and I'd say your heater leaves something to be desired." Ruth glanced at the cloud issuing from her friend's mouth and couldn't tell if it was vapor or smoke. The defroster was going, but sent little warmth up the windshield.

"Don't worry. I have most of the civilized amenities. We're almost there."

"How you can tell in this beats me!" Nettie commented. She said nothing as the wheels spun momentarily, throwing the car into a partial skid.

"I haven't driven in weather like this since college days," Ruth said, "but it's sort of like riding the proverbial bike, I guess. I haven't forgotten how." She turned into the driveway, marked by the splash of light from the post lamp on the edge of the lawn. The lights in the windows glowed stagily through the swirling flakes, and Ruth thought the scene would look perfect on a Christmas card.

As she struggled out of the car, Nettie continued to complain. "Ye gods, Red, how can you stand it out here? What in the name of heaven do you do with yourself when you're not on the job?"

Ruth laughed. "It's easy to see you've never been in a small town for any length of time. The trick is to keep some time for yourself." She put Nettie's suitcase down inside the door.

They sat down in front of the fire with a brandy each, and Ruth handed Nettie a large envelope she had brought from New York months before. "Before I forget. I've made time to read these and I thought they were great. I liked them even better than the first lot you gave me. Thanks, Nettie. I appreciate your letting me see them."

Nettie took the envelope and laid it on the coffee table in front of her. "Well, a person learns to appreciate any readers she can get. You're welcome."

Ruth leaned back in the wing chair. "Don't laugh, but your poems have got me going. Those, and maybe something about this place, I don't know. Anyway, I've been writing too. Oh, not poetry. I don't know what you could call it. It doesn't rhyme, or most of it doesn't." She risked a direct look at Nettie to see how she was reacting.

Nettie's eyes were focused sharply on Ruth, who could see no hint of laughter, as she had feared she might. "That's good."

"Yes, well, I doubt if it's good, but it's been … it is an interesting experience. Funny, how you can start off with an idea, and then it can sort of get away from you, and you say things you didn't even know you were thinking."

Nettie cocked her head. "Learn anything?"

Ruth thought for a moment before she answered. "Yes, I think so. Yes. I've begun looking at things, at objects and nature and even people, differently. Maybe I should say, more consciously. I notice all sorts of things I never used to, now that I try to describe them. Writing things down seems to give a little bit different view, and you get— insights, I guess you could call them. And the stuff I remember! It's as if a lot of my life happened to somebody else."

Perfectly seriously, Nettie said, "It did. You're not the same person you were twenty years ago, or ten." She lit a cigarette, leaned back, and looked at the smoke rising. Ruth watched, wondering if she would ask to see what she had been writing; wondering if she wanted to be asked.

Typically, Nettie surprised her. "Honor's dumped Alex. Did you know?"

Ruth felt her stomach lurch. "No. How would I know?" She tried to keep her voice steady.

Nettie continued as if Ruth had not spoken. "I saw her with another man twice last month in Rabino's. So I asked Jake."

"Jake?"

"Yeah. You remember. He did the lights for the Castoffs. He said the group all fell apart after Alex directed a play she had the lead in. I forget what."

Ruth was silent. She had a momentary vision of Honor's pouting expression, her languid movements, spotlighted on the stage. She saw Alex standing beside her, leaning toward her. Ruth cleared her throat. "How is he?"

"Well, I haven't seen him, but the scuttlebutt is that he's hitting the bottle pretty bad." Nettie leaned forward to tap her ashes into a saucer on the coffee table. "It's too bad. I figured he'd see the light before this. Never dreamed he'd hang in there that long with her."

"That's a shame," Ruth murmured, in the voice of someone commenting on the death of a stranger, though she found her middle was vibrating.

"So," Nettie said, stubbing out her cigarette, "let's have a nightcap and then you can let me get some shut-eye."

"Of course." Ruth got up to get her another drink. She stifled her yearning to hear more about Alex, and they spoke of other things until bedtime. Was it the wind that made her spend such a restless night?

In the morning, Nettie was up before her. Ruth found her standing in front of the window in the kitchen, drinking orange juice and half smiling, her eyes moving over the snowscape, crinkling with pleasure. Apparently in deference to the country, her head was swathed in a red and white cotton bandanna instead of one of her more exotic draperies. She was wearing a huge, out-of-shape fisherman's sweater and a pair of olive green wool slacks.

"Good morning."

"Morning. This is enough to inspire anybody. You forget all snow isn't grey. Look how it's stuck to some of the branches. What do you do if you have to get to work? It can't always snow on Friday night."

"I hire somebody to come with a plow so I can get the car out. He's usually here by eight-thirty. On Saturday he does the weekenders first." Nettie shook her head skeptically, but seated herself at the kitchen table while Ruth prepared their meal.

They ate a lot and had three cups of coffee each, squinting against the glare of sun on snow, but unwilling to shut it out. Blue jays flashed to and from the feeder, and the smaller birds flitted in after seeds that they carried away. Their names: chickadee, titmouse, junco, nuthatch, that Ruth had not thought of in years, came back to her. They laughed at a squirrel, frustrated by the wire suspending the feeder, who tumbled into the snow half a dozen times before he gave up.

"You've really settled in here, haven't you?" Nettie said, as they washed the dishes. "Don't you miss the old town?"

Ruth smiled. "I was sure I would. And I suppose if I'd left my job to come here, or if the—circumstance—had been different, I might have, but maybe the timing was right. And maybe if I hadn't found just the right house, but as it is, no; I really don't."

"And Alex? Do you miss him?"

"Nettie, you know you don't take the prize for tact."

Her friend said casually, polishing a plate with the dish towel, "I don't give a damn for tact. I want to know how you feel."

Ruth sighed. "Probably I do. I don't know. I'm finding myself better company than I thought I would, though." When Nettie said nothing, Ruth said, "Yes. Of course I miss him."

"You want him back?"

Ruth put her dish towel down on the counter and sat down at the table, looking out the window at the glitter of snow crystals in the cross light of morning sun. The calm that had soothed her since she had come to this house made it possible for her to think about the question without shrinking. Now she knew part of the answer, at least. She said, "You know I've been seeing Malcolm Gentry, don't you?" Nettie grunted affirmatively. "He's going to California. I saw him for the last time before Thanksgiving." Nettie kept silent while Ruth marshaled her thoughts. "He was good for me. I doubt if I could have kept my head after—after the split with Alex if it hadn't been for Malcolm. Does that sound crazy?"

"Not to me."

"Well, it seemed very queer to me while I was going through it. He's a wonderful man."

"I asked you about Alex," Nettie reminded her.

"I'm getting around to him. Give me a minute to figure out how to put all this into words. But I have been thinking about it. You see, I do want Alex back ..." Ruth saw Nettie's expression change. "But I don't think he'd come. And I have to face the possibility that we may never get together again. That's not easy. Don't laugh, Nettie. I guess I'm old-fashioned. We took vows, and I can't forget those." Nettie seemed on the verge of speaking, but Ruth went on, "In spite of Malcolm. If I lived to be a hundred, I'd never forget my husband. But the fact is that if we could ever have another chance, I'd never again be the wife he knows. *I* think I'd be better, but there's no way he'd know that. And I couldn't be his wife on the old terms."

Nettie asked softly. "What do you mean, 'old terms'?"

"Well, for one thing, I'm more—maybe *awake* would be the word—than I used to be. I'd never settle for the same kind of unvarying routine that I used to have. For another, I'd make him confide, explain, talk to me, or I wouldn't be able to live with him." Ruth risked a glance directly at Nettie. "And I'd be sure to do my own talking too." She moved restlessly in her chair. "There must have been so much that went on in his head that I didn't even guess at! It makes me ashamed." She shook her head. "Oh, it was his fault too, because most of the time he wouldn't open up. Well, I wouldn't settle for that anymore. I'd insist that we somehow get to understand each other."

Nettie raised her eyebrows. "Very commendable, I'm sure, but how do you think you can do that now, if you couldn't do it in more than ten years of trying?"

Ruth looked into Nettie's eyes and narrowed hers. "But that's just it! I didn't even know I should be trying. And on top of that, I never thought there were things about myself I wanted another person to know. Things they might not figure out for themselves. I was always afraid to show too much and thought he didn't want to either. I just assumed that ...what does that funny guy on TV ... Flip Wilson say? 'What you see is what you get.' I made the mistake of thinking that was enough."

She stood up and sat against the window sill with folded arms. "Don't you remember how you used to try to get me to imagine what wasn't obvious? Well, at first I thought you were talking about things like, oh, details of the color of an apple on a plate, or how the fog smells when it comes off the river, or the way those trees wave in the wind out there. Finally, I hope not too late, I figured out you were talking about what goes on inside other people's heads." She rubbed her eyes with one hand. "The more I thought about it, the more I saw I had to get away, from the old place and especially the old habits."

She moved from the window, pacing slowly back and forth. "You can't change a whole point of view, set of mind, just by deciding to." Ruth smiled wryly. "I guess it's like anything else. You have to work at it. That's why I decided to try the country for a while. I hoped the change of scene might help me make other changes. Well, whatever happens in the end, it's been worth it. If I ever got a chance to do things over again, I hope I'd do them differently." She glanced at Nettie. "Not a very novel remark, is it? And maybe it would all work out the same way. Anyway, now I'm about ready to try to take up the option on this house. With my job and lower expenses than I've had for years, I can handle a mortgage. I'm afraid I better begin to learn to do without what I want the most." She stood straight, away from the window sill. "But you know something? I'm still not ready to give up. Not yet. You tell me Alex is hurt right now. Maybe I can help him, and maybe if I can make him feel better, he might be willing ..."

Nettie exploded. "Jesus H. Christ! Are you serious? '*He* might be willing'? What rights has he got? Who walked out on who? I don't care if you *are* still in love with him! You can't mean you'd ... If you ever see him again, you ought to tell him where to head in and what to do ..."

Ruth laughed. "You're a good friend, but you don't see the problem. We're no different from most couples. Our problems have two sides, you know."

"Balls," Nettie snapped. "You sound like a psychology textbook. Who're you trying to kid? This is me, old Nasty Nettie."

Ruth shrugged, and took the coffee pot off the stove. "More coffee?" She wondered at her lack of annoyance with her friend, at her own deep optimism. Like someone who has discovered an important piece of information from a map no one else has seen, Ruth knew she was going the right way, even though she wasn't sure what the end of the journey might be like.

Nettie held out her cup. "Okay. I get the message—again. Well, to each his own poison. I'll butt out." She sounded matter-of-fact, as always, and Ruth smiled at her as she filled her cup, wanting very much for Nettie to see how grateful she was for her interest. She also hoped it was clear that her mind was made up. She was prepared for a long wait.

The balance of the weekend passed companionably. Nettie did not mention Alex again. She did ask to see what Ruth had been writing. They parted with their friendship cemented more strongly than ever. At the station, Ruth said, "If you find out anything about Alex you think I ought to know …"

"Count on it," Nettie interrupted tersely and climbed onto the train.

CHAPTER TWENTY

It was the middle of April, days were lengthening; so it was not quite dark when Ruth left the supermarket. Treetops and church steeples were visible as silhouettes against the eastern sky that glowed palely behind them, reflecting in puddles on the asphalt. Ruth pushed her cart to the back of her car, opened the trunk, and loaded the bags inside. When she slid into the driver's seat, she noticed an odd smell: sweat and dust, as if someone had been there. She turned out of the lot onto the main highway.

"Just keep driving till I tell you to turn."

She gasped and jumped, making the car lurch as she clutched the wheel. The man's voice came from directly behind her right shoulder. A sting of terror made her suddenly limp. She was afraid she couldn't control the car. Desperately, she tried to think how she could get help. But in the dusk, passing automobiles were nothing more than headlights, without visible drivers, like robots. More headlights showed in the rearview mirror—remote, tantalizing, completely inaccessible. The smell became overpowering, a mix of stale sweat, the dry odor of old soil, plus a sweetish overlay like the aroma of a fragrant herb.

"Keep your eyes on the road, lady, or you'll get us killed." His voice was grating, rough, accented with a drawling touch of the South. She felt his hand drop on her shoulder and she began to shake, terror liquefying her insides.

"You take the next turnoff, you hear?" When she did not answer, he shouted, "You hear me?"

Speechless, shaking and icy, she managed to nod. She drove with jerks and hesitations, unable to keep her foot steady on the accelerator.

"There. Turn off right up there." She signaled and turned onto the road he indicated. "Slow down, damn it! Wait—there's a good place. Turn there. *Now!*" He grabbed her shoulder again, causing her to wrench the car awkwardly into the dirt road to the left.

He was murmuring now, his tone muffled, a tremor in his voice. "Now you drive nice and slow, and when I tell you stop, you stop, hear?" It sounded like "heah."

Again she nodded. Her hands were cold but slippery on the wheel. She slowed to a few miles an hour. The road was rutted, narrow, overhung with tall trees, the shoulders dense with undergrowth. It was fully dark here, the afterglow cloaked by woods. The car rattled and bounced over stones and holes in the road.

"Up there, where that bend is. You park the car."

"But, I can't get off the road."

"It won't matter. We won't be there long. You do it."

She pulled to the right until the wheels dropped into a ditch, and branches scraped the side of the car.

"Turn off the engine," he growled.

"'Now you lean forward so's I can git out the back."

Ruth opened the door and started to get out herself, to allow the seat back to be pushed forward, but the man clamped his hand viciously on her shoulder, pulling her against the seat, shouting. "Here! I said you lean forward!" He released her shoulder and struck her hard on the side of her head. "You do like I say!"

Ruth cried out when she felt the blow. With her ears ringing from the clout and from shock, she pressed herself against the steering wheel as she felt him force the seat against her back so he could get out. In the light reflected by the headlights' glare on the trees, she could see him now. He seemed to be tall, extremely thin, clad in a denim jacket and pants, his hair long and curly.

"Turn off the lights," he ordered. She did. At first she was blind in the darkness, but he must be too. For an instant she thought of trying to run, but he had taken a grip on her left wrist that was painful. He gave a violent jerk, and she fell sideways out of the car, onto the gravel and mud in the roadway. Again she cried out. As if she had made no sound, he tugged at her arm, dragging her along like a sack, while she struggled to gain her feet.

"I'm tellin' you, don' try to fight me, lady. It'll be all over a lot sooner an' a lot easier if you jes' relax."

They were around the front of the car now, and he paused for a moment, apparently feeling the way he wanted to go. Ruth managed to get to her feet, though she was still bent over by the intense pressure on her arm. He suddenly twisted so as to throw her to the ground again.

Suddenly, she thought she would choke. She tried desperately to turn her head away as his callused hand closed over the bottom half of her face. The smell of his skin—musty, rank—was repellent. She struggled as strongly as she was able, even tried to open her mouth, thinking to bite. He struck her again, this time with a full swing of his free arm. The blow stunned her.

She realized fuzzily that he no longer was twisting her wrist, but she couldn't free her head. He was forcing her flatter to the ground with the terrible pressure of his arm against her neck, while mashing her lips against her teeth with his other hand, half smothering her. Her hair came loose. His weight fell on her as if dropped, driving the breath from her.

He was dragging the hem of her coat and her skirt up to her waist. She was dazed; a great roaring sound like wind in a cavern filled her ears. She tried to arch her back, force him away, but he was too heavy, and she was too weak. She fought to get her elbows against his chest, to push him away from her, but his position and the arm across her neck with one hand on her face kept her from reaching him. She grunted in pain when he thrust a bony knee against her clamped legs, prying them apart the way one opens a clam shell. Gagged by his raspy hand, she made whimpering sounds as she strained to scream. He tore her stockings and she hardly felt the sting of the nylon straining against her flesh. When he entered her, it seemed as though she were enduring something like a combination of a knife and a club. She was torn and bludgeoned at the same time. Lights flashed behind her eyelids, the noise in her ears increased, and she thought she was drowning in some unnatural way, without the clean solace of water. Time was nonexistent.

❧ ☙

At last, incredibly, she could breathe again. The weight was gone from her chest, and she smelled the odor of dead leaves, the clayey tang of wet soil. Her legs and stomach were bare, and she was freezing. She continued to lie on the ground, wracked with convulsive tremors, unaware of the little moaning sobs she was making. She lay twitching, sprawled, pale in her white office clothes like a ghost in the darkness.

❧ ☙

It was about five o'clock in the morning when the phone rang in Alex's apartment in New York. A man with a wheezy, high-pitched voice asked for Alexander Duchamp. He said he was a state policeman, calling from a hospital in a western Connecticut town to notify Alex that his wife was a patient there.

Groggy with sleep, Alex could not think of the right questions to ask because he had trouble figuring out what he was being told. Ruth—something about Ruth. He fumbled for a pencil and obediently wrote down the information the man was dictating to him. After he hung up, he sat on the edge of the bed and stared through the window at the weak glow just beginning to edge out the black of night. Hospital, injuries? Ruth!

❧ ☙

Later, Alex remembered little of the trip. He had packed a sweater, a change of underwear, shirt, socks, and shaving gear in a canvas sports bag, checked his credit cards, and put his checkbook in his inside pocket. Then he rushed off, carrying his raincoat, slamming the door much too loudly for the early hour.

Taxis right after dawn were few, but he found one; the streets were incredibly quiet and free of traffic; he remembered having to wait a good while for a bus at the terminal. The trip seemed hours long though it was only seventy miles. He was rigid with fear, his mind virtually blank, for he dared not imagine what might have happened. He functioned like an automaton.

When at last he entered the hospital lobby, he noticed that it smelled strongly of freshly brewed coffee. There was a steaming Styrofoam cup on the information desk in front of the woman who directed him to Ruth's floor. His stomach growled audibly, and he had to swallow as he got on the elevator, half nauseated and chilled.

He got off, and like a thief, hurried slightly crouching, along the corridor toward the number he'd been given downstairs. Since he saw that the door to her room was open, he slowed his pace as he approached it. He groped frantically in his mind, trying to remember if the man on the phone had told him what had happened to his wife. Would he find her unconscious, swathed in bandages, hooked by tubing to machines or oxygen? His mouth was now as dry as a blotter, and he was sweating. Though the corridor was carpeted, he began to tiptoe.

Ruth was in a small semi-private room, but there was no one in the other bed. She was sitting up, morning sun shining through the window. The backlighting made her hair glow, but her face was drained; not just pale, but more as if she'd been bled. Bruises around her eyes and mouth showed she must have been beaten.

She turned her eyes to him as he came into the room, and he remembered vividly those timid, proud, sensitive horses he'd loved when he was young. She lowered her lids slowly, then opened them again. Alex saw tears brimming.

"They told me they called you," she said in a quavering voice. As if she were an observer of herself, seeing herself through a thick pane of glass, she was aware of an awful distance from what her brain told her was the here-and-now, but which she registered only dimly. The insensibility pervading every facet of her consciousness overbore every other impression. She wondered whether she was still under the influence of the sedative they'd administered the night before. Alex. She tried to look into his eyes, but could not make her own obey the impulse.

Alex could say only, "Yes." He was drowning in alien feelings compounded of pity and fury. He wanted to embrace her, comfort her, stroke and soothe her. Yet, curiosity kept shouldering aside the more empathetic feelings, making him feel he was guilty. How could he question her? Looking at her flickering, fearful gaze, he was afraid to touch her. The table with her breakfast tray on it stood in his way between them, so he pushed it aside and sat down on the edge of her bed. He licked his lips, trying to moisten his mouth so he could speak normally. "What happened, Red?"

Gazing past his shoulder at the window, she took a very long, tremulous breath and closed her eyes. She groped for a tissue on the night stand and blotted the tears that squeezed out under her lids. Now that he was close to her, Alex could see that her mouth was swollen, but the dark marks around her eyes might be from fatigue or shock. He trembled.

"It's too bad you had to be bothered," she murmured. He leaned a little forward to be sure he could hear everything she said. She seemed so weak, broken like an abused flower. This Ruth was a fragile stranger.

"Just tell me about it," he said gently.

"Stupid," she was saying, shaking her head, her hands busy with the crumpled tissue. "I was just getting a couple of things at the supermarket …" Her whisper trailed off. He waited. She looked out the window, avoiding his eyes.

"Go on," Alex urged, struggling to keep his voice almost as low as hers.

She cleared her throat, spoke as if she were in an empty room, musingly, as if to herself. "I didn't bother to lock the car. I had only a short list. I never thought of looking in the back seat. I just put the groceries in the trunk, and then got in the car." She reached for a new tissue. Alex took the box and put it on the bed between them.

He waited. "Can you talk about it?"

In her odd, faraway voice, Ruth said, "There was a man. Hiding behind the seat. I didn't see him until I was on the stretch of road between …" She looked at Alex then, as if he were a stranger to her. "It was dark, you know. I'd been at work. It saved a trip the next day to stop then. I never lock the car. It's not a new one, and it doesn't even have a tape-deck or anything." She looked away again, into space beyond him.

Alex clenched his fists and began to develop a stiff neck while he strained to keep still, to be patient, not to press her too hard, all the while willing her to tell him—tell everything.

It took a long time, getting the story. Some she was able eventually to tell him, the rest he gleaned from the police. A state police cruiser on routine patrol found her near midnight, dazed, standing on the highway shoulder, trying to flag down a car. She couldn't answer questions, still too deep in shock. The police examined her identification, which showed her husband as next of kin. At the hospital, when the staff was able to confirm what the police suspected had happened to her, they had called Alex without giving him any details.

Alex had read about those things, had heard about how women are overwhelmed and brutalized, but he had trouble associating this knowledge with the fact, with Ruth, with his wife. What little she said was disjointed, fragmentary. Alex did his best to listen, to say only enough to encourage her to talk. Sitting on the edge of the bed in Ruth's hospital room, trying to engage her frightened eyes, Alex found he had done few things in his life that took more restraint.

He wanted to swear and smash something. He felt as if a head of steam were building up under his skull. He actually shook. Something warned him not to let Ruth see how he felt, so he struggled for control. Once he was sure she was finished talking, he reached instinctively for her hand, craving the touch of her flesh. She snatched it away, pressed herself back against the pillow, away from him, eyes rimmed with white all around, her mouth opened slightly. Then she seemed almost as shocked by her reaction as he was, and he saw her try to overcome her reflexive behavior. Yet he felt as if he had received a blow, and he, too, cringed. Though Ruth's face showed terrible confusion, and he understood her reaction was involuntary, Alex felt that she might have stabbed him without causing him more pain.

He got up and stood looking out the window with his back to her. He needed to hide his face. His mind was a turmoil of hurt and seething fury. Less than twelve hours ago his sluggish life had exploded around him, and he was reeling from the impact.

Ruth was silent behind him. Like someone who has survived an earthquake, he looked out the window, as if in the parking lot and the receding ranks of unfamiliar domestic roofs he could identify landmarks to get his bearings.

As the silence between them lengthened, gradually he began to see he faced two problems: Ruth's pain and his anguish over her fear of him. He turned to look at her.

She lay motionless, eyes closed, biting her lips to stifle the sobs she felt rising through her chest. Behind her closed lids, she seemed to stare into mist that boiled like storm clouds, occasionally breaking into nearly transparent shreds, only to reform into impenetrable walls. She had not the strength to open her eyes and look at daylight.

As if nothing had separated them for the past nine months, as if he had never known Honor Ringwold, in his depths Alex felt himself Ruth's husband still—possessive and jealous and afraid for her. Overwhelmed with his own seething and conflicting emotions, he could scarcely comprehend hers. He knew only that he must somehow recover her, his wife.

CHAPTER TWENTY-ONE

Ruth watched Alex's back disappearing as he went out the door. Still woozy with sedatives, images surfaced like flotsam in a flood, hideous and frightening. She was dimly grateful that Alex had been there. Grateful, and for a moment, surprised, before she fell back into hazy confusion. She was in pain, but not sure how much was physical and how much emotional.

When a nurse came in to tell her she could dress to go home, she felt a wave of panic that almost made her cry out. She bit her knuckle and tried to slow her breathing. She forgot that Alex had been there.

The nurse was kind. She took Ruth's things out of the closet, found her lipstick in her purse, helped her to comb her hair. She tried to brush the mud stains off Ruth's clothes and found a pair of stockings for her. Since she had been wearing her office uniform, the white nurse's hose looked fine, but she felt as if she were about to be forced out into an exposed position, back into danger. She could hardly put her hair up, her hands were shaking so much. She was amazed when Alex appeared at the door again with her discharge slip in his hand.

Despite those anxieties, she was also in a sense as numb as a cheek at the dentist's. Her hearing was affected; sounds were muffled and distant. Even though Alex was there, she was no more interested in him than in the trooper who had picked her up, or the doctor in the emergency room. Drumming in her depths was a command that above everything else, she must be calm and dignified. No one must know.

Out in front of the building, she saw her car parked behind a state police cruiser. Did they expect her to drive? A trooper came up to them, holding the keys out to Alex.

"As soon as you feel able, Mrs. Duchamp, we'll expect you to come and see if you can give us an identification from the mug books." Ruth looked at him blankly. She thought they had asked her a lot of questions the night before, but she could not remember them, or the answers she had given.

"We'll be there as soon as we can," Alex said. Both men were looking at her. Seeing that something was expected of her, Ruth nodded.

Alex helped her into the passenger side of her car, then got in himself and started the engine. She was shivering. It was a bright blue spring day; the sun was warm when it touched on skin, but the air was damp and chilly in the shade. Alex gave her a quick glance and turned on the heater as they moved out onto the street.

"Can you tell me how to get you home?" He spoke in the sort of cheerful, tentative voice one uses around people who are very ill or senile. She looked at him, surprised, then remembered he had never been here before.

She gave single word directions as they went along, telling him when to make turns. Watching the traffic, the passing streets and people, then the thinning houses and shops as they got into the country, she was immensely grateful that he was driving. They stopped twice for traffic lights she'd forgotten were there and that she didn't see were red. She felt Alex's swift glance from time to time, but he said nothing except when he was unsure of where to make a turn. Ruth had to concentrate to tell him in time because everything looked strange, as if she had been away for a very long time.

When they got to her driveway, Alex turned in and pulled up. He sat for a moment, looking at the house, then turned to her, trying to force a smile. "It's nice."

He took the keys out of the ignition and handed them to her. He got out, went around the car and opened the door for her. She had not moved, except to take the keys. When he put his hand gently under her arm to help her into the house, she flinched, but he supported her, and as she began to walk to the porch, he took his hand away. Ruth unlocked the door, and turned to see if he was following her. He had stopped on the step, which placed his eyes a little below hers. She looked down on him, confused, afraid he was leaving.

"If you let me have the keys back, I'll empty the car." She handed them over. She had forgotten her groceries. The ordinary thought came to her that it was convenient that nothing would have spoiled overnight, since the weather was still so cold after dark.

When she walked into her front hall, she had the kind of sensation she recognized as what one has when a fever is broken, and there is the certainty of recovery in spite of shaking knees. The broad mantel with its brass candlesticks and dried flowers, the black iron kettle hanging from the crane, the books and the pictures on the wall—everything seemed to welcome her. She dropped into the wing chair and waited for Alex to come in.

He put the things away in the kitchen, not asking where anything belonged. Then he walked slowly around the house, from room to room. The sound of his footsteps overhead gave her comfort. Eventually she heard the kettle begin to whistle in the kitchen. Alex came back into the living room. "Coffee? Tea?"

"Tea, please." Still, she sat motionless. In a few minutes he brought a cup. He sat on the couch to drink his, as near to her chair as he could get.

Alex watched her for a long moment before he spoke. "Is the bed in the guest room made up?" he asked quietly. She nodded and watched him take his bag up the stairs.

෨ ଔ

Ruth was aware only of the passage of time, not of how much slid by. She spoke seldom. If Alex told her to come to the table and eat, she could do it, but she was incapable of initiating any activity. Like a small child, she got up when he woke her, ate when he put food in front of her, went to bed when he said it was time.

She was always so tired. She was glad that Alex did the cooking, that he suggested a walk in the warm sun to look at daffodils along the wall, that he gently got her to go to bed. She remembered having scarlet fever when she was about eight and how she felt convalescing. A similar lassitude governed her now as she began this recovery.

Without insistence, Alex made conversation from time to time. He tried to interest Ruth in things, to get her to speak. He explained about how he was launching himself as a freelancer by searching out clients, industrial accounts, instead of advertisers. He talked about the interesting problems of photographing machinery and gauges.

At first he was disappointed that she did not ask him about himself. In fact, she wasn't particularly curious. She had no desire to do more than let every day just slide by. He perceived this and determined to be patient. It was Alex who called Dr. Jessup, Ruth's employer, to explain why she wouldn't be at work for a time. He asked her only necessary questions, then took care of arranging things like her time off, like keeping fresh milk in the refrigerator and doing laundry. Ruth was not particularly anxious when he left the house to do errands or buy food, but she gradually realized that the certainty he would be back was what kept panic at bay.

The police called. Alex behaved like someone with a frightened child who has to be taken to the dentist. He got her to the state police barracks, as he had said he would, with a combination of firmness and tact. She looked at hundreds of pictures, or so it seemed. She saw nothing familiar in any of them.

The attack had happened near eight o'clock at night, and naturally she remembered more about the man's voice than about his looks, since it had been so dark in the woods, and that was hard to describe. Though she did try, she could not produce the sort of information they could make much use of. She found that she could hear that voice in her head, every word he had said, though when the police found her, she remembered nothing except being dragged out of the car, thrown onto the wet weeds and stones at the roadside, struggling against the man's iron hands and his weight crushing her chest, his knee bruising hers as he forced her legs apart, and the blows to her face and head, then his forearm across her throat. She could not see his face, but whether because of terror or the darkness, she was not sure. She might have lost consciousness for several minutes. The pressure on her throat had been agonizing. Then, many days later, she had a clearer recollection of his voice. It was medium range, but gravelly and soft, the vowels drawn out and drawled.

"He might have been from the South," she said.

Once she had made the visit to the police, Ruth began very gradually to realize that the whole thing was really in the past. It was something she could begin to spend the rest of her life forgetting.

After a month, with Alex encouraging her, she went back to her job and her routine. In the lengthening days, she got home before dark every night. She began to cook for the two of them, to do the laundry, pull weeds, and run the vacuum cleaner. Alex continued to be quietly there when she returned from her job. They would talk about ordinary things, the weather, the news on TV, food. Two more weeks elapsed.

One evening when she came home, Ruth noticed that Alex had dug the vegetable garden up. He was still out there with a rake, breaking up clods, when she drove in.

"How about letting me take you to work so I can have the car tomorrow?" he asked over supper.

"That's fine," she said. "What do you want to do?"

"Get some seeds and plants; get your garden in for you. It's already halfway through May."

All at once, what he was saying sank in. For the first time, Ruth looked more than a day ahead, and she felt as if her chest were expanding with the first full breath she'd taken in months. If you plant, you do it to reap the harvest!

That evening, she began cautiously to acknowledge to herself her delight that Alex was still there. She even dared to wonder how they were going to go on. The thought of deciding on what kind of tomato plants to buy and where to put the pole beans somehow brought her closer to normal than anything else had. It woke her to the fact—so astonishing —that Alex was still with her.

After supper, they sat at the table with a sheet of paper and laid out the garden plan. "Is it too early to put out tomato plants and cauliflower and eggplants?" Alex asked. "It stayed so cold up where I come from, we wouldn't dare to do it for another two or three weeks."

Ruth said, "Around here they say that when the maple leaves are as big as the palm of your hand, it's safe to put out tender plants. No problem with cauliflower or broccoli, I'd say. And in two weeks, even tomatoes and peppers and eggplant, I think."

Alex looked up from his diagram and smiled. The expression on his face opened some internal dam in Ruth's mind—releasing present sensations as well as memories that all unrolled with Alex at their center. His beauty overwhelmed her again as it had not since before the night she'd ridden the ferry. She felt dizzy and put a hand to her eyes. As if more than a year had evaporated into the ether, the man she married was sitting to her right at her table, lamplight glossing his hair, highlighting the modeling of his arms below the rolled sleeves of his shirt. Alex gathered up the papers and pencils, blew eraser crumbs off the table and reached for the switch to turn off the lamp. "Bedtime?"

She realized his tone was the same casual one he'd been using since he had come. She nodded. Before she went up, Ruth went to her desk in the small room she used for a study to take out the notebooks she had been writing in since she'd moved, but not since the attack. One was filled and another nearly full. She took them upstairs with her, but when she began to read, her mind flitted away. The present was beginning to press on her at last with more weight than the past. She lay awake a long time.

Ruth was aware that Alex would have to go back to his business soon, but what else was he going back to? They had said nothing more important to each other here than they had in the weeks before he left. Yet the climate in which they moved now was as different from that one as spring is different from the dead of winter. Questions began to churn in Ruth's head. Other than what Nettie had told her, mostly gossip, she knew nothing of what he'd been doing. More important, what had happened to him on the inside? He looked fit now, not as if he had been drinking heavily.

She felt as if she were waking up after a long sleep. She began to know she was going to have to go back to being a part of the ordinary, busy world again; she couldn't just keep going through motions. It was time to notice the headlines again, balance her checkbook again, make appointments, get the car serviced.

And she also knew that she and Alex would have to talk. They had lives to lead and they had to make decisions about how to go on with them. Ruth's respite, her adjustment period, had come to an abrupt and traumatic end. Now her recovery was going to have to become final too. There was a lot to do. When she finally fell asleep, it was with a mental list running off the bottom of the page.

She dreamed of Alex, hanging in a cage above her head, like a giant parrot. When she spoke urgently to him, he would not answer, so she cranked her little organ on its monopod faster and faster, and Alex's cage turned slowly back and forth as he smiled silently inside. The dream faded when her arm became so tired, she thought she could not give the little handle another turn.

༄ ༅

They planted the garden, beginning the next day, which was Saturday, and were so tired by dinner time, Alex asked if she'd like to eat out. She looked down at her hands, scratched and filthy with ground-in dirt and suddenly the idea of sitting in a public place appealed to her. She could get her nails clean again, after all, with a little effort and a brush, just like anyone else.

They went to a good, unpretentious French place nearby. They sat in a window overlooking a river. The warm light of a fair weather sunset bathed the scene before them in rosy hues. Alex was reading the menu. Ruth looked at him, flushed with afterglow, sunburn, and the ruddy color natural to him. She noticed faint creases at the corners of his mouth and some white hairs glistening among the dark waves above his brow. He caught her studying him and when he looked up, she tried to smile. She saw his expression become more serious. His eyes darkened visibly, and for a moment she thought he was angry.

Her look disconcerted him, forcing Alex to face the growing tension. In the dark of his solitary nights in the guest room he had made his resolution. He had no right, yet daily she was cementing him ever more firmly to her. "I think I should go back to town on Monday," he said. "How would you feel about that?"

She swallowed. "Of course you must. I'll be fine. No need to worry. Not now."

He put the menu down and began to reach across the table, but drew his hand back suddenly, as though he had touched something hot. His eyes left Ruth's. *She* must make the first move!

"I could spend weekends here with you, if you'd like me to." He looked at her, then at the roll on his plate. "Only if you'd like me to."

Ruth gathered herself, as if getting ready to meet a challenge, before she managed to speak. "Thank you for coming in the first place. Thank you for all you've done for me."

Alex broke in, raising his eyes. "I could take care of the grass and help you with the garden and see to repairs." His voice sounded breathless, as if he had been working hard or running, and she felt the intensity of his gaze. It recalled the feelings he'd roused during their courtship. She was afraid, yet yearned to renew those feelings the way she craved air.

"You'd want to spend your weekends doing that sort of thing? You must have other things ..."

"Nothing," he interrupted. With heavy emphasis he said, "I have nothing better to do."

The waitress came to get their orders. Ruth was grateful for time to let his words sink in before she would have to respond to them. Alex ordered a bottle of wine to go with their dinner. When it came, he raised his glass.

"Would you like to drink to ..." He paused. She saw him flush even more deeply, the color darkening his skin, a sheen showing on his forehead. "Could we drink to a better tomorrow?"

She thought she should smile, make light of his toast and join it, but she could not. Her mouth seemed frozen, and she could not take her eyes from his. She remembered how he had pinned her with his piercing looks when she was first in love. Though unnerved, at the same time she was filled with a rush of hope and energy. She lacked courage to reveal her feelings, so she lifted her glass, touched his with it, and then dipped her face to sip. "Of course."

CHAPTER TWENTY-TWO

During the weeks Alex spent with Ruth after the rape, though he began to accept his revived feelings for her, much of the time he felt like a kind of good Samaritan. It was clear that she was shocked and ill. He was surprised that his own uncertainties and soreness were so effectively soothed by the knowledge that he could help. He made up his mind that he would work as long as it took to get her back to ordinary life, to restore her to her old self. The woman he loved, after everything, in spite of everything, was still his wife!

Thank God the police had called him! This awful event had made it possible for him to go back to her in strength, had saved him from crawling, from apologies. He could scarcely decide which was greater, horror over what had befallen her, or gratitude for this opportunity to be, in a sense, her rescuer.

Though he suspected such a concept was sophomoric, he could not escape his memory of the sense of spiritual loss he had experienced after being forced to face the ugly facts that had made him turn his back on Honor. Her disdain, her cruelty, had suddenly made him know what a stray dog must suffer when it cannot get home. The feeling of helpless isolation had terrified him. Though he had had a good share of being footloose and alone, he had never been through anything like that. He had let Honor unman him. Strange, archaic, descriptive word! Thinking about it in sober retrospect, he realized he had allowed himself to be transformed, torn away from the person he had been and turned into a species of sexual slave.

Observing Ruth now, he saw that she, too, was afloat, separated from ordinary experience and almost surely from her real self. Degradation had made each of them virtually unrecognizable to themselves. Alex ached with the sorrowful knowledge that there is no loneliness more profound than that.

During his own desperate time, he had been able to go from place to place on the subway or a bus without getting lost, but by the end of the day, he could not have cared less about where he was. Much of the time he could not even remember where he had been. His apartment was a place with a bed in it, and so he would go there to sleep. Now, back from his sojourn in the country, he spent an hour sitting in Central Park near the sea lions, eyes on people going by, but his attention elsewhere. It gradually dawned on him that he had a specific task to accomplish. He needed to take stock, make plans.

He watched children with their parents. They held bunches of balloons and squealed at the animals, who would slide into the water, frolicking and barking. He saw couples on bicycles, teetering when they reached for each other's hands, endangering everyone on the walkways. Alex began to try to imagine what each person or couple or little group might be like at home. Pictures formed in his mind of apartments with sooty window sills and dark china cabinets and hassocks in front of television sets. He imagined looking past those to kitchens glaring and steaming through narrow doorways, where the mother in an apron moved back and forth between stove and refrigerator. These visions were microcosms that glittered enticingly like *faux* gems in a jewel box.

Such fantasies did not, as they might have once, make him feel sad or deprived, just oddly curious. There was a peculiar, palpable pleasure in those imagined scenes of the ordinary lives of others who were nameless and faceless. He enjoyed sitting dreaming. It had been a long time since the days when the boy had only to look out a window to fall off the edge of the earth he knew. It was a small, happy discovery that he could regain something of that old feeling. He had thought it must have died along with his delusions the night he had run from Honor's jeering laughter.

The weeks with Ruth in Connecticut had opened new windows. Once again he felt at liberty to drift toward possibilities, just as he had when young. And that thought raised another disturbing one. He was no longer so young.

It dawned on him eventually that he was trying to figure out what kind of place he might belong in, since he had separated himself so completely from those he once had been able to claim. He understood that what he sought was not just space for his body. What he needed was a home. Watching Ruth in her house had shown him that.

Even though the woman he thought he knew had behaved as though under sedation for weeks, now she appeared comparatively serene. He thought her lack of hysteria was due largely to her place, which she occupied so contentedly. It seemed that there was something physical between Ruth and her house. It affected him too. He longed to claim a part of it. And again, that thought led to another. If he were to succeed, he would have reclaimed Ruth as well.

Though he had disliked the convent and the sisters, he had been at least accustomed until the Duchamps came to release him. After that, for a time, knowing nothing else, he had felt he belonged with them. When suddenly he no longer felt that way, he was a drifter. It had been mostly a problem of food and shelter when he was young. He had failed to notice that he was displaced, since he kept looking around the next corner or into the next county so eagerly. After that, he would have said he belonged with his wife. It struck him as odd that he had never thought of it that way until now, when he saw, so nearly too late, that he might not fit anywhere at all.

With Ruth, near stranger though she seemed to him at times, in the old house in Connecticut, Alex began to envision what it might be like to belong again. He was not thinking just of four walls or geography. There was more to it than that, something harder to grasp.

Here was another of those unfinished patches in his life. The idea came to him as he ruminated on the park bench that he needed to stand back, to try to see himself from an outsider's point of view. Objectivity was a concept he'd thought about only as it applied to film making. Now a fearsome upheaval had occurred, obscuring some of his more bitter memories of the near past. Now was the time to make changes. He realized that to redeem himself with Ruth, he must be wiser than he'd ever been before in his life. Certainly he was not full of admiration for what he saw in his mirror in these days!

He had paid Nettie a visit, full of trepidation. She answered her door with a look on her face hard enough to frighten a terrorist. Somehow, he persuaded her to let him in so he could report on what had befallen Ruth.

"Please understand that I don't expect you to think any better of me, but I've been staying with her. She's pretty much okay now, I think. I'm going back on weekends to help take care of her and the house and all."

Nettie had said little. He could tell by the expression on her face that she was far from convinced that he was sincere. In his heart, he couldn't blame her. He understood that to her, to Ruth, to anyone he cared about, actions could be his only proofs. He did not say so to Nettie, but he knew he had to make up his mind, now that he was beginning to think again, about how he could try to find a way — where? Back to Ruth? He scarcely dared to think in those words.

On his park bench, he acknowledged to himself that he needed to get his affairs organized. Not only did he need work to keep the bills paid; he needed to order his priorities. What had given him the courage to say what he had about spending his weekends in the country? He sensed that Ruth was truly grateful. He thought of her refusal to give him a divorce when he wanted one, of his frustration and anger. Now he thanked heaven. How, and more important, why, had she faced out his wrath and lunacy and been so steadfast? Then he wondered with a mental shudder, what if she merely pitied him? It occurred to him to wonder how much she knew of the misery he'd endured at Honor's hands. What would it take, in short, for her to let him back into her life? How could he woo the woman he had been married to for years? A bitter twist to his lips at the irony made a passing walker give him a suspicious look.

Maybe it was all those confessions and absolutions he had been through in childhood, but Alex was determined to force the past to stay where it belonged — in the past. While he was on his own in the city, he could gain control over his own life, and then return to the country and Ruth, but he was almost afraid to hope. He got up suddenly and walked briskly out of the park.

Alex began to work harder than he ever had in his life. He made up careful presentations, wrote proposals, scheduled calls. He hired a temporary secretary to man the tiny office he rented. He began to think about what he could do with a camera that could not be done in a magazine article or in still pictures. Successful work appeared to be the fastest route to becoming a new man, and he was willing to take any that came his way. At night he was too tired to do much more than fall into bed, where he slept heavily until the demands of another day presented themselves, and he addressed them eagerly.

He discovered that the act of trying to create something was like sledding downhill on ice. The momentum was a little frightening, and he could not slow it down, but in the same way, it was exhilarating. Often he was so tired at night that he just called Ruth and then went to bed without bothering to eat. In spite of the pace, he felt well, strong, full of hope, and even younger.

When he went to the country, he behaved like a good house-guest. He worked hard, ate well, and tried to ignore the fact that the hostess was his wife.

His stock-taking had begun a string of unbidden memories. In time he discovered that a person may want to leave the past behind, but often it will not release him. For the first time in over a decade, he thought of his stealthy departure from his Canadian home. Were Mariette and Gabriel still alive? Were they all right? Had he hurt them beyond forgiveness? He would try to escape these questions, but they began to intrude relentlessly among his other thoughts.

Finally he wrote his parents a short letter giving the bare facts of his life. He mailed it with a sudden stab of fear that it might be returned unopened.

Then one day, when he got back from work, he found in his mailbox a thin blue envelope with a Canadian stamp. He sat down and carefully tore it open. Mariette had written in her schoolgirl hand, in French, naturally. Just looking at the language was like falling into a time warp. He had been speaking English for two thirds of his life and discovered he had forgotten some words. But reading was as if he could hear her voice speaking. He held the pages to his nose, as though he might get a whiff of the delicious smells from her kitchen.

She told about selling the gas station after Gabriel had fallen ill with ulcers. They lived quietly, going to mass twice a week and to the bingo games at the church for amusement. Now that he could no longer drink, Gabriel had taken to woodworking in a workshop he'd made in the cellar. He sold dollhouse furniture and bird houses to a gift shop that had opened out on the highway near the old garage. There were more tourists now.

Alex tried to imagine what a tourist could find to look at in St. Agathe.

Mariette did not write a word about him. He had written that he was sorry to have left so suddenly, that he was married, prospering, naturalized. He said he hoped they had forgiven him for running away. She did not refer to any of that. Alex thought as he read that she might have written her letter to an old school chum she did not remember too well. It had that hesitant, slightly formal, unrevealing tone. He read the letter three times before he began to notice how careful her sentences were. There was no hint of emotion in a single word. It was then that he realized how much hurt he had inflicted on those kind people. They had not even had the comfort of a grave to visit. He crumpled up the thin paper as he clenched his fist. *One problem at a time.*

ಶಿ ಅ

Alex continued to care for Ruth with gentle concern, while spring rushed in and warmed and softened the countryside. Ruth was getting her color back, partly because they could spend time out of doors, but it seemed to him that it was partly because she was beginning to escape from the memory of what had happened to her.

The irony was that just as she began to recover, it was as if Alex only then began to feel the event fully. He had trouble looking at her in the shorts she was wearing for gardening. When she put on a bathing suit and lay on a lounge chair in the sun, he felt like running out to throw a sheet over her. He caught himself staring at her whenever he could, looking for some outward sign of what had happened. The bruises he had seen in the hospital had long since faded, but he was nagged by the idea, though intellectually he knew it was false, that she was marked for life with some stigma he was unable to see. There was a subtle disgust he would not admit to feeling even to himself every time he failed to detect any overt reminder, as if she were deliberately hiding a shameful scar. He was ashamed of his feeling, prayed Ruth was unaware of it, yet he could not banish it.

One day he told her about the letter he had written home.

"Alex," she said with shock in her tone, "how could you do that?"

"You mean run away, or write?"

"Well, actually both. Years ago you made me see how you were feeling before you left. I guess I'm upset at your writing after all this time. They must have become used to not knowing anything, and now you've given them a terrible shock. Think how upsetting this must be for them."

"Yes, it must be," Alex had to admit. "And of course, now it means I can't stop there. I'll have to go and see them sooner or later."

"How will you explain ..." She stopped.

He knew he referred to their separation. "Well, I won't go right away," he said hastily. "There's much too much for me to do right now to think about making a trip. I'll have time to figure out everything before I start off." He spoke with mental fingers crossed. The truth was that he had no idea how he would deal with the confrontation, for so he imagined it.

The season advanced and the fields were filled with wildflowers. Weekends were busy and physically tiring. It was possible to devote attention to outward needs. When Ruth brought up another matter that Alex had given no thought to, he was jolted.

"I'm going to have to make plans to visit Mother. I was wondering if you would ... if you'd consider taking time off to go with me."

He wondered for the first time what she had done the previous summer, when he was unavailable. His first inclination was to say he would go whenever she wanted to, but he had a mental picture of the two of them registering in one of the motels where they had always stayed to break the journey. Then it occurred to him that there might be considerable awkwardness in the March house, after his absence the previous summer, if she had gone. In addition, he was fairly sure that Ruth would have told Dan the truth, and Alex dreaded facing him. So he hesitated.

Noticing this, Ruth said hurriedly, "But I know how busy you are, getting things going in your business. I shouldn't have asked without thinking."

"No, please don't feel that way. I just have to do a bit of planning, that's all. When would you want to go?" He would have to face it some time.

She looked at him intensely before she said, "Let's talk about it another time." She picked up her gloves, and went outside to weed the corn rows, and Alex followed her. He was uncomfortably aware that he might be forced to make good his resolve to tidy up his life even sooner than he had actually been prepared to.

CHAPTER TWENTY-THREE

It had been a quiet month. With the advancing season, Ruth had seemed to come alive again like the grass and trees and flowers. Alex was with her regularly, and she relied on his presence even though nothing was as it once had been. Her perspective had altered so that everything about their relationship called for reexamination. Alex's presence seemed to restore a facet of herself she had thought was lost. She saw that for a long time her life had been compartmented, separating work and her personal life, with the priority on the former. Now the emphasis was reversed. During the time they had lived in New York, Ruth's job had been the most important thing for her, except when falling in love distracted her. Once married, she had accepted her life and Alex's together unexamined—had gradually taken it for granted.

Her world had been shattered twice: first by Alex's betrayal, then by the rape. Now her life was again separated into two parts. Everything that went before Alex deserted her was now distant. Not insignificant, just far away. Perhaps that was why she was able to think about it in such detail. She still shrank from facing the fact of her affair with Malcolm, but now even it seemed unimportant in the light of what had happened since. It was too late for guilt anyway—Alex's or her own. Events had rendered that emotion meaningless, but in that thought were demons. She wondered whether she would ever regain what had been lost on that dew-wet roadside at the cold-blooded hands of a stranger.

Alex was scrupulous about arriving on the train on Friday nights. She would drive to the station to meet him. Every time she saw him step off the car and begin to walk toward her, she felt anew the same spark of pride she remembered from when they first were married. She had to make herself resist glancing around to see who else might be looking at him too, this man who was—no—this man who had been hers.

Weeks passed tranquilly. They would go home to a late supper. Usually they finished before dark, serenaded by the liquid songs of thrushes and thoughtful, quiet chirps of small birds going to roost. Cool air drifting from the woods would foretell the need for a blanket. By the time the crickets had tuned up, the field and hedgerow were sparking with fireflies, and overhead the blue-black sky stretched, pricked with starlight that for so long they hadn't seen in the glare of urban nights. After the dishes were done, they would sit in the living room, warm light shining on their books, music turned low. They almost never turned on the television, though three channels were available. Thus Ruth continued to renew her acquaintance with serenity.

But she knew this static peace had to come to an end. She dreaded it because she could see no certain outcome. That was why she began to watch Alex closely. She needed to know what his thoughts were on what should come next. He must give her some sign. She lacked the courage or initiative to make decisions. The last time she'd felt so doubtful about herself was when she recognized Alex on the tennis court. It had been a mistake to ask him to go with her to Maine. At first she wasn't sure why. Later it occurred to her that sleeping arrangements might be what troubled him.

ಬಿ ಆ

A couple of weekends after Ruth had asked about going to see her mother, Alex brought it up again. He was studying the road atlas. "We could go up through western Massachusetts and Vermont instead of through Boston this time."

Ruth said hesitantly, "Well, I've been thinking, and I realize you shouldn't take the time."

He looked up. "I've got my schedule for our next film worked out, and we can't begin until after the fifteenth of August. You could go before then, couldn't you?"

"I thought I'd fly up. Dan would be willing to meet me in Portland. That way you needn't interrupt your work."

Alex looked intently at her. He felt a stab of disappointment. She thought she saw both relief and a question in his expression. "If you think it would be better for you go to alone ..." She wanted to say how far from the truth that was, but was afraid to. She was afraid he might want to avoid making good on his offer.

They both felt the burden of too much left unspoken. Ruth shook her head, smiled, and went to get some ice cream. When she came back with the bowls, they spoke of the garden and of other things.

At bedtime, Alex leaned to give her the kiss on the cheek that had become their ritual, but he took her hand and squeezed it before letting it go. She felt his touch like a warm, sweet current, as strong as ever before, but now like a transfusion that conferred a sense of well-being she'd never thought to reclaim.

Again Ruth lay a long time awake, her mind darting from one thought to another like wasps trying to get out of a closed room. Alex seemed so changed. He was so calm and so serious. He seemed older. Yet he looked almost as he had the first time she saw him. But she was nothing like the girl she had been. Though they could not wipe out the past, there must be some way to benefit from it. She made up her mind that she had to make it clear that she forgave him. How? Could she, truly? She knew that in her heart, she had already.

Alex need never know about Malcolm. Yet, if she hid that part of her life, she would be a liar as well as an unfaithful wife. Did that matter? So much had changed since then!

She heard barred owls calling and calling, then her mother's voice seemed to mingle with theirs, as sleep crept over her. In her dream, Elizabeth appeared in an old chambray house-dress, remembered from childhood days. She stood on the back steps, a wicker laundry basket on her hip, calling Ruth with the diphthong sound on her name she always used over distance. "Ru-uth, Ru-uth!" She was standing up among the long grass next to the fence, and was surprised because it reached only to her knees. She had thought she would be almost hidden from her mother. But the voice continued to call, and call as if Ruth were invisible, though she was less than a hundred yards away. Ruth wanted to answer, but could make no sound. It was one of those dreams in which one struggles desperately to do simple things. She kicked the blanket off and woke cold, lying in moonlight that spilled across the foot of her bed.

Until dawn, she lay trying to assess the new phase she and Alex had entered. The only thing she was sure of was that she would never regret her refusal of divorce. Surely good will and steadfastness could rekindle love?

The next day Alex was laying a flagstone walk from the edge of the driveway to the huge stone step at the front of the house. In the years they had lived together, Ruth had become accustomed to his ability to handle the usual small repairs, and of course, his familiarity with tools and small machinery and cars. But now she was astonished at his obvious pleasure in the heavy work he began to do in the country. He had spent a fair sum on gardening tools and clearly enjoyed using them; for tilling, mowing, rebuilding fallen sections of the stone wall, and now the walk.

On the porch, Ruth shelled peas and watched him turn a slab of bluestone from corner to corner across the grass. "Have you seen Nettie lately?"

Alex stood up and wiped his brow with a wrist, supporting the oblong of stone against his leg. "No, not for a while now." He bent over again, heaving the stone onto one corner and dropping it over the bed of sand he had prepared. He continued to work with his crowbar, aligning and leveling.

Ruth was acutely aware of several things simultaneously, as if she had suddenly developed a more refined sensitivity—to time slipping away, to Alex's presence, to the faint, wild cry of a hunting redtail hawk, to the subtle security of her home. She felt a flood of courage well up. "We haven't said anything yet that's going to have to be said, have we?"

Alex straightened abruptly, almost dropping the crowbar. He stood for a motionless moment, like a model for a life drawing class, the bar supporting his unbalanced stance, his head turned toward Ruth, the muscled curves of his perspiring neck and shoulders glistening. He spaced his legs and turned his body so he held the iron bar in both hands exactly between his feet. Then, as if physical balance provided what he needed to be able to answer, he said, "No, we haven't."

Having taken the plunge, now Ruth had no idea what to say. What had Alex said once? Love was like facing an icy lake, and the only way to cross it was to swim. "You haven't said anything more about ..." Even with her new bravery, she had to force the words out. "About getting a divorce. Do you still want one?"

He shook his head slowly. "No."

"Would you—would you want to tell me about—about you and Honor?" She saw a faint ripple of shock cross Alex's features. He licked his lips. She went on, "Were you—was it very hard on you when—you parted company?"

"Very." He remained motionless. Shadows cast by the sunlight masked his expression.

Ruth was determined to penetrate his reticence. "Are you contented living by yourself in town?"

"Reasonably."

"Are you living by yourself?"

"Of course!"

Ruth looked down at the green pod in her hands. It was split, the peas still lying in their perfectly graduated row. She didn't want to disturb that symmetry. It seemed destructive to uproot them and tumble them into her bowl. She ran her thumb lightly across the cool bumps. Then she looked up at her husband, standing bathed in sunlight, his skin glossy with moisture from his exertions, his head poised at a questioning angle. Despite the shadows that hid the expression in his eyes, she was acutely aware of his body. He stood as if rooted.

"I don't want to go back to the city," Ruth said. She looked down at the dewy green globes under her thumbs. She needed to tell him how she felt about this house. He needed to know how it had been for her all those months alone.

The telephone rang inside, breaking the spell holding them suspended. Ruth set her bowl down, and went to answer it. It was ringing for the fourth time before she got to it. When she picked up the receiver, there was only the hum of the line. She said, "Hello," a second time.

"Is that you, Ruth?"

"Mother?" Immediately she recalled the evening she had received the only other call from her mother since her marriage, and she stiffened as if bracing for a blow.

"Yes, Ruth, I think you had better come up as soon as you can."

"What is it? What's wrong?" Ruth forgot the warm sun and Alex standing outside.

"Dan has had an accident."

"What, Mother? Tell me. How bad?"

"We aren't sure exactly. Will you come?"

"Yes, of course! But, please, Mother, tell me what happened!"

"A scaffold collapsed." Elizabeth paused, as though something had caught in her throat. Ruth waited, feeling her heart beating. "His back is broken."

"Oh, God! Mother, I don't know how long it will take for me to get there, but I'm coming. Don't worry, I'm coming." As she was about to disconnect, she thought to ask about Lacey and the boys.

"She's taking it well." Elizabeth's voice failed on the last word.

Ruth had the phone in both hands. "Give her my love. I'm coming. Goodbye." She put the phone down and felt nausea. She took a deep breath before going back to the porch. Alex was still standing leaning on the crowbar, his head down, as if studying the ground at his feet.

They found in short order that to make air connections was going to be so time-consuming that the only sensible thing to do if they were to set off immediately was to drive. Ruth's anxiety overrode everything. She never thought to ask Alex if he could go with her; she simply behaved as though she knew he would.

Alex felt as if he had been given a gift.

Once again, he took over practical matters. He notified necessary people, reminded Ruth to call Dr. Jessup, and put soft drinks in a cooler. They changed clothes, packed, put suitcases in the car, and locked the house.

Alex drove, and as they turned out of the driveway, Ruth looked back at the house, safe and contented, nestled under the great maples, sunlight paling the field at the back. She noticed the crowbar lying beside the half-finished walk, where Alex had dropped it.

CHAPTER TWENTY-FOUR

It was a relief to Ruth to be on the road. There was nothing they could do until they reached Devonport. The journey would provide a respite before she must face whatever awaited them. Later, the trip remained in her mind like an odd venture into another plane of being, the strangeness of which made certain isolated details linger sharply in her memory, like symbols. Instead of sensing the speed of their motion, there were long moments when it seemed to her that they were fixed, and the world was racing past them.

Alex saw their situation in a different way. He realized it presented an opportunity, but more clearly than Ruth, perhaps, he feared what might be coming at the end of their journey. He was ashamed to be thinking of himself, but he feared that disaster for Dan would pose a threat to the two of them. He understood his wife's love for her brother. More than anyone, he knew her loyalty. Whatever awaited them in Maine might force her to some unforeseen choice that would take her away from him. He had the notion that only by being useful, necessary to her, would she allow him to remain with her. The thought brought a lump of terror to his throat. Perhaps if he showed his own vulnerability, he could touch her and make her aware of him again, but he was afraid of intruding on her private worries and unsure of how to say the things he wanted to, so he kept silent for a long time.

As the miles sped past, each became more conscious of their silence. Finally, after they got past Springfield, Alex spoke.

"Can you think about anything besides Dan just now?"

"It surprises me, but yes." Ruth kept her eyes on the road ahead. "Now we're on the way, there's nothing to do but travel. We can only hope and pray."

"Then maybe this is a time for me to tell you some things you should know." Ruth heard a thickened timbre in his voice, and something in her tightened again, as if she were preparing her body to withstand blows. She dreaded revelations or confessions, while she knew it was important to hear what he would say. It was like teetering on a brink, like the feeling she had on her wedding night—that what was coming might be painful, but might be the way to happiness.

She murmured, "I'd like to hear."

Alex began to talk. She was aware that he was trying to be objective. Though it was not the first time he'd made an effort to talk about himself, she now sensed the intensity of his wish to reveal honestly as much as he could, rather than trying to conceal as much as possible. She'd anticipated hearing about Honor, but he started much further back than that. Sometimes in his recital, she felt compelled to look at his face, especially to concentrate on his lips.

Alex kept his eyes for the most part steadily on the highway. "I guess I've never been too good at facing, or accepting reality. I've tried to live in my own world, or one I dreamed up for myself from ideas I picked up, I don't really know where from, but mostly books, I suppose. When I was a kid, I used to swipe them from the library at school. All kinds. Most of the time, I sneaked them back when I'd finished them, but I kept some of my favorites. I wonder if Mariette and Gabriel ever found them and saw the school stamp. They gave me a flashlight for Christmas that first year I lived with them, and I'd use it to read under the quilt till I fell asleep." He chuckled. "They couldn't understand why I used up so much of my allowance on batteries."

"We read a lot at home too," Ruth said.

He spoke as if he hadn't heard her. "For me it was pure escape. If

I happened to learn stuff at the same time I was imagining how it would feel to reach the top of a mountain, or to find a new bacterium under a microscope, or fantasizing the blow of the flat of a sword on my shoulder, that was a bonus. I read for the windows books gave me to see out to unreachable places. A glimpse of Timbuktu, of history or science or glory..." Alex paused and swallowed. "The possibility of joy." He glanced at Ruth, and she saw him flush before he looked back at the road.

His choice of words surprised her almost as much as the peculiar intimacy of what they described. Furtively she looked for telltale signs that he was being ironic, but saw only a solemn droop to his mouth and marks of tension at the corner of his eye.

"I didn't get a chance at much fiction in those days. The school library ran to basic and outdated reference materials, biography, and the local newspaper. I didn't miss stories because I was happy imagining myself as an explorer, a scientist, or maybe a tycoon. Everything I read seemed impossible, so it didn't matter if it was fact or not.

"I'd read about all kinds of true adventure by the time I left high school. Not all of it physical. It was a Catholic school, don't forget." Now his lips curled in an ironic smile. "There was even a time when I thought well of saints. But as I got older, the town felt as if it had a wall around it as high as the one around the convent yard. It felt—claustrophobic." He clenched his jaw. "I'd actually get panicky. I think maybe that has made more trouble for me—and for you too, I guess—than anything else."

She gave him a startled glance. The whirl of thoughts sparked by only a few words was astonishing. Only his profile was visible, yet she read a compass of emotions on his face in the brief moments when he was silent. She realized with a stab of anguish that the years of watching and loving that face had made it possible for her to detect much that was hidden from other eyes. She was torn with remorse about what she'd failed to notice.

A maxim of her mother's rang like a knell in her mind: *There's none so blind as those that will not see.*

Alex went on, "I should tell you about what ... what happened with Honor." Ruth began to say he need not, but he interrupted. "It's your due. I regret everything. It was shaming. It's over, all over, and

I've been taught—I guess you could call it a lesson—in values. I told Nettie, but I don't know if she believed it, that I never meant for the whole thing to turn out the way it did. I mean, I didn't set out to hurt you, or myself, for that matter. I was such a fool, to think I might have a little—adventure—without doing any damage!"

In spite of herself, Ruth took an audible breath. If he heard her, Alex did not show it. "But they talk about playing with fire. I've never tried drugs, except for alcohol and a couple of reefers when I was still a kid, but tangling with Honor was kind of like the way dope is. She could invent ways to keep a man coming back the way unscrupulous hunters bait deer to a salt lick. And I was like the poor things that go to it, even when they sense the danger. Once I got a few tastes, it got so I couldn't do without more."

Ruth's imagination was rioting suddenly, showing her fantasies of surreal intensity. Few pornographic images had ever crossed her path, but even the descriptions she'd heard now tangled with suppressed memories of the rape, weaving a waking nightmare like the Hieronymus Bosch painting of hell she remembered seeing in a museum: swarming, naked, little insect-like human bodies—the damned.

She rubbed her eyebrows and turned in her seat so she could look at Alex's face, superimpose its beauty on the horrors she was imagining. He slowed the car a little and chewed his lower lip. She kept silent, trembling.

"But I wasn't so hooked I couldn't see when she was getting way beyond me. I knew I had to get out, and I did." She saw the muscle over the angle of his jaw bunch again. "But it was like quitting heroin cold turkey." Ruth closed her eyes. For the first time, an inkling of what he might have gone through touched her.

After a pause, he went on in a lower voice, "I'm glad you didn't see me then. Pete hauled me up out of the bottom of the hole I let myself fall into—by main force."

She said involuntarily, "I wish I could have been there to help."

Alex threw her a black look. "I was in bad shape, but I hadn't entirely lost my pride."

She felt stung. After years of sharing a life with this man, learning how he brushed his teeth, the order in which he removed his clothes, the sound of his breathing when he was on the edge of sleep, the shape of his broken little toe and the precise location of a mole on his right thigh—learning to know all those things and a thousand more, she hadn't learned what his heartwood was like. Nettie had seen deeper. She, his wife, had not perceived what would threaten him or what could break him. Indeed, she realized now that she knew little enough about herself. Small wonder he had been a closed book.

When she heard Alex's voice again, she could not look at him, shamed by her own thoughts. "I'll never forget some of the dreams." To her now hypersensitive ears, his voice sounded hoarse and strained. "In one, I sailed out on a lake that looked just like pictures of Kashmir, in a boat like a sort of floating surrey with a fringe on top. Honor was steering while I rowed. She was wearing some gauzy material that floated around her in the breeze. She smiled at me and leaned back on her elbows, pushing her boobs into the air. I tried to reach for them and dropped an oar. She pulled off some of her wispy clothes, very slowly, smiling, while I leaned sideways, still watching her, trying to catch the drifting oar. I couldn't take my eyes off her, so I couldn't catch it.

"Just as I stretched my hand toward her again, I saw that the cushion she was leaning on was swarming with butterflies, crawling with them, and they were multiplying, so they were beginning to cover her like a blanket, vibrating orange wings enveloping her like something in a horror movie." He swallowed. "I snatched my hand away. She'd turned into an awful, pulsing mass. Then I was standing in the yard back at the convent. I was crouching, trying to get away from Sister Joseph-Madeleine's knuckles. She was poking my scalp as she twisted my hair. It hurt. She forced my head down and down, while at the same time she lifted the hem of her habit with her other hand. My knees scrunched into the gravel, and that hurt too. I saw black stockings above the laces of cracked, black shoes and I was terrified of what I might see next. Then I woke up, sweating."

Ruth shivered and looked down at her lap, unable to think of anything to say. What Alex had just described flamed before her mind's eye. The tires hissed, and the roadside sped by in a blur.

Alex resumed, his voice level. "Things looked wrong when I was awake too. How could I mix that nun with Honor Ringwold? I tried to blot out the feeling I might be going nuts by getting—staying— drunk. Naturally, that made it worse. It was a long time before I began to see things without distortions. It was like living among the crazy mirrors at a fun park. Months later, people told me how strange I'd been."

Ruth discovered her jaw was aching and opened her teeth behind closed lips.

"And then you…you needed help, and finally I came back to the real world. I mean that literally. There was a definite feeling of nightmare about that whole … mess, as I think of it now." He shook his head several times rapidly, as if he had water in his ears. "You'll be glad to know I'm as ashamed of myself as I can be. More than ashamed. She made me … I was demoralized, almost immobilized. Disgusting and disgusted both."

"I'm sorry," Ruth said after a long silence. "You've been so unhappy, haven't you?"

He curled one side of his mouth. "If I have, it's been ninety-nine percent my own doing. I know I've got a hell of a lot to make up for."

For a while Ruth watched the road unrolling toward them. Alex kept silent, grimly guiding the car on the almost empty highway. Ruth longed to soothe him, to make some gesture to show her good will, but what was the right thing to say? She wondered whether it been some sort of premonition that bolstered her determination to hold on. At long last, she was able to feel for him. Was there a way, a safe way, to let him see that? She had once been so confident, so certain that right would prevail. Now she was too battered by events and tardy understandings to trust herself.

Alex's silence seemed an acceptance of hers. It dawned on her that she could not forget her own pain, that she had been beginning at least to push it aside, and then, after so much anguish, just when she thought she was regaining her footing, she had fallen victim again.

And now, here they were, speeding toward yet another crisis. If only she could escape the feeling of helplessness, of being at the mercy of events! She looked again at Alex's profile, backed by the blur of passing trees and other cars. His expression was calm.

Her mind leapt back to the rape. How must Alex think of her after that? With an effort to concentrate on what he'd been telling her and to sound practical, she said, "Well, it's all over now. Maybe we have to start thinking in terms of new days."

"I'd like to think so," he replied. She saw his lips tighten. Then she thought of Malcolm, knowing she should clear her own conscience, but was too irresolute to speak.

They stopped for lunch at a highway cafeteria whose fluorescent lighting made the patrons look as though they might be ready for autopsy. Ruth stared uncertainly at the artificial-looking salads and jewel-toned gelatins, and then helplessly at Alex. He chose sandwiches for them both, and coffee. They ate mechanically at a table littered with crumbs and sticky with spilled ketchup.

It was a relief to return to the private haven of the car. Ruth didn't offer to drive, and they set off once more into the stream of traffic and the featureless landscape of the interstate. Alex turned on the radio, shattering the swishing silence with a burst of thumping music. He searched the dial, static sputtering between fractured phrases and broken chords. The reception was impossible, and he gave it up.

In the absence of any distraction, Ruth tried to gather courage to say what she needed to. "Alex, I ought to tell you …"

"You don't need to tell me anything," he broke in gently.

"Yes, I do. When you left, I was devastated. A lot has happened to us both since then. But I had some help along the way. I had an affair too."

Alex took his eyes off the road to look at her. She was staring straight ahead. He maintained silence, his jaw set. When she was sure his attention was on the road again, with her lips trembling, she looked at his face. It seemed impassive, but she saw him swallow.

"What happened?" His tone was tentative, gentle.

With a flood of gratitude, she said, "We had separate ways to go. I'm not sure how I could have managed without—I'm grateful to him."

"So am I, Red," Alex said quietly. He took one hand off the wheel and laid it on her knee. After a while, she let her head drop against the back of the seat and closed her eyes. In a few minutes, she fell into a doze.

ಸಾ ಲ

As they drove into Devonport, the sky was fading from cerise to lavender, the ocean dull purple under the afterglow. Ruth limped into the hospital waiting-room, stiff from sitting. Alex followed. When Ruth saw Elizabeth, she felt sudden panic. She had been sure their mother would be upstairs with Dan.

They embraced briefly. "Thank you for coming," Elizabeth said. "It may be that you'll wish I hadn't called you." Ruth tried to ask how Dan was, but Elizabeth went on, "He's what they call 'stable.' Lacey is with him, but they don't want anyone else. He won't die, they say." She put her clasped hands up to her mouth. She looked haggard and incredibly old. She seemed not to see Alex at all. She stood in the center of the small room as if she had been abandoned there and did not know where to go.

Ruth dropped onto the edge of a plastic-covered settee as if she'd returned from a long hike. She looked up at her mother, tears beginning to blur her eyes.

"He may be paralyzed," Elizabeth said.

All at once, Ruth wanted to wail, to keen and shout, to curse ... What? Fate? God? It made no difference. Her beloved Dan! She was overwhelmed with a compulsion to give voice to her terror at a world she had once thought so benign and that had turned so barbarous. As if in reaction against all that had happened to her in the past year, she felt herself losing control, on the verge of some manic demonstration.

Alex saw her shaking and bent over her, his hand touching the back of her head lightly. Feeling faint, she bent forward. Putting both hands to her mouth, she bit the knuckles of her fists to keep from screaming. Alex sat down next to her, put an arm across her shoulder, drawing her against the comforting bulk of his side. She squeezed her eyes closed, her body vibrating like a wire in wind.

Watching his mother-in-law, he realized that Elizabeth knew nothing of what had happened to her daughter. "May we take you home?" he asked.

Somehow they made their way back to Ruth's car without saying a word to each other. Alex drove them both to the house.

The glare in the kitchen hurt Ruth's eyes. She let her mother lead her upstairs to the room where she and Alex always stayed. There she sat down on the edge of the bed. After some time, Alex came in with a steaming mug in his hand, and Ruth drank the cocoa without having moved.

"Your mother had a cup too and she's gone to bed," he said quietly.

Ruth nodded. "You're tired out, Red." She looked around, saw he'd brought their suitcases into the room. He said, "She didn't mention another room. I could go sleep downstairs on the sofa ..." He allowed his voice to trail off.

Ruth looked up at him, the cup still in her hand. He was frowning, his eyes hollow with fatigue. She stood up and carried the empty cup to the dresser. In the mirror, she saw her own pale face. Behind her stood Alex, the lamp on the nightstand behind him darkening his image. Framed in the mirror, their shapes overlapped, like a double portrait against a softly glowing background.

Without turning around, Ruth said in an uninflected voice, "No, it's too uncomfortable."

Perhaps it was the familiar warmth of her husband's body, or the sounds of the sea in the distance, or exhaustion, but she fell asleep almost immediately.

CHAPTER TWENTY-FIVE

Details of the time in Maine blurred in both their minds. Alex felt like a useless appendage, though he did errands, acted as chauffeur, tried to look after the house, and cooked more than half the meals. Through it all, his attention was riveted on Ruth. His own life had come to a standstill, its reanimation dependent on his wife's. He thought of her vulnerability, and how he felt when he had seen her desperate and traumatized. From that moment, he made up his mind that he could face whatever was to come, so long as it might end with Ruth's love and respect.

Ruth was naturally preoccupied with fears for Dan and his family, but several times every day she would look at Alex and silently thank providence for his presence. Though she could not muster confidence enough to imagine the future, she was grateful for his company at the end of exhausting days when she could sink into oblivion next to him. It had once again become the natural thing to do. He gave her comfort merely by being there.

They stayed in Maine for two weeks, visiting the hospital daily, waiting for the final assessment of Dan's injuries and for a prognosis on his recovery.

In the hospital, Dan lay encased in plaster and threaded with IV tubes, his eyes at first vague, later frightened, and finally defiantly darting from face to face. He did not talk, as though something had happened to his ability to form words. The doctors insisted that nothing about his accident had anything to do with this. Ruth was terrified by his silence. She feared as well that the thread of their old intimacy might be snapped. She and her mother did not discuss this. Ruth assumed Dan behaved differently with Lacey, but had no opportunity see whether this was the case, since the number of his visitors was restricted. She hoped.

As he came gradually to full consciousness, those watching could see him begin to struggle with the full knowledge of his misfortune. Ruth thought she saw her private fear realized. She confided to Alex, tears in her voice, "I don't know when he got to be so—so manly! I watched him grow up, but now he's turned into a stranger." She smiled tremulously. "With a familiar face. Oh, Alex, what's going to happen to him? Someone so capable, whose physical strength and talents have always been not just his livelihood, but what made him himself—made him Dan?"

Alex reached for her hand. He had nothing to offer, but she saw in his eyes the sympathetic response she craved and was comforted.

Dan's sons came daily to stand at the foot of their father's bed, eyes large as nocturnal animals', speechless and reverent. Only the rigidity of Dan's lips betrayed his fear.

Finally, one day, when he was allowed more visitors, he smiled when Ruth and Elizabeth went in. Lacey was sitting with his hand between hers, as they usually found her. She would always smile and talk as if they were visiting someone with an ordinary cold, and they had all followed her lead.

Elizabeth became the staunch one after the group of doctors had agreed that with months of therapy and a lot of determination, there was a chance that Dan might be able to walk with leg braces some day and that he would regain most of the use of his arms. Ruth and Lacey both went limp, as if they had needed the strain of uncertainty to stiffen them. When he came to pick them up, Alex found them in the drab waiting room drenched with tears and almost without the strength to walk to the car. Elizabeth, on the other hand, looked ten years younger. She led them outside, her head high, and her mouth a grim line, a living example of fortitude.

During the whole time they spent in the March house, Ruth and Alex shared a bed. For him it was a period of dreadful uncertainty and nightly penance. He would lie beside his sleeping wife, picturing the rape in lurid scenes that flickered in his mind, while he tried to black them out. He alternated between anger and pity, repeating inwardly, *She was helpless*. Why should he be thinking of that now? He should not be dwelling on that awful experience. He should be supporting and comforting her. His inability to suppress an insidious notion that something about his wife was changed by what had happened to her shocked and shamed him, even as he recognized it; still he could not escape it.

Thus, by the end of their stay, Alex, too, was emotionally exhausted. Thinking back on those two weeks, he came to be glad in a blameless way that Dan's tragedy kept him so effectively disconnected from Ruth. It gave him time to come to terms with the inner conflict between his rediscovered love for her and the aftermath of what had befallen each of them.

For Alex, one of the peculiar things about that period was that the sharpness of his own sense of guilt was gradually blunted. He watched Ruth when she was unaware of it, comparing her now with the girl he'd married. This was not just a matter of matching her looks with that memory, but of seeing other, more subtle changes. Of course, time alone was responsible for some of them, but there were other things visible, apart from her fears for her brother. A steely note would sound in her voice sometimes that was completely new to him. Yet she would gaze at him now and then with a pleading look that brought their first days together rushing to the forefront of his memory.

By the time they left Maine and its crisis behind, they were each both subdued and expectant. Separately, each was becoming acutely aware of the future as another entity to be faced and perhaps battled through.

ත ଇ

Once home again, Alex made up his mind to activate his resolve to straighten out his life. Accordingly, he made plans to go to St. Agathe. He did not ask Ruth to go with him, partly for practical reasons and partly because he felt they had too many unresolved issues of their own to be ready to meet his foster parents together. Besides, he was superstitiously afraid to acknowledge his springing hope, and couldn't bring himself to speak of it to Ruth. Instinctively, he wanted to postpone her meeting with his parents until he could be sure he and his wife could be reconciled. Whatever he did took on the force of omens in the back of his mind. Finally, there was the notion that it was necessary to face his duty to those he'd deserted before he dared to try to take Ruth back.

He made an attempt to explain tactfully why he wasn't asking her to go with him. "Let me feel them out, alone, first. They're shy, Red, and I don't know how they're going to take me. It's been a long time, and they'll have enough to accept, just seeing me again. Maybe they won't welcome a prodigal son. I'd hate for you to find yourself in the middle of something like that."

"I do understand." She touched his arm. "I'm so glad you're going."

Alex looked at his hands, clasped between his knees. "It's overdue. Let's hope it's better late than never."

On the road again, Alex had more than enough time to worry over what he was doing. What would he say to Mariette and Gabriel? After so many years without giving them any news, he couldn't decide what to include, though he knew what he'd prefer to leave out. Just because they knew nothing, he had the choice of what to tell. Wryly, he understood that what he wanted most was the absolution he could acquire only by complete honesty and wondered whether he was capable of it.

He'd developed no strategy by the time he drove his rented car between fields of fading stubble and into the sparse outskirts of the town. Overcome with *déjà vu*, he parked and got out. It was as if he had ventured into a crystallized dream. The deserted look of the place in late afternoon was a dramatic contrast to the crowds of New York, or even the busy main street of the town nearest to Ruth's house in the country. It was late in the season, and already most of the leaves had fallen; the fields were brown and empty, except for the cow pastures. The distant bark of a dog emphasized the absence of visible humanity. Alex stood for a minute, trying to decide whether to ring the bell at the front door, or go around to the kitchen, as he used to when he lived there, and decided that would be to presume too much.

He took his suitcase and went up the front steps. Before he could press the bell, Mariette opened the curtained door. Alex tried to absorb her with a quick glance. In the dark hallway, she might have been emerging from a cave. He could see that her eyes, squinted up as if in pain in the warm light of afternoon, were filled with tears. Her once round cheeks were lined and pale; she had become a thin old lady. The waxy cast of her skin looked entirely unnatural to him, and for a moment he thought she might be someone else.

"*Bienvenu.*" She held out her arms. Alex's throat ached. He put down his suitcase, and embraced her, kissing first one cheek, then the other. She had shrunk, and her body felt rickety in his arms. He wasn't prepared for the melancholy that washed through him. He closed his eyes against the pain of it.

They went into the house, which had changed not at all. It still smelled of furniture polish, fresh bread, and cinnamon. Gabriel was sitting at the kitchen table, holding a newspaper. What hair he had left was entirely white, but otherwise he looked very much the same, though diminished, as if he too had shrunk. He rose stiffly when he saw Alex. The men shook hands awkwardly and silently.

Alex thought the two days he planned to spend with them would seem an eternity, if they were to continue like this—wordless and brimming with emotion.

Gabriel went to get a bottle of Calvados. He poured them each a small glassful, then they sat in the kitchen as Mariette got a meal together. Neither could keep his eyes off the other, but the restrained and hesitant tone of their polite talk made Alex want to get away. Gradually, slowly, the tension was dissipated by the homely kitchen, the sounds and smells of cooking, and by the brandy. The old people began to ask tactful questions, always speaking French. Finding himself rusty after so many years speaking only English, Alex answered everything as well as he could.

He did not know how to explain the gap in his marriage, so left it unmentioned. He had brought snapshots of Ruth and himself and he tried to fill in the years, at least the salient facts of them. He was overcome suddenly with a longing to feel like a son again, instead of a stranger. He talked carefully, showing as much of the truth as he dared, from the day he had run away. The two old people kept staring at him, and he realized eventually how different from the stripling who'd made off with a customer's car and a brand-new muffler he must look, now a man over forty, with such a checkered career already behind him.

They said no word of reproach, nor did he try to apologize to them. What could he say? It comforted him that they seemed to understand that what was so long past was no longer of importance. He grasped the fact that there were no amends he could make, in any case.

He inquired after their health and how they spent their days. What Alex told them was facts, without embellishments or interpretation, and what they told him was the same. Everything of internal importance was avoided with scrupulous delicacy. They discussed nothing personal, just as one would never recite details of his sex-life to elderly parents. Alex's now halting French became more fluent as time and tension passed.

After two days, he left with utmost relief. He was glad to be going now, lightened by his decision not to leave them to die without word of him. He looked back to see them smiling as they waved goodbye from the porch, side by side, not touching each other, like folk carvings.

Thinking, thinking on the long drive home, he came to see that their love made his hope for atonement irrelevant. He had just been given the perfect example of forgiveness. At last he thought he saw the way to reach his wife.

CHAPTER TWENTY-SIX

Ruth welcomed Alex's absence. As anxiety for Dan subsided, she needed to think over the time she and Alex had spent together since he'd come to her after the attack. His presence reinforced the certainty that he was necessary to her, absolutely vital. Like the instinct for self-preservation, her determination to bind herself to her husband again overshadowed all other motivations. Despite the fact that it had begun in an innocence that bordered on ignorance, she found her love for him had endured. As if the damage it had sustained had strengthened it like a broken bone that has healed, she felt it growing, expanding, and demanding expression.

Not just Alex's gentle helpfulness encouraged her; it was more than that. She was certain she detected respect and affection, even desire. In the days he was in Canada, she made up her mind to risk her new independence, her hard-won self-sufficiency, especially her pride, on the only worthwhile gamble she could imagine.

Alex, by this time, understood that complete honesty had an outside chance to effect a full reconciliation, but he wondered if he had the courage for it. Or was he doing Ruth an injustice? She had never said a bitter or even critical word to him since they had been together again. All she had done was ask a few questions and flinch once or twice at the answers.

When she said to him once, "What about Honor made you want her so much that you decided to leave me?" he wanted to refuse to answer, or at least to fabricate something equivocal. The look in her eyes had prevented him, as well as his newfound sense of obligation to her. Humbled as he was by her refusal to give him up, supported by her staunch faith in the marriage that he realized he'd carelessly broken without making any attempt to preserve it, he'd done his best to give her an answer.

"What I felt then, and what I know now don't really have much to do with each other." He had to reach deep for every word, as though he were discovering it as he went along. "At the time, I thought she was someone extraordinary, exotic, unconventional and exciting. I was overcome by ..." He felt heat rising in his face. "I guess just raw sex. She was so voluptuous and so ... bold. I thought she was courageous, when what she really was, I see now, was merely outrageous." He longed to forget gestures and events that had snared and then bound him so tightly.

Ruth nodded slowly. "At least it's over now," was all she said, but in that short remark, Alex heard some of what he had failed to perceive before: the strength it must have taken for her to cling to her decision to wait it out. Looking at Ruth's straight back, a chill passed over him like the proverbial ghost walking over one's grave. What if she had been weaker, or even merely less trusting of her own instincts?

One Friday night, some weeks after he returned from Canada, they were sitting in front of a fire. The noise of katydids was silenced by the unaccustomed cold, and the house was very quiet. Alex got up to put a record on. They had begun to listen to jazz—Bushkin, Mingus, Coltrane.

While he searched for one, Ruth spoke. "Do you think you could work from here? Have an office this far from New York?"

He looked over his shoulder at her, but she faced the fire. He returned to his chair, trying to conceal his surprise at her question and his upsurge of hope. His new company had been as busy as he wanted it to be, with work coming in whenever he went out to look for it. The four special films he'd made had been well received by the clients. He had been given two word-of-mouth referrals that he was working on at the moment, but he had never given a thought to trying to work away from the city. His mind spun with the implications of what she had just said, and with fear that he might be inferring more than he should.

He tried to sound casual. "I don't know. Maybe it's possible, but it wouldn't be easy. I'd have to commute at least four days a week, if I continue to do my own directing. If I were just selling the service, it would be different."

Ruth stood up and went to look down into the flames. "Well, I've been thinking about the future." Her hair was almost as bright as when he first knew her; the firelight made it shine, ruddy as a Titian *signorina's*. Alex heard his own heart, thumping hard enough to shake him.

She said a little too loudly, "You've been very helpful to me, Alex, since ..." He heard a tremor, which made him long to touch her, to tell her she need not say it, but she went on, "since the rape." She hugged herself, her eyes still on the flames. Stiffly, like a headmistress, she said, "It seems to me that we've been getting along well."

Alex had a light sweat on his forehead. He was afraid to speak, lest whatever words he uttered should fail to convey what she wanted to hear, or what he longed to say. Ruth turned around abruptly and looked him in the eye grimly, as if she were about to reprimand him. "Would you like to consider—going back to the way we used to live?"

She was very pale, and Alex could tell her mouth was dry. In the long pause while he tried to think of the best way to give her an answer he saw her try to wait calmly. A spate of thoughts raced through his mind. *She needs not just someone—she needs me!* Alex understood suddenly, like the revelation of a coded message, that he might have a place again, a place where he would be truly necessary. Suddenly it all seemed so simple.

He gathered himself. "Red, I'll work it out. I want to be what I should be—your husband again." His voice dropped to a whisper, "If I can." The fire crackled and flared suddenly, but Ruth stood absolutely still, looking intently at him. "Thank you for asking me."

They remained like a pair of statues for several breaths, staring into each other's eyes. Then Ruth inhaled deeply, like someone coming up from under water. Alex went to her, took her hands in his and said, spacing his words out, "Ruth, I love you."

An odd expression passed over her face; her eyelids fluttered, and for an instant he thought she might faint. Finally she whispered, "And I love you." He lifted her hands, still within his, to his lips, and she leaned into his chest with a sigh. His arms imprisoned her against his body. Nestling into his embrace, she absorbed his strength in order to remain upright. She wanted to stay like that for a lifetime. He felt as if he had come to rest after an odyssey. The fire emitted a tiny, whistling song. Each listened to the breathing of the other.

Ruth raised her head after a time. "Darling, I owe you a story, to make an honest woman of me."

Alex felt a hot shaft of unease, as when the dentist picks up a new bit to fit into his drill. "You don't have to ..." he began, but she cut him off, raising her face and gently pushing herself away from him.

"Yes, yes, I do." She turned to the couch, and sat down, facing him squarely. "In a way, we could be meeting for the first time just now, so much has changed." She clasped her hands very tightly, but he saw they trembled. "I think—I really think you've changed as much as I have, and I'm not even sure just how much that is yet, but we can't just pick up where we left off, can we? We have to start almost from scratch." She frowned. "We must!"

Alex sat down next to her. She looked at him with gratitude, but went on determinedly. "I've already told you, I've been unfaithful too." She looked up to see that he was gazing at her with mournful eyes. His lips had parted almost imperceptibly, but he waited in silence for what she would say. "It was ..." she licked her chalky lips, "... it was Malcolm Gentry."

Alex sighed deeply, drawing himself erect. "I have no right ..." He took her hand. "It's all right."

Ruth said quietly. "He did help me through the worst time of my life. But I knew from the start, it wasn't going to be a permanent thing, I think. It's been over for months. He's gone to California. I've had time to learn to be alone, the way I thought I'd have to be indefinitely."

Alex stood up and pulled her gently to her feet. "Neither of us has to be anymore," he murmured, his lips brushing her brow. Then he hugged her to him, his face buried between her neck and her shoulder, stroking her hair with one hand. His eyes burned and his throat hurt. He placed his lips on her forehead very softly. Ruth was limp, not just in body, but in the inner part of herself, where for so long she had been only a stony skeleton.

"My love," she whispered. A log settled with a sibilant sound and a fountain of sparks, but they did not move, their forms so close they might have been a single body, standing in the flickering firelight.

☙ ❧

It proved to be a slow process, learning each other again. Ruth couldn't will herself to be pliant, nor to forget. Nor could Alex. After he tried unsuccessfully to make love to her, she pressed his head onto her shoulder, laid her chin against the top of it, and stroked the back of his neck until he slept. In the morning she spoke, something the old Ruth would never have done. "Were you thinking about the rape?"

Alex closed his eyes, breathed deeply and nodded, sad, shamed, but compelled to admit the truth.

"I don't blame you," she said quietly. "So was I. If you're willing to be patient, I think we can get over it." Alex went to her and hugged her to hide welling tears.

CHAPTER TWENTY-SEVEN

December was nearing its end, cold as any city-dweller could want. Ruth and Alex spent a day out in the woods, cutting branches to decorate the house. The first snow was sifting down so gently they had to hold their breaths to hear its tiny whisper. It dusted dry leaves and grass and small plants like sugar on a cake.

Ruth intended to make ropes to twine the banister, swags for the fireplaces, a wreath for the front door, and numerous table decorations. They already had a bucket full of bittersweet vines covered with berries on the porch. "If you'd cut some more white pine, I could carry another few branches," she called to Alex's back. He was ahead of her, the bunch of hemlock and spruce he was carrying waving rhythmically over his shoulder as he walked. Through the scrim of snow, ranked trees made a somber backdrop for his red and black checked jacket and the feathery branches.

"Okay. On the way back, we'll get more from the tree near the house. I want to see what that is, up ahead, by the stream."

He waved the pruning shears. Through intervening trees shone tiny spots of bright red. They pushed their way through undergrowth, tugged against insistent thorns, and found a large clump of black alder with red berries clinging in clusters on stiff, black twigs.

"Oh," Ruth breathed, "they're beautiful! Like jewels, or drops of blood. They're too perfect to cut."

Alex turned to her, the green of his burden against his reddened cheek, and his knitted cap frosted with snow. He radiated color and vitality. "If we take only a few, it won't make any difference. Look how big the bush is." He smiled and winked. "Why, I think it would be wasteful, even ungrateful in a way, not to accept such a gift, don't you?"

She smiled back and nodded, scratching her chin against the bristly burden in her arms. "I'm so glad you found them! It's going to be the final touch to make it perfect."

Alex beamed at his wife. Snowflakes glittered on her russet hair, collecting among the threads the wind had loosened. Her cheeks were pink from cold and so was the end of her nose.

"We'll have to make another trip if we don't have enough." He carefully chose and clipped berry-laden twigs. "Neither of us can carry any more now. Too bad it didn't snow sooner. We could have taken a toboggan and brought back a lot more at once."

"We don't have a toboggan," said Ruth.

"It would have been the perfect excuse to get one, don't you think?" He leaned forward and kissed her, pushing the scratchy branches away with one hand, his nose cold against her cheek.

They made a wreath for the front door from hemlock and the bushy spruce, a red velvet ribbon, and twigs of black alder. More berries, feathery white pine, cedar, dark yew, cones, candles and brass candlesticks made every room fragrant and festive.

"This house was made for Christmas decorations," Ruth said, as she stood back to admire the living-room mantel. Christmas carols played softly on the new hi fi Alex had brought from the city.

Alex said, "I think it was made for you too." Ruth turned to him with a smile and a kiss. "You should have your picture taken against that background—the dark green and twisty twigs of orange and red bittersweet. You know you're beautiful, don't you?"

"Thank you," she murmured, suddenly hot with embarrassment. She leaned into the curve of her husband's arm and gazed at their handiwork. "Okay. Now it's time to get serious. Aren't you hungry?"

∞ ◎

"Do you think Mother will mind sharing with Nettie?" she asked, probably for the fifth time, as she finished clearing up after supper.

"Red," he said with a chuckle, "think about it. It's only for three days, and what's her choice? Maybe Nettie'd rather use a sleeping bag in the study with the boys. Who knows? She could tell stories to them all night. We can make adjustments after everyone gets here." He came up behind her and kissed her on the ear. "This house, with you in it, would make a perfect Christmas for anyone. They'll have a wonderful time." He felt as though he'd never had Christmas before. Like a child who hopes for the gift at the top of his list, he was full of eagerness for the day to arrive.

"You don't think I was too hasty? Asking my relatives and Nettie together?" Ruth turned in his arms, looking up at him.

"Well, maybe it'll turn out to be a mistake, but I think they'll get along. Your mother might have a little trouble with some of Nettie's choices of words, but it won't hurt her. And Dan and Lacey will be fascinated. I predict the boys will fall in love." He grinned as Ruth raised her eyebrows. "Well, maybe not in love, but I bet they'll take to her. They're old enough now to appreciate her."

From childhood, Ruth had tended to date things in her mind in relation to Christmases. She remembered events that took place before or after special holidays, like the one when Dan got an electric train, or the one when they both had mumps, or the year they each were given one book because that was all Nathan could afford. There were times when they had lonely guests from among their parents' acquaintance in and near Devonport. Until they died, Elizabeth's parents had always been with them and Nathan's as well. All children should have grandparents. March Christmases had hummed with guests and laughter, as at no other times.

So Ruth lay in the dark, thinking about the Christmas to come. It would be the first since Alex and she had been married when they would have a family celebration. This gave it a special significance. Most of Ruth's nerves came from her superstitious fear that if the house party did not turn out to be as happy as she hoped, it might be an ill omen for her future with Alex. This was to be a landmark

Christmas.

Alex's memories of Christmases were marred by their unique solemnity. At first, in the convent orphanage, later in the religious home of the Duchamps, it was the babe in the manger and the man on the cross that had always dominated the holiday. He remembered the frigid sacristy where, dizzy with fatigue, he prepared to serve the midnight mass. He had loved the carols, but the dirge-like tempo favored by the sister who was the organist had seemed to take the joy out of them. To the child exhausted from church duties and the day itself, overfed on Mariette's surfeit of holiday food, the carefully chosen practical gifts had always seemed dismally anticlimactic. He did not doubt that this year would erase memories of past Christmases, including those he and Ruth had celebrated so sensibly and meagerly on their own in New York. On Christmas Eve, Alex slept as soundly as a tired and happy child.

Ruth understood why Alex had refused to invite his own parents. When she suggested it, he had said, "Those two shy people have been through too much already on my account. I wouldn't feel right about subjecting them to strangers at holiday time. You can't imagine how foreign we'd seem to them, apart from the language," he added hastily when he saw Ruth's frown. "Please don't misunderstand. I want you to meet them, but this wouldn't be a good time—for them."

Ruth looked forward to meeting the people who had reared Alex, who had known him when he was suffering the growing pains that propelled him out of his home and across the continent, but she appreciated his concern for them and was convinced he was right. Still, she was beset by spells of doubt. She remembered times when aftermath of gift-giving had been unanticipated. Like the year Nathan had decided to outfit Dan for hunting. He had given him a rifle for his birthday the year before, and it had never been fired except during that weekend when his father was showing him how to use it safely. The next Christmas, Nathan gave Dan hunting boots and a jacket with ammunition pockets, a game bag, and a hat with ear flaps. Dan was aware that he was expected to come home with a grouse or a duck or some other dead creature some day.

For Dan, however, hunting had proved to be a chance to steal periods of solitude that he'd always been shy of claiming. Feeling obligated, Dan had tried, but the pheasant he brought in one day was the first and last he ever shot. He had refused to eat any of it. The gun became his ticket-of-leave. Ruth wondered whether their father had ever noticed. Her thoughts about a hopeful future and Christmas had stirred their opposites: ghosts of the past, but now dimmed so that what she had experienced seemed to lack normal contrasts, like poorly exposed photographs. Yet they hovered still, mocking the confidence that made her feel safe in her house. She was ashamed of her introspection, but knew she was changed and she thought strengthened, and took heart.

Then had come the horror of the rape, all the greater for her misplaced confidence. Now she dared to wonder what she would have done if Alex had not come to the hospital. Would she ever have regained her taste for life, if Alex had not succeeded in reawakening her love? But then it had never died. She turned over, placed a hand on his hip, and sighed lightly. The proverb about an ill wind passed through her mind as sleep drowned her restless thoughts.

ಸಿ ೧೩

Ruth was glad that her relatives arrived before Nettie. She had been afraid that her mother would feel as though there were a subtle alignment in opposition to the Maine contingent, if they had arrived to find bumptious, aggressive Nettie already ensconced. Alex thought she was being silly when she told him that.

As it was, Elizabeth arrived with Lacey and Dan and the boys in a flurry of hugs and laughter. Ruth and Alex delighted in welcoming them, showing them around, arranging their gifts under the tree in the corner of the study. They installed Dan and Lacey in the downstairs bedroom, easy for Dan on his crutches, where there was floor space for the boys' sleeping bags and a TV set. The boys quickly found a channel showing *M*A*S*H* episodes. They lay on their stomachs on the floor and watched entranced. Dan and Lacey closed the door on them. It was time to meet Nettie's train.

Elizabeth had gone up to lie down, and Dan and Alex set to work on a jigsaw puzzle, leaving Lacey and Ruth to meet the train. The snow had left only spotty reminders of itself in shaded corners of fences and against the north sides of tree trunks, but the dull sky seemed to promise more. Juncos and chickadees were mobbing the feeders. Yet the weather did nothing to dampen Ruth's spirits.

"I'm so glad you all came!"

Lacey said, "Once Dan talked Mother into it, it was all settled. We wanted to come." She paused, then said, "It's the first place Dan has *wanted* to go since the accident." Lacey seemed to be relaxed; she showed none of the strain Ruth had anticipated. Lacey went on, "He goes to work without fretting, but he still hates to be seen at a social occasion."

"That's a little hard on you, isn't it?"

"Not especially. I know he'll get past it eventually. We're both getting used to the new way of living and we're both so happy that he's come so far. We know we have to be patient. It's working out," she said serenely. "We're fortunate we had insurance; Dan's lucky to have competent, trustworthy men who work for him, so he's able to make a living. The world hasn't come to an end, even if it has shaken us up a good deal."

"You're pretty brave, you know."

"It's not too hard when you don't have to do it alone," Lacey replied with a little smile.

Nettie, presumably in honor of the occasion, arrived turbaned in red, green, and gold, looking not unlike an oversized, animated tree ornament when she dropped from the train step in her black cape, burdened as she was with glossy shopping bags bulging with colorful packages. She set those down on the platform and accepted her suitcase from a man who handed it down to her.

"Merry X-mas, Red," she said gruffly, giving Ruth a one-armed hug. They stowed her things in the trunk of the car. "You must be Lacey." Nettie climbed into the back seat. "You're as pretty as your picture. Happy to meet you at last."

Lacey laughed. Ruth drove home with her passengers in a spirited conversation about the relative merits of rocky cliffs and smooth sand beaches, Lacey defending the former, and Nettie the latter. Ruth relaxed, seeing them warm to each other.

Once home, Nettie became, in spite of her brilliant plumage, as formal and dignified as a matronly goose. She watched and she listened. Ruth and Alex supposed she'd make notes after bedtime, but she proved to be a perfect stimulant for Dan's shyness and

Elizabeth's reticence. She teased Josh and little Andrew, drew them out, made them laugh, and as predicted, enchanted them.

After supper, Ruth followed her mother to the guest room, intending to sound her out about how she felt about sharing it with Nettie, so she might make a tactful change of plans, if necessary. Elizabeth sat on one bed while Ruth turned the other down.

Gravely she said, "This is a lovely house. You were fortunate to find it. You've done a fine job furnishing and decorating it." She paused, studying her daughter's face. "I know you and Alex will be happy here."

"I'm glad you like it too." Ruth sensed that her mother was implying more than she was saying.

Elizabeth pointed to her suitcase. "If you look there, you'll find a package. It's a combination housewarming and Christmas present especially for you."

Ruth found the parcel and sat down on a chair to untie the ribbon. "Oh, Mother!" White tissue made a nest around the carved sandalwood box—her father's tribute to his wife, given so many years before. She lifted it to capture the faint, warm fragrance. "Thank you," she whispered, with tears in her eyes. She gave her mother an awkward hug, bending down with the box in her hand.

"Please assure Nettie that I don't mind how late she may want to come to bed. I hope you'll all excuse an old lady for retiring early." Elizabeth was smiling.

Ruth thought of how rare such smiles had been in past years. Her mother was thinner, a little bent, her hair white. She looked as if age were softening her. It occurred to Ruth that she'd never seen her before, except in crises, in a situation in which she hadn't been in charge. Here, she was a guest, and perhaps she was going to enjoy having someone else worry over the meals and whether there were enough blankets on the beds, for a change. "We're so glad to have you here." Ruth gave her another impulsive hug.

Perhaps it was the truth of that remark that gave the entire weekend its aura of closeness and gaiety. After the gifts were opened, while the other women went to the kitchen, Nettie saw an opportunity to challenge the boys at archery, using the gifts she'd brought them. Dan exchanged a wink with Ruth from his chair, as he observed the interchange.

Josh asserted, "We know how."

"It's easy," Andrew put in.

"If you two think you're such hot shots, I'll be happy to keep score for you. Then I'll show you how to do it right." Nettie was helping Josh and Andrew string the bows. "Just because I live in a big city doesn't mean I never learned a thing or two about anything else."

Skepticism written all over their faces, the children went out to set up a paper target against the spring-house. Dan swung himself to the window on his crutches, where he and Elizabeth went to watch.

"They'll lose all their arrows in the grass and weeds," he said, chuckling. Nettie was measuring off the distance in giant steps, while the boys tacked up the target.

"She's not going to have them just let fly, is she?" Dan was saying. "Look how she's insisting on correct form. Where did she learn to do that?"

"Andrew hit the target!" Elizabeth's voice was merry. "You thought they'd lose their arrows, didn't you, Daniel?"

"Josh's bounced off, but it just fell in front of the wall, so maybe they'll find it."

From the kitchen, Lacey and Ruth could hear occasional shouts of encouragement and whoops of delight when a shot went well. Ruth wanted Alex to mash the potatoes for her, but discovered he had gone outside too. He stood, aiming, looking like a Greek athlete in Abercrombie clothes, bowstring under his chin, while the boys gestured instructively at him. Nettie was planted, arms akimbo, supervising the group. A few fluffy snowflakes began to sail slowly down through the still air, to complete the picture.

During the meal, everyone laughed, teased one another, and ate hugely. Candlelight and a crackling fire in the increasing gloom of the winter afternoon warmed cheeks already flushed with cold and excitement.

Andrew said, his eyes large with respect and fatigue, "Miss Zabriski knows an awful lot about archery!"

"Yeah," Josh broke in. "And she can sure shoot too!"

"Well, guys," Nettie said, "None of us got a bull's eye, but it wasn't too bad for a bunch of amateurs, was it?"

"I'm gonna practice till I can hit the gold every shot," Josh declared.

"Nobody could do that," Andrew put in.

"What about Robin Hood and that guy with the apple?"

"Those are just kid stories, dummy."

Nettie intervened. "Maybe all the tales about splitting arrows and perfect shooting aren't *exactly* what happened, but you should practice. That's how you'll get better."

"Well, I'm going to practice until I'm as good as—as the guy with the apple. What's his name?" Josh was looking stubborn.

"William Tell?" Dan asked.

"That's the one. I'm gonna shoot every day."

"Wait a minute," Nettie interrupted. "You're going to have to have a little common sense. You can't shoot in the rain, or you'll ruin your arrows and you'll have to be sure you set up where you have a good chance of finding them if they don't go into the target. Don't forget the safety rules you learned today."

Ruth refrained from showing her amusement at Nettie's sounding maternal. She looked at Dan. He sat with his crutches leaning against the back of his chair. She searched his face for the shadows she remembered seeing there when he was a boy, and they'd been best friends. Even in his present circumstances, with so much to overcome, she failed to see any. His brow was smooth, mouth relaxed. He listened to his offspring, now and again glancing at Lacey with a smile.

"You know, son," he said, "Mr. Tell might never have shot that well in his life before. Do you remember the story?"

"They put an apple on his kid's head and he had to shoot it off, didn't he?"

"That's right. What do you think would have happened if he'd shot a little too low?"

Josh's eyes got big. "He'd have killed him."

"Right. And what would have happened if he'd missed high or to one side?"

"I dunno."

"He'd have lost his own life. So you see, he had a pretty powerful motivation to do it just right."

"What if he was nervous?" Andrew inquired.

Alex said, "You can bet he was shaking in his boots." He glanced at Ruth so swiftly she wasn't certain his eyes had sought hers. "But sometimes, if it's important enough, you can do what you know you have to do."

"Can I have some more stuffing, please?" Andrew asked.

"May I, Andrew," said Elizabeth. Then, when they all burst out laughing, she smiled too.

Alex directed a penetrating look toward his wife at the opposite end of the table, across the candles and greenery and scattered plates and serving dishes. Moving his lips very precisely, he mouthed, "Merry Christmas!" and smiled.

CHAPTER TWENTY-EIGHT

Even though Alex had enjoyed himself, he was glad when everyone was gone. It had been three days of gaiety, of big meals and holiday fun, but it had been a strain. He felt as if he and Ruth had just been through some kind of test. Now he was impatient to be alone with his wife again, to discover whether they had passed.

"How did you think it went?" Ruth asked after he returned from taking Nettie to the station.

"I was just going to ask you. I thought it was great. Everyone had a good time, don't you think?"

She nodded, smiling. "Yes, I do think so. The boys made it perfect, didn't they? Still, I was worried about Dan. How did he seem to you?"

"Adjusted," Alex replied. "He told me he still wakes up in the middle of the night, and then the goblins come around sometimes, but he figures there hasn't been enough time yet to get used to being only about half what he was before the accident."

Ruth nodded. "Lacey told me that too. I still can't get used to it, that he's really crippled for life."

Alex thought of the many injuries people sustain. "Well maybe ... I don't mean to sound like Pollyanna, but maybe he isn't crippled *for life*." It seemed vital that he find words of comfort for her. "Maybe he can't walk without crutches, but maybe in himself he's stronger than you or me. It's a bitch, but he looks at it a bit differently. He's grateful it wasn't any worse." Ruth said nothing. "Maybe that's the way we should look at things too."

She swallowed, then looked at her husband. Trying to see into his mind, she read in his eyes a plea. Perhaps the test they had both felt implicit in this holiday had been different from the one she had imagined. Suddenly, she saw that honesty was his due every bit as much as hers. Yet she had not yet found the courage required. She felt it was safer to respond as though his surface meaning were all she caught.

"Yes, of course. That's Lacey's attitude. You're right. We're fortunate, maybe more than we deserve. We can all learn from disaster, can't we?" She turned away quickly, afraid of tears. Alex came close to her. She asked with a falsely bright tone, "How did Mother seem to you?"

Alex touched her arm, yearning to embrace her, but aware of her struggle for self-control. He withdrew his hand almost at once and went to sit on the couch. "She seemed fine to me. She's not getting any younger, but I think she's getting maybe a little less starchy as she gets older. Her health seems good, and she's not too lonely since she has Dan and Lacey nearby. Don't worry too much about her." He realized he wanted to quiet all Ruth's fears, even the ones she hadn't expressed, even the ones that had no connection to him.

She sighed. "You're right." She went to sit next to him on the couch and curled her feet up. He put his arm around her, and she dropped her head to his shoulder. "Dan's remarkable, and so's Lacey. I guess we all expect Mother to be a rock, the way she always has been. Funny she should seem softened at the same time."

They fell silent, close but apart. In the new quiet, the house seemed oddly animate, as if clasping them organically, like the shell of an animal—a turtle or a snail. Alex laid his cheek against Ruth's hair, and a wave of desire washed over him, despite the sense that he was out of step with her mood. "How about a cup of coffee?" he said.

᪻ ᪺

Soon after the holiday Ruth broached the subject of visiting Alex's parents in Canada. At first, without quite understanding why, he resisted. In all the years he'd been away, all the years of their marriage, he had never thought of going back himself, until so recently. He'd been unprepared for the callus that time seemed to have formed to shield Mariette and Gabriel from the shock of his belated arrival. It was not that he felt cheated of some scene of high emotion, only that he'd been braced for one. He had not yet come to terms with what he had found, and he did not know how to assess their sensitivity. If he took Ruth to meet them, would they notice that something was out of tune in his relationship with his wife? But Alex knew that his and Ruth's new life together depended on trust. Thus, finally he allowed her to persuade him. If Mariette and Gabriel were to surmise that the marriage was less than perfect, he would have to take the risk. In spite of his fear that he might be tempting fate, his greatest concern truly was that the Duchamps might be so shy with Ruth that she would feel rebuffed.

ಖಾ ಛಾ

It was late spring by the time they went. Driving into the main street of St. Agathe from the highway bordered by blue-green oat fields was like taking a turn out of the twentieth century and finding oneself back in the nineteenth. It was the first time Alex had entered St. Agathe with someone who'd never seen it before. Ruth thought the modern automobile parked in front of the post office appeared out of place. Swaybacked barns on the road into town, buildings with false fronts, faded signs and grimy show windows projected a discouraged air. And there was the red brick church looming, its silvery roof glowing like neon in the apricot light of sunset, flanked by the school and the brick wall, behind which she could see the dormers of the nuns' and orphans' enclave. Ruth took everything in without comment. Alex tried to see it through her eyes. When they turned into the side street, budding trees and intervening buildings shut out the ecclesiastical view.

At the door of Alex's childhood home, Mariette kissed Ruth gently, first one cheek and then the other and then led her up to the spare room. Gabriel stood formally and silently in the doorway to the parlor and bowed his head with a shy smile to Ruth when Alex introduced them. The old peoples' grave expressions, their polite murmurs in halting English, made Alex apprehensive again. As he might have guessed, it was domesticity that saved them from agonies of embarrassment.

After she washed her face, Ruth went to the kitchen with Mariette. Almost immediately, they worked out one of those strictly sex-linked relationships of amicability that revealed itself in the dinner, when it was served. Alex would have recognized Ruth's salad dressing anywhere and the way she folded a napkin. The balance of the meal was pure Mariette: ample and spicy.

Thin as she had become, he thought her cheeks showed a little of their old rosiness. Questions and answers about Alex's doings satisfied conversational requirements, and Gabriel kept looking from his son to Ruth, and back again with a twinkle in his faded blue eyes. When they got to the coffee and maple sugar pie, Mariette seemed to have recovered her sense of belonging in her own home, and Alex, too, relaxed at last.

His mother leaned toward him, her face solemn, and said in slow French that he was sure Ruth would understand, "*Pourquoi pas des petits-enfants?*" Alex felt the blood rise in his face; he glanced at Ruth. She had the startled doe look in her eyes. For her sake, he wanted to sink out of sight and out of reach of questions and take her with him. Looking for the gentlest way to tell the truth and forestall further questions, he hesitated.

Ruth said, "Is she asking why we have no children?" Alex nodded. "Explain that we *have* tried, but that I can't," she said calmly. "And you should let her know about how my job seemed to fill the gap—for me, anyway," she added.

"*Comment?*" Mariette said.

So Alex told them what Ruth said. He assumed they'd make a comment, ask more questions. But Gabriel shook his head gently with lips pursed, and Mariette reached over and touched Ruth on the shoulder, like someone comforting a child with a broken toy. Ruth, to her own surprise, was able to smile. Alex thought then that doubtless this failure was something important they had in common with the old couple.

In bed later, in the unironed sheets smelling of laundry soap and sunlight that Alex remembered vividly from his childhood, Ruth lay on her back. "Could we visit the orphanage?"

"What on earth for?" The notion struck him as something analogous to viewing a corpse. When she said nothing, he suddenly felt willing to try to exorcise the memories of his time there. Perhaps to see it once again from such a different perspective might accomplish what his former attempts to come to terms with his past had failed to do. It would be, in fact, the first time he had faced what so often haunted him, or acknowledged its existence.

He reached out for Ruth's hand and squeezed it. "Maybe that's what we really came up here for. We'll go tomorrow."

✥

As they entered the convent grounds through the Gothic doorway, Alex thought how little changed most of it appeared. While in his day, the children had been clothed in castoffs and resembled the motley crew they actually were, now they were uniformed, but he saw little else that was different. The porteress let them in and gave a neutral smile when Alex identified himself as an alumnus of the institution. She nodded to Ruth when he introduced his wife, and left them sitting in the guests' parlor, in what might have been the same chairs where he first saw Mariette and Gabriel.

Alex was tongue-tied, listening to the nun's footsteps and the clicking of her beads fade away. Ruth sat, feet together, hands folded in her lap, as though she too had been brought up by the strict sisters. The joyous trilling of a robin filtered through the closed window like the siren song of another world.

Presently, the nun who'd let them in reappeared with another sister, who took them on a tour. Alex watched Ruth as they looked into the nursery where four infants were being cared for by a young nun all in white, like an overgrown swan. He could see his wife was making an effort to hide emotion. They passed the classrooms, stopping to peer through the netted glass panes into the sanctums where rows of heads were aligned, facing dusty blackboards. A *music room* had been added since Alex's time, where four or five-year-olds trilled *"Sur le pont d'Avignon"* to the accompaniment of an out-of-tune upright piano, played by a nun in novice habit, whose thick spectacles made her eyes appear to be brimming with tears.

A frown pleated the skin between Ruth's brows when they inspected the cheerless dormitories, but she maintained an unbroken silence. She had not expected the mere fact of habits to make the nuns seem so alien to her and, therefore, so inappropriate as guardians of little children.

The overwhelming impression Alex derived from their tour was one of dreary disinterest. Perhaps he had prepared himself for too much emotion; he was surprised that he was close to being bored. Cream-colored paint, fumed oak, tiled floors, stained glass, and the unrelieved black-and-white garb of the women seemed to dim even the bright eyes of the children and the colors of the flowers so stiffly arranged in the parlor and on the altar in the chapel. Even the refectory was unchanged as to paint and decoration. The tables were still dark brown, scarred, and bare except for salt and pepper shakers and cruets of vinegar. He felt as if he had never actually lived in this lackluster place. He looked under their wimples at each nun he saw, wondering whether he'd recognize his old nemesis Sister Joseph-Madeleine, if she were still alive—she would have been at least in her seventies—but he recognized no one. No one except the children. It was as if they were the same ones he had felt lost among when he was one of them.

As they were leaving by way of the playground gate, they skirted a shouting group of boys, scrambling on the stony dirt after a soccer ball. A rotund, carrot-topped young priest with a whistle hanging around his neck stood by the wall, shouting encouragement into the fray. Unnoticed by the rest of the group, a tow-headed little rodent of a fellow was sitting on a stone off in a corner where creeper was just breaking into leaf on the wall. His head was down almost between his bare knees. He was studying something on the ground.

Ruth touched Alex's arm, and nodded in the child's direction. They followed the wall around to his corner.

"Comment t'appele toi?" Alex bent down so the child could hear in the din of the game behind them. The boy looked up; his eyes were hazel, clouded with an expression of dreamy confusion. Alex repeated the question.

"Michel."

Overcome with a wave of compassion almost too forceful to contain, his throat half closed, Alex stammered, *"Qu'est que tu fait?"* The boy pointed to a line of ants undulating across the patchy grass that survived along the edge of the playground. The procession disappeared under the chipped bricks and eroded mortar of the wall.

"I wonder if he'd like to follow them," Ruth murmured, gazing down at the child. Alex looked quickly at her, then back at the huddled boy.

"Au'voir," he said softly and drew Ruth away. He turned to wave to the boy, who half raised a listless hand before he went back to studying the ants. Alex and Ruth hurried out of the convent like people with an appointment to keep.

They didn't speak of the visit to the orphanage. Ruth because she'd seen that Alex longed to reach out to the pathetic little boy, Alex because he feared hurting Ruth with a reminder of her barrenness.

They left for Connecticut the day after the trip to the orphanage. After breakfast, Mariette took Ruth upstairs, while Gabriel and Alex carried bags with the jars of preserves Mariette was sending home with them out to the car. As always, the two men spoke French. "It's good to see you and Mariette looking so well," Alex said, unhappily aware of the stiff politeness of the remark.

"Your Ruth—she is a good wife," Gabriel said. Alex nodded to him, wondering if he were going to add anything about how he saw his son as a husband. Gabriel had rarely missed anything Alex had wanted to hide from him when he was young, even though it had seemed to Alex that he so often failed to understand what he perceived. But Gabriel said nothing more.

The women emerged, Ruth with a small white box in her hand. "Look what Mariette has given me." She took the lid off the box. I inside, Alex saw an old-fashioned gold pocket watch, with a chain and seal attached. "She said it was her father's and she wants us to have it." Ruth raised her eyes to Alex's. "In case we should want to pass it on. I'm quite sure that's what she meant, but perhaps you should ask, to be sure I understood."

Mariette was smiling, nodding her head. "She understand, I t'ink," she told him.

"Merci, merci, Mariette!" Ruth gave Mariette a hug, received her

kisses on each cheek and handed Alex the box. He felt a hollow in the pit of his stomach, like the day when the plane taxied down the runway for his wing-walking. He put the box in the pocket of his jacket, and held out his hand to Gabriel, who drew him into a quick embrace. Then Gabriel kissed Ruth, first one cheek and then the other and opened the car door to help her in. They waved out the windows and Ruth called, "*Au revoir, au revoir; à bientôt!*" as they drove off.

Alex was thinking, with no sense of irony, how even to a grown-up, the journey home always seems so much shorter than the one away.

CHAPTER TWENTY-NINE

A new rhythm, or perhaps more accurately, an older one, imposed itself on Ruth and Alex Duchamp's lives after the trip to Canada. Each became more aware of the world around them. Dawn and nightfall, seasons and weather that they had once only imperfectly noticed amidst bricks and mortar, now became vivid. Together, they found renewed pleasure in the sensual world. They even mentioned how their perceptions had sharpened as a result of their renewed pleasure in the processes of living.

Ruth enthusiastically tended their country home and it flourished and sleekened under her touch. Each time Alex returned to the house, it was with conscious, incredulous, gratitude that he was home at last. If either felt a lack, it was one that did not bear mentioning. Hearts' bruises began to fade away. Ruth occasionally surprised Alex by voicing a thought she would never have mentioned in the old days, but they seldom referred to the troubled time. Alex behaved toward his wife with the delicacy of a bridegroom.

Ruth kept a spiral-bound notebook on the desk. Alex wanted to know what she wrote in it, but hesitated to ask her, since he assumed it was some kind of diary. She saw him watching her one day when she was writing. "You wouldn't be interested, I'm sure."

"Why do you say that?"

"Well, it's just a sort of journal. It wouldn't interest anyone but me." She flushed. "Most of it's just—therapy—and a few poems, a couple of pieces you might call essays, but mostly nothing." She smiled wryly. "And yes, I would be embarrassed, so please don't look."

"Poems? Couldn't I see those?"

She considered seriously, then nodded. "I'll type copies for you."

He looked at her with renewed respect. He thought with chagrin of how superior he had felt once, assuming he was the creative one. How incredulous he'd been when Ruth told him about Nettie's poems. He noticed now with some pleasure that he relished these surprises, rather than feeling, as he once would have, threatened by them.

By the time Ruth got around to making her copies, Nettie had published a book, so Alex could compare the work of the two. He read thoughtfully, and then reread. With pride in her, he judged Ruth's work gentler and deeper than Nettie's. One piece hung in his mind, about a hurdy-gurdy man she'd seen once in Washington Square. The sight had quelled her own joy on a beautiful day, when she perceived what it cost the man to perform. Like a metaphor for all the hidden miseries of helpless people, it had haunted her, and she had made a poem about that.

> I smiled at tinkling chords,
> The tiny simian side-kick,
> Shoddy gilt and threadbare velvet,
> And a bright blue view of Napoli—
> But all was changed from gay to grim,
> From festive revel to mirthless charity
> When I looked into the player's eyes.

Alex thought wryly of the many misapprehensions he had been prey to as a result of first impressions. He saw Ruth's poems as emblems of the changes that had transpired between them, of their mutual, new attention to undercurrents, particularly in each other. He wondered if he was getting sentimental.

☙ ☙

The visit to St. Agathe was a turning point. As though it marked a boundary beyond which lay a territory where yesterdays lost their power over the present, Ruth and Alex began finally to surrender to happiness. Ruth wrote a bread-and-butter note to Mariette that Alex assured her would need no translation. She put the watch carefully away with her jewelry. They did talk over details of the trip. Ruth had questions about what they had seen.

"You said once how you felt regimented. Weren't the nuns kind? Didn't you make any special friends? Were you so lonely? You weren't like little Michel, were you?"

Alex did his best to answer her from the distance he had so deliberately placed between that time and the present. The impressions that had loomed so vividly when he told Ruth about that period of his life had begun to lose their power, he realized with surprise. At last, they seemed to be diminishing in the necessary dimming and healing of time.

"I guess they were kind, as you put it. But we were too miserable, too conscious of our isolation to notice, I think. In some ways, I probably was like Michel. I got lost in my head to escape. He's probably doing that too."

Their fourteenth year of marriage was the best they had known. It seemed as if the turn of seasons seen together in their beloved house enriched a fertile place where love could flourish. In the dense quiet of country nights, Alex would turn back the covers in order to look at Ruth in moonlight. Still young, her body had only ripened, he thought. She would drink in his beauty with the eagerness of one deprived. They would sleep after love entwined, like children in a fairy tale.

☙ ☙

The next spring, they were planning a trip to visit their respective families in Maine and Canada when Ruth said, "That little boy we saw, all alone in the playground at the orphanage—I haven't been able to get him out of my mind."

Her words renewed the stab of sadness experienced almost a year ago, when they saw the child together. Alex said, "Yes. He seemed to be a bit of a maverick, didn't he?"

"Would he have a chance of adoption, do you think?" Ruth smiled. "He's not a pretty child."

After a thoughtful silence, Alex answered, "I'd say his chances weren't very good."

※ ※

On the way north, Ruth and Alex stopped to stay a few days with Elizabeth in Devonport. Ruth and little Andrew were standing at the edge of the cliff, watching the gulls bobbing in the air like corks floating, their perfect equilibrium maintained by the trim of their tails and the angle of their wings. Sailing past the figures on the grassy crest, almost at eye level, they turned their heads to train incurious yellow eyes on the earth-bound.

On the bluff, the wind snatched at a rainbow kite, whose string Alex fed off the reel. With none of the easy grace of the birds, the bright-hued shape dipped and dived and quivered, its tail spiraling behind it, like a mismanaged marionette. Alex tilted his head back to keep his eyes on the kite, garish as a giant parrot against the gathering mackerel clouds. As the kite shot up, then spun and hurtled toward the ground, Alex shouted, paying out string and running backwards.

Elizabeth and Lacey stood at the fence, watching. At Alex's shout, Andrew turned from Ruth and ran back across the field to his uncle. He jumped up and down, reaching for the spool. Once the kite steadied in the air, Alex carefully placed the reel in Andrew's hands, and stood back as the boy watched his captive, straining against the tether as if it were alive.

Ruth ran toward Alex and Andrew, the wind dragging her full skirt against her legs. The watchers saw Andrew turning, offering the reel to Ruth, who bent to reach around him and place her hands over his, with the child between her arms.

The two women at the fence heard the sound of a car door

slamming on the driveway behind them. Dan lurched slowly toward them on his crutches, with Josh running ahead of him. They stopped at the fence with Elizabeth and Lacey, watching the three with the kite in the middle of the greening field.

Dan said, "It's fun to see Andrew with Ruth and Alex. They're great with the kids." He looked down at Josh. "Why don't you go and try the kite too?"

Josh scurried under the fence and ran out into the field. The wind carried the shouts of the kite-fliers to the watchers' ears. Dan lifted an arm from his crutch to place it around his wife. They watched Josh, who with casual expertise was making the kite loop and dive and soar again, while the others stood still, heads back. Then Andrew jumped up and down and clapped his hands.

"My," Lacey said, as the quartet came closer, following the antics of the kite, "it's astonishing how good looking Alex is. And Ruth, with that wonderful hair. Too bad she cut it, but they *are* a handsome couple!"

Elizabeth said dryly as she turned away from the fence to walk back to the house, "Handsome is as handsome does." Dan and Lacey exchanged a look that spoke of how close to the bone the remark cut. Then they smiled again, watching Ruth and Alex and the children.

ಸಿ ಐ

That night, moonlight laid a cool finger across the quilt on the bed where Alex and Ruth lay curled together. A breeze redolent of sea and new leaves stirred the curtain at the open window.

"It seems strange to be here so early in the season," Ruth said sleepily.

"Mm-mm." Alex adjusted the position of his arm under her neck.

She said, "Now that you've made me retire, it's going to be so nice to have weekdays to work in the garden this summer, instead of only weekends." She thought, but did not say, how much fun it would be to show a child how to plant radishes, which give such a speedy reward.

"Well, just don't kill yourself, trying to do everything alone. Save some time for me." He kissed the warm curve between her neck and shoulder.

She chuckled. A screech owl shrilled in the woods, its tremulous whistle sharp against the distant breath of the ocean and the whisper of leaves.

"I wouldn't be surprised if Gabriel never touches his new pipe. He probably won't want to bother to break it in," Ruth murmured.

"If you give it to him, he'll smoke it. Do you think the coral necklace is okay for *Maman*?"

Ruth snuggled closer. "If you give it to her, she'll adore it."

Alex's breathing slowed and deepened. Ruth pulled away from his shoulder as gently as she could and turned on her side. She could see the outline of the door frame faintly, and a shard of moonlight reflected in the mirror on the dresser. It faded while she watched, dimmed by the thickening clouds they had seen building in the afternoon.

Ruth closed her eyes and saw again the dancing kite, like an errant ballerina, sweeping its colors across the sky, while little Andrew squealed and raced under it. Alex's profile arrested her eye against the heavens, the line of his neck and jaw exposed by his open collar and the angle of his head, tipped to follow the gyrations of the kite. The curves and angles of his head, the chiseled nose and lips, the shape of his skull, she thought for the thousandth time, would suit a coin. She remembered his laughter.

"Darling." Ruth half-hoped he wouldn't hear.

"Mm-mm."

She searched for words.

"I'm not asleep," he murmured. "What?"

"I was wondering—could we go back to the orphanage again?"

Alex opened his eyes, though he lay still. He said nothing for several long seconds. In his mind's eye he saw Ruth, bending down above the tow-headed little boy with his chin on his knees, watching ants marching under the wall. Her unconscious posture was as graceful as the child's was huddled and furtive. The mental picture changed to Ruth in the wind on the cliff, gazing up at the kite with Andrew and Josh, just this afternoon.

"Michel?"

"You don't know how often I've thought of him." She felt Alex nod. "Please understand, I don't want to press you to …"

"Everyone needs a home, especially when we're small." Alex

reached across to draw her against him again, back to chest, curved with knees behind hers. He cupped a breast with one hand and kissed her nape softly. "We'll pay him a visit while we're up there." He thought of his parents. "We might make *Maman* and *Papa* very happy too."

"Thank you for understanding."

"Thank you for trusting me to," Alex replied, his voice so low she felt more than heard it. She put her hand over his on her breast and closed her eyes. A puff of wind billowed the curtains at the window. The wan light of the moon was gone. Alex pulled the quilt higher over their shoulders, tucking it against his wife's neck and under his own chin. Faint in the distance, the owl trilled again, like a departing phantom.